Tales of the Spinward March

Book Two: The Red Queen

By David C. Winnie

Thank you Rene,

Please Enjoy!

[signature]

2017

Dedicated to:

HRH Queen Alexandria Victoria
Doctor Marie Salomea Sklodowska-Curie
Jeanne d'Arc
Doktor Angela Dorothea Kasner-Merkle

And to all the great women who come small in body, but mighty in achievement...

Acknowledgements

My Thanks to the following:

Cover Art: Bogdan Maksimovic

Book Cover Design: Creative Publishing Book Design

Author Photograph: John McAlpine

Credits:

"Hammer to Fall" from the album "The Works" by Queen 1984

"Drowned "from the rock opera "Quadrophenia" by The Who 1973

"The Final Reflection" by John M. Ford.   Pocket Books 1984

All story tellers are slightly mad. Thanks to the Friday Night Poker Group, both members who have passed on and the present players who keep me sane. I raise a Joe. DCW

FORWARD TO DAVID WINNIE'S *THE RED QUEEN*

He outlined the Spinward Series to me over two pots of coffee (and several bathroom breaks) over 15 years ago. I was fascinated with the concept then, and now, as I am finally privileged to edit the output of this *avant garde* emerging writer, I continue to be enthralled. *The Great Khan,* Book #1 in the series, is one of the finest first novels I have ever seen in my 70 years of reading science fiction.

The Red Queen, Book #2, will not disappoint you, as it continues the saga of the Spinward March through otherspace and the known and unknown universe. Feisty little Khan Annika Russolov will win your awe, respect and perhaps your heart, as she dedicates her entire life to the expansion of her Terran Empire.

A word to those who are hesitant to invest in self-published books: Times have changed in the publishing world. Remember Frank Herbert's *Dune,* felt by many to be the best science fiction novel ever written? 50-odd years ago it was rejected by traditional publishers <u>twenty-three</u> times, in a day when those publishers were often taking a chance on new and emerging writers. Today it takes a miracle of space and time for the new author's novel to be picked up by the downsizing and beleaguered traditional publishers who depend upon their already well-known and well-loved authors' output for the profit on their bottom lines. Thus, the emergence of the many self-publishing outlets. (I self-published my first novel, *Three-Point Shot,* for young adults, and it won a Writer's Digest award that year.) Self-publishing is, today, the best way to get the new author's work into the reading marketplace.

Read and enjoy *The Red Queen,* recommend it to your SF-reading friends, and wait as I do with bated breath for #3 in the Spinward Series. Thanks for buying books.

J. R. Nakken Award-Winning Author of the memoir
Confessions of a Martian Schoolgirl
Autumn, 2017

Here we stand or here we fall
History won't care at all
Make the bed, light the light
Lady Mercy won't be home tonight...
-Queen, 1984 A.D.-

Prolog

From "The Law of Angkor Khan."

Section 3: Laws of the Khan

    3:1.1 The Law of Succession. The Khan can only be succeeded by one of the eight heirs. The eight heirs will be designed by the heir File Committee. Each file will have its own committee that is responsible for designing the perfect heir. They File Committee will be advised by the File Council. The File Council will consist of members as assigned by the Khan.

    3:1.1.2 The Khan is free to select his or her bond partner from any Terran in the Empire. After the pair are bonded and before they consummate their bonding, the File Committee will extract genetic material from each partner. This material will be combined to create the basis for the heirs. The File Committee will adjust the genetic pattern to match the design of the perfect heir. Once matched, the pattern will be impressed onto a zygote and gestated using the Angkor/Vinithri egg system.

    3:1.1.3 At the biological age of five Terran years, the heirs shall be presented to their parents and the Empire in keeping with the Traditions of Khalkha Tribe.

    3:1.1.4 At the age of eighteen, the File Committee will select which of the heirs has achieved perfection as the reincarnation of the Emperor Angkor Khan and is worthy to rule the Empire.

    3:1.1.5 Upon the death of the Khan, the designated heir is the Khan, with all the honors, duties and responsibilities of the Khan.

    This Law, as all my Laws, is written by my own hand.

    ANGKOR KHAN

Imperial Offices, Mongolia 3070 A.D.

Chapter 1

Imperial Palace, Amaar, Capital City on Argulea, Terran Empire.
5031 A.D.

It was perhaps as fine a day in May as could be remembered.
Weather control ensured the conditions. The Emperor was known as
a creature of comfort. So, of course it was a fine day.

A light rain had fallen. It ended at precisely at 3 a.m., giving
all the gardens in the old city a good soaking, but not so wet as to
spoil the day. With so many Very Important Persons coming in
from across the Terran Empire, it would not do to dampen a single
well-heeled slipper.

At sunrise, the last of the cleaners left the streets. The city
was perfect. A slight breeze blew, carrying the scent of fresh blooms
through the entire region. The Empress was fond of roses: large,
well-tended beds and planters filled the whole of Amaar.

In the heirs' nursery, the eight children were roused.

Today, they were to be presented to the Imperial Court.
Though clones, their parents, the Emperor Robert De L'Orange
Khan and their mother, Empress Lorraine, had supplied their basic
DNA. The File Committee then altered the genes, enhancing
preferred traits, removing undesirable. The result were these eight
children, brothers and sisters, but each unique. Tall, short, and one
tiny. Hair color ran from as dark as the void to golden as the sun.
Curiously, they were not a balanced eight. Rather, the committee had
created five boys and three girls.

Compromises had been made. You simply could not stuff
every desirable trait into a single child. For instance, one could
design the child to have excellent night vision. But the tradeoff
might be that he (or she) would have smaller hands. These children
were the result of over two thousand years of genetic mapping and
manipulation. Each was to have unique physical or mental

advantages over the others.

The symmetry and balance was traditionally maintained. For the yin and the yang to be biased this way, most unusual.

They were alike in the emerald eyes with an Asian fold, sign of their family line. And an unshakable belief in their own infallibility. Each was perfect. Everyone else was inferior. It was the basis of their programed genes. And the Proctors reminded them of it constantly.

The Proctors. The daily constant in the children's lives. They were teachers, counselors, coaches and disciplinarians for the eight. They sat on the File Committee and had helped design these children. The very future of the Empire depended on the Proctors. They helped to create the eight, and they were responsible for development of the Empire's next Khan.

Even with the importance of the day, routine must still be followed. The children arose at sunrise, had their morning exercise. After bathing came breakfast, then on to lessons. For the one with the experimental superior brain, today's lessons were a direct download. The others sat in a classroom under the watchful eyes of Proctors. After lunch, they were dressed in their ceremonial clothes. Each was inspected by an eagle-eyed Proctor. All of them were reminded repeatedly, "*Stand straight, head high! Not a wrinkle your uniform, not a hair out of place.*" This was the standard for these children. Anything less than perfection was unacceptable.

Precisely fifteen minutes before the Khan was to enter the Throne Room, the children were inspected again, making sure each was exactly as it was supposed to be, perfect. One would expect eight five-year-old children to wiggle and resist all the attention and waiting. These were not ordinary children. They were heirs. One day, the best of them would be Khan.

The Emperor Ming si Haun Khan and his wife, Empress Lorraine, entered the Great Hall. As they strode down the center aisle, the mighty and great of the Empire bowed and curtsied as the royal couple passed. Citizens all, regardless of the color of scales or skin, number of legs or multiplicity of orbs, their homage was proper. The Imperial Guard, imposing soldiers in royal purple and gold, made sure of that. Ming si Huan Khan had only been Khan for two years, following the assassination of his brother, the Emperor Robert De L'Orange Khan. There were quiet whisperings of his violent anger and of what happened to those who didn't show him the proper deference.

The royal couple seated themselves in their thrones on the dais, as ministers and military officers entered side doors and stood at stiff attention. Ming si motioned with a finger and a door at the side of the dais opened. With great precision, the eight marched out and stood, facing the royal couple. Seven of the children gave a deep bow. The last, the tiniest child and dressed all in red, did not. The Khan took notice, and forced a small smile. Excellent! The child provided him with an opportunity to appear fatherly. "Child, is this how you show respect to your Khan?" Blush suffused her slender neck, but she clinched her jaw firmly before favoring him with a barely perceptible nod.

The Khan sighed. It was not starting well for her. He remembered when he was one of the eight. Every misstep, every tiny mistake for the next thirteen years would be noted and filed away. He dismissed thoughts of the child and lifted his finger again.

A holo appeared and projected the story of the Great Khan, who had unified the people of the old Terran Union. How Angkor Khan had given them his law. How his cleverness had defeated the great Vinithri empire. His wisdom had forged an alliance with that alien nation. How it had led to the creation of the File Committee, whose job it was to continue and improve the Line of the Great Khan himself.

The Khan scarcely listened. He had heard the story in many times over the years. The heirs were constantly reminded of their royal lineage.

On his Naming Day, Ming si expected to be named the next

Khan, only to learn that his brother, Robert, was to succeed. Oh, the years he waited, hating his brother. Robert De L'Orange had been a popular Crown Prince, traveling across the Empire, making the important speeches. The people came to adore him.

Ming si, as an inferior heir, had been expected to live a productive life out of sight, out of mind, bearing the family name of ne-Khan forever. Of the Khan's family, but not the Khan. His brother married the beautiful Lorraine. By law, ovum and seed were extracted from them before they consummated their marriage. That, in turn, was sent to the File Committee to be assigned and modified to create the brats now in front of him.

Then the Khan at least had had the good graces to get himself killed by an assassin's bomb. The Imperial Council panicked, naming Ming si Khan immediately, as clearly the children weren't ready. He wasn't concerned in the least about these children. Yes, one of them would replace him one day. But he was young and fit. He had the entire apparatus of the Empire at his disposal. He had the beautiful and dutiful Lorraine. Any threat to his crown would be dealt with severely.

He studied the little, insolent child covertly throughout the boring presentation. It wouldn't do to punish her here. He'd get through the ceremony, then tell the Proctors just how displeased he was with her. He remembered corporal punishment when he was that age. A good beating for rudeness might be just the thing.

She was a homely little thing. Barely three feet tall. Her eyes were a bit too close over a pug nose that hovered over a pointed chin. With her golden hair pulled back in a queue, she seemed less a threat and more an object of his pity.

Red sensed the Khan's contempt. It mattered little to her. She listened to the thoughts around her, noting who she trusted and who would bear watching. Black was doing the same. He was an ally. After the death of their father, he had sworn his obedience to her.

She focused herself on the Empress, who was visibly startled as Red caressed her mind. **"So, I take it you are our mother, yes?"** she asked. **"Tell me, Mother, what were you thinking, marrying such an ass? Was it simply politics, or was there something else? Well, no matter. I am bored with all of this."**

Lorraine put her lace handkerchief to her mouth. She hadn't been aware any of the children had mindspeak. Robert hadn't.

Or, at least he had never told her of it.

Red sighed. Aloud. Murmurs crossed the court. Such a thing was simply unheard of and unspeakably rude. She sighed again. The holo stopped, unsure of what to do. The Khan's voice was stern. "Behave, Child," he admonished. "I cannot believe a child of mine would ever be so rude."

"That's because you are not my father." Red placed tiny fists on her hips and lowered her gaze ominously. "My father was a Great Khan. You are merely an imposter, a pretender, a fake. You are not Khan!" She pointed to the Empress. "She is the mother of us," Red cried, "mother of the heirs, wife of my father, the Khan!" She mindspoke to her brothers and sisters. **"There, she is the one. She is our mother. Go to her, comfort her."** Six of the children broke with their training and rushed the Empress, who encircled them in tentative arms and issued quick kisses. The seventh, Black, hesitated, his gaze vacillating between his mother and his sister. He wavered, but stood his ground.

The Khan reached out to probe the mind of the child, Red. When he touched it, he froze, then recoiled. Icy fury radiated from her, not just blocking his probe but sending it back with such force that he was physically moved back in his chair. His mouth gaped as burning mental fingers tore into his head, ripping and tearing as he gasped and choked. Then she was gone from his mind, placid, her head tilted to look regally down her nose at him.

"I'm bored. I need a chair," Red announced. There was a commotion behind the throne; a small wooden chair was produced. "That shall do for now, I should suppose," she said. The servant who had produced the chair moved to place it beside the Empress.

5

"No," said Red, "my chair belongs there." She pointed to a spot to the right of the Khan. The trembling servant looked first to the stupefied Khan, then scuttled over, placing the chair in the designated place. Red, strode up the stairs, followed closely by Black. She seated herself as if the nondescript little chair were a throne. Black moved behind her and stood at her right as she folded her hands calmly on her lap. "So, Uncle," she ordered him. "Let's complete this ceremony. I have studying to finish."

The whole of the Terran Empire exploded.

On each of the one hundred fifty worlds there were protests. The Law of Angkor Khan were lessons every Terran learned in school. That was part of the Law. No one could break the Law and say they didn't know. Nor could the Council or even the Khan himself could violate the Law and not be exposed.

The Law of Succession was the easiest to understand. The most perfect of the eight was to be the new Khan on the death of the predecessor. Since each Khan was the reincarnation of Angkor Khan, his successor must be perfect as well.

The child had pointed out the unthinkable conundrum the Imperial Council faced just two years before. Never had a Khan died before the successor was ready to assume the mantle and title. The law had no specific direction for the situation.

The Empire suffered in the rule of Robert Khan's father. Emperor Robert L'Orange Khan was a popular choice to lead the Empire. Upon Robert's death, they met in a panic and decided on a course of action. The Empress Lorraine had agreed, on the promise that Robert Khan's children would remain heir.

She had married Ming si. He wasn't a bad man by any means, other than being terribly vain. And he didn't make too many demands on her. Being named Khan seemed to be good enough for him.

The Empire was in an uproar. For the first time, it had a close look at the heirs, and the Red child reminded them not only of what they had lost, but how the Council had erred by failing to follow the law. Riots broke out on every world. There was talk of revolution. Ming si's order went out. Imperial troops brutally quelled any disturbance.

On Biafara Prime, a news commentator suggested that perhaps it was time to do away with the monarchy. He was dragged from his ground car by a mob led by his own son. They tore him to pieces.

The Council remembered well the lessons of the so-called democracy revolution during the devastating reign of the eighth Khan. His own daughter had removed his name for all time over the devastation he wrought on the Empire. That mistake would not happen again. They raced back to Terra's Giza Palace, capitol of the Empire.

Terra was the only place the Leaders of the File Committees would meet with *oust landers,* those not Terra born. They were the highest priests and nuns of the Temple of Angkor Khan. With them, all final decisions of the designs and selections of the Khans were made. They rarely left their temple and never left Terra.

Tahn was First of the Temple of Angkor, Leader of the File Committee and not coincidently, leader of the Red File. He settled back in his seat of the hovercar that was transporting the eight leaders that were the File Committee. He and his staff for Red File had meet after the Presentation Ceremony incident. She had responded to the download and stimuli perfectly! Even better than anticipated. The second sigh was the marker, showing that she indeed knew herself to be superior to the Khan.

Tahn had summoned the rest of the File Committee even before the ceremony concluded. They reviewed her sequencing and training. They observed her reactions to the stimuli, right down to which hand she placed upon the other when she sat. The discussion was short. Tahn and his team had succeeded magnificently.

A few anomalies existed, of course. Most could be repaired or adjusted. But the defective genetic sequence in the line of the

Khans was present in young Red. She would require the Descendent to complete the sequence for her heirs. The search for the Descendant was well underway. He must be found and soon. When Red became Khan, she must be bonded with him.

The very future of the Empire would depend on it.

The Imperial Council was in disarray as they arrived. Cacophony in the streets was reflected in the council chamber. Tahn and the File Committee sat in tranquil thought as minister after minister yelled and disputed what should be done to correct their momentous error.

Some argued the children should be destroyed and new heirs drawn from the new Khan. Others argued that both the current Khan and his wife be executed and the best of the children be installed as Khan, with the Council serving as the advisors and teachers. The Council would retain all authority, until the Khan showed he (or she) was capable of ruling. A small minority nearly caused its own riot when they suggested that perhaps it was time to move away from the monarchy, that perhaps it was time to try democracy again. They were shouted down and physically assaulted. One of their number later succumbed to the pummeling he took. None dared forget the lessons of the Eighth Khan.

Finally, Tahn stood and spoke quietly. "There was good reason why Ming si Haun was not made Khan," he said. "He is selfish and vain, interested only in what he can get for himself. The qualities we found in Robert Khan have transferred to this latest line. We are seeing evidence with in terms of leadership and wisdom. This class also is demonstrating the balance of boldness and restraint needed in Terra's Khan. The File Committee believes these traits alone would clearly improve the line and lead to an even greater future for the Empire.

If we destroy these children and use Ming si Haun as the template, we cannot fully remove the selfishness that is Ming si and he would doubtless pass that on to his children. This would be a disaster for the Terran Empire. No, the File Committee agrees, these children are the ones that we must use to select the next Khan. It is to you to decide what the Empire is to do until the new Khan is ready."

There was no more discussion on the question of succession. In thirteen years, the new Crown Heir would be named. After more debate, it was decided to leave Ming si Haun in his place, changing his title from "Emperor" to "Regent." His name would be returned to ne-Kahn and he would rule the Empire only until the heir chosen ascended to the Throne. To protect the Empire further, they decreed the new Khan would be announced on the Naming Day, but wouldn't assume the title until age twenty-five. They hoped that the Crown Prince or Princess would put this time to good use in preparation for their responsibilities of the Terran Empire.

It was done. Ming, of course, was furious. It was enough that the title of Khan for which he had always been destined had again been stolen from him. But he was also reduced in name, back to ne-Khan. Of the Khan's family, but not Khan. No one ever remembered a ne-Khan.

He sat in his Palace at Argulea, smoking. Usually, the cool vapor would be enough to calm him, along with the kind ministrations of whichever slave he had selected for the evening. Tonight, it availed him not. The girl they had sent displeased him, and guards had already dragged her broken body away.

Ming considered option after option, but unless he could eliminate the entire Council or murder the eight, he was consigned to be a footnote in history. The small nothing between the fifteenth Khan, his worthless, dead brother, and the sixteenth Khan.

Ming si Haun ne-Khan reached for his comm.

Chapter 2

The assassin moved quietly through the darkened corridor with a practiced grace. A faint glow came from the light fixtures but, since it was evening, the lights would be low to replicate Terra. He didn't mind; the darkness was his friend.

This would be the assassin's last job. The boss had told him this one thing would set things right between them. Ross had screwed up royally, all right. The contract the boss had put on his life had proven that. But all would be forgiven if he pulled off this one little job. He'd get paid and a long-range scout ship that would take him far, far away.

Whoever had ordered the hit had pull and money. The scout ship proved that. It was nice to do a job that, while dangerous, seemed to have enough protection from above that he had a better than even chance at succeeding.

Ross knew who the target was. You couldn't go anywhere in the Empire and not know who THAT kid was. It didn't bother him, a hit like this on a kid. It was going to square a lot away for him and give him a chance to start over. And, if he failed, well, he wouldn't have a spacing to anticipate.

He found the child's room straightaway. Only one kid had hair of gold, and there it was, glistening on the pillow in the faux moonlight. He slipped into the room noiselessly and closed the door. The knife slid from the concealed sheath on his forearm, cold glitter in the room's pale light.

He moved on cat's paws to the side of the bed. Stretched out his arm to lift the blanket.

Or he tried to. His right hand held the gleaming knife, his left arm was trying to reach. Trying. Hard. He couldn't move the knife... Or his arm. He suddenly realized he wasn't breathing, either.

"Ooooo," he heard in his head. **"That's pretty.**

Arcimanium, isn't it? Can I see?" His eyes worked. She threw aside the blanket, her emerald eyes never leaving his face, and easily took the knife from him. **"Nice,"** she commented. **"Let's see, how does this go?"** She held it against her thin arm. **"Oh, poo, it won't fit. I think I'll keep this as a souvenir."** Swiftly, the knife disappeared. **"Now, my brother, Black, is interested in spies and assassins and stuff like that,"** she said. **"I think this is the perfect time for him to practice. Black?"**

A boy appeared from the darkness. **"Get it all out,"** she instructed him. **"Every bit. We need to know who ordered this, for our enemy list."** The kid in black just looked at Ross, his eyes bored into the assassin, who screamed in silent agony. Sharp claws ripped into his skull, tearing it open and pulling it to the sides. The boy was rampaging through his head, those eyes exposing everything Ross knew, everything he had ever done or attempted. His fears were exposed, his weaknesses. His terrors. The Black heir flipped through Ross's memories as though he paged through a manuscript. Nothing was sacred, nothing missed.

He needed to piss, but wasn't even allowed to do that. When the boy was finished, his victim's mind sundered, he nodded at his sister and disappeared again into the shadows.

"That went well," she told her captive. **"Black is very pleased. You told him some things he needs to know and gave him valuable practice. As a reward, you may breathe once."** Air left his lungs once, then he inhaled. And was frozen again.

What to do with you," she mused. **"I can't very well let you go, because you'd just go back to being a bad guy. That is, if that Tony guy, the boss, doesn't find you first."** Red's face brightened. **"I'll give you a choice in deciding what happens."** His hand moved of its own accord and emerged with his small slug thrower. He also found himself shuffling to a spot beside the door, raising the weapon to his forehead. She giggled.

"Here's your choice," she said gaily. **"You can have five more breaths. Just five! Then you can shoot yourself. Or, you**

can stand there and not breathe at all. It'll take longer, but you'll die anyway. So, what's your choice?"

A few moments later, there was a soft pop, followed by a heavy thump and the rattle of air leaving lungs for the last time. "That was a good choice!" came a little girl voice.

Chapter 3

Ten years later

Celtius 4 was an unusual find for the Empire, a century ago.

While like many Terran worlds in terms of gravity and atmosphere, it differed in several ways. It orbited around both stars of a binary system. The planet had water ice, but was curiously completely devoid of life.

Scientists poured over the planet, convinced they had missed something. But it was Celtius 4 that had missed something. Life.

The Empire established a terraforming facility on the surface. While close to habitable, the ecosystem needed adjusting. It was estimated that it would take a full century for the planet to support a full, viable colony.

The eight were sent to the newfound colony, Celtius 4, for two standard months. It was to provide both an excellent opportunity for the children to learn firsthand the terraforming process and to perhaps get a sense of ecological responsibility. The research station would provide the stimulus they needed and there would be ample work to do.

The assignment also provided the heirs with a wide-open playground. By now, the atmosphere had thickened enough to support human life. This allowed for traveling around the planet unencumbered by pressure suits. Various grasses had been seeded planet-wide, one of the first steps to making the planet biome self-sustaining. While much of the travel was done by air cars and wheeled vehicles, horses were brought to the planet as an inexpensive transportation alternative; the added benefit was that horses were more enjoyable for the residents. The eight all soon became adept horsemen and seized every opportunity they could to take off on a ride.

It was Red who suggested they leave before the Proctors awoke and race to weather pylon twenty-five miles away. It would be a long ride, but it would have the combination of upsetting the Proctors' precious schedule and allowing the children a day of doing as they chose. At fifteen, they were prone to rebellion from time to time, Red most likely of all. So, they all rose quietly and went to the barns. Food for the day's adventure was acquired. They geared up the horses and sneaked out on the plain in the predawn light.

There was no need for a signal or countdown as there would be with any normal children. Red tensed and mindspoke, "**GO!**" They spurred their horses and took off across the wide open plain. It was close for the first miles but slowly, Red and Blue began to take the lead. Within another mile, the gap widened. Red, being smaller and lighter, wasn't as big a burden to her horse. Soon she was pulling away from Blue. She could feel Blue laughing with joy. The wind streamed her long, golden hair. She held her eyes open wide against the stinging wind. The big gray, his nose flaring, was steady and powerful beneath her.

She could see the pylon. Straight in the saddle now, her victory assured, Red released the reins and raised her arms in a victorious "V".

"VICTORY!" she screamed, laughing. "VICTORY FOR ME! FOR THE NEXT TEN THOUSAND YEARS! I AM VICTORIOUS!" Her brothers and sisters heard her savage cry.

Then her horse stumbled. She grabbed at the reins and missed, her legs squeezed the sides and she nearly regained her balance. She fell anyway, tumbling and bouncing once she hit the hard surface of the plain's new sod. She felt her left foot catch, her knee twist and tear. She screamed, not in pain, but in anger and fury for having fallen so. Still screaming her rage, she finally tumbled to a stop.

Red tried springing to her feet, but her destroyed knee betrayed her. She sat pounding the dirt in frustration, her horse calmly munching a few yards away. Blue and the rest rode up, laughing and commenting on her fall until Blue realized she wasn't getting up.

"**Come on, Red, No fooling. Get up!**" he mindspoke.

She shook her head. "**I can't,**" she responded. "**I really screwed up this time. Something broke inside, I think.**"

The rest of the children heard and stopped at their fallen sister. Yellow leaped off her horse, knelt and looked at Red's leg. She rubbed her hands together and began to move them over the swelling left knee. "**Oh yes. Torn. Several ligaments. I believe your patella is fractured as well, along with your tibia. Red, you need a doctor, right away.**"

Blue responded in kind. "**All right, she can't walk, means she can't ride. Green, White, lift her up to me, I'll carry her back.**" Yellow splinted Red's knee as best she could. Orange held the horses while Red's brothers carefully lifted their injured sister to Blue.

Unobserved, Purple trotted over to the pylon and touched it. "I win," he announced.

Orange handed Blue some of the food. There was no hesitation. The eight touched minds, and then five wheeled their horses about and raced across the green terrain.

Black hesitated.

"**Well, go on. I'll see you at the station in a few hours,**" Red told her faithful brother. Black looked to his brother.

"**Go on. We'll be fine,**" Blue insisted. "**We need you to get the Proctors.**" Nodding, Black turned his horse and raced after the others.

The first hour, they said nothing. Red was acutely aware of the powerful, handsome brother who carried her. It was his size, strength and beauty that angered her. Everyone loved Blue; surely, he was the front runner for ascension to the Khan's Throne. Red was none of these things. Small and scrawny, her overabundance of golden hair seemed to have a life of its own. She was brilliant and her psionic powers frightened everyone. She was of late more

17

irritable and outspoken, defying the Proctors and arguing constantly with the others. Red demanded more of them as she pushed herself harder and harder, attempting to stand out amidst siblings who had so much going for them. To her, even the staid, quiet Black seemed to be more favored by the Proctors.

The twin suns continued their march across the sky. The wind across the wide plain rustled the grass as waves on the sea. Red had not until now noticed the smell of the new grass, a sweet fresh odor. Her eyes grew heavy in the warm sunlight and buzzing grass; she even found riding this way with Blue was comfortable. He wasn't holding her too tightly and seemed to be focusing on walking the horse so it only occasionally jolted. When it did and she hissed in pain, he apologized immediately.

Soon, he began a soft hum. Red recognized the tune. The Proctors had taught them their ancient ancestors were nomads, born to the saddle and created a mighty empire. They learned much of their culture, handed down from the Great Khan himself. Included were a variety of songs that it was said the Great Khan enjoyed singing. Blue was humming a travel song. Red joined in the humming, then began to sing in her soft, pure voice. Blue joined her in the ancient tongue. *"The trail, it leads out in front of me. To where it goes, only the Gods of the Sky, Wind and the Grasses know. And they tell my horse, who gladly carries me. Onward to the endless steppe!"*

They sang and laughed, as they rode along. Red hissed in pain from time to time, but carried on singing. After three hours, a hovercar came speeding toward them. "Thank you, Blue," she whispered. "I don't know what I would have done without you."

He smiled, happy and confident. "You're welcome, Red. I only did what was needed. Were the roles reversed, I know you would have chosen the right thing to do." A quick, brotherly kiss landed on her nose.

Would I? she asked herself. *Were the roles reversed, would I do the thing I know to be the right thing?* She was still pondering

18

that question when the Proctors stopped the hovercar and loaded her into it.

Chapter 4

The clinic on Celtius 4 was a new building on the edge of the station compound. It boasted a large glass front facing the open plains. A Proctor carried her from the hovercar into the clinic where a matronly woman ushered them into the examination room. Red was laid on a bed; her leg was elevated quickly and efficiently. The nurse placed a cool pad over the injured knee. Red felt relief immediately.

She had seen hospitals before, but none quite like this. The walls were a pleasant, cool pastel color. The light came from an open skylight above her, the odor from the sweet grasses outside. There were no cabinets or counters covered with mysterious jars and boxes. A low table to one side boasted a bowl of wildflowers.

A tall, gangly man entered the room, followed by the matronly woman pushing a cart that held a boxy device. "Good afternoon!" the young man said. "I am Doctor Yuri Russolov, the research station physician. I'll be treating your injury today. So, tell how you did this while I examine, yes?" He removed the cool wrap and positioned the device over her knee. "This is a blue laser scanner," he said proudly. "It was originally invented nearly three thousand years ago, in Russia. I have found it is the most efficient way of examining injuries such as yours."

His deportment irritated Red. She snapped, "What do you mean you're the doctor? You're much too young!"

"Yes, I am young. I'm only twenty-two. But I graduated college at fourteen, which is younger than you, and medical school at eighteen. That means, for all intents and purposes, that I am smarter than you. So, answer my question, please." His voice was both smug and cheerful.

Red gritted her teeth. Acid dripped with her words. "I fell off my stupid horse. I was racing my brothers and sisters and I had won the race. Then I fell off the stupid, stupid, clumsy horse." He had started the machine and was staring at it, writing-WRITING, on a clipboard. "If you're so smart, why are you writing on that stupid paper instead of using a voice pad?" she asked.

He looked up. "If I use a voice pad, I can't very well listen to you," he answered. "Since you're the one who did all the falling, why does that make the horse stupid?"

Red growled and wrapped her arms over her head, wishing he were finished. Finally, he stood and said, "I'll be right back. Don't go anywhere." He pushed the machine back and replaced the cool cover on her injured leg.

It seemed forever before he came back. Dr. Russolov pulled up a chair and said, "O.K. What you've done is tear both your menial collateral ligament and your anterior cruciate ligament. Those will be easy enough to fix, however I will need to do a surgery. Your bigger issue is: you broke the ends of both your tibia and your fibula, along with your patella."

Red interrupted. "You use a bone stitcher and I'll be right out of here tomorrow, right?"

"Nope," he replied. "The ligaments will require surgery. That would have you down for several days at best. I spoke with your Proctor. You have a genetically enhanced bone structure that a normal bone stitcher can't fix. Normal bone is more compartmentalized, which is what the stitcher can mend. But your structure is more fibrous, so when it fractured, all three bones splintered. While I'm in your knee fixing the ligaments, I will also have to wire the bones back together so they can heal correctly. You'll just have to stay here for up to two months while the bones heal."

"That is totally unacceptable," Red stated flatly. "We are to depart next week to continue our studies elsewhere. There are more important things at stake here than your rudimentary skills. Doctor."

Her emphasis on "Doctor" was sarcastic. But young Dr. Russolov didn't rise to the bait. "Important or not, your opinion of my skills, or not, the facts are the fact, little one," he said. "Barring a medical miracle, you will be guest in my facility for the next two months."

"Well, we just see about that! I want to see my Proctor. Now!" Dr. Russolov's smile was guileless as he opened the door and beckoned.

Her Proctor entered, a tall, thin black man with a long, narrow face. Typical for his position, he was hairless and dressed in a long, flowing robe that matched the color of his assigned file, red. "You wish to speak to me, Child?"

"Yes!" Red snapped, "This "doctor" seems not to have the requisite skills or equipment available to handle my injury. I demand we depart immediately for a hospital that is equipped properly so I can return to training immediately. Make it happen."

"Indeed?" Her Proctor's voice was smooth as his head. "I reviewed the doctor's vitae thoroughly prior to our arrival and consider his skills more than adequate to repair your injury. I take it that you object to the course of treatment?"

"Of course, Proctor," she replied. "He says I have to stay here eight weeks. That is simply not acceptable!"

The Proctor sighed. "It is indeed unfortunate," he said. "We have changed our departure to tomorrow, as we have discovered a red giant star going into imminent collapse. It should be spectacular and provide an outstanding educational experience for the other seven."

"But I must go!" she protested. "I've always wanted to see a red giant collapse. You must simply let me go!"

"Red, my child, I have often counseled you on the consequences of your actions." Her lifelong Proctor's face was sad. "Now you are getting first hand a valuable experience with consequence. I am sure you will not enjoy it, but it will be a lasting lesson for you."

"It isn't fair," she pouted. "I, more than anyone, deserve to see it. If that stupid horse hadn't stumbled…" her voice trailed off, then she had another thought, frightening. "What about schooling?

If you leave me here, I will fall behind in my schooling! That won't be fair. I'll be too far behind if I'm left here for two months!"

"Ah, you are most fortunate there. Dr. Russolov is a scholar, as fine as any Proctor. He shall make you a more than adequate teacher while we are gone. As a doctor, he is qualified to maintain and administer direct your downloads." The Proctor smiled, "Really, for you this will be the best possible solution."

Red pouted while reaching out to scan the doctor. If she could find some weakness. But when she touched him, he wasn't there! It was as though she were passing her mental probe through empty air. "Proctor!"

"Ah, you've discovered my secret," chuckled Doctor Russolov.

The Proctor steepled his fingers. "Yet another reason for using the good doctor while I am gone," he said. "He is esper blind. He cannot be touched, or scanned or manipulated by anyone with psionic abilities. For me, that makes him the perfect companion for you. Someone to whom you must listen and respond. It will do you immeasurable good."

"How am I supposed to communicate with someone who is so stupid he can't hear my mind?" she asked contemptuously.

The Proctor smiled. "You talk," he said.

Surgery occurred the following morning. Red's brothers and sisters visited beforehand, concerned for her but excited to be off to see the rare event. "We'll send you images," promised Blue. Orange gave her a surprise kiss on the cheek, and Yellow hugged her almost too tightly.

"We'll see you soon, Sister," whispered Yellow. The others held her hand for a moment, then hastened from the room.

"Wa-wa-water." she croaked, in what seemed only seconds since she was wheeled into the operating theater... A hand slid under her head, a cup found her lips. "Shhh, just a sip for now," came a calm voice. She took a sip, then another at the voice's encouragement.

"More water," she croaked. Again, the gentle hand held her head and put the cup to her lip. She emptied the glass. Soon she felt stronger and could open her eyes. Her leg was in a contraption that fastened to her calf and thigh. As it rotated, it lifted and bent her knee, then extended it again, all without pain.

"The surgery was very successful," she heard. "Better than even I could imagine." Dr. Russolov stood beside her, glass in hand. She recognized the electrolyte and reached for it. The doctor let her take it, but kept a hand close by as she drank. She felt stronger still.

"What is this thing?" she asked, pointing to her knee. "Is this why it doesn't hurt?"

"I've placed a neural blocker on your leg for now for the worst of the pain," he explained. "Pain is your friend right now. It will let you know you are pushing too hard. If it hurts, don't try and bully your way through, understand? As for my little machine - it dates back more than a thousand years. It keeps your muscles moving and active, while reducing the pressure on your leg. Don't worry, we'll have you up within the next week."

For you, now, for the rest of the day, the best thing is to sleep," he instructed. She could feel herself getting drowsy. "We will talk later tonight, little Red." Before she could reply, she was fast asleep. Each of the several times she awakened, the doctor decreased the neutralizer. By the third awakening, the pain was noticeable. By the fifth, it had started hurting. She told him and he backed it off, just a little. "That's what we're looking for," he told her. "Just below where you realize it hurts."

When she awakened the next morning, the machine was moving in a larger arch and slightly faster. Dr. Russolov brought her breakfast. And a pad. "You've shaken the anesthesia now," he told her. "Your Proctor left a lot of school work for you. Best you get started now..."

With the anesthesia out of her system, she assessed this young doctor whose mind she could not touch. Tall and gangly, with a full brown moustache that was nearly dwarfed by a large, hooked nose. But his eyes were deep and empathetic, his hands perfectly formed and gentle. As for doctoring, perhaps he wasn't so bad, after all. Red sighed and turned to her lessons.

Once an hour, Dr. Russolov would return and quiz her on what she had studied. She noticed that he wasn't looking at the pad when she answered. Either he knew what she was reading, or he was being condescending. She decided to check. On one question, she answered incorrectly. Sharply, he corrected her, and without checking the pad.

The day went on that way, Red studying and then being questioned. He would occasionally accelerate the machine or reduce the neutralizer. Always she was on the edge of pain; he seemed to know the perfect setting. By the end of the day, the arch was near normal and the pace was brisk. She was pleased to hear him announce that her physical recovery was ahead of progress. But he warned her that it was just the ligaments that were healing quickly; the bones were not ready to bear weight and would not do so for several weeks. After supper, when she would normally expect more lessons, he came in and sat in the chair next to her bed.

They talked for hours. Just talked. He told her about growing up in New Russia on his parents' farm. She told him about her life as an heir. He chuckled at one point, saying, "Ah, so you are a little Red heired girl." Her brow furrowed. Surely, he could see her hair was blonde, not red. Then she thought about it and laughed when she caught the pun. Finally, he bade her goodnight, dialed the machine to a slower pace and, leaving, extinguished the lights.

On the third morning, he disconnected the machine and had her sit up with her legs hanging over the bed. He placed a splint on her leg and allowed her to stand for a few minutes without putting weight on it. Red gritted her teeth, not wanting to admit how it hurt.

It was also the first day he performed the download. He wheeled the familiar teaching machine into her room. From experience, she donned the headset and began the download. Her eyes turned black, and moved side to side while her head jerked back and forth, up and down. After an hour, the machine stopped. She took the headset off and gulped the electrolyte and water he gave her. Then he took out his pad and began his questions. It wasn't items that required thought or required calculations, just simple recitations of facts.

It was boring.

That evening, he brought a book. She was surprised; very few people, museums and the palace archives, had books these days. "It is poetry my great, great grandmother Annika gave me when I left for school," Yuri explained. He read a poem which spoke of the grassland of the steppe, the grass waving as the sea. She stared dreamily as he read, seeing the endless lands of wavering grass. She imagined dancing to the rhythm of the wind, spinning about and falling to the ground like a seed.

After supper the following day, he brought a hoverchair and they went outside. The air was cooling and a light wind danced through the compound. A scrap of paper skittered about. Workers passed by and greeted Red. She enjoyed being out after having been cooped up for so long. Sitting with Doctor Yuri Russolov was pleasurable, too. They sat quietly and watched the suns go down.

Red found she was liking her young doctor. The conversations weren't serious, discussion based debates. Rather, she mused, he talked to her like a friend, an adult! She found by not being able to read him, she had to listen carefully to what he said and depend on what he said to understand him.

And, she secretly admitted to herself, he was not bad looking. His shock of curly brown hair was too long, sticking up and about his head like tree branches. She didn't much like the wiry moustache that hung past the edges of his mouth. He had an easy

27

smile that showed nicely white teeth. But his nose. Oh, his nose! It was a great big honker, that nose!

Her physical rehabilitation was going well. After two weeks, the neutralizer was removed completely. Doctor Yuri (as she was beginning to call him now) escorted her to the small gymnasium for therapy. He presented her with a pair of crutches and she began to hobble around the station. Although her leg tired rapidly, she enjoyed stopping to rest and visiting with the scientist and workers of the terraforming station.

At fifteen, she found fascinating the variety of people she got to meet and talk with. They were all immensely proud of their work and eager to show it off, from the massive oxygen scrubbers to the composting pits that were supplying the natural fertilizer to help feed the young planet. "In twenty-five years, you won't recognize this world," the station master told her. "Already we've planted out first forest a hundred miles from here. We've achieved enough atmospheric stability now, so we are working with the polar caps and soon hope to be able to create seasons here. Imagine, perhaps in a few years, we might have snow for Christmas."

Red had never spent much time on holidays. The eight heirs had studied holidays, of course. With one hundred and fifty worlds in the Empire, the future Khan would need to be at least familiar with the traditions of the people. Holiday messages to her subjects would be a requirement. For herself, the only day that would matter would be her Naming Day, when she hoped to be named the Crown Princess.

It was less than three years away.

Her Proctor showed up after the first month. He met with Red and Doctor Yuri in his office, going over the surgery and the progress she had made rehabilitating her leg. He sat and reviewed her downloads and studies, then gave her an examination. The results were, as to be expected, excellent. After the examination, the Proctor stared at his charge for several long moments. Red squirmed a bit, nervous as always at the line of examination she was expecting.

Finally, he spoke. "How are you feeling, Child?"

Red furrowed her brow. What a ridiculous question! How did she feel? "I don't understand the question, Proctor," her cross voice announced.

He sighed, "Red File," he told her, "the question is quite simple. You've been away from your family for a month. You've missed an exciting scientific event you were anxious to see. You've been rehabilitating an injury while living with a group of strangers without…" he lowered his glare and continued quizzically. "I am assuming you had the good graces not to scan your hosts?"

Red was taken aback… Astounding! Since she had come out of the surgery, it had never occurred to her to scan any of the residents of the station. They had been so nice, so kind. They had welcomed her and made her part of their family. Becoming comfortable talking to Doctor Yuri, she had then talked with everyone else.

"I…feel…. good?" she answered, "Yes, good, I feel good, Proctor. Strange, I haven't tried to scan anyone since I woke up. Did they do something to me?"

The Proctor's smile was beatific. "Yes, they did," he answered. "They taught you a lesson. They are showing you how to be human. You, in turn, are learning to live amongst humans.

"Of all this line of heirs, yours is the file that has created the most discussion and concern. We gave you a bigger, more complex brain. We had to do significant modification to your human form, borrowing from many Terran creatures and a few alien patterns. We have been concerned, though, with your emotional development. Frankly, there have been serious discussions over discontinuing you. But director Tahn wanted to see if you were capable of normal, healthy emotional development. I'm glad to see that you are making progress."

Discontinuing me? Red thought. N*ot fair! I work harder than any of my brothers and sisters! I must! The file managers gave them more to work with! That wasn't fair, either! And because of that, they discussed discontinuing me!* Inwardly seething, she caught her breath and forced herself to show no anger.

Her Proctor departed the next morning. The station manager was there with Doctor Russolov to see him off. The Proctor was effusive in his praise for Doctor Russolov and the entire staff of the research station.

Meanwhile, Red focused on what she had been told. She had nightmares of doctors with long needles chasing her endlessly through the halls of the Giza Palace. Her dream siblings cheered them on, the Regent and her mother, the Empress, laid wagers with the staff on who would catch her first. Several times during the night she woke in tears.

Morning came. She didn't want to get out of bed when the nurse came to rouse her, but eventually dragged herself out of bed and hobbled to the shower. The nurse admonished her for not using her crutches. Red ignored her and dressed sullenly. The girl complained of being tired and demanded the nurse take her to breakfast in the hover chair. The nurse did so, pushing the angry teen to breakfast. Red wasn't hungry and resisted when Doctor Yuri checked her electrolytes. The nurse took the Doctor aside and described the actions Red had displayed that morning. Her electrolytes were low, so he made up the vile cocktail and insisted she drink it. She whined and complained, sipping it slowly. "You must have mixed it wrong, it tastes like glarpshite!" she admonished him. She had drunk half and he figured it would have to do; it was clear she was going to be obstinate today.

Morning class with the doctor was a disaster. She refused to don the download and flipped through the pages on her pad, not really paying attention to any of it. She sighed heavily when he asked her review questions. After an hour, she declared, "This is dumb. I don't want to work anymore. I want to go for a horse ride."

Doctor Yuri shook his head. "Out of the question. Your leg isn't healed enough to safely ride. You'll fall off and reinjure it."

"I-DON'T-CARE!" screamed the girl, "This is stupid. I am bored, I want to go on a horse ride, NOW!" She threw her pad across the room.

Doctor Yuri sighed, picked up the pad and set it on the table before her. "We do not throw things here in my clinic," he told her. "Now, pick it up and prepare for the review."

"NO!" she shouted. "I want to go horseback riding."

Dr. Yuri shook his head. "Your leg isn't healed enough to go riding. And riding is a reward for good behavior."

Red set her jaw, reached for her crutches. "Where do you think you're going?" he asked her.

"To the barn," She stood and hobbled away. Doctor Yuri watched her back with caring eyes and a knowing smile on his thin face, followed her at a distance.

She picked up a saddle, but couldn't figure a way to get it on a horse while on her crutches. Dropping the crutches and carrying the saddle didn't work; she fell to the straw-covered ground. She growled and tried to regain her feet. "Help me," she ordered her doctor, amused and leaning on the barn's door jamb.

He shook his head. "No, you put yourself there, you take yourself out."

Red would not beg. She humped her bottom across the floor, dragging her leg behind her, then used the wall to rise. "Hand me my crutches," she demanded. Dr. Yuri threw them across the barn in the opposite direction.

"Get them yourself."

"You're MEAN!" she screamed, and attempted to walk across the dirt floor, but stumbled and fell again. Her bad knee was wrenched, so she crawled, grumbling all the way, to the nearest crutch. Standing with its aid, the angry teenager reached the other and fell again trying to pick it up. Sputtering and filthy, she

31

screamed at the last straw. The fifteen minutes to lunch bell rang. And she was hungry.

Sullenly, she hobbled back to her room, took a quick shower and changed into clean clothes. Red felt her spirits rise until she arrived at the dining room and was furious to see Dr. Yuri already there, calmly eating his lunch.

"Quite a treat there, young lady," said one of the dining workers. "Our first crop of carrots! I like them fresh, but they made a delightful dish, butter sautéed carrots. Try it!"

Five carrots sat on the side her plate, each about four inches long and fat. They swam in a thin butter sauce. "I don't like carrots," she announced to the cosmos. When finished, all that remained on her plate were the five orange vegetables.

Dr. Yuri appeared. "Don't forget your carrots."

"NO! I don't like carrots."

"Really? Just try one."

NO!"

"Come on Red. Be a good girl, just try one. You may like it."

In one vicious movement, the girl stabbed one carrot, brought up and into her mouth, chewed a couple of times and made an ugly face as she spat it out.

"I don't like carrots!" was her agonized scream. "Why won't you idiots listen to me for a change?"

An immediate buzzing began in her skull and she felt her body stiffen. Unseen by Red, the nurse who had approached her from the rear smiled and signaled with a thumb up. An older woman used a napkin remove Red's spat carrots, then seated herself across the table. "That's another function of the neutralizer," she explained. "You have no control over your body now. And this," she affixed a pad to the girl's forehead, "neutralizes your psionic ability. So, you will not get your way. You can agree to stop this nonsense immediately or you can sit here and whine like a baby until you do. Then you will eat your carrots like a good little girl would, anyway. Understand?"

"You can't do this to me!" Red screamed, "I am the heir to the fifteenth reincarnation of our revered founder, the Great Angkor Khan! I will be all you dummies' Empress in three years! Why won't you listen to me?" Everyone in the room laughed. She yelled and cursed; they just finished their meals and went on their way.

A group of technicians walked by her table. "Seems to me the fifteenth reincarnation of the Great Khan needs to have her fanny paddled," someone said, instigating a further round of laughter.

Doctor Yuri finished his meal and went to his patient. "Missus Adams is a farmer, but her work is done for the day. She has already raised three daughters, so I wouldn't be so pig-headed with her."

The big woman, Mrs. Adams, still sat across from her. "Are you ready to be good?" she asked.

Red glared.

"O.K." the older woman said. "I'll see you in an hour." True to her word, Mrs. Adams checked every hour on the hour. After one, Red was still glaring. Two hours and she was sniffling. Three and she was crying. "Please, Miss," she begged, "Can I please go?"

Mrs. Adams crossed her arms. "Will you be good?" she asked.

Red sniffled. "Yes," she agreed in a tiny voice. The older woman patted the girl's shoulder, smoothed an errant golden lock.

"No more conniption?" she asked.

"Nuh-uh," Red answered.

"And you eat the carrots," Mrs. Adams finished.

Red began to weep once more.

"I really don't like carrots," was her tiny-voiced reply.

Mrs. Adams tipped her head. "Was that any way to let us know? Next time you don't like something, you say so politely. Then I'll warn them not to serve it to you."

33

Red ate supper with Mrs. Adams that night. They chatted together for a bit after, then the girl hobbled over to Dr. Yuri. "I'm sorry, Doctor. I was bad today and I said things I didn't mean."

"You need to talk when you feel this way, little Red," he said finally. "It's the only way we can help." Red nodded her understanding. "So, do you need to go to your room and study or do you want to go watch the sunset first?" he asked.

Her rare smile was more brilliant than the dual sunset they would see. "Sunset, please," she said.

They sat away from the other sunset viewers. She cuddled up next to him, still sad and afraid. Hesitantly, she told him about the Proctors, how they had considered discontinuing her. The thought of not becoming Khan terrified her. She turned her face to his chest and sobbed. Red File had never cried in her fifteen years. Clearly, it would be a sign of weakness. Here, under the starry skies, she released fifteen years of pent up tears. Yuri held her close and gently stroked her hair.

Red entered a funk. She went through her rehabilitation and school work without enthusiasm. She would occasionally hobble about the research station visiting the residents she had befriended, but most of her free time was spent staring at the plains outside the station. She was quiet at meals, speaking when spoken to, responding in a low voice. There were times she would seem to be brightening, but would soon return to her silent, almost sullen mood.

The station residents became concerned. Katy O'Brien, an Irish botanist to whom Red had attached herself, had a long talk with the girl one afternoon. "She's a teenager," Katy said. "'Tis what happens to teenagers." The women of the station agreed and set about figuring out what to do about Red and her mood.

Yuri was oblivious to Red's darker mood. He had assigned some of the other residents to help with her schoolwork. She fussed with her assignments, unless Yuri was about. When he was, she brightened and worked harder, eager to please him. She wouldn't always sit with him during meals, but would sneak glances at him when she didn't. In the evenings, though, they would spend hours watching the sunset and talking.

The women of the station noticed; some would cluck their tongues at the young doctor and his teenaged charge. Mrs. Adams would set them straight. "Well, it's plain to see she fallen for him and why not?" she would say. "He's young and handsome enough. And quite responsible, as you all know. He's got a good head on his shoulders and we've nothing to worry about. Leave them be."

The idea for the party came from the station master himself. During an informal meeting, he suggested the party for young Red before she left, three weeks hence. Everyone thought it was a grand idea and they set about planning immediately. Doctor Yuri took it upon himself to call the Proctor.

"Delay her departure for a week for, a what?" The Proctor seemed genuinely confused.

"A sweet sixteen birthday party," Yuri explained. "It's a custom from some of our residents. Some of the women here had them, others had a coming out party when they were that age. With the depression she's been in, I think it would be a good event for her."

Red's Proctor was nonplussed. "We have never considered such a thing before," he admitted. "We tell the children when it is their birthday, of course. It's considered a milepost and gives them a specific goal and timeframe. But the Great Khan never made much attention to his birthday, except when the children are presented and when they are named. Still, I see no detriment. Might I attend the party and observe? Perhaps we will use this "Sweet Sixteen" in the future."

Yuri showed up one morning with a sidesaddle. He mounted it to a horse and Red could ride again without putting too much stress on her recovering knee. Three days before the party, as they were preparing to go riding, Yuri told Red, "I have a word. Raudona. Do you know what it means?"

35

Red concentrated for a moment. "Yes, Old Vietnamese. It means red."

He lifted her into her saddle and helped her put her feet in the stirrups. "I think it much better suits you. I believe I will start calling you Raudona." He tilted his head. "Raudona. Yes, it's a prettier name than just plain old Red."

She blushed. She couldn't recall being called pretty.

They spent all the time they could together the last week. She had discarded the crutches and was walking much better, although she still needed the brace. They had taken to holding hands and that got the tongues wagging again. The Proctor observed them and said nothing. But he could be seen from time to time with a small smile on his face.

The afternoon of the party, the women took her away. "What is going on?" the confused girl asked.

"A party," they explained. "You're our guest of honor and it won't do to wear your everyday clothes." Red protested, but didn't fight as they supervised her bathing. The station barber made an appearance. Red balked. Her one vanity was her hair, and this barber also worked in the composting pits. She was finally convinced to let him cut and arrange her hair. When he showed her the mirror, she gasped. He had spiraled her hair up several inches, then allowed it to flow down her back, "Oh my!" was all the stunned girl could manage.

They produced a formal dress, made from the crepe and silks requested from the Proctor. It didn't fit perfectly and there was little time to adjust it, but Red loved it all the same.

Her mirror image left her speechless. Red looked and felt like a princess. She blushed and turned to her friends, "Thank you," she gushed. "I don't know what else to say. Thank you."

They led her to the gaudily decorated cafeteria, where the station manager was waiting outside the door. He was wearing his formal uniform, though it had clearly seen better days. He wasn't wearing his customary ball cap, either. Red was slightly surprised that what she thought was a thick mop of hair was instead an unruly ring. His pate shone under the artificial lamps as he bowed formally and offered her an arm.

They entered the cafeteria and were announced. "Residents of Celtius 4, station manager Rory Gant is pleased to present Miss Raudona of Terra." Everyone was there and all applauded as he escorted her to the front of the room, followed by all the station's women. Over her head, a large sign read, "Happy Sweet Sixteen, Raudona!"

She was overwhelmed. Mrs. Adams presented her with a wrist corsage. The station manager handed her a box, "From the whole station." Inside was a thin gold bracelet, with the word "Raudona" spelled out. He helped her place it on her wrist.

Then Dr. Yuri stepped forward. "This is from me, Raudona." Inside his gift was a gold necklace, with a small ruby setting. Mrs. Adams held Raudona's hair up as Doctor Yuri fastened it around her slender throat. Red, Raudona, fingered the gift, then stood on her tiptoes and kissed his cheek.

The party went into full swing. The station manager claimed the honor of the first dance, but soon she was dancing with everyone. Mindful of her knee, they were sure to give her frequent breaks to sit and visit. Holo-cameras were produced, since everyone wanted an image with the heir. She laughed and danced, ate cakes and danced more.

Finally, Dr. Yuri produced a hoverchair for her. "It is late," he explained, "And she is still a student, after all." There were groans all around, but he resolutely put the tired girl in the chair and returned her to her room. "Did you have a good time, Raudona?" he asked her.

She nodded, strangely shy. "It was nearly perfect," she replied. "It just needed one more thing."

Dr. Yuri puzzled, replied, "What would that be?"

"This." She stood on tiptoe again, put her arm around his neck and kissed his mouth. "My first real kiss," she explained.

Then she turned and rushed into her room, closing the door behind her.

Chapter 5

They were walking through the fields, at the doctor's insistence. His excuse was to have her get more exercise for her leg. It gave them time to hold hands and talk. Raudona was thrilled spending time with Yuri. He had asked her to call him by his given name, a very grown-up thing, indeed.

Yuri had exciting news for her tonight. "I have received a letter from Christ the Savior Hospital in New Moscow," he told her. "I am offered a residency in surgery. I have accepted and will be there in three months."

"Oh, Yuri, that is wonderful!" Raudona exclaimed. "I know you have been working so hard for that job. And you'll be so close to Giza! Less than an hour by sub orbital!"

Yuri chuckled. "Yes, so close, if I could afford such a thing. More likely, I will have to rent a flier and take half a day to see you there. That is," he grew quiet, "if you want me to come see you there."

"I do," she said softly. "I will be busy with school, but I'm sure I can ask my Proctor for time to see you. And," she was mischievous now, "we have a fleet of transports at Giza Palace, including a couple of sub orbitals. Getting you to Giza from New Moscow shouldn't be a worry."

They continued to walk through the gathering dusk. Returning to the station, the suns finally set and the sky went dark, illuminated only by the seemingly endless sweep of stars from the Sagittarius Arm. Annika took Yuri's hand in hers, their fingers intertwined. "I am told by my Proctors that when I consider the night sky, I am considering the past, given the speed of light and the time it takes to reach my eyes where I stand at this very moment," she said. "But given my position, given who I am and what I know I am destined to become, I'm sure I can see into the future."

"What do you see in your future?" Yuri asked.

"I see my Empire," her voice was firm. "I will be the Khan, Yuri. I know it. I just hope…" her voice trailed off. She swallowed and said, "I just hope you come to see me at Giza Palace, Yuri. Promise me you will."

He kissed her slender fingers. "I will."

It was the day for her to leave. Raudona arose and donned her red unitard, shorts and jacket. Her things were packed in the small valise that came with her. She looked longingly at the party dress the station ladies had made for her, then stroked the smooth silk and crisp crepe and sighed. There would be no opportunity to wear it when she got home. And she had no way to pack it, anyway.

A tap on the door brought forth Katy, Mrs. Adams and the women she had befriended. Katy saw the dress in the closet and asked, "Here, now, what's this? Surely you're not running off and leaving it behind!"

"I don't have room on the shuttle to transport it," Raudona explained. "At Giza, we are issued uniforms, so I won't have an opportunity to wear it."

Mrs. Adams took Raudona's hands and explained. "Dear, you aren't taking this dress to wear again. You take it and put it in your hope chest. One day, you'll have a daughter and you'll show it to her when she turns sixteen. She may wear it, or use it as an idea for her dress. So, you hold on to it, O.K.?"

Raudona chuckled as she pointed out, "When I become Empress, I will have at least four heir daughters."

Chatter abounded as the females ate; Raudona blew Yuri a kiss when he entered and waved to her. The couple didn't sit together. Raudona was surrounded by her women friends; the conversation was lively and there were constant shrieks of laughter. Yuri sat to one side, not eating, focused on his cup of coffee.

The room became silent when the Proctor arrived. He found a seat next to Yuri, but the spell was broken. The women issued tearful, hurried goodbyes and, red eyed, went about their duties.

Soon, only Mrs. Adams, Katy, Raudona, Yuri and the Proctor remained. There was an awkward silence until the Proctor stood, saying, "Child, I'll be waiting at the ship. Take care of your goodbyes."

Yuri moved next to the sniffling girl. The huddled together for several minutes, before Raudona said, "I'd better go." He took her hand and they walked through the station to the landing pad, followed by Mrs. Adams and Katy. Friends called out to her as she passed.

The Proctor waited for her at the shuttle. Katy marched up to him and thrust a box into his surprised arms. "This here is her party dress from her birthday," she intoned in her sweet brogue. "It is very important to her. You will see it's safely stored aboard and when she gets home, you'll see it's put away for her. Do you understand?"

The Proctor held the box away from his body, as if it were strange and unpleasant. But he nodded and disappeared into the ship and returned a few minutes later telling Katy and Mrs. Adams, "It is as you asked and will be done as you have said." Mrs. Adams grunted and the two women gave Raudona a final hug, then returned to the building.

It was as though they were alone. He held her tightly, never wanting to let go. She clung to him.

Her Proctor cleared his throat.

"Until New Moscow, Raudona. Three months."

"New Moscow, Yuri."

"No crying now."

"Of course not."

Raudona, her head down, entered the ship. She turned at the hatch and blew Yuri a kiss.

"I shall make sure we schedule some time for you two to see each other," the Proctor stated. "I cannot guarantee as much time as you might like. But I'm sure we can work something out." He held out his hand.

"Thank you." Yuri clasped the Proctor's hand.

The hatch closed with a hiss as the Proctor entered the ship. Liftplates glowed and the ship slowly raised, turned and flew up and away. Yuri watched, his heart aching. Three months. Dejected, lonely already, he put his hands in his pockets and went for a walk in the fields.

She was asleep. He closed the door and went to the secret comm station, the one that used otherspace to carry the message. Even the military didn't have it. He tuned it in and waited.

The File Master appeared.

"I greet you, Master," the Proctor said.

"And I you, my servant. She is aboard and well?"

"Yes, Master. There will be continued rehabilitation on her knee. It is likely that will be a weak point for some time. But I believe it will not handicap her for long."

"Very well. What of the emotional program? Did it activate as we designed?"

"Yes Master. She is exhibiting the range of emotions as we had hoped. Normal, teen age instability has exceeded expectations slightly, but the research station was an excellent training ground for her to gain control over her more, shall we say, unsavory outbursts."

"We can expect compliance, then?"

"Not entirely, Master. I believe that they instituted some controls in her she wasn't aware of. She will still occasionally have outbursts, but the lessons she learned from the station personnel and the social interaction she was forced into will serve her well. I predict that we shall see some defiance, but by Naming Day, she will be ready."

"What of the romantic programing? Has she imprinted with the partner as we had need?"

"Without a doubt, Master. The doctor is an outstanding choice. Transferring him nearby, but not too nearby, was an equally brilliant stroke. I predict the romance will flourish and we can expect she will choose him as her partner."

"It was not so much brilliant as it was necessary. The doctor is what the Empire needs to bring back into the Imperial line. You are to encourage this relationship carefully and quietly at every opportunity. I expect the marriage to be in no more than ten years. Sooner than later would be preferred. We shall have the files ready before then."

"It shall be as you command, Master."

"See to it that it is. We shall see you in seventy-two hours when you arrive at Terra.

Chapter 6

Three years later.

Terra! Ancient and traditional home for the Terran Empire. The wellspring from which all Terrans sprang. The blue sapphire floating in space, the jewel that pulls at the heart of every man and woman born.

At the very heart of Terra is the Giza Palace. When the Third Khan, Hinabrian, was touring the war-ravaged cities of Terra following the third Galactic Council War, he awoke one morning to see the sun rising from the cliffs of Giza. He gazed in wonder as the sun backlit the tombs of the ancient God-Kings of Egypt. He decided he would build the new capital for his young Empire in the place of these ancients.

The construction of Giza Palace would outlast the 80 years he was on the throne and two hundred years beyond. It became a magnificent edifice, blending natural stone with traditional construction and modern flair. The campus extended from the desert floor to dozens of stories, high over the rim of the plateau. It arced in each direction, from the air a sweeping crescent. The ends of the palace tapered to a single building block, as though wide, circling arms embraced all who walked to the plaza.

The plaza itself was a seamless white expanse, measuring a square mile. During Great Events of the Empire, millions of beings would crowd the plaza and bear witness to events regarding the Royal Family and the Empire. They rejoiced in the encircling arms of the piazza, the center of the citadel holding a broad balcony where the Khans would appear to their worshipping subjects. On either side of the balcony rose a pair of towers, the Tower of the Dawn to the east, the Tower of the Evening to the West.

And the palace itself! Thousands of offices, warehouses and barracks. Vast apartments and suites. Parklands and gardens, all set

45

to open air and fed from the River Nile through a clever series of aqueduct, sluices and ejectors. There was no need for pumps in the palace, nor expensive cooling systems. Emperor Hinabrian Khan had planned well. Great turbines supplied power, the very force of the river created all manners of plumbing and cooling.

Today was a rebirth for the Empire. For the eight, the course of their lives would be set. In the culture of their ancestral tribe, the Khalkha, they would announce their chosen adult names, becoming adults in the eyes of their people.

For seven, there would be a disappointment. Their quest would end. They would be greatly respected, both in personal and professional circles, living for the rest of their lives as ne-Khan. Of the Khan's family, but not the Khan.

And the eighth. The eighth who was first. He or she would be named the Crown Heir. The Crown Heir would still need to continue to grow, being instructed on the responsibilities and the task of being Khan of the Terran Empire. No detail would be too small, no plan without their permission. Theirs would be the direction over trillions of Terrans spread throughout the Empire and beyond, as well as the partners, client states and the subjected. The new Crown Heir would wait seven more years, completing school and training before he or she would assume the title and name of Khan.

The eight waited in a large chamber at the center of the palace. Each was deep in personal thoughts. Orange didn't want the job. Black knew he wouldn't be Khan; his talents lay elsewhere in the service to the Empire. Green and Purple were unsure where they stood, each hoping for the title, even more unsure what they would do with it. Blue was completely relaxed. He knew he had done all he could; there was nothing more to be done. Whatever happened today, he was genuinely excited to be starting the next part of his life.

White was anxious for the day to be over. Today, finally, he would have his freedom. Let the others fight over the crown, after today, he would emulate the brother of the ninth Khan and disappear forever.

Red, however, was certain she was to be the next Khan. She had excelled at every test the Proctors could invent, every physical challenge.

There was no one, living or dead, who was ever more prepared to rule the Empire. She was the only one qualified to be Khan; anyone else was already less than she.

Without her, the Empire would be diminished.

She simply had to win.

A fanfare sounded. The family elders, other notable members of the Royal Family and members of the court were filing into the lower level balconies of the palace. The eight could make out the cheers of the crowd through the thick stone walls.

Violet sat dangling his fingers in the room's fountain, occasionally slapping and splashing the water. He was wearing a handsome velvet suit, with ruffles and breeches. His hose shone brightly and a stylish ribbon controlled his hair. Yellow and Green wore long, flowing robes. Red had donned a brilliant unitard, over which she wore a long, flowing dress open in front and flowing to the sides, more like a dramatic coat than dress. Her hair, as always, was tied back in a severe braid. She had thought about wearing the dress her friends had made for her two years before, but decided impression of the Empire was more important.

Another fanfare. The Regent Ming si ne-Khan and the Empress Lorraine were making their entrance. The cheering was louder. The eight knew their Uncle was reveling in the worship, believing the cheers were for him. Each knew they were superior to him.

All had devised their own method for getting rid of him.

Dohlman appeared. "It is time," he announced. They lined up as they always had. Today would be the final time. They would never return to this room, together like this, again. In mindspeak, each wished the others well.

The Regent and Empress stood proudly at the center of the balcony in full view of the plaza. The eight turned to the couple and bowed, although Raudona's subservience was a bare tip of her head. Then the siblings turned to face the waiting throng below.

The Regent spoke, his voice carried by hidden microphones. "Citizens!" he cried. "Terrans! Terrans here and throughout our Empire! Our companions! Our Allies! Our Honor Guests! I present to you today the sons and daughters of our dearly, departed Khan, my brother Robert! Today, these children are children no more. Today we celebrate the traditions of our forefathers, going back to ancient times. We celebrate the Law laid down two thousand years ago by our Great Khan himself."

The crowd was roaring. The Regent had to wait until the deafening cheers abated.

"This morning, for the last time, my brother's dear children awoke as youths. Now, before the tribesman in this place, all those who bear witness here and all the Terrans wherever they may be viewing today's ceremony, I invite our new men and women to step forth and declare themselves before the Gods!" The volume of the crowd began to build again.

White stepped forward first. "Today, I am Tomas Blanco."

Then Black voiced his name. "Noire" was all he said.

Purple spoke, "I declare myself as Victor. Victor Royal."

Orange stepped forward, fierce and beautiful. In a strong voice she declared, "I am Anja de L'Orange. See me and despair!"

Green bowed low in his flowing robes. "I am Jiro Hijau."

Blue bounded. "Hello, everyone!" He was expansive, his arms flung wide. "I am Blaise. Blaise Bleu!"

Yellow stepped forward and curtsied. "I have chosen to be called Teresa Curie. I vow to serve."

The last of the eight to step forward was Red. Confidently, she looked over the crowd, turning to Yuri's section last. She could see his curly head and the smile he wore. She grinned back and said, "I am Annika. Annika Raudona."

Annika. Named for Yuri's great, great grandmother. She could see his face break into a huge grin.

The Regent began to speak. "Citizens! Our new family…" His voice trailed off and he squinted, looking north toward New Cairo.

The crowd stirred, confused. Many turned and saw the small craft racing toward the palace. As it passed over the edge of the plaza, little black objects tumbled away from it. They exploded over the crowd, shrapnel tearing through flesh. Hundreds died instantly. Before anyone could react, an identical ship roared over from the east, depositing more death. Then came one from the west.

"RUN!" someone screamed in the mindspeak.

They scattered as a ship came in from the north. It fired a rapid gun, spitting rounds across the balcony and into the crowd below. Bombs fell from it and more died in the carnage. The ships continued to loop, make their runs, raining death.

Annika found herself scrambling on her hands and knees. There was a pop and a wet smack as the body of a soldier nearly fell on her. His gun clattered to one side. She stared at the dead soldier, then grabbed his gun, stood and began firing. She was blinded with fury, firing into the sky and through the thick, acrid smoke around her. She roared aloud as she fired.

"ANNIKA!" She heard the scream in her head. The softer, **"Annika! Here, turn around!"** She spun around and took her finger off the trigger just in time. Noire was standing there, calm in his entreaty. **"Sister, hand me the gun. Please."** She handed the gun to him blankly, oblivious to the death and destruction around them. **"Come, Annika, we need to find cover from the attack."**

"NO!" she insisted. **"We need to find the others."**

"Don't…" he begged.

She looked about, trying to get her bearings, then went to her left. Unsure, she still felt it was the right direction to go. Within

49

yards, the wind blew the smoke back and Annika could see where she had been standing only minutes before.

Carnage. A slaughter house.

Victor was face down. Or would have been, if his head wasn't gone. Jiro and Anja were in pieces. Annika recognized the orange slipper on the lower leg and could see a pile of green robes, saturated with viscera. Blaise lay on his back, staring at the sky, blinking. He was trying to hold his stomach in, failing to notice his legs were gone.

"BLAISE!" she cried through the link. "Oh, GODS above, don't move!" as she hurried to him. She shook as she knelt next to him, desperately trying to remember what she should do. His eyes turned and focused on her.

"Annika?" he asked, "Why? Why, dear sister?" His head fell to the side and he seemed to lose focus. Then she heard him whisper. "Avenge us." She felt him slipping.

Then he was dead.

A raider flew over, continuing to spit death. There was a motion behind her. She spun but there was only Noire. "Annika, we have to go, it's not safe," he begged.

A soldier stumbled past, his arms held out in front of him. Annika suppressed a cry. He was on fire. He stumbled a few more yards and fell. She searched for her gun; she wanted to make sure he wasn't suffering.

Screaming on her left, the Empress was holding a prone Regent, who bled from his head and abdomen. Screams and cries all around, explosions, fire. Smoke encompassed the abattoir like the deepest of fog.

Annika flinched and ducked as another of the raiders flew over, low but not firing. Moments later, a smaller, spearhead-shaped vessel painted in Imperial greens and browns screamed past, chasing the raider. Here was a succession of snaps; the fighter was firing on the raider. *Good, our fighters have finally arrived.*

50

Yuri. She had to find Yuri. She turned wildly, trying to decide which way to go. Noire grabbed her arm, begging her to come with him to safety. She stepped back, tripping over Blaise and landing in the middle of the remains of her sister and brothers. Terrified, she tried to stand, slipped and fell again. Her body was soon coated with the gore of her siblings' bodies. This time she couldn't hold back her scream.

A soldier appeared. He lifted her unceremoniously, flopped her over his shoulder. "Miss, are you able to walk?" he yelled above the ongoing din.

"Wha-wha…" Annika stammered. "Hey, PUT ME DOWN!" she screamed. She began to beat his back with her small fists. "I must go find Yuri."

Her captor ignored her and began to run, screaming into the microphone at his mouth. "O.K. I'm bringing in the Red; Black is with me. No, I haven't seen the other two."

He entered a door and ran down the corridor, turned a corner and stopped. Other soldiers gathered round as he let Annika to the floor. She beat on his chest screaming, "I must find Yuri! Take me to Yuri!"

The soldier grabbed her wrists. "Listen, LISTEN!" he hollered. "Get yourself together. Someone just tried to cut the head off this government and right now, for better or worse, you are the one in charge. I need you to calm down and listen!"

He got through to her. Annika stopped yelling and hitting. She was shivering now, but her eyes took on a steely resolve. "Yes, you're right," she said in a strangely calm voice. "What is your name, soldier?"

"Campion," he replied. "Captain Morris Campion. 2nd infantry."

"Well, now you are Major Campion of my personal body guard," Annika said in the calm voice. "Right now, you need to get me and my brother to the command bunker. Now, soldier!"

He spoke into his microphone briefly, then asked her, "Can you walk? I can carry you if you can't keep up." Annika huffed, narrowed her eyes and stormed down the corridor.

Chapter 7

They hurried down the passage, following Annika. She entered an elevator and dropped dozens of levels, then exited. Major Campion wondered how she knew where she was going. **"I'm taking directions from you, Major. It's quicker this way,"** she mindspoke.

At a washroom, she paused. Her entourage took up guardian stations outside the door. Inside, a wreck looked at her from the mirror. Hair in disarray, black smudges and…blood on her face. Annika gasped and scrabbled for the faucet. She scrubbed with fury, watching the gore go down the drain. Her control slipped and she found herself escaping into hysterics again.

"Calm down, Sister," Noire mindspoke. **"Just presentable is all you need for now."** His matter-of-fact demeanor restored her control. There was nothing she could do about her clothes, and she could only smooth down the worst of her hair. *Not a hair out of place…* echoed in her head. *Well, no time for that now.*

The soldiers at the door of the Command Center stiffened as she arrived. She pushed her way past them and through the doors.

The Command Center was circular, with three tiers. Consoles lined the walls, with a busy army of soldiers scurrying from one to the other. A large holo emitter above the lower floor and stretching to the ceiling displayed Egypt and the Mediterranean Sea. Red and green arrows danced across the map.

She was soon recognized. "Holy glapsh…I mean, attention on deck!" a passing soldier yelled. Immediately, the whole room stiffened. Annika whispered to Major Campion, "Now what do I do?"

"Carry on!" he bawled. He winked at her, obsequiousness gone since her trip from the balcony over his shoulder. "Better get used to it." A short, aging, bald officer appeared in front of her and bowed.

53

"Miss, I am General Han, Deputy Commander of this facility. I am pleased to see you and your brother made it here safely."

"Thank you General. Any word on my other sister and brother? I know about the others. And the Regent? What is his condition?"

General Han took her by the arm and led her down the stairs toward the holo table. "Your sister Teresa has been recovered, but she refuses to leave the Plaza," he said. "She is aiding in establishing a triage station. I have no word on your other brother. The Regent has been taken to the palace hospital. He is grievously wounded, but expected to make a full recovery."

He pointed to the hologram. "This is a live time tactical display of what is occurring at this moment. There were twelve raiders that attacked the Plaza. Two squadrons of fighters were scheduled to be overhead during the ceremonies. Odd, the launch orders were canceled."

Annika studied the dancing arrows. "You said you are deputy commander?" she asked. "Where is the Commander?"

Han shook his head. "General Teague was here at his post this morning. We chatted for several minutes. I haven't seen him since." Annika and Noire shared a sideways glance; her brother nodded his agreement.

"General, I want this General Teague arrested," was Annika Raudona's first official order to her army. "Put him in a cell and my brother will... interview him." General Han nodded and quietly gave the order to a nearby aide.

"As you see, we have already downed eight of the raiders," the General announced. "The others are heading north. I have ordered fighter command in Europe to launch more interceptors, but I intend to leave two unharmed to follow back to the mothership. These raiders are too small to be interstellar."

Annika decided she liked this General. She gave him a quick scan and confirmed that she could trust him, also. "Have we secured the space around Terra?" she asked.

Han shook his head. "No. That requires an order from the highest level."

Annika glowered. "As for right now, General, I am the highest level of government," she hissed. "Shut down all the space around Terra. All shipping lanes in and out of the Sol system are to be searched. Not a ship in or out without a physical search. Any ship that refuses is to be detained."

The General grinned and bowed. "As you order. I will make it so."

Annika asked, "How bad on the plaza?"

General Han touched a control. "We had over two million guests on the Plaza today for your ceremony," he answered. "I had thirty thousand troops on security. We are fortunate indeed that the raiders were only using high explosives as opposed to incendiary devices. The casualty lists will be high, but not as high as I fear they might have been. I have also alerted the nearby garrison in Persia; there will be another fifteen thousand troops here by evening. Our biggest difficulty right now is due to the sheer size of the event. Already, the hospitals in Cairo are overwhelmed. We have begun to transport the wounded to the surrounding communities, but I am afraid many will die before they can receive treatment."

The numbers were numbing, but the would-be Khan grasped the situation quickly. "General, you have my authorization to use whatever means you deem necessary, for the duration of the crisis."

Then she felt a surge of panic. "General a…friend of mine is a guest. He was in the Plaza when the attack started. I need him found. He is very important to me. I must know he is safe! Please, General!"

He sighed. "Captain," he snapped, pointing to Campion.

"Major." Annika corrected.

"Major. I see she has attached herself to you. Take a platoon of soldiers and secure this friend of hers... Will that do?" he asked her.

Annika realized that was a huge concession, given the situation. "Yes, General, that is exceedingly generous." She gave Campion Yuri's description and where he had been sitting when the attack occurred.

For hours, she sat and watched the activity as it swirled around the command center. Reports came in, the data would be sent to whomever was responsible and rapid decisions made. Aides reported to General Han and hand him a slip of paper or a data pad. He acted quickly on each piece and move on. Officers would cluster together, have a hurried discussion, and then move on. It looked chaotic, but she could see the pattern, the organization, the fluidity. The teamwork.

Teamwork. Annika began thinking of her siblings. The Proctors would give them assignments that forced them to act collectively. Not to find any one weak spot, but to enforce the importance of working together and presenting a united front. Blue always excelled at these games, confident and charismatic. He always seemed to know just the right thing to say when she or one of the others would disagree. Once they hit puberty, she and Orange could seemingly never agree on anything. But Blue was always there, laughing and cajoling, so that in the end, the two sisters could work closely together.

Orange. Anja. Annika closed her eyes and tried to see her dead sister's face. But all she could see was the orange slipper on the lower leg. The rest of her was gone. Annika bit her lips and tried to see Blaise. She could feel the blood on her hands. Victor's headless body swam into her daydream. *Jiro, where was Jiro?*

Annika began to shake. A tall, muscular sergeant was passing by, stopped and dropped to her knee. "Hey," in a soft voice that belied her size. "Are you all right?" Annika didn't see her, only saw Blaise trying to mouth his final words, and her tremors increased in violence. "Crap!" said the sergeant. "O.K, Honey, stay right here." She ran over to General Han, who saw Annika's condition and nodded assent.

Returning to Annika, the sergeant knelt and took the heir's face gently in her large hands. "Hey, Sweetie, listen. I'm Pamela. I'm the Quartermaster for this part of the facility. What say you and me go for a little walk, maybe let you freshen up and have a bite to eat?" Annika allowed herself to be guided. Then a door opened and they entered a three-room suite.

"Look Annika, a shower. Why don't you undress and clean up? I'll order us some supper and rustle you up some clean clothes."

Annika nodded, listlessly undressing on the spot, her clothes falling to the floor. In the bath, she stared helplessly at the controls. Pamela, hearing no noise from the shower, hurried in, turned on the water and directed it on the young girl.

Annika found soap and washed herself. The warm water sluiced over her, relaxing her tense muscles. She began to feel herself lifting slowly from her catatonia. Fighting down the images running through her head, she resolutely washed the remainder of the dirt, grime...and blood, that streaked her body. She untied her hair and washed the stink of the day from it, too.

Finished, she stood and soaked in the hot water for a time, trying to wash the horrors of the day away. She took the soap and scrubbed herself again. Rinsed again. Soaked for a few minutes, then reached for the soap once more. "Hey, hey there, now, that's quite enough," declared Pamela, opening the shower door. She held a huge, soft towel. "Come on, Sweetie, that's enough scrubbing. Time to dry off and get dressed. Supper will be here soon."

Annika willed herself to step towards Pamela and the towel. The older woman embraced the shuddering girl who was briskly dried and rubbed down. Pamela had her sit while she brushed out and braided Annika's once again golden hair.

"Sorry about the clothes, Sweetie, best we could do on short notice." A uniform lay on the bed. An Imperial Officer's uniform, although there was no rank. The underwear fit well enough, but the rest of it was too large for the slight girl. The pants were worst; she couldn't get them to stay up. Exasperated, Annika tried to bite and tear a strip from the bedsheets. Pamela pulled a switchblade from her pocket and cut the bedsheet into a makeshift belt to hold the pants up. The jacket covered the pseudo belt.

The meal was simple fare, soup, bread, cheese and fruit. Annika was surprised at her appetite. It had not occurred how many hours had passed since she and her siblings had been together and eaten.

Her siblings. She stopped chewing and tears clouded her eyes. Once again, she quivered and shook. Pamela quickly wrapped her arms around the girl. "When I was not much older than you," she whispered, "I was on a combat drop. It was a pissling little planet that only the Gods below knows why we were taking. They were pretty well equipped; it was taking more effort than it should have.

"We were dropping on what we were told was a command and control site. They were shooting damn good that day, and suddenly the other side of the drop pod was gone, along with a half dozen crack Imperial Troopers. All of them my friends. We entered a spin and I braced myself. The Gods above must have been looking me over that day; I was awake the whole crash. We hit and tumbled, which tore our craft to pieces.

"The impact killed most of the rest of my friends. I found out later I had broken my back, but when what was left of our pod stopped moving, I was hanging from the wall that my drop rig was hooked to. There were some moans around me, so I knew I wasn't the only survivor. I had to get out.

"I struggled and got my harness to release…and promptly fell on another Trooper. Rodriguez. From one of the farming colonies. He was trying to make enough scratch to buy his own farm. He was still alive, I know, because he cried out when I landed on him. I could tell he was a goner. He looked at me with his one good eye." Pamela swallowed and went silent for a minute.

"Yeah, I got out," she said, her voice strong again. "I crawled over fifteen of my friends. Most of them were dead, smashed to a pulp. But a couple were like Rodriguez. Still alive, but dying. There was nothing I could do but get out." She put her hands around Annika's cheeks again and stared into her eyes. "I can still see each one of them."

Annika sighed. "Does it ever stop?"

Pamela shook her head. "I still see them every night."

There was a tapping at the door. The messenger announced, "The General would like to see you back in Central,"

"I'll stay with you," Pamela stated," We'll be fine." They followed the messenger back to the command center.

Annika startled when everyone leaped up and stood in brace. "I understand tradition and the respect you're giving me," Annika smiled, "but for the duration of the crisis, would you all please stop all the jumping up and down when I enter a room? It's really starting to make me jumpy." A nearly audible chuckle rolled around the room. "Now, do that stand easy thing, would you?"

At the holo on Level One, General Han set to his report. "First," he said, "The Imperial Council, along with the File Board, wish to see you in the Grand Council Room at ten hundred local tomorrow. I will make sure we have a proper fitting uniform." Annika nodded, pleased. The uniform she had on was much too big; the hint of acceptance from the General in his offering of a uniform was a welcome relief.

"Second, unpleasant news, I am afraid." He pointed to the holo. The map was of the North Sea. There were Green arrows, but no red. Instead, there were two red X's. "The first turned and engaged the fighters out of Norway sent to intercept them. The fighters had no choice. I approve of their decision to shoot down the enemy. The second was more disturbing." He touched a control. The view changed to a cockpit view of an Imperial Buccaneer. "This is view from the flight leader. As you see, he is head on with the raider. Now watch."

59

The enemy craft flashed into view, then lifted its nose and began to climb. The fighter pointed its nose and decreased the range, climbing faster. Suddenly, the raider arced over, and dove straight down. The fighter turned and followed, breaking away at the last possible moment. The enemy did not, smashing into the sea at least two thousand miles an hour. The plume of water was impressive.

"Gods below!" exploded Annika. "May his soul be cursed to cleaning the crack of the Eighth Khan!"

"My feelings exactly," said Han, "until one of my junior officers offered up an idea. Lieutenant?" An officer who seemed barely older than Annika appeared.

"I am Second Lieutenant Beckman, Ma'am," he reported. "I am from historical records. I am serving the command post intelligence division, offering historical data when it seems appropriate. My family has a long heritage of military service. Back in the early years of the twentieth century, one of them served in the Kriegsmarine of the nation state of Germany. His specific service was on a submarine. I was studying the course of the raiders, puzzling with everyone else why they were taking such a course. They could have been leading us away, a decoy, so the mothership might slip out of orbit, but I quickly dismissed that idea as every scanner on the planet was looking for them. Then I thought of my many times great grand-sire. I thought 'What is the difference between a jump capable ship and an ancient submarine?'"

Annika quickly grasped the idea. "You found them. Where? How?"

Han smiled. "When he told me his idea, we went back to the time he mentioned. There was nothing there. However, within one hundred years, Russia had developed what was called a blue light scan laser. The blue spectrum is capable of penetrating fluids, such as water."

I am familiar with blue light scan lasers, Annika thought.

"We adapted some satellites, extrapolated the raider's course and found this. He touched a control and the view changed to map mode. It rolled over the northern polar cap and stopped over a body of water.

"Bering Sea?" Annika asked. "There? Why?"

"It is a very remote location," explained Han. "A clever idea, really. From there, they could have lifted right through the radiation zone of the Van Allen belts. Under the best of circumstances, it is difficult to track anything through there."

"When do you take them?" Annika asked.

"Soon," Han replied. "We have assembled assets to capture them when the surface. Better to take them once they leave the water, less of a chance of an accident that way. They are ours, they will not get away."

It was the best news she had heard all day, Annika decided. On a terrible day, good news at last. "Will that be all, General?" she asked.

"No," he answered slowly, "I have one more bit of news for you." He broke into a wide smile.

"Hullo, my little Red Heired girl." Annika whirled about.

"YURI!" she screamed.

Chapter 8

Annika leapt into Yuri's arms, her arms around his neck. She kissed his face over and over, then buried her own face in his chest. Her body shook, relief coming at last in tears. Yuri was alive and right here with her. She couldn't contain herself.

"Annika, Annika," cooed Yuri, stroking her hair. "It is me. I'm here for you. My beloved Annika."

"Thank you," she said, turning to the room. "Thank you, everyone. Gods, Yuri, it's really you." She buried her face again. "What happened, where were you?"

"I remember you announcing your name," he said. "I made the connection right away. You chose my great, great grandmother's name, yes?" Annika nodded. "You have no idea how honored I am that you did that," Yuri said.

"Then the first bomb exploded.

"It happened so fast. The bombs started falling; everyone went into a panic. I was buffeted about, but fortunately I didn't fall. Many were killed by the bombs, but many more were killed when they fell and were trampled by panicking people trying to escape. I remember seeing a big bomb hit the stage where you had been standing. I nearly collapsed; I thought for sure you were there. I had to get to you. I don't know how long it took and I remember throwing punches at people who wouldn't move out of my way fast enough. I saw your sister and brother's remains. Someone had covered them up. I'm so sorry for your loss, Annika."

"Thank you, Yuri."

"I didn't see any sign of you, alive or dead. But the smoke was clearing and I could see and hear there were thousands on the Plaza who needed help. I am a doctor first and last, Annika. I swore an oath, I had to help. There were others, doctors, nurses. But most were just ordinary people, who helped.

"We began to go through and save who we could. A soldier showed up. I explained to him how a triage works and he helped us organize. More soldiers showed up and we began to make good progress. A lot of people died today, Annika. But a lot more were saved because of your citizens and your soldiers. They did a fine job.

"Finally, about an hour ago, your Major Campion came to our triage, looking for me. He told me you were in trouble and needed me right away. There are doctors there now and I had to come if you were in trouble. And so, I am here."

Han cleared his throat and said, "Well, Miss, I have nothing more for you today. I would suggest you and your friend go get a good night's sleep. You've had a very hard day and I expect you will have many in the days ahead." He called, "Attention!" Everyone snapped to brace again, then bowed to the young woman. Annika let go of Yuri, braced and returned the courtesy.

"On behalf of the Empire," she said, "thank you for the magnificent job you all did today." She held her bow for a minute, then straightened, took Yuri by the hand and gestured to Pamela to lead on.

The suite Pamela led them to was larger and more ornate than the earlier one. Bedrooms were on their right, each with a large bed, the bath to the left. Yuri explored and returned wide eyed. "Good Lord," he gasped. "How big a bath does one really need? We could bathe my whole family in that tub and still have room for half my cousins!" Annika shrugged. She had been seeing such things all her life.

"Good that you found the bath, Yuri," Annika teased. She wrinkled her tiny nose. "You certainly need it."

Pamela had moved to the window and opened the drapes. "Oh, my!" she said, stepping back. She tried to close the drapes. Yuri stopped her.

The suite overlooked the Plaza. The sun had gone down and the Plaza was dark as the void. Here and there in the dark were

64

pools of light, exposing frantic efforts. Other, smaller lights were moving about, amongst the stationary pools of light. Lines of lights swept along, stopping and frantically signaling. A transport lifted from one lighted area and raced away, another arrived right on its heels.

"I'm so sorry," Pamela said. "I had forgotten the direction this suite faced." She was clawing again at the drapes. She finally stopped, grabbed Annika by the arm and said, "Come on, let's go. I know of a better suite."

Annika held up her hand, "No, we'll stay here," she said quietly. She watched for a while, then turned away.

"Dohlman," Annika called.

Dohlman appeared. A tall, stately man, dressed in a high collar suit with a blue plaid cummerbund and white gloves. His hair was slick and parted in the middle. Below his upturned nose was the thinnest of moustache. Although only a holo, he was programed as the head of the house staff and served its master and mistress exclusively. "Yes, Ma'am?" he queried in a voice reminiscent of the highest level of elegance and perfection.

Annika ordered, "Pour a bath for my friend Yuri and get him a set of pajamas. Send a servant around to his hotel and fetch his wardrobe. Order a light supper for three..."

"Two, Ma'am," interrupted Pamela. "I have to be getting back to my husband and children."

"Two, then," continued his mistress. "Arrange transportation for the sergeant. Yuri and I will be dining in tonight." Dohlman tipped his head and disappeared.

Moments later, they could hear the bath running. Annika shooed Yuri to it and he was soon splashing away. She changed into a soft, flannel set of pajamas, topped by a long robe. Then, resting her head on the windowsill in one of the suite's luxurious teal chairs, she watched the work below. Yuri exited the bath and the supper cart came, but Annika scarcely noticed. Her eyes were locked on the Plaza.

Yuri ate in silence. Occasionally, Annika would turn and take a bit of bread or fruit. But she returned immediately to the window. Finished, Yuri poured himself a coffee and moved his chair next to hers. For hours they watched, silently. The lights were less frantic and the fliers were no longer rushing in and out. Yuri understood all too well what that meant. They were no longer searching for survivors. The mission had changed to recovering bodies.

Annika yawned. Yuri said quietly, "You have a big day tomorrow. Maybe you should go to bed."

Annika pointed down at the Plaza. "How can I sleep when they aren't?" she demanded. But she yawned again and dozed off. He stood and lovingly lifted his petite friend. In her room, he called, "Dohlman?" When the servant appeared, Yuri nodded at the bed. Dohlman turned down the covers and Yuri kissed her forehead and tucked her in. As he was leaving, her eyes opened.

"Yuri?" she said. "Please stay, just until I fall asleep. Please?" He sat on the edge of the bed, stroking her hair. Smiling, her eyes closed and she drifted off to sleep. He started to stand and she woke.

"No, Yuri, please stay."

She made room and he lay on top of the covers, holding her. He stroked her head softly and again she drifted off to sleep.

He removed his arm and started to slide off the bed again.

"No, Yuri, don't go. Not yet." Her grip was steel on his arm.

Yuri called Dohlman again and gave him specific instructions. Minutes later, a servant arrived, carrying a cup of warm milk. "It is what my mother gave me when I couldn't sleep," he told her. A little white lie. It was the milk and nutmeg his mother would give him, but he had also added a relaxant to help her sleep. She needed rest more than anything right now, the physician in him said.

It worked as he hoped. Annika drifted off again, only this time when he removed his hand, she curled her own hand to her chest and continued to sleep.

He went to his own room and crawled into bed. Were he not so tired, he supposed, he would have marveled at the soft, silken sheets and thick down comforter on the bed in his own room. He soon drifted off to sleep.

And awoke to screaming! The clock said it had been less than an hour. Surely, it couldn't be Annika! He leapt from his bed and ran across the suite to her room where she sat, bolt upright in her bed. Her hands were gripping and tearing at her hair, her eyes wide open, unseeing. Her scream was long, drawn out. She would exhaust her breath, whimper, and scream again.

Yuri sat on her bed, wrapped his arms around her and began to gently shake her. "Annika! It's O.K. You're safe. I'm right here, Shhhhhh..." he repeated over and over. She finally stopped the screaming, gasping, gulping and hiccupping. Her face was wet and her eyes red, but she was focusing now, not on the terrors of her dreams, but of her room, safe in the palace. Yuri held her and continued his soft chant, managed to lay her back on her pillow.

He sat longer this time. "They're all dead, Yuri," she whispered at one point. "They're all dead. I couldn't stop the bad people. How can I ever make up for all of them dying? How can I? I'm supposed to be able to protect them all, Yuri. That's what it is to be Khan. To protect all my people. Oh, Yuri." She started to drift off again, but snapped her eyes open once more.

"Yuri, please stay tonight with me," she pleaded. "Here, in my bed. I can't be alone tonight. Please, Yuri!"

Yuri was perplexed. Although they were both of age, Yuri wasn't sure how the palace would react if he was caught in bed with the young girl. "But," he argued with himself, "there is nothing improper going on. She needs me; I must be with her." Annika immediately rolled over and snuggled in close. Her sigh was deep as

67

she fell asleep instantly. Yuri wrapped a guardian arm around her and drifted off to sleep as well.

Chapter 9

Annika awakened slowly, aware of the warm body next to her. She wasn't surprised; of course, it was Yuri. With sleepy eyes widened, she examined the face alongside hers.

His nose was awfully large, she giggled to herself. It wheezed as he exhaled. And he snored! A great, snorting snarl escaped from his gaping mouth and nose as he inhaled. Then the funny wheeze as he exhaled. In his sleep, Yuri's brow had relaxed, softened. It was as though someone had drawn two thin line across and added fine, brown hair. His hairline was higher than she remembered. *Would he go bald*, she wondered? She liked his hair. He had trimmed his moustache, thin like his brow. She wasn't sure how to feel about that. His chin, below his gaping, snoring mouth, was squarer than hers.

Annika admired him for long minutes before laying her head on his chest and listening to the air whooshing in and out of his lungs each breath. And the steady thrum-thrum-thrum of his heart. *Does his heart know I am here?* She wrapped her arm around him.

"Well, I suppose I could get used to sleeping in a castle if I got to wake up to a beautiful princess every morning," Yuri rumbled, stroking her hair.

Annika rubbed her face against his nightshirt. "Well," she replied, "I'm used to waking up to more comfortable pillows. But your scrawny chest will do, I suppose, in a pinch."

Dohlman appeared. "Good morning, Ma'am, Doctor," he announced. "I have taken the liberty of holding breakfast service at the door until you are presentable. Your baths are drawn and clothing laid out. Doctor, a servant brought over your belongings from your hotel; you'll find them laid out in your room and bath. Ma'am, your bath is also waiting. General Han sent a new uniform over last night. I examined it and have had the appropriate alterations made. I should hope it fits better. I will have your schedules ready when you come out for breakfast." The holographic butler disappeared.

"Well, he didn't send in the troops to drag me off," Yuri noted.

"Nope," Annika replied, "They work for me. Still, I've learned when Dohlman says your schedule and clothing are laid out, it means you're probably running behind." With a quick kiss, she left him to the duty that called her, first padding to her bath.

After quick, brisk calisthenics to get the blood pumping. Annika decided against the bath for a quick shower. A servant appeared and helped her braid her hair. The already made up bed boasted an Imperial Army uniform, smoothly laid upon the bed's gold eiderdown. She fingered the material of a sleeve. The dark green cloth and brown leather were authentic. General Han was sending her a message, of that she was sure. *Good,* she thought. In the days and years ahead, support of the armed forces would be critical.

She dressed carefully in the perfectly fitted uniform. *How does Dohlman do it?* She admired herself in the mirror after she dressed. The high collar, so loose and irritating the day before, was trim and comfortable *Overall perfection, I'd say.* Annika Raudona was ready for whatever the day might bring.

Breakfast arrived. Yuri had already poured his coffee when she joined him at the table, selected a slice of toast and marmalade with a cup of tea. "That's all?" Yuri asked.

"Yes. I'm not very big, so I don't eat much in the mornings. Plus, this is when I service my electrolytes." She produced a small, tapered device that she pressed against her neck. After a moment, she examined its surface and raised a single finger to one of the servants.

Annika finished her toast just as the servant returned with a tray bearing two glasses and a pitcher. One glass was filled with the silvery-grey colored fluid. Annika drank the solution, then reached for a glass of water, drank it quickly, reached out for a second, then a

70

third glass. She was gasping slightly when she finished, wiping her mouth delicately with a napkin. "Eighteen years and I still don't like the taste," she told him.

They regarded the schedules Dohlman provided. Yuri would make rounds in the local hospitals for his assigned patients from yesterday's attack. Annika saw her schedule and groaned. Her day was to be tied up with the Imperial Council. Bureaucrats and politicians. She shuddered, knowing she was surely the lead topic of their day.

Breakfast finished, the young couple embraced, and went to face the day.

The Imperial Palaces throughout the Terran Empire are as varied as the one hundred fifty worlds upon which they were built. Yet, there were common elements to each palace.

The first were the Throne Rooms. Each was a large, airy room with plenty of light and color. A raised dais with thrones for the Khan and their partner stood at one end of the chamber. Artwork of the world was displayed to recognize that area's contributions to the Empire.

The Imperial Council chambers, however, were anything but as grand and glorious. Most were located under the Throne Rooms, as to remind all that they were the foundation of the Empire, that their work kept the Empire growing and thriving.

On Terra, the Council room was dark with a low ceiling. The walls were of chiseled stone without decoration. The room was circled on three sides by forty heavy timber desks, their number physically divided by a stairway up the center of the far wall to the Throne of the Khan. To the Khan's left was the Prime Minister and the nineteen ministers assigned to the posts of managing the domestic affairs of State. On the right was the Defense Minister and the nineteen assigned to the physical safety and stability the Empire.

The Throne of the Khan was always the largest and least elaborate chair in the room. It was unpadded, the legends say, to ensure the Khan would remain attentive to the affairs of state.

A lit spot was in the center of the room. Here, supplicants would stand in full view of the Council for examination.

Annika stood in the circle of light and studied the final outstanding feature of the Khan's Throne. Sitting on the unpadded seat of the unadorned throne was the Crown of the Empire. It sat on the throne when the Khan wasn't present. In this case, the crown represented the last Khan, dead for sixteen years.

Her father.

As with many of the symbols left behind by Angkor Khan, the crown was dazzling in its simplicity. It was a plain, unadorned steel circlet, two half hoops arching across the top. A rivet joined the hoops where they intersected and a ring of ermine wrapped around the lower rim of the crown. Her father had been Robert L'Orange Khan of the Orange File. Thus, the cap inside the crown was a regal burnt ginger.

Annika waited, calm, with her hands behind her back. A neural blocker had been placed on her head; the ministers did not want this witness to read their thoughts. They were the guardians of the Empire for now. They wanted her to know it.

And some had very good reason to not allow her in the room with her telepathic powers. They had much to hide and far more to lose.

Morris Stype, the Prime Minister, stood. A tall, gaunt man, his ninety years disguised by a powerful presence and energy. Minister Stype had allowed his hair to turn a distinguished white, not bothered by the signs of aging. Morris had gentle eyes on his patrician face, a combination that would put the subjects he scrutinized at ease while being verbally dissected and exposed.

He had served the Empire for more than sixty years. The girl, Annika, reminded him of his great granddaughter. He was inclined to be gentle.

The Prime Minister cleared his throat. "Greeting, Heir Red File, Annika Raudona. Please accept the condolences of this Council for your loss. If you would please, explain your actions for the horrible incident yesterday. Be thorough, my dear."

Annika spoke for over an hour. Of the ceremony and her participation in it. The attack, and finding her brothers and sister, dying and dead. Her escape to the command center. Finished, she set her jaw and awaited the Council's questions.

The ministers talked amongst themselves for a few minutes, then the Prime Minister gaveled the room back to order. "We shall begin our interview now, beginning with my counterpart, Minister Gavin Howland, of Defense."

The Defense Minister clasped his hands together and asked, "Miss, one of your first actions yesterday was to order the arrest of General Teague, commanding officer of the Central Command. Might I ask why?"

"Certainly, Minister," Annika answered. "When I arrived, I found General Han, his deputy, running the center. I asked where General Teague was. Teague had been there earlier in the morning, that much was confirmed. Before the attack began, he slipped away, abandoning his post. I ordered him arrested, pending the investigation of the attack that killed members of my family."

"Has General Teague been found and arrested?" she heard someone ask.

"General Teague is still missing," replied the Defense Minister, "and several of his key officers are absent as well. I find this curious. I have enlisted the aid of the ministries of Imperial Intelligence and Internal Security. I agree with the heir; I would like to know their whereabouts as well." He motioned in Annika's direction. "I have one more question. Why are you wearing an Imperial Uniform?"

Annika raised her chin. "When I arrived at the center, my clothing was torn and soiled with the blood of my family. General Han sent me to clean up and change. They found me a uniform to

73

wear. This morning the General sent me a uniform that fits better. I believe he was honoring me for yesterday. It is my hope that I honor both General Han and the rest of our soldiers when I wear it."

Many of the ministers nodded. "You do well to honor us for your actions yesterday, Annika Raudona," cried a voice from her right.

"If I can be so bold and ask a question." The voice wheezed from a minister to the left of the Prime Minister, who recognized the minister of Justice.

The Justice Minister, an odious, obese man gurgled as he scowled at Annika. "While I respect the actions of young Miss Raudona, I have a question I need answered. Miss, after you left the Command Center last night, you were seen in the company of a young man. Might I ask the name of this young man?"

"Why, certainly," Annika replied, "you may ask away." She stood there for a long moment.

"Well?" wheezed the Justice Minister.

"Well, what?" the girl asked.

"Well, are you going to tell us who the young man was?" He gurgled now.

"No," was her answer.

"NO?" asked the surprised minister, unused to being denied anything.

"No," she said. "Who he is and what we did or did not do are not your business."

"I believe it is my business," came the angry reply, "as it may relate to the good of the Empire."

Annika glared at the leering man. She wished she hadn't agreed to wear the glarpshite neural blocker.

"Are you asking this question as part of a criminal investigation?" Annika asked.

The minster blustered. "I said nothing of a criminal investigation," he condescended. "I merely asked the name of the young man you spent time with last night in your suite."

74

"And I refuse to answer," was Annika's forceful reply. "I am now an adult by Terran law. If you are not conducting a criminal investigation, then I am invoking the Law of Privacy. If you cannot show the intent of a criminal investigation or the evidence of a crime, then I have no need to tell you who may or may not have been in my suite last night, no matter how much your perverse self desires to know." The room erupted in laughter.

A page hurried to the Prime Minister and handed him a note. "I declare this hearing suspended," he announced after reading it. "We have an extremely important witness who wishes to address the Council on a matter of grave importance to the Empire." The Council murmured and grew still as the doors were opened.

Chapter 10

Two rows of four elderly men and women entered the room. All of them were balding and wearing saffron robes. Each robe had a sash of a different color. They formed a line eight wide behind Annika. One, wearing the red sash, stepped forward to the center of the Council and bowed deeply. Standing, he announced, "I am Tahn, chair of the Red File and first among the File Committee. I will speak to this Council."

The Prime Minister nodded. "You honor us with your presence, Master Tahn," he said.

Tahn began. "After the tragic events of yesterday, the File Committee met last evening to discuss what was to be done. After our discussions, we retired to our rooms to reflect and meditate on the question: did the events of yesterday prevent us from doing our assigned job of selecting the next Crown Prince or Princess, and thereby the next Khan? This morning, we assembled again and voiced our consciences. Nothing about the selection of the new heir has been disturbed. Our deliberations and meditations on this subject have not been affected. We have decided to reveal who each of us has determined to be the next Khan."

He stepped back in line. All eight File Committee members called out, "As laid down by the Laws of our benefactor, leader and father of our modern law, the Emperor Angkor Khan, I affirm I have sought the guidance of the Gods above." Each reached into their robe and removed a golden envelope and held it above their head with both hands. The eight continued their chant, "As has been revealed to me, I now reveal to you. Here is my selection for the fifteenth reincarnation of the Angkor Khan."

There was a single ripping noise as they tore the ends off the envelopes. They reached in together and extracted a colored card.

Eight Red cards.

The entire room immediately leaped to its collective feet and bowed deeply. Annika reveled in the achievement of her dreams. It had happened. It had really happened. Whether before a crowd of millions or in the closed chamber of ministers, the Gods had spoken.

She was superior.

All before her were inferior.

She was Annika Raudona …KHAN!

She ascended the stairs to what was now her throne. Reverently, she lifted her father's crown. "My father, Emperor Robert De L'Orange Khan, has passed from this world and into the lands of the eternal. Father, rest now as I, Annika Raudona, assumes the mantle of our duties." She handed the crown to a page, ordering, "Place this in my safest stronghold until I ascend to my Throne." He bowed and carried it from the room.

The throne was set to the height of her father, tall even for a Terran man. With one hand on an armrest, Annika made a hop and twisted into the chair. Hands in her lap, she held her royal head high.

Morris Stype straightened from his bow. "Highness, receive now the affection of your Council." The whole of the Council raised their hands high above their heads, calling out, "HooooOOOO, HooooOOOO, HooooOOOO!" Enthusiastic applause followed.

A nearly imperceptible nod of her head acknowledged her ministers' acclaim, and she pointedly removed the nullifier and handed it to a page. "I believe this is no longer necessary," she said. Several councilmen looked stricken. Particularly the Justice Minister. His eyes bugged and his mouth gaped like a fish removed from the water. She reached out and touched his mind. The old fool believed he could block her by thinking of nursery rhymes and working math problems. His defenses were easily swept aside. They would stop an inferior. Not her. Especially not now. She found what she wanted. Pointing to him, Annika announced, "Arrest him. I shall forward the charges later. Contact my brother, Noire. He shall personally supervise the interrogation."

She settled back on the chair. "There is a ceremony that occurs at this point, formally anointing me as the new Crown Princess. Given the nature of the current crisis, I propose we forego this tradition for now and get straightaway to work." The Council voted. As Crown Princess, they would favor the future Khan with her wishes.

Tahn bowed. "Since we are no longer required, we shall take our leave of this hall and depart for our monastery in the morning."

"What is the condition of the Regent?" asked Annika. A minister on her left stood.

"Health and Welfare, Crown Princess. I am in contact with the palace hospital. While grievously wounded, none of his injuries are life-threatening. He is through surgery now and recovering. He was shot in the chest, stomach and one arm by what was probably friendly fire.

"His lung was nicked and collapsed. His liver, stomach and intestines were all punctured or perforated. His right arm was shattered; the bone has been regenerated. Given his physiology and excellent health, I anticipate he will be able to return to his duties within two months.

"His distaste for Giza Palace is well known. The Empress has expressed she would like him to be fit to return to Argulea as soon as possible. I estimate he should be fit to travel in a week. In the interim, he has been moved to the Imperial Army Hospital in Thebes."

Annika nodded assent. "Very well. Do whatever is required to return my uncle to health. Please express my regards for my uncle and tell my mother I will visit tomorrow."

She changed the subject. "Casualty numbers from the attack?" she asked. The Defense Minister stood.

"Majesty," he said, "General Teague has still not been located. General Han would have come himself, but he pointed out that it would be inappropriate to leave his post as Deputy

Commander of Central Command with General Teague missing. As such, he has sent Colonel Forrester to give that report. Colonel?"

Colonel Forrester was a broad, heavy man with a thick, wide moustache. His accent was Terran Australian. "Ma'am. Overhead imagery showed the attendance at the Plaza was approximately two point three million beings. The enemy dropped forty-eight high explosives. They also fired nineteen hundred rounds of mid-range energy weapons. We have accounted for approximately one hundred thirty-seven thousand dead, including your family. An additional fifteen thousand are missing. We have sixty-five thousand injured that are requiring hospitalization. Fortunately, we have the Seventeenth Fleet available. They provided two hospital ships and supplemented our shuttle fleets. Casualties triaged as savable have been spread around the planet and are being treated now. There were, in addition, four hundred ninety-seven thousand who had minor injuries, were treated and sent home."

The Council was silent. Nearly one hundred forty thousand dead. The number was unfathomable. However, Annika was trained not to be overwhelmed by numbers. "And the attackers, have they been tracked down and captured yet? Do we know who did this?" The Colonel swallowed and read his pad. He sighed and responded.

"Augmentons," he intoned.

Augmentons. The bastard children of Terra's genetics programs. Modified beings who used mechanical components to enhance themselves physically. The drawback was that the enhancements drove the augmentons insane. They were banned throughout not just the Empire, but throughout the quadrant as well.

General Han was keeping the raiders' mother ship secret. Good. Until she and Noire, along with her loyal officers, could find all her enemies, she would withhold that information from the council.

The Prime Minister interrupted. "Crown Princess, it is getting late in the day. Might I suggest we adjourn to dinner and resume this meeting when there is more and better information available?"

Annika checked her chrono and swore. It was nearly supper! She had missed lunch with Yuri. "Yes, of course, adjourn the meeting," she said as she hurried without ceremony out of the hall. Major Campion waited with four soldiers to escort her back to her suite, protection for the head of state.

"Out of uniform, aren't we Major?" she asked him. "Still wearing Captain's bars."

He blushed, "One, I haven't had time. Miss, er, Majesty. Two, the official order hasn't come through Command. Three..."

"One and one only. You work for me now." Annika was firm as she traversed the hall, encircled by her guards. "Get those oak leaves on, Major."

Yuri was already in the suite. Supper was on the table, but he was at the window, watching. "They've already filled the morgues," Yuri said, "Here, in Cairo and the surrounding areas. The army is setting up refrigerated cars and converting warehouses as quick as they can. It's an impossible job, Annika. Some will be identified. Many will not." She moved to him; he wrapped his arms around her. They watched the search for bodies in the Plaza for a time until Dohlman appeared and cleared his throat.

"Majesty, Sir, your supper will be best if you eat it before it gets cold." He watched them silently until they relented and sat to eat. Then he closed the curtains and programed a holo of the ocean before he disappeared.

"Ah, I forgot. Congratulations on your ascension. I am so proud of you. I know you worked so hard," Yuri said.

"I didn't win anything," she said quietly. "I worked hard, yes. But it was all to prepare me," Annika flourished a hand in the direction of the window, "for this. I've been taught what to say, how to think. They poured terabytes of data in my head and challenged me to make sense of it all.

"I am as prepared as any Khan before for my task," she hesitated. "Except for..."

"Except for me," Yuri finished.

"You are a complication," Annika snapped. "I know how to run my Empire. You..."

"Are a complication, yes," Yuri finished. "I've been many things in my life. A complication is not one of them."

"Yuri, be reasonable..." Annika started.

"Reasonable?" Yuri nearly shouted. "I thought I was your friend."

"We are friends," Annika argued.

"But with all your new duties, I am an unaccounted variable," Yuri spat. "A miscalculation in your perfect programing."

Dohlman appeared, holding a silver tray bearing a note. He extended it to Annika. It was in elegant script, clearly handwritten: *"I will have tea with you at dawn. The Dawn Tower. Please come alone. Tahn."* She folded the note and tucked it in her left sleeve, under the sheath for her knife. She got up from the table. "I'm sorry, Yuri, it's been a long day. I have a lot to think about." She turned and went to her room, firmly closing the door.

When her nightmare returned that night, she cried out to Yuri, who came at once, wrapped his arms around her and sang a lullaby.

Chapter 11

Flanking the center of the Imperial Palace at Giza were two elegant barbicans towering over the plateau. The western was the Tower of the Evening; the east was the Tower of the Dawn. Neither had an easy way to the top, only the spiral staircase that wound through the interior. There were no landings to rest upon; one was expected to start and finish in one long climb.

Emperor Hinabrian Khan had them built this way. The stairs started at a small door on the ground level of the palace. Hinabrian wanted only the most fit and honorable to be allowed to scale either meditation tower.

Annika woke before Yuri, and slid out of bed. She dressed and kissed him on the forehead before leaving. After last night, she wasn't sure she wanted to face him. Not yet.

Annika hoped the old man, Tahn, would be able to make the climb. For her, it was a strenuous workout, but easy enough for someone as superior as herself. She was surprised to see the shadow of Tahn framed by the window facing the sunrise. "Ah, my old friend, Angkor, welcome. I am glad you made it!" the old man said, joy palpable in his words. "It has been a long time, my old friend. Here, sit with me. The sun shall be up soon."

Annika selected one of the plump and colorful cushions scattered across the floor, and sat at the low table next to Tahn. The eastern sky was beginning to glow, a golden white light on the distant horizon, chasing the stars once more to their daytime caverns.

"Here now, watch closely," breathed the old man. A brilliant drop of liquid gold heralded the sun's first appearance. It spread as the disk formed, growing brighter and brighter. The gold faded to orange, then to white ringed with gold as the whole of Sol appeared in all its glory, the golden light reflecting on the few clouds visible.

Tahn raised his arms, smiling broadly as the sun shone on his weathered face and warmed his heart. "Of all the vistas I've been to, of all the sunrises I've seen, each is always better than the last," he said. "It fills me with great hope for the new day." He closed his eyes. "Thank you for sharing the sunrise with me, Angkor Khan. It seems so long since we have done this together."

"Master?" Annika asked, wondering who he was talking to.

The old man chuckled. "Do not worry, Girl," he said kindly. "I know you are Annika Raudona Khan, daughter of Emperor Robert De L'Orange Khan. I am not senile.

"I knew you before you were born," he continued in the same gentle voice. "I knew you before you were even conceived. I knew you before you were a sample in a Petri dish on the table in my lab." He closed his eyes, remembering. "You are the second Khan I have designed. The first was your father, although I simply finished him. You, I oversaw from your beginning. After your Father was named Crown Prince, I was assigned to head the Red File. My team and I wrote much of your code before your father met your mother. You may have noticed I gave you my chin!" He smiled and stroked his pointed chin. Annika laughed and imitated his gesture.

He leaned forward. "I snuck that in," he confided. "I wanted to give you a piece of me I could see. I'm glad to see it worked so well. It makes you so attractive!" His smile faded. "You are my greatest creation. Unfortunately, I fear I failed miserably."

"I don't understand, Master. I am the superior, the Crown Princess. Where am I lacking? What is it I need? I'll do what you ask, Master!"

"I know you will try, Child," he said sadly. "But I failed in your humanity. You are the most brilliant mind we ever created. Yours is the brain that every Khan will be measured against from your progeny until the end of our Empire. But I failed in in making you human. My dear, you are stunted emotionally, only able to respond to that for which I programed you. You've made progress.

If there is one area I feel you may never be able to measure up, it is your ability to be human. Not just act human, but be human."

"I don't understand, Master," said the confused girl.

He added tea to the pair of gilded cups on the table and handed her a cup of exceedingly bitter tea. Annika made a face. "Yes, exactly," Tahn said. "The sunrise was so brilliant. The moment is perfect. So how can the tea, with all things in perfect harmony, be so bitter?" He held his hand out for her cup and threw it against the wall, smashing it. Two more cups were produced and the tea made again, this time adding a helping of sugar.

"That's better, Master," she said.

"Yes, but now the sun is up, the moment lost. How sad, when the sun was perfect, the tea was bitter. Now the tea is perfect and the sun…is just the sun."

He pressed his lips together. "Daughter, when it was clear you were to be the next Khan, we have been doing everything we could to create humanity within you. When you were injured at fifteen, I had hoped it would be the fulcrum to your emotional development. I felt that experiment was an outstanding success!"

"Wait," Annika asked. "Are you saying my leg injury was a result of a File Committee plan?" Her anger began to arise.

"No," he said. "We can only create circumstances that lead you to make decisions. Immature decisions, as it turned out. That was what I hoped for. Your poor decision led you to being injured. That made the lesson even more valuable. Telling you that we were considering discontinuing your file was the most successful part of the whole experiment. I wept for joy when you had your emotional outburst!"

Annika was shocked. "I thought you were going to kill me when I got home," she gasped. "I thought I was going to be dissected and examined! I thought I was a f-f-f-f-failure!" Her lip quivered and her eyes reddened as tears began to form.

The curator of the Red File was overjoyed. "Oh, better and better! Some of your programing works! Perhaps there is hope yet."

"Tell me, Child, have you been having nightmares since the attack?" he asked clinically.

Annika nodded.

"And have you turned to Dohlman for assistance or this young man of yours?"

Annika answered in a small voice. "Yuri has come to me when I cried out. He has comforted me and helped me to sleep."

"Excellent! Perhaps there is hope yet, like the new dawn. Or the bitter tea."

He sipped his cup again, but it had gone cold. He threw the cup against the wall and nodded to Annika. Hers had gone cold as well, so she tried to copy Tahn's action, but her cup flew over the wall and out the window. "Look out below!" he chuckled.

Two more cups appeared, but this time her Proctor indicated Annika should pour the tea. She added the tea and sugar, then the water. Watching closely, she handed Tahn his cup. He sipped it and smiled. "Yes, perfect."

He sat back in the cushion. "Tell me, what you think of this young man of yours?"

Annika shrugged, "I like him," she said, "but I fear for him. I have trained my whole life to be Khan. I don't think he knows what it will entail. I'm afraid if we continue our relationship, that he will be hurt by what I must do as Khan. All the scrutiny, all the attention." Her eyes moistened again. "I don't want to hurt him!"

"But if you send him away, that will hurt him even more, no? I like this young man, Yuri. I have studied him for some time. I think you need him more than you know.

"It is written we are all born as half people," said the old man, "and we spend our lives looking for our other half. Do you remember the story of Angkor's wife, Sophia?"

Annika's face brightened at the remembrance. "Yes, Master. He saw her in the market in Delhi and followed her. He said she was the most beautiful woman he had ever seen. It took him days to muster the courage to talk to her, even more to ask her out. In the

86

end, though, he won her heart and they married. When she died, he nearly died from grief."

"Do you understand why he nearly died?"

Annika snorted. "That's easy. It's because he loved her."

Tahn shook his head, "Ah, so close. I thought maybe the programing was right. You are so close." He tapped her forehead. "Listen and think, Child. Why did Angkor Kahn nearly die when Sophia died? Why can I feel my own wife, although she is three thousand miles away at our home in the Angkor Khan's temple? Why is it, when you are in pain, you call for your friend, Yuri?"

Annika scrunched her brow. "Is it because you believe he is my other half?" she asked.

Tahn shook his head. "Closer and closer," he said, "but not there yet. Well, if she can't get it, then maybe in the next file."

Annika didn't like the sound of that.

"What next file?" she demanded.

"You are Khan now," he told her. "We have already started to lay down the patterns for your heirs. It will require you choose a partner. Fortunately, we have time, as you seem unable to complete the formula yourself."

Annika sat back, pondering. What was he trying to teach her? She thought about the sunrise and the tea. When the one was perfect, the other was not. When the other was made perfect, the moment was passed and there was still imperfection. Then it hit her.

"Master, when did the File Committee know I would be Khan?" she asked.

"Ah, the light comes on," Tahn said happily. "Child, we knew when we reviewed the patterns before we planted the embryos into their Vinithri eggs. Your brothers and sisters were there all along to make you ready to arrive at this point. But you haven't answered my question. Why is Yuri so important to you?"

"Because he is my other half." She was solemn as she voiced her truth. "Without him, I am incomplete. Without him, I will never be Khan. Not like my father." I need Yuri."

"You need your Yuri," agreed Tahn, "Tell me, Daughter, how do you feel about your Yuri?"

She closed her eyes. A tear escaped her right eye, coursed down a perfect cheek. "I love him," she answered.

Chapter 12

They came down the stairs together. Annika escorted Tahn to his shuttle surrounded. Tahn joked that since he was such an old man, perhaps he guards should have carried him. Having made the climb up and down the Tower of Dawn's staircase herself, Annika wondered if perhaps he could carry a guard.

They talked quietly about things of little importance. At the shuttle, Tahn turned to the girl. "You and your Yuri. You must come to the Temple of Angkor Khan as soon as possible. There are secrets that you must know to be Khan. And there are things you must do." He lay his hand on her forehead and mumbled a prayer. Then he boarded the shuttle, not looking back.

Major Campion was wearing the correct collar device today, she noticed. Good. She liked the young officer who had taken charge of her during the attack. Today the detail was to escort her to her office. She had never had her own office before and was eager to see what it looked like. Naturally, she read Campion and led the way. Major Campion was becoming used to the rapid pace the Crown Princess kept. He staged guards along the route.

She arrived at the office in short order. In the outer office was an efficient looking woman working at her desk. She looked up and said crossly. "You're late. I shall contact the Prime Minister and let him know you are in. Well, go on, you have work to do." She pointed to the doors over her shoulder.

Her office was immense, at least 50 yards long. Behind the desk was a sheer glass wall, covered with ornate draperies. She couldn't see what it overlooked. The remaining walls were covered with rich tapestries and shelves of statuary. The desk was simply too large. She tried the chair, which slipped away as she tried to hop up into it. Frustrated, she pushed it against the desk and tried again. She made it in the chair, but then had to kneel on it to spin around and face the desk. She felt like a child looking over the Proctor's desk.

Fortunately, there was also a pair of couches. Red couches. *Did they just put them in here?* She was still unhappily perusing the desk when the woman from the outer office entered and announced, "Crown Princess, your Prime Minister." He swept into the room, bowing nearly to the floor. When he came up, he stopped. Annika could see he was struggling not to laugh. She supposed she did look silly behind the oversized desk, and blushed furiously for looking so foolish.

Prime Minister Moritz Stype indicated the couches. "Perhaps this will work better, Crown Princess?" She slid from the chair and scurried around the desk. The couch was not high so she maintained most of her dignity attaining a seat.

Annika assumed a regal pose and said, "Prime Minister." He indicated the woman who stood on the threshold. "This is Miss Norris, your personal secretary. She is responsible for your daily schedule and the management of your office. I'm sure she will make arrangements for your desk."

"Yes, Crown Princess. Of course, if you had been on time this morning," Her voice was stern. "We would have made the appropriate alterations to your office prior to the Prime Minister's arrival. Which you were also late for. I would suggest you pay a bit more attention to your schedule in the future." With that, she spun on a heel and left the office.

Moritz Stype shook his head. "She was both your father's and grandfather's secretary. She was quite put out when the Regent opted to use his own secretary. Miss Norris has been maintaining this empty office since your father died. I expect she is much happier now that she has some real work to do."

Annika reached out and touched the minister's mind. Instantly, he jumped up and yelled, "Stop! He threw down his pad. "I have been Prime Minister for both your father and the Regent," he thundered. "I served on the Council with your grandfather! That alone should convince you of my loyalty. But if it is not, then all you need to do is demand my resignation and I will leave immediately."

"Please, Prime Minister, stay," Annika asked in a small voice. "I meant no offense."

The old man breathed heavily, but seated himself again. "I am an empath," he explained. "I can't broadcast or read like you can. But I can tell when I am being scanned. To scan someone in polite society is the moral equivalent of rape to me." He recovered his breath and said, "O.K. Now I am ready. Go ahead."

Annika was confused, "Sorry?" she asked.

"Scan me," he ordered. "Let's get this curiosity of yours out of the way so we can get to work." He closed his eyes and sat back. Annika bit her lip. "No, if my father trusted you, then I suppose I should trust you. Thank you, Minister."

"Very good," he said, his tone still curt. "Our first order of business - your schedule for most days. You and I will meet daily; generally, I prefer the morning. For today, we'll skip most of the business. I understand you want to go see the Regent. Miss Norris has this slotted for after lunch. That's fine, but most afternoons will be either meetings with various ministers or visitors. Your mornings will consist of briefing sheets and reports. Miss Norris will have them ready when you arrive. I will have read them already, of course, and I will notate my opinions on the border of the reports. You should either accept, ask for more information or reject each in hand.

"Which reminds me," he continued, examining her closely. "We need to schedule your upgrade to receive military and advanced grade downloads. We will do that this tomorrow. Our experience has shown that when you come out of the download net, it is preferable to have someone familiar at your side, a partner or close friend, who will help you recover. For both your predecessors, it was your mother. She will do, unless your friend is available. I can have orders issued to have him come in today for the necessary training, if you wish. As a doctor, he is probably your best candidate."

"No, not order," Annika replied thoughtfully. "I will ask him this evening." The minister raised a brow, but said nothing and went about acquainting Annika with the duties of her Empire. Hours passed while she learned; the Prime Minister was patient, calm, and she felt comfortable.

For lunch, he escorted her to a grotto. A long, still reflecting pond of glowing blue waters illuminated the dark cavern. A single round table with a white cloth sat near the shoreline.

"This is the Garden of the Blue Waters. Your father enjoyed it here," he told her. "As Crown Prince, he and I spent many of our lunches in this garden. I had resigned as Prime Minister after your grandfather passed. I was working as the Minister of Internal Affairs. Your father convinced me to return to the Prime Ministry."

He fell silent, remembering.

The food arrived, monk fish. "Fish is good brain food," quipped the minister. "You of all people should eat plenty of fish."

Miss Norris had been busy while they were gone. The heavy desk had disappeared and in its place, a smaller, more delicate white desk with a golden filigree. The red cushioned chair fitted her perfectly. Annika smiled, fingering the old-fashioned desk lamp and soft red leather pad centered on the desk. There was a stack of papers in an enameled box, an empty box next to it. "I will leave you to your duties," said the Prime Minister. "If you need anything, don't be afraid to ask. Majesty." He bowed and was gone.

She set to work. The first report was "Effects of Standard Terraform Techniques on LaGrange Asteroids in the Perce's System." It proved to be mostly dry, technical material. She initialed it and went on to the next. It wasn't any better. Through the afternoon, she read and initialed report after report. She grew thirsty and crossed the huge room to peek out and ask Miss Norris about some tea. Miss Norris escorted the Crown Princess back in the office to show her how to call her in the outer office. "Anything else, Miss?' she asked, sniffing.

Oh, Gods below, I don't even want to ask. Perhaps I should just explore. But urgency overtook her reluctance. "Um, yes? The washroom?"

When Annika was finished, she came through the concealed door behind her desk to find a steamy pot of tea on the credenza. And more paperwork. Sighing, she went back to work.

At precisely four, Miss Norris entered and announced that Annika was done for the day. "There is a hovercar waiting to take you to the hospital to see your uncle," she announced. "It will return you to the palace when you are finished. Dohlman has scheduled your supper for six. There will be time after supper for you to work on some of the reports you didn't finish today. I would suggest you go to bed early; you have a taxing day scheduled for tomorrow."

Major Campion and her detail were waiting outside the office. They hurried off to the hospital, where a crowd had gathered outside. As she moved from the hovercar to the building, the crowd gave her a polite smattering of applause. Annika stopped and waved, Campion grabbed her arm and hustled her inside. "Best not to be too much in the open right now," he told her.

Guards were everywhere. She was taken to the Regent's room high in the hospital tower. Her mother was there, holding her husband's hand. Another woman was also in the room, wearing a plain brown suit and a vacant look on her face. Annika had an immediate headache.

"Daughter! I see you're becoming acquainted with our banshee, Grenna," her mother cooed. "I suppose your Proctors never told you about them. Poor dears, they're not very bright. But they have a wonderful talent, I'm sure you can feel right now. They transmit directed telepathic white noise, rendering you and any of your telepathic friends quite blind, as it were. It keeps you from meddling in people's heads."

93

It was certainly effective. There was a constant buzz in her ears and pain centered in the middle of her head. "It hurts, Mother," Annika complained. "Would you ask her to stop, please? I promise not to scan your husband."

Her mother shrieked with laughter, "Stop? If it were possible, I would have Grenna cause you even more pain. Stop, indeed." She kissed the Regent on his forehead and strode from the room.

Her uncle glared at her. His lower body was concealed by a tent, tubes and wires running beneath it.

"So, Little Red, how was your first day of work?" he rasped.

She gritted her teeth, "I have a name, Uncle. I expect you to use it."

"Oh, yes, what was it? Annika? Annika Raudona? Named for your boyfriend's mother, I understand."

"His great, great grandmother," she corrected.

If it was possible to be malevolent amid tubes and bandages, Ming si Haun was the man to accomplish it. "Yes, how sweet, showing love and devotion to your little doctor friend." Then he brightened, his sarcasm dripping. "Tell me, little Red, has he been playing doctor with you?"

Instantly and without thinking, her assassin's knife was in her right hand, she moved towards the Regent until there was a shrieking in her head. The knife fell from her hand, clattering to the floor. Annika grabbed the sides of head and fell, screaming noiselessly. She writhed as the Regent watched, smiling.

"Amazing thing, these banshees," his words oozed poison. "They're barely smart enough to keep from soiling themselves, yet when their master is threatened by a telepath, they're quite adept neutralizing the threat, as you are experiencing right now." He leaned as far as the wires and his wounds would allow, admiring his handiwork. "Excruciating, is it?" he asked." You have no idea how much I am enjoying watching you suffer, Little Red. But, I suppose if I were to allow her to kill you, there would be too many questions. Grenna, release her. Next time, Child, I would suggest wearing one of these beauties. Blocks the banshee's scream." He tapped the neutralizer.

The pain eased immediately. Annika gasped and choked as her system recovered, then was sick all over the sparkling tiles. The Regent clucked, "Now I suppose I shall have to call someone to clean this mess. Well, my dear, find your little toy knife and go. I will let you know when I am ready to assume my duties again. Do try and keep up. I know it's probably a bit much for a child like you to handle. Be gone." He dismissed her with a wave of his hand.

Outside the hospital room's door, Annika's head still spun, she couldn't focus, she stumbled and fell. The Regent's laughter echoed from his room. Campion gasped, grabbed his sidearm and headed for the door.

"No, no," gasped the girl. "Just get me out of here. Now."

"I have the Crown Princess," he spoke into a clip microphone at the car. "We'll proceeds straight to the palace. Have the med team waiting."

As soon as she left the hospital, she began to feel better.

"Major, the med team will be unnecessary," she said. "Just get me home."

Arriving at her suite, she stripped and stepped into the shower. She considered her confrontation with the Regent. Clearly, he meant to keep power, even after she became of age. She had the law on her side, but the law would only go so far as she would be able to enforce it.

And she had Yuri to consider.

They dined at a pleasant desert rock garden of Dohlman's choice. The day was warm, ice-cold fruit juice and water greeted them at their table. They ate in awkward silence. Annika was trying to compose herself; she could tell Yuri was angry.

Given what she had said the night before and how she had sneaked out this morning, she couldn't blame him for being angry.

"Yuri, we need to talk," she finally got out.

He set his fork down and folded his hands on the table. "All right," he said evenly, "Talk."

She took a deep breath, "I'm sorry for what I said last night," she apologized. "I didn't consider what I said before I said it and more importantly, I didn't consider you. I can see what I said hurt you. I don't want to hurt you, Yuri. Now or ever."

"Yes, what you said is hurtful," he agreed. "But do you understand why it is hurtful?"

Sugar in the tea or enjoy the dawn? The dawn, with its bitter tea... "Please tell me, Yuri, I am listening," she answered.

"It's your damned condescending, superior attitude," Yuri snarled, "I know you were created to become leader of this Empire. But I've gotten to know Annika Raudona. Not the Crown Princess, not the Khan. Just Annika. You know what? I like her. I like her a lot. I want to spend more time with her. Maybe all the time. But you've got to quit pushing me away. I won't let you do that to me. I can't be there only when you need me. You must be willing to let me be there all the time, or," his breath caught, "none of the time. I won't be a part time friend with you, Annika."

Annika's eyes clouded with tears. *Enjoy the dawn, with its bitter tea...* "I don't want you as a part time friend either, Yuri," she choked. "But I don't know what to say or what to do. I'm confused, Yuri, because I never want to hurt you. I want only what will make you happy." She gazed at him and confessed in a small voice, "and I want to be with you all the time, too."

Yuri rubbed his eyes. "There must be something in this room," he said. "My eyes are getting watery. Maybe something in the plants."

"Me too," she said, "Maybe we should just go for a walk?"

That night, Annika didn't have to call for Yuri. She went and climbed into his bed and cuddled up against his warm body. He wrapped his arm around her and held her close, nuzzled the back of her head and gave her a kiss on her neck.

Their dreams were pleasant.

Chapter 13

Yuri and Annika left their suite hand in hand. She was fidgeting, nervous. She had been downloaded many times, with major upgrades once a year. Today was to be different. She was to be reformatted, upgraded to a full adult brain, capable of receiving the weekly accounting of the affairs of the Empire. Including secret military reports

Their journey from the suite to the lab was short. The room was white, sterile. A raised, chrome chair dominated the room; an arm dropped from the ceiling, holding a video screen. A kind-faced nurse in a surgical uniform greeted the couple and led Annika away to the changing room.

"Good morning, Doctor Russolov. I am pleased to see you again." The Proctor who had come to Celtius 4 gave Yuri a deep, respectful bow.

"Good morning, Proctor," Yuri replied. "I had not expected to see you here."

"I am responsible for the education, training and development of Annika Raudona," he explained. "Now that she has been elevated to Crown Princess, my role evolves. I believe the upgrade to her brain will be successful. File Master Tahn agrees with me. Of more concern to me will be her progress after this exercise."

"The download?" Yuri asked.

The Proctor nodded. "The Crown Princess will be adjusting and learning to use her new programing for the next few weeks. In a perverse circumstance, the attack provided an outstanding opportunity to test what we have come to call the super brain. What I am referring to is afterwards, when the Regent Ming si Hahn neKhan resumes his job. She will not have a specific role at that time to guide her training."

Yuri nodded. The last few weeks living with Annika showed him that while she was brilliant, she had large gaps in her ability to communicate and interact with people. She was socially awkward and seemed to miss many of the social cues blaring obvious to most people. Too often, she reacted emotionally, childlike, rather than in the manner of an adult.

"I understand you have a tenured position at Christ the Savior University Hospital in New Moscow, Doctor," the Proctor stated.

Yuri nodded. "I have a few days before I have to return," he explained. "I very much like my job and it is close enough to my family. But I am worried about Annika. What will become of her after the Regent returns to work?"

The Proctor smiled. "I think I may have a solution to both of our issues, Doctor," he stated. "I have connections at your University. Would you be willing to take a six-month sabbatical? I can arrange a research grant if you would have Annika stay with you and your family. I think the exposure to family life she would experience on your father's farm would be beneficial for her. She has decisions to make for herself and I believe living away from the trappings of Imperial power would be beneficial for her. Given the nature of your relationship, I think you would find benefit as well."

The Proctor certainly had a compelling argument. Yuri loved his family; he was certain she would receive positive benefits from the family farm.

And there was the added benefit of spending more time with Annika.

"I shall give your proposal careful consideration," Yuri replied.

A technician beckoned to Yuri. He showed the new electrolyte new mixture. "We're breaking fresh ground here, Doctor," he was told, "The patient will call for you as she comes on line. We must administer the fluids correctly as she requests them. She will not be in fully in control of her motor or cognitive functions, so you must exercise control for her."

98

Annika was led into the room. She now wore white, a loose-fitting pair of pants and top. Wires hung from the sleeves and legs of the garments. More wires dangled from her face and skull. She called for Yuri after she had been seated in the room's dominant chair. While he held her hand, technicians busied themselves connecting her wires to various consoles around the room. Lights, screens with numbers, letters and symbols flared to life. There was a cacophony of noise as well. The only one Yuri could hear, however, was a thrum-thrum-thrum. Annika's heartbeat.

A Proctor in brown robes entered the room bearing an opaque box containing the download headpiece. Wood-grained in appearance, it circled Annika's head at the brow, extended down her cheeks and arched further down to her neck in the back. Tabs stretched over the top of her head. Technicians added extensions to the arms of the chair, data pads attached. Annika gave Yuri a last squeeze and placed her hands on the pads. She inhaled deeply and exhaled. "Ready," she announced.

Her body gave a jolt and she gasped. Yuri could hear her pulse begin to accelerate and saw her begin to quiver. Fingers began to slowly tap a tattoo on the pads. Annika's head snapped up, green eyes turned black and began to move side to side while her head nodded up and down. Yuri heard the pulse increase. He checked the monitor. Dear Gods, 250, 300, 350…500 beats a minute! It was accelerating. Surely, they had to stop. Her heart should have exploded by now. The technician at the station smiled. "Almost there," was his cheerful pronouncement, "and look at her fluidic electroglands! They are producing at 150% above expectations! Outstanding!"

Yuri wanted to walk away. By all measures of medical science, Annika should have come apart at the seams by now. The tattoo of her fingers was a steady buzz, her eyes couldn't be tracked. From her open mouth issued strange noises, definitely not human and the noise from her pulse was a high-pitched whine. Everyone was watching her, enthralled. Not Yuri. He had given her downloads at Celtius 4, but it was nothing like this.

After half an hour, the staccato tapping of her fingers slowed. She was no longer making the odd noise and her head was turning in smaller and smaller circles. Yuri grabbed the cart holding her electrolytes and pushed it next to her. He listened to her pulse as it slowed, praying.

There was a large "SNAP" and the displays around her all went blank. An attendant removed the pads under her arms, even though her fingers still wriggled and writhed. Annika's head stopped its frantic nodding. She stared straight ahead, the black in her eyes fading to a flat rendition of her emerald green. Every breath in the room was stilled.

"Yuri?" came the ragged whisper. "Yuri, my love, I am ever so thirsty." He held the first glass to her lips, the silver-grey sludge sliding past her pale lips. He saw her throat work as she swallowed the entire glass of the vile smelling liquid. "More!" she gasped. Yuri tried to place the next glass in her hand. She grabbed at it, swinging too hard. It flew across the room with a crash. "YURI!" she screamed, "MORE!" Before she could react, he had another glass at her lips, holding it with both hands.

"Shhh, Annika, I am here." She put her hand on his as she drank the revolting potion.

When the glass was empty, she breathed heavily. "More, please," she asked in a stronger voice. With closed eyes, she held Yuri's hand and now sipped the mixture.

Annika's eyes lost their flat green stare, began to sparkle their natural emerald green. "One more, please," she entreated. Her mouth formed a small smile as she drank neatly, then asked for five glasses of water, one right after the other. Her clothes were stuck to her body from perspiration, hair splayed about. Yuri smoothed her hair as best he could. She turned her head until he could caress her cheek.

"Proctor, may I rest now?" Annika asked. "I am so tired." She held Yuri's hand to her cheek, closed her eyes and fell asleep. Applause rippled through the room.

"A success," the Brown Proctor told Yuri, "a complete, absolute success! Well done, Doctor." He took Yuri's hand and shook it vigorously.

"I don't pretend to understand," responded the confused doctor. "All I did was hand her fluids."

The Brown Proctor shook his head. "You don't work much with computers?" he asked. "Red File has entered a restart phase from her reformatting. You were a big key. Had you not been there or if someone unfamiliar had responded, she would have gone into self-preservation mode. She might have attacked everyone in the room until she was subdued or she could even have initiated a self-destruct sub routine."

The chair in the center of the room had folded into a gurney. A nurse removed his hand with the gentle touch. "Please, Sir, we're taking her in for a bath and changing. We'll transport her to your suite when we're finished."

A bustle of activity filled the room as the gurney was escorted from it. Attendants put away equipment, polished surfaces and left. The Proctor offered to walk with Yuri back to the suite, provided they stop along the way for lunch. "Doctor, she'll be sleeping now for 24 hours. I rarely have a chance to just sit and talk with anyone outside my order during meals."

In the hallway, Yuri was delighted at the Proctor's words. "Tell me, please Doctor. Have you ever watched baseball?"

The Proctor was spot on in his estimate of how long Annika would sleep. Yuri was holding her hand a day later when she stirred. Her eyes opened with a snap and she sat up. She shook her head and said, "Whoa! That was something! Yuri, my love, have you been sitting there all night?" She scrambled out of bed and began to flex and stretch. "Man, do I feel good!" She danced about, began

101

stripping her pajamas as she hopped and skipped to the bathroom. "Yuri, darling, would you call Dohlman and get breakfast going?"

Yuri watched in stunned disbelief. Annika, usually modest, was prancing and leaping about naked. She whirled in circles and cried, "Hurry, hurry, Lazybones, I'm hungry!" She pranced into the bathroom.

"Dohlman?" The butler appeared. "Would you set breakfast for two, please," Yuri asked. "And notify Red Proctor. Let him know Annika is awake." The Dohlman nodded and disappeared.

Annika was…singing? A wild tune in an unfamiliar language issued from the bath. He couldn't recall hearing her sing. Breakfast arrived and interrupted his thoughts, he was drinking his coffee when the shower shut off and Annika bounded into the room.

Completely nude, water still dripping from her body.

"Oh, goody! Food! I am so hungry." She raced across the room, eyeing the setting.

"Annika," croaked Yuri. "Didn't you forget something?"

Annika stopped, looked down at herself and cried, "Oh, yeah, be right back." Off she ran to her room, returning seconds later. She pointed to her feet. "Slippers!" She began to grab food and shove it in her mouth.

Yuri was just starting to call for Dohlman when a knock came at the door. Before Yuri could respond, Annika, spraying food from her mouth, yelled, "Enter!"

The Proctor entered. "Good morning, Crown Princess, good morning, Doc…oh!" He reached into a pocket and pulled out a golden band. "Red File, please put this on."

Annika shook her head. "Can't," came the answer. "Eating." More food sprayed out of her mouth.

The Proctor sighed. "Child!" His voice raised. "Put the transducer on now!"

She spat the food in her mouth on a plate and took the band, placing it around her head. The Proctor produced a pad from yet another pocket and tapped a few keystrokes. Annika froze.

The Proctor continued to tap away at the pad while talking to himself. "Ah," he finally said aloud. "Of course. You've been a very lazy child." He tapped the pad once more.

Annika came out of her stupor. "Proctor, good morning! I was just, AHHHHHHH!!" she screamed, trying to cover herself. "May I be excused?" she called over her shoulder as she bolted for her room.

The Proctor shook his head and gave Yuri one of his small smiles. "Well, the manners sub-routine is working," was his wry remark. "She did excuse herself."

"What just happened?" Yuri asked.

"Ah, well, in simplest terms, I had to adjust some of Red's Files..."

"Annika."

The Proctor inclined his head. "Annika," he corrected, "has a series of emotional settings that are adjustable. We found we had to write them into her as she didn't develop them naturally. There are the more basic emotions, like you saw today. Modesty. Gods above, that was difficult. As small children, we allowed the Files to live naked. We felt it would help break down some social taboos for them. When the time came, the other children developed degrees of modesty as we had them dress. Not Annika. She couldn't understand why she had to wear clothing. It took two months until we found the anomaly. We were able to override it, but adjusting the files associated with it took time. Some will still require thought on her part and interaction with others."

"But she will be all right."

"Oh, yes. I think what happened during the reformatting; her modesty setting was reset to an earlier age. Twenty months, it seems to have been." The Proctor continued to poke at his pad.

"Ah, the nudity, the singing and the poor table manners." Yuri stated.

"Singing?" The Proctor sounded surprised.

Yuri confirmed, "Yes, she was singing in the shower."

"Interesting." The Proctor began to tap away at his tablet.

Annika returned to the table, looking contrite. "I apologize, Proctor, for my appalling behavior."

"Yes, Child, appalling is a good word. How do you feel?" he asked.

"Embarrassed."

The Proctor looked pleased. "Excellent! You didn't have to search to understand what you feel! Very good, Annika. Now, why do you feel embarrassed?"

"You and Yuri saw me nude," Annika said shyly.

"I have seen you nude many times, Child."

"Yes, but I was much younger," she explained.

"And now you are older. Why are you embarrassed Yuri saw you?" he pressed.

Annika said, "He's never seen me that way before."

"He is a doctor; he's examined many people naked. Why does this embarrass you?"

She chewed on a *petchya* rind, her brow furrowed in concentration.

"I don't want him to think I am ugly," she whispered.

"I don't think you're ugly," Yuri interjected. "I think you're beautiful."

"Really?" Annika sounded hopeful.

The Proctor raised a hand. "We are losing the point of the lesson, Child. Why do you think Yuri would find you ugly?"

Annika hung her head. "I haven't been taking care of myself properly."

"Exactly. What did I find in your physiological scan?"

"A low endorphin rate."

"When did you last work out, Annika?" the Proctor asked.

"The day before the Naming Ceremony. The day was so busy, I skipped it from my schedule. In the days after, I didn't make the time."

Yuri interrupted in his Doctor Russolov mode. "What are your reactions when you allow your endorphin levels to get too low?"

"Fear. Self-loathing. Poor body image. Self-destructive behavior. Irresponsible actions."

"Exactly," said the Proctor. "I am resetting your schedule. You will change into your workout uniform and go to the gymnasium. I will have Major Campion and Sergeant Swartz direct you into a proper routine once more."

"Yes, Proctor." Annika left the table and went to change.

"And you, Doctor? What are you doing today?"

"I was going to walk with Annika to her office, then go work in the city hospital. But I think I will just go straightaway to the hospital."

"Yes," agreed the Proctor.

"Higher, higher!" screamed Sergeant Pamela Swartz. "Superior being, my ASS! Get that weight off your chest and get it up. Now!"

Annika gritted her teeth and pushed. Pamela was her old friend from the first day of the crisis; she had been pleased to see her. Pleased right up until the workout began. Then something evil emerged. Annika had read about demon possession and wondered if that was what happened to Sergeant Swartz.

The weight reached the top. Pamela grabbed the bar and helped guide it into the bench. Annika, breathing heavily, her arms above her head. "What!" cried Pamela, "a rest? We'll rest when we're dead. Come on UP!"

Wearily, Annika got off the bench. She twisted, stretched, loosening and limbering her body. Rolling her neck, she joined Pamela on the track for a two-mile cool-down jog. Annika couldn't speak. A mere Terran, albeit an adult soldier, had outperformed her physically. She burned with embarrassment.

105

Finished, they entered the locker room and showered. Pamela had a fresh uniform to wear; Dohlman had delivered a loose suit for the girl. "Well, off to work," Pamela quipped. "Best way I know how to start my day. See you tomorrow?"

"*NO!*" Annika wanted to scream. Instead, she smiled. "Looking forward to it."

"Sweetie, today was just a start. I know you can do better and you and I are going to find out just how good you can be. Look in that mirror. Tell me truthfully how much better you feel already?"

Annika looked. Her hair was a mess. Normally, she had help with that. But, she had to get to work. She took a second glance. Her face was ruddy from the strain. But she was already feeling...better. "Maybe you're right, Pamela," she replied, "Whoops, off to work."

As always, Annika led her small troupe to her office. Miss Norris didn't look up. "You're late!" she cried as Annika hurried by.

"Yes, I know," Annika called back. "Tea, please, Miss Norris."

This day established Annika's pattern for the next two months. She would work on reports until nine, when the Prime Minister Stype would arrive. They would go over the events of the day and the reports she had read. Annika appreciated the old minister. He was patient when explaining the finer points she didn't understand, corrected her so she didn't feel foolish. Most of all, he encouraged her and allowed her to make her own decisions.

At eleven, she ate lunch at one of the dozens of gardens and grottos near her office. Her favorite "The Garden of Eternity", was open aired, facing the plateau of Giza. The view was of the Sphinx and three ancient pyramids. She found solace viewing the weathered stone monuments to ancient kings as she ate. As often as he could, Yuri would join her. When he couldn't, any number of ministers gladly accepted the invitation of the Crown Princess. There was rumor around the Imperial Ministry that this young woman was formidable, working hard at being accessible and cordial. Annika was developing a following.

The afternoons were more reports and too often, meetings. Annika struggled in meetings. She didn't like to sit still that long. Most of the meetings were with members of the court and government trying to curry favor or be noticed. From time to time, she broke the Prime Minister's taboo and looked into some of her visitors' heads. Most of the information was benign, but some she noted for future use.

A few of these scans she shared with Noire. There would be quiet investigations and quieter arrests.

On the seventh day after the attack, she and Yuri arose early. Dohlman had laid out somber clothing. Noire and her sister Teresa joined her for the state funeral. Their mother and the Regent joined them, along with two dozen members of the family who had survived.

Four boxes containing the cremated remains of her sister, Anje, and their brothers sat on a plinth at the front of the plaza. In even rows were the remains of the forty dead members from the Royal family. Annika had never met them, nor any of the other survivors arrayed before her.

The ceremony was mercifully short. After the priests and bonzes representing the Khan's family chanted their prayers and waved their incense burners, the thousands gathered bowed in silent respect for the mourning Crown Princess and departed the plaza.

The interment was likewise brief. Annika placed the four boxes containing her siblings in the sepulchers carved in the bowels of the palace for that purpose. She hesitated with the orange-ribboned box, that of Anja.

A Khan does not cry, she told herself. *But a sister does...*

Yuri wrapped his arms around the weeping girl and led her away.

Chapter 14

"How many dead, Minister?" Annika demanded.

Morris Stype checked his pad. "One hundred thirty-eight thousand, four hundred seventy-nine."

"How many whole families?" she asked, dreading the answer.

"At least fourteen thousand. It will take time to go through the remains. Some are only DNA samples."

"One hundred thirty-eight thousand." she repeated. "I'm afraid so many will go unclaimed. Whatever shall we do? I can't bear the thought of so many unclaimed and unremembered in a warehouse."

"Commonly, a memorial would be erected near the disaster site…" Minister Stype began.

"That's it exactly. Two weeks. I want the proposed plans on my desk in two weeks."

Minister Stype rubbed his neck. "That could be very expensive."

"For the favor of the Crown Princess and future Empress? I think we'll have far more designs proposed than we have victims. Two weeks, Minister."

Three days later, General Han requested a meeting. Annika, ever looking to escape the disapproving glare of Miss Norris, raced to Central Command. General Han met her at the central holo. "We got them," he announced, his grin wolf-like in stark contrast to his respectful bow.

An image of a wild ocean was up on the screen. "Set time scale back one hour," he directed, "and then advance at five-minute increments." The image scrambled, then froze. It began to move again. They double backed north, to the Arctic, "he indicated. "The ice there is at its thinnest and we were able to trace them easily with the blue light laser."

Flashes of fire erupted from the ice. "They cut their way through, expecting to be able to rise up through the Van Allen belts. But I had a squadron of Buccaneer fighters and two scouts orbiting the breakout. If they got past them, I had a full destroyer division in low orbit. They weren't going to escape."

The holo screen showed a ship rising from the ice. Instantly, smaller ships were dancing around, bombarding the ship with bolts of energy. A scout swooped around, fired larger missiles into the hull. "It took quite a pounding before it faltered," Han continued his report. "The crew, fifteen total, all augmentons. The ship hit the water and sank. I had submersibles and divers nearby. Once all the biological components died, we could retrieve thirteen of their brain processor units undamaged. Once revived, it will not take long to determine the perpetrators of this heinous crime."

This time, it was Annika who bowed low to General Han. "Crown Princess, you honor me!" gasped the startled General.

"No, General," the future monarch ruled, "It is you who honors my Empire."

Annika was snuggled with Yuri in bed. The terrors still came to her in her sleep. Yuri was her shield, her knight in shining armor. In his arms at night, nothing could touch her, nothing could harm her.

Dohlman appeared. He shook Annika's shoulder. "Crown Princess! Wake, please."

She had been having such a pleasant dream. They were riding together, back on Celtius 4. It was late summer; the air was still. The sudden shaking was annoying. Yuri calling her Crown Princess was even worse. Wait, what?

Annika roused. Yuri snored beside her. "Dohlman! What is it? What time is it?" she snapped. It had been a lovely dream.

"It's 0243 hours, Crown Princess." He handed her a piece of paper. "He was most insistent, Ma'am."

A deep breath, exhaled forcefully. Take the note. Read it. "Gods above and below!" she exclaimed as she scanned the missive, was dressed and at the door in minutes. An Imperial Intelligence agent was waiting. He clicked his heels, and led her away. They were joined by two members of her personal guard. The black Intelligence Ministry van carried them swiftly to the squat, somber building. The van hadn't stopped when Annika leaped out and raced inside.

"Noire!"

"Here Annika."

"It's him? Truly?"

"Yes. And the conspirators as well."

"All of them."

"Yes. Would you like to see?"

"Of course!"

Noire escorted her to the elevator. It dropped 10 levels in seconds.

The elevator discharged them into a short, dimly lit hallway. There was a single plain door opposite of the elevator. Annika restrained herself from running.

Beyond the lonely door was a conference room like any other found in the Empire. Wood paneling, a vid dominating one wall. A table and chairs.

A man in an Imperial Army uniform trousers and white shirt. A General's jacket was laying on the floor and kicked aside. He was splayed akimbo against the right wall. His white hair was disheveled, his eyes bulged, bloodshot, his mouth in a rictus grin.

Annika could see no restraints, though the man was struggling as though to get free. She examined him closely, confirming what she thought she saw. Or rather, didn't see.

"This is your work, Noire?"

"Yes, a suggestion given to me by Minister Blount. The detainees believe they are being held into place and then I use stimulus to terrorize them. The late Justice Minister managed to break his arm trying to get free in this method of restraint."

"Impressive. Your skills have grown since you came to Intelligence."

"Thank you. I am quite proud of this detainee. I have implanted a stimulus that should have him ready to give me the information I seek."

"Can he hear me?"

"Please. It will be entertaining. You are the image I am using on him right now."

Annika arched her eyebrows and smiled.

"General...Teague, is it? "she asked, "Of course you are." Her face took on an orgasmic look of pleasure. "You cannot possibly imagine how pleased I am to finally meet you," her voice dropped to a sultry purr. "And I am, of course, Crown Princess Annika Raudona Khan." She bit off each syllable of her name, stretching it to its full import.

"I 'm sure you know who I am." She traced a finger along his cheek. Frantic noises came from his throat and he began to shake with even more terror. "You tried to have me killed," she pouted. "Bad general. That wasn't very nice of you."

Then she stretched tall, assumed a regal pose. "No, not very nice indeed. I wonder what it takes for a man of forty years in my father's and my grandfather's service to turn on his future Empress. Money? Power? None of that matters now, General. You killed members of my family. You killed one hundred forty thousand souls of my Empire. You tried to kill me. In the end, General, I shall kill you. Your family, your officers and their families will likewise suffer for your treason."

She whirled away.

"Noire, I want this done."

"Yes, Sister."

112

"Teague and all of his conspirators are to be court marshaled. By officers known to be loyal to us. Contact General Han, he can provide a list. I want it done by next Friday, all of them. The Regent reassumes power the next day; I will not leave this to him."

"Yes, Sister."

"And I want the arrests to start immediately and quietly. I will pass sentencing for them before the council."

"As you have ordered, my Khan."

Those who saw her leave that early morning cowered. Her face wore eyes of emerald flame. Her mouth was a thin, pleased smile.

Chapter 15

It was to be her last day ruling the Empire, for now. Annika had risen early and taken the walk up the Tower of Dawn. She considered inviting Yuri, but decided this was to be for her and her alone.

It was prepared in the fashion she requested. The water already hot. Annika measured the tea and sugar. The sky lightened, the fiery orb appeared and began its ascent. The tea was, as Master Tahn would say, the perfect tea at the perfect sunrise. She hurled the cup against the wall. The Crown Princess spread her arms as the rays reached out and embraced her, the warmth wrapping around her like a blanket, the glow reflected on her upturned face.

A falcon circled above the desert. It rode a thermal up and down, ever watching the ground below. It arced onto a wing and dove. Just as it looked like it might hit the ground, it flared and struck its prey. It rose again, bearing its next meal.

The perfect sunrise with the perfect tea.

The future Khan was pleased.

Annika sweated and strained through the last workout she would have with Sergeant Pamela Swartz. In just a few weeks, she had become pleased with the way she looked and felt. Her mental well-being and self-confidence had returned. In the mirror as she stretched, she was pleased with the way her body moved under her unitard. Smooth, practiced moves showed her grace, form and …beauty. She studied each tendon as it stretched, as each muscle contracted and expanded. Exquisite. Perfection.

They showered and dressed, Pamela in her uniform, Annika in her preferred loose pants and top. They gave each other a peck on the cheek.

"You will be at my suite today? Before I leave?" asked Annika.

"Of course, Sweetie," responded her best friend. "I wouldn't miss it for the world! A chance to see you off on your first real vacation!"

Annika savored her walk to her office. Normally hurried, today she was going to enjoy every moment.

Major Campion had arranged her detail like a relay race, as the Crown Princess would normally outrace her combat ready escort. Her saunter today caught them pleasantly surprised.

As always, Miss Norris greeted her with, "You're late!" Annika snickered; it was a familiar routine she would miss.

"Yes, Miss Norris," she called back. "Please send in tea, Miss Norris."

Inside the door, she whispered, "Dohlman?"

He appeared, as always at her elbow. "Yes, Ma'am?"

"You have it?"

"In your desk, Ma'am. Bottom drawer."

"Thanks, Dohlman, you're the best."

"Indeed." He disappeared.

Annika excitedly waited for Miss Norris to bring in the tea and set it on the credenza. As the older woman turned to leave, Annika cleared her throat.

"Miss Norris, a moment of your time?"

"Yes, Crown Princess?"

"I want to thank you properly for all the help you've given me. I know I've been difficult, but I've tried, really tried. And you taught me so much. Thank you."

"You're welcome, Crown Princess. Will that be all?"

Annika blurted. "I wanted to give you this. A memento of our time together." She handed Miss Norris a small, beribboned box.

The older woman accepted the gift. Inside, she found a golden pendant watch. The cover was inscribed with the message: *To my friend and teacher, Miss Norris. Crown Princess Annika Raudona Khan.* Under that inscription, in tiny letters, it read:

Annika's time. Miss Norris read the inscription twice, not understanding the last part of the inscription. Then she noticed the watch face.

The hands ran backwards.

Miss Norris, one not easily amused, displayed her tight-lipped smile, corners of the mouth barely lifting. Nonetheless, her fondness for the young princess hovered in the room. "Thank you," she said as she fastened it to her sweater. "I shall cherish it always."

"One more thing," Annika asked. "When I come back, I'd like you to be my secretary. If you would. Please."

Miss Norris invested in an almost perceptible nod. "We shall see. Now, you have work to do."

At nine, the Prime Minister arrived. They set to work immediately. After an hour, Moritz Stype set the last of his papers down. "Crown Princess, we have the memorial decision to make this morning. The architects are waiting in the lower conference room."

Annika was disappointed. Each architect's rendering seemed to follow similar themes, whether tall spires or blocky, odd looking lumps of rock and stone, with fountains and ponds galore. Nothing that was exciting or inspiring. She was about to close her eyes and just point, when she noticed a young man sitting on the edge of the stage, sketching on a pad.

Annika wandered over to have a look. He was an assistant to one of the great architects, an unkempt looking boy, his rumpled clothing out of place in her palace.

Annika took his book while he spoke of his drawings. He showed her the drawing on which he was working. It was an image of her wandering through the exhibit, and captured the disappointment on her face!

Then she stopped. An image struck her. It spoke to her. "What is this?" she asked.

He searched his memory for the source of the drawing. "Oh, that," he finally responded. "It's village ten klicks from here. It was built centuries ago following some damn war or another. Refugees

117

moved in and just never left. They used the methods that have always been used here, straw reinforced mud brick, covered with a gypsum paste to reflect the heat. The roofs are made from leaves and branches taken from forests."

"This is what I'm looking for!" she gasped. "Look, like this." She took his note pad and drew an oval. "This is the Plaza. At the open end, we build the village. It doesn't have to be full sized. And we leave the roofs off so sunlight is always shining in. We put a plinth inside to hold the sarcophagi. We'll try to keep families together, of course. This will be a memorial, not just to those who died on that terrible day, but a memorial to anyone who dies in service to my Empire!"

She called the Prime Minister, voiced her plan. He looked dubious, but finally agreed. "This Necropolis of yours would seem to be an excellent plan for our future, Crown Princess..."

Annika beamed. She dismissed the other architects and ordered work to begin, immediately.

Annika returned to work. She had only one meeting in the afternoon with Gavin Howland, Minister of Defense. Despite her original misgivings about this minister, she had found him a loyal and dedicated servant to the Empire.

She would need that loyalty in council.

"Everything is in readiness, Crown Princess," he announced. "The court martials were finished this morning. All conspirators guilty on all counts, as expected. Intelligence has rounded up the families as we discussed. They are being held, awaiting your decision."

"No regrets, Minister?"

"None Crown Princess. If we don't nip this in the bud now, how far would it travel? No! Execute the traitors, now, publicly. Punish the families. It will be a harsh warning to anyone who considers attacking your Empire."

"Very well. Send the message. Convene my council in an hour."

He bowed and left the room.

In her quarters, Annika fingered her uniform sadly. It might be years before she donned it again. This uniform meant the universe to her. The acceptance of the Imperial Army assured she would have the muscle to enforce her law. Today would serve as a warning to any who would defy her.

She dressed carefully. The uniform must be perfect. A servant brushed and braided her hair. *"Stand straight, not a hair out of place."* It rang through her head over and over.

Finally, it was time. Major Campion had selected the five finest troopers in the Empire. They wore full combat dress per her orders. Save for a single attachment. Each wore a blood red sash. Thus adorned, they marched behind their Crown Princess.

The doors opened the moment they approached. Annika led her entourage directly to the throne. It had been lowered to her diminutive size. No repeat of her first visit here.

Gavin Howland stood. "Bring him," he commanded. A side door opened and a pair of soldiers dragged an older man to the center of the chamber. He shook them off, stood painfully and saluted. "General Mason Teague, reporting as ordered."

"Noire has done his work well," thought Annika.

"General Mason Anderson Teague, you have been found guilty of the crimes of murder, assault, dereliction of duties, abandoning your post, disobedience of orders and treason with malice toward the crown by a court martial of your peers," read the Defense Minister. "The mandatory sentence for these crimes is death. Are you prepared to receive sentencing before the crown for the crimes for which you have been found guilty?"

The general wavered. Then in as firm a voice as he could manage, he responded, "I do not recognize the validity or authority of this court. This tribunal is illegal by the laws of..." he got no further; one of the guards punched him in the stomach.

The whole room was quiet save for the coughing of the old general. He struggled again to his feet.

Annika sat regally. "You don't recognize the legality of this court," she said. "You do not recognize my authority. The authority laid down by the laws of my ancestor, the Great Khan himself. You refute the traditions and regulations you have faithfully served for forty-three years.

I was prepared to be merciful, General," her voice rose. "Look at what you have done to me! You have attacked my Empire using filthy mercenaries! Augmentons! You used augmentons against me! Me, your sovereign! You attacked and murdered one hundred thirty-nine thousand of my loyal subjects! You murdered my family!"

She was breathing heavily. "I see no room for any mercy for you. You, your co-conspirators. Your families. Your officers are sentenced to death, to be publicly hung by the neck until dead. Their families are to be taken to the mines of Nikuman, to be of service to my Empire until death. Your wife and children will join them."

Her eyes narrowed. "Now do you respect my authority?"

Then General worked his mouth. "Freak!"

The Crown Princess moved too fast to see, taking the rifle from the nearest soldier and in nanoseconds was standing in front of the general, the rifle raised. She fired the rifle in full automatic. The General's body jerked and twisted, falling in a messy heap. She continued to fire, emptying the weapon into his body. When it was finally empty, she stood over the remains, her breath coming in great gasps. Annika handed the rifle to one of her guards, then pointed at the body.

"This. This is the price for standing against me. This is the price for standing against my Empire!"

She braced herself to her full four feet ten inches and marched from the council chamber.

Pamela was in the suite, waiting. They stripped Annika's uniform off and carefully folded it for storage. Annika took a quick shower, changed into a bright floral sundress. She spun in front of a mirror, delighted with her reflection. Never had she dressed this way. It was light and comfortable. She looked and felt beautiful.

"Pamela, am I pretty?" The older woman took her young friend's hands. "Sweetie, you're beautiful. Yuri is such a lucky man." Annika beamed and picked up a clutch purse. "Am I holding this right?"

The girls giggled. "My knife doesn't fit in here," she complained, after trying to put it in the clutch.

Pamela snorted. "Do you think you'll need that to use on your man?" She took it and promised, "I'll pack the wicked thing in your bag."

They strolled through the palace, chatting amicably, to the garage. Yuri was waiting by a flier. "I'll see you soon," Annika promised her friend as she skipped to the flier.

Pamela watched the couple embrace and leap into the air car. It lifted off the platform, turning slowly. Annika twisted and waved to her friend as the ship climbed and slipped away. She waved until she could no longer see the air car. Dejected, Sergeant Pamela Swartz returned to her job.

Chapter 16

Yuri guided the craft up and over Cairo and the Nile delta. He slid the top of the flier back and they enjoyed the warm sun and cool breeze. He placed his hand behind his head and sighed, loudly and happily.

"On vacation," he smiled, "At last!" Annika copied his movements, tucking her hands behind her head.

"This is great," she exclaimed. "Now what do we do?"

He shook his head. "We're doing it. Nothing."

"Oh," Annika sat quietly for a moment. "How long do we do this?"

"You've never taken a vacation before?" asked Yuri.

"Nope. First time." Annika quipped. "Growing up, every minute was planned for us. Eating, sleeping, and studying. Even toilet. Working in the office the two months have been the same thing."

"No wonder you are so neurotic." He chided.

"Who said I'm neurotic?"

"I did."

"Doctor Yuri or boyfriend Yuri?" Annika stipulated.

Yuri got a faraway look in his eye. "Hmmm, boyfriend Yuri. I like that."

"Don't evade the question," she snapped.

"I'm not. I just choose not to answer. Besides, Doctor Yuri is on vacation."

Annika rolled on her hip, facing Yuri. "So, my boyfriend thinks I'm neurotic," she demanded.

"All boyfriends think their girlfriends are neurotic."

Annika rolled her eyes.

Then she slid the roof all the way back, unfastened her safety belt and stood on her seat, oblivious to Yuri's frightened yells. The girl leaned until her legs were against the windscreen and screamed joyously!

"Look, Yuri, I'm flying!" she cried, "Victory! For Ten Thousand Years! I am Victorious! Wheee!"

Yuri held the air car smoothly, fearful of jolting Annika from her pose.

Eventually, Annika grew bored. She plopped back in her seat. "Hey, let me drive," she said.

"Can I trust you?"

"Probably not. Come on, please?"

He released the controls. Without waiting, Annika grabbed the control and pulled it back. The air car climbed steeply. It started to stall. She rolled the car over and dove for the sea. "Wheee!" she screamed again. A twist of the control and the car rolled over and over. Yuri was feeling green as Annika laughed and chortled, flipping, looping and rolling the car.

"Annika," Yuri pleaded. She leveled out the car and reset the autopilot.

"That was fun!"

"How long have you been flying?"

"Years."

"Seriously?" he asked incredulously.

"Well, flown about. They didn't want to take too many chances with me."

Yuri asked, "How many times have you piloted, then?"

"Counting today?" She gave him an impish grin.

"Of course."

She seemed to be tabulating. "Counting today," her voice trailed off, "once."

"Seriously?"

"Yup."

"You're incorrigible."

"That's why you love me." She bestowed a peck upon his cheek.

"Hey, what's that?" Yuri pointed above them.

Annika squinted. "Buccaneer fighters," she informed him. "Our escort."

"We have an escort?" Yuri queried.

"Yup. Only way Major Campion would agree to let me ride with you instead in the back of a sub-orbital," she stated. "He's in a shuttle behind us, along with the rest of my bodyguard."

"Seriously?"

"You say seriously a lot," she quipped.

"I am finding out I need to be serious with you," he responded. He aimed a thumb upwards. "Necessary, I suppose."

"If Major Campion says it is. It doesn't bother you, does it?" Annika asked.

"I guess not. I've never had an escort before."

"Well, technically, it's for me. So, you should plan on staying close on this vacation," she informed him.

"I plan on it." He slid closer to her.

They continued north and east. Soon, a chain of rocky islands appeared. "Thasos," Yuri pointed. "I went there as a student. It has magnificent beaches, great restaurants and an amazing market. I was able to get us a suite near the waterfront, with a balcony." He thought for a moment. "But you knew that."

"Don't be angry, my love," she soothed. "The Major already found out. It's easier and better this way."

"Do I want to know how he did it?"

"Nope."

Supper was lamb in a fine restaurant. They shared a bottle of wine, Annika's first alcohol. She enjoyed the crisp, sweet drink, but choked a bit when some slipped down the wrong part of her throat. Shortly, she began to feel ill.

They cut the night short and hurried to the hotel. It was an uncomfortable night for both. Annika was woozy and had difficulty trying to sleep. "The room is spinning," she complained. Finally, she slipped out of bed and was ill. Yuri entered the bath as she was finishing. "So, I think we've discovered you can't drink alcohol. At least not very much." That was Doctor Yuri speaking, Annika decided. She had to agree. Yuri half carried her back to bed.

Wisely, he let her sleep it off.

When she did finally wake, she was thirsty for her electrolytes and water. She didn't want breakfast, so Yuri packed a basket for the car with fruit and cheese. They left later than expected.

"I say it was the lamb," Annika stated primly.

"I would point I ate the lamb, too, and wasn't sick." Yuri replied.

"That's because you're Russian. That makes you weird."

"And your ancestors were Mongolian. What's that make you?"

"Blessed," she smiled.

"Yes, I see you are very blessed right now." He feigned vomiting.

"Be nice. I'm sick. How long until New Moscow?"

"Six hours."

"Good. I think I'll take a nap."

New Moscow was the pride of the Russian Federation.

The ancient city had been flattened in the War of the Five Cities. The resolve of the Russian people was legendary. It took four centuries, but the city was restored beyond its former glory.

During the rebuilding, the vast rings of streets were still centered on the Kremlin Fortress and Red Square. The colorful domes and towers of Saint Basil's were rebuilt. Entrepreneurs recreated the famous department stores, Gum and Voyentarg.

The Cathedral of Christ the Savior property was expanded and boasted one of the finest universities of the entire Empire.

126

Old Moscow had been proud of its many gardens and urban forests. New Moscow had carefully grown and nurtured larger parks and gardens. Gorky, Sokolniki and Izmaylovsky parks were far vaster than before.

It was said that from the air, New Moscow looked more like a forest growing a city, than a city with a forest.

Yuri steered the air car to the villa he had rented. From the outside, it was a large set of ivy covered walls. Inside, the courtyard was a stately garden. The walls themselves held all the rooms, most of which opened to the garden.

Importantly, room enough to include Major Campion and his team of bodyguards.

Annika was the consummate tourist. Having been raised traveling the Empire for months at a time, she settled quickly in her new home, and then set about exploring the city. Yuri enjoyed showing her his adopted home. She was intrigued by the many churches, stopping the car to walk around the Cathedrals.

Yuri took her to the theaters. At the Bolshoi and its ballet, she turned up her nose. Vaakhtangov Theater was of more interest; they were performing an ancient musical. She was enthralled and spent days singing parts of a song: *"Let me fall into the ocean, let me fall into the sea. Let me be stormy and let me be calm. Let the tide in and set me free..."*

Yuri loved the sound of her voice. It was high and pure, like a breeze whistling through a beech wood grove. She sang other songs as well, some in strange languages. One sounded happy, a bouncing twirl that she would skip about singing for a few minutes, before her voice tailed off and she would get quiet and pensive. Always she wanted to be alone for a while when she sang that song. He asked her once why it made her sad.

"It was Blue's and my song."

One sunny day, Annika announced after breakfast she wanted Yuri to take her shopping. They took the car to Red Square, where the finest stores coexisted with a vast, open market.

She brought a net bag with her and a small list. "I've been helping Greta, our cook," Annika said. "She's sent me with a list to see if I can find a few things." The couple had great fun moving from stall to stall and examining the wares, finding the items. Annika was a good negotiator, talking and cajoling vendors for better prices and higher quality goods.

They had arrived outside the famous Gum Department store. One of the icons of the old city, it had been faithfully reproduced. The young couple wandered through the aisles examining the goods. She selected a pair of running shoes she liked. Yuri chose a new shirt and jacket.

The second floor was more clothing, mostly for children. Annika giggled, showing Yuri the baby and young children's clothing. The third floor was toys. Yuri expected to continue to go to the next floor, but Annika wandered in. As they traversed the aisles, they would pick up a shiny top here or a glittery ball there and show them to the other. Yuri had stopped, looking over a vexing puzzle made of glossy colors and odd shapes. He was going to show Annika.

She wasn't there.

He carried the puzzle with him while he looked for her. He found her staring at a vast display along the back wall.

"Dolls." She said softly, "Yuri, look. Dolls."

He came to her side as she looked from side to side in slow motion, trying to take in the inventory. "Well come on, take a closer look." He urged her forward.

Annika moved slowly, in awe. There were dolls of every size, shape and color. Dress up doll, play dolls, talking dolls, baby dolls. She began to stop and touch them, then would pick one up and hold it, examining it as if looking for something.

She stood for five minutes staring at a princess doll dressed all in ruffled pink, a tiny tiara on its head. Toward the end of the aisle, she gave a small cry and picked a plain rag doll from the bottom shelf. She stared at it as she had the others, then hugged it tightly to her chest

"Would you like that one?" Yuri asked. Annika nodded, holding it tighter.

He paid for their purchases. It was a good time to go home.

Annika wouldn't set the doll down, clutching it to her chest on the ride home. She fled into the house and slammed the bedroom door closed.

She came out at supper, her eyes red. The doll was still firmly hugged under her left arm.

It was a quiet evening. Yuri sat on a bench next to the garden, working on his puzzle. Annika sat on another bench, hugging and talking softly to her new friend.

It grew late. Yuri held out his hand and said, "Come on Annika, time for bed." They went to their room, changed and climbed into bed. They spooned, with Annika still holding her doll.

"When we were seven, Yellow, Orange and I saw some other little girls playing with dolls in one of the gardens. It looked like great fun, so I asked the Proctor if my sisters and I could have a doll. He said that dolls defined an unhealthy female model and had little or no educational value. So we made our own, out of old socks and cleaning rags we found. It was great fun after lights out, the three of us playing with our dolls. Mine was Miss Breezy, Orange's was Tabitha and Yellow's was Kitty Kat. We thought it was a funny name, but it was Yellow's. Oh, the fun we had, making up stories and adventures, singing songs and dancing with our dolls. We had to hide them carefully, so the boys and the Proctors wouldn't find them."

"But they did. The Proctor made us watch as he fed them into the recycler, reminded us of our responsibilities and how important it was that we prepare to become Khan one day.

"I miss Yellow. But I really miss Anje."

She buried her face in the doll and cried herself to sleep.

129

Chapter 17

They left Moscow for the fall harvest.

Yuri flew his air car up into the eastbound flight path and set the autopilot. The ship flew swiftly above the Ural Mountains and over the vast plains. As they left the foothills, Yuri pointed to vast blue/green fields to the east.

"There's the beginning of my parents' farm," he told her, "Those are the algae bogs used to make food proteins. That is the bulk of the harvest, but it's largely automated. We'll be working the local family farms on the collective to bring in the foodstuff harvest. The whole of our community is able to feed itself and we feed much of Terra with the algae bogs."

Yuri dove the air car back toward the ground, heading for a large clump of buildings. "My parents' house," he announced.

As the engines wound down, there was a cry. "Yuri-i-i-i-i-i!" A handsome woman wearing a long peasant dress came flying out of the main house and embraced him as he climbed from the car. "Yuri, my precious son. You're home!"

"Mama," he cooed as she grabbed him by the face, covering his face with kisses.

As Annika stepped around the car, Yuri released his mother and said, "Mama, this is my friend, Annika. Annika, this is my mama."

"Clara," the auburn-haired woman said, releasing her son. "Uh, what should I call you? I mean: Crown Princess, Majesty?"

"How about just Annika?" She flashed a wide, toothy grin as she was enfolded into strong, maternal arms.

"YURI!" A bear of a man stalked purposefully from the barn. His thick, black hair swayed like the mane of a lion. A fierce beard, streaked with grey, covered his lower face and raged half way down his chest. He was dressed in a utilitarian blue coverall and was wiping his hands with an old red rag.

Yuri was engulfed in a massive bear hug, and kissed on the cheek. Andrei began wiping his son ineffectively with the rag, chanting, "Sorry, sorry. Working on a balky tractor."

Ah, so this must be Annika. I am Andrei. Please call me Papa." Before she could move, the beast had her in his apelike arms and was giving her a surprisingly warm and comfortable hug. "Oh, damn, sorry. Sorry. Damned tractor anyway." Andrei now wiped Annika with his dirty rag.

"Papa! Quit mauling the poor girl," Clara cried. "Such an ill-mannered brute I married!"

Andrei looked terribly contrite. "I am just so glad to see my son and meet his friend."

"Fine, you've met them. Now back to work! You can meet her again at supper. Now, *boh*!" ordered Clara.

"Son, I am working on a tractor in the barn. Why don't you come help me when you and Annika settle in?" His father ambled back to the barn.

Clara followed him as he walked away. "He really is the sweetest man," she confided to Annika. "But he gets so excited, like a little boy sometimes. Maybe that's why I love him so." She clapped her hands together. "So, children, I have you in the guest cottage. Yuri, you know where it is. After you are settled, Yuri, you go help your father. Annika, how about if you come find me in the kitchen?"

Annika had attended many dinners as one of the Eight on dozens of worlds throughout the Empire. Nothing had prepared her for supper at the Russolov table.

Andrei, as the father, sat at the head of the table. Annika sat on his right as their honored guest.

Everyone else filled in haphazardly on a mixture of chairs and benches. Yuri had been consigned far to Andrei's left. Annika was not sure how many people dined that evening. People would come sit, eat, leave, and then come back minutes later. Clara was kept busy refilling the dozens of bowls of meat, vegetables, rolls and salads. After Andrei had offered a grace, the food began to circle the table. In both directions! She would hand a bowl to Andrei only to have him hand her a platter. Before she could get any food off the platter, the woman to her right would be handing her another vessel while relieving her of the one she had just been handed.

It was maddening!

The circling food finally slowed and stopped. Annika had managed to put some food on her plate. How had everyone managed to heap their plates so high?

And the conversation! Everyone seemed to be talking at once. Shrieks of laughter would break out suddenly, then be cut off by a joke from the other end of the table.

Meekly, she ate, smiling occasionally and laughing when it seemed appropriate.

Finally, the ordeal was over. The women got up and, with a few of the men, cleared the table. Annika tried to stand, but Andrei patted her hand. "Not this time, little one," he rumbled. "Tonight, you are our guest. Now tomorrow, we may make a scullery maid of you." He tipped his head back and roared with laughter. Annika joined him. What would Moritz Stype say to the future Empress of the Terran Empire scrubbing pots and pans?

Yuri moved next to her and took her hand under the table. Clara reappeared, bearing tiny glasses and a chilled bottle. She passed out the glasses and began to pour everyone shots. Annika placed her hand over her glass and said, "None for me, Mama."

"Eh?"

"She doesn't drink, Mama."

Thank you, Yuri.

"Ah, right, she's not Russian," reasoned Andrei.

Clara brought Annika a glass of juice, explaining, "It is bad luck to toast with water."

133

The toasts started. Everyone had something to celebrate and drink to. Some were quite funny. Others were somber, remembering someone long past and fondly remembered. Annika stood and made a toast of her own. "To my brothers, Blaise, Victor and Hijau. And my sister, Anja." Yuri stood. "To my lovely friend, Annika." There was a raucous cheer and the drinks went down again.

Andrei stood, his glass held high. He wobbled about and belched. "To my son, Yuri, returned home at last. And his beautiful woman, Annika. May your lives be filled with happiness, joy and childr…" He toppled forward and passed out on the table.

Astoundingly, Andrei, Yuri and the rest of the revelers were up and working the next morning, albeit slowly. Yuri nursed his coffee and had a few slices of toast before heading out the door mumbling about finishing the damned tractor for his father.

Clara walked to the guest house to gather up Annika. She escorted her around the family farm, gathering eggs, milking the goats and cows, feeding livestock. It was hot, dirty work. Annika loved it. She spent the afternoon on the back porch, shelling peas and talking with Clara.

"With all the algae fields, why are you growing food like this?" asked Annika.

"Because we always have grown our own food," Clara explained. "Farmers across the Empire have a connection with their land. They work hard and the land will reward them with their bounty. Besides," she waved a pea pod, "these fresh peas will taste much better than any protein."

Supper that night was in their guesthouse. Clara packed the couple a basket, explaining, "Last night celebrated you children coming home. Now we go back to work. It will be harvest time soon and we need to get ready for that."

She kissed Annika on each cheek and sent her on her way.

Baskets of hot breakfast were at their door every morning. Every evening, Annika brought a basket of a prepared dinner to the guest house.

She worked hard in the kitchen, reveling the experience of the plain, simple peasant work.

She found herself asking the Proctor's question: *Child, how do you feel?* She found she didn't have to think about it. She felt wonderful. She had the familiar parts of her routine to be followed. Electrolytes first thing in the morning. Exercise with her bodyguards before breakfast. Her days filled by chores. Visiting with the other women. Clara took her out in a hovercar and she watched the massive harvesters collect the algae. "It will go from here to the processors," Clara explained. "From there, various food companies will purchase the proteins to be used to make foodstuffs."

Sundays, Annika and Yuri saved for themselves. They would rouse late and spend the day enjoying the others company. One afternoon as they lay in the grass watching the clouds, Yuri cleared his throat. "Annika, I have a question to ask you of the upmost importance," he said.

"Oh, what could be so important a question on such a day as this?"

He rolled on his stomach. "I've been thinking. The village doctor has recently retired. There is a small office available and the community needs a doctor. We could let the villa and New Moscow go and settle here on the farm. What do you think?"

What do I think? Oh, Yuri!

"I think it should take some careful consideration. You're giving up a lot at the University," she said tactfully.

"Yes. But I am needed here. And you seem so happy."

"I am happy," she sighed.

"So, we'll stay."

"Yes, until spring. I have to go to the Temple of Angkor Khan in the spring."

An icy wind swept across the prairie, foreboding the imminent arrival of winter. Frost coated the windows of their cottage and tendrils of arctic air crept through gaps of the snug cabin. Annika had snuggled as close as she could to Yuri, trying to leach warmth from him. She tried climbing on top of him, but that didn't work. She gripped the blanket they shared and rolled over, wrapping most of it around herself. That was better.

Yuri rolled on his back. His snoring increased tenfold. Annika clamped her hands over her ears and gritted her teeth. It didn't help; the noisy sawing noise was too much. She poked her face out of her bedroll.

"Yuri! Hey Yuri."

There was a grumbling noise, then the snoring started again.

"YURI!"

More grumbling.

She gave him a push "Hey YURI! Wake up!"

"What do you want?"

"You're snoring. I can't sleep."

"I'm not snoring."

"You are. Like a great big pig. *SNORT-SNORT-SNORT!*" Annika pushed her pug nose up as she imitated a pig.

"Funny. You are making oinking noises like a pig, seeing how you're a blanket hog."

"A what?"

"Blanket hog. Who has the blankets and who's freezing?"

"I was cold!" she protested.

"*SNORK-SNORK-SNORK!*" Yuri pushed his nose up as Annika had just done.

She sat up, still wrapped in the blanket. "That's not funny. I am not a hog!"

WHAP! Annika was knocked on her side. She righted herself, still wrapped in most of the blankets. WHAP! Down she went again. She sat up screaming.

"HOW DARE YOU..."

136

WHAP!

She went down again. Yuri sat over her with a pillow in his hand.

"What are you doing?" She was angry now.

He looked confused. "Pillow fight?"

"Pillow fight?" Then she understood. She wrestled her hand out and grabbed a pillow of her own.

WHAP! Down went Yuri.

WHAP! -WHAP! -WHAP!

The fight was on. Annika was at a disadvantage, wrapped in the blankets as she was. To compensate, she grabbed a second pillow and began swinging wildly. WHAP-WHAP-WHAP-WHAP!

There was a sudden tearing noise. One of Annika's pillows split wide open and feathers flew about the room. Annika shrieked and laughed as a cloud of feathers drifted slowly about them. Yuri leaped forward and tackled her on the bed. She struggled.

Not too much.

The door was flung open. Major Campion and two of his guards pounced into the room, weapons at the ready. Annika gave a small shriek.

"Yes, Major?" Yuri asked.

Campion looked at the scene. He recovered quickly. "Nothing Ma'am, Sir." he said. "Just seeing if you were ready for the morning workout. I see you're otherwise occupied this morning. Very well. Carry on." Her bodyguards backed out slowly and closed the door.

Yuri still held Annika pinned to the bed.

"You give?"

Annika chuckled naughtily. "No way!"

He kissed her.

"Well, maybe."

He kissed her again.

"Hmmm. I think my defenses are weakening."

Another kiss. Longer this time.

137

"Hmmmm," she purred, "maybe I will surrender. Only if you keep torturing me this way."

He collapsed on top of her. They kissed long and passionately, stopping only when the alarm clock finally went off.

"Time to get ready for work," he sighed.

"Yup."

He looked around at the feathers and ruined pillow.

"Don't tell Mama!"

Chapter 18

Winter blanketed the steppe. The oceans of grass were now covered in thick mounds of snow. Arctic wind howled across the empty plain, clutching any who ventured out in its deathly grip.

Annika and Yuri were happy, snug in their tiny home. Daily, Yuri would get into his hovercar and drive to his new office. Annika struggled through the drifts to the main farm house to collect the food for a few days and visit with the women there.

Andrei paid Annika a visit one clear, frozen morning. "Annika, I have a favor to ask. Christmas is next week and we have no *Snegurochka!*"

"Papa, Christmas was last month," she answered. "And what is a *Snegurochka?*"

"Bah, Christmas was last month if you are a stinking Roman! We are Russian. Christmas is January 7th. Four days from now."

"You didn't answer me. What is a *Snegurochka?*"

"You don't know the story of Grandfather Frost and his granddaughter, the Snow Maiden? Were you raised by Cossacks?"

"Proctors."

"Same thing."

"Yup. What is the *Snegurochka?*" she repeated.

"Not so far from here and many years ago, lived a good couple, Ivan and Myra," Andrei said. "They were kind people, always helping everyone. They had so many blessings in their life, save one. They had no children.

"One Christmas, Ivan went out and built a little girl out of snow and named her *Snegurochka*. Grandfather Frost came around and saw how much they loved her, so he touched the girl with his magic staff and gave her life. She was a wonderful daughter, Ivan and Myra loved her as proudly as any Mama and Papa. One day, she met a fine young man and fell in love. She gave him a kiss and vowed to be with her parents and the boy forever. But she was still made of snow, so when spring came, she melted. The legend says, every Christmas Grandfather Frost brings her back for Ivan and Myra and all the children, to help him give out candy and gifts. Until her true love comes and takes her away."

"So, all I would do is help Grandfather Frost hand out gifts."

"And candies, yes."

Annika flashed her largest smile. "How can I say 'no,' Papa?"

Yuri didn't go to his clinic that day. He had gotten up early and left a note for Annika, telling her he was going to Moscow. She shouldn't wait up, he'd be home late.

He hadn't lied entirely. He drove his air car to the city and caught the sub-orbital to New York City.

It hadn't been easy to contact Noire, whose position in Imperial Intelligence kept him busy. Noire was in New York today and agreed to meet him at Lennon's, a fine restaurant in Midtown. He hadn't seen Annika's brother since that terrible day in the Plaza, where the boy wore his despair on his sleeve so he was surprised to see Noire sitting at a booth, sipping from a cut glass and smiling. "Yuri! How wonderful to see you!" Noire didn't get up. He directed Yuri to sit in the booth across from him.

Noire ordered drinks. "I'm sure Annika doesn't let you partake very often. Her intolerance to alcohol and all. So, what can I do for you?"

Noire smiled, but his eyes did not. *An akula stalking its prey,* thought Yuri.

"Noire, you know Annika and I are very fond of each other. I love her and I believe she loves me. You are her closest blood relative and I need to ask your permission to ask her to marry me."

Noire's smile faded, immediate and with purpose. He shook his head.

"No."

"May I ask why?"

140

"Certainly," Noire began to explain. "You deserve as much. I am a loyal Terran and I have vowed to serve my Empire and my sovereign. While my uncle is Regent for now, Annika will be Empress one day. If she marries you, she will want to stay on your farm and raise children. I can't have that. You must let her go, just for a while, to learn how to be Khan. If she feels this way about you in three years, then I will gladly give you my blessing. But, today, the answer is no."

Yuri insisted. "I think you underestimate Annika. She plans on attending classes at Moscow University. If you allow us to marry, I can be sure she'll finish school."

"I'm sure you believe that and you may very well be right. But I must be certain. The future of the Empire depends upon it."

"But I love her," Yuri said, desperate now.

"Yuri, it is not a question of love. I know my sister loves you. If she was any normal Terran woman, then I would be happy to give you my blessing. But she also loves our Empire and must do what is best. If you marry her now, then I can guarantee the Empire will fail inside one hundred years. We – Terrans - may even become extinct. Can you live with that?"

"But what if she changes in three years?" Yuri asked. "What if I change?"

"If either of you change to the point where you two are no longer compatible, I would be stunned," responded Noire. "There are times when I am talking with Annika, you are all she talks about. But, I know her heart. If you asked her now, she'd say no. As happy as she is, she must prepare to assume her duties as Khan."

Yuri recalled the conversation that night in Giza. Annika had warned him of this, after a fashion.

"Yuri, if you truly love my sister, you'll have to trust her," Noire said evenly. "Because this is what she was born to. Give me what I ask. Three years."

"And if you try to force the issue one day earlier," Noire said in his dried bone voice, "you'll not see your wedding day."

Annika smiled and raised her arms. In the mirror, the Snow Maiden looked back at her. Her normal braid had been brushed out and flowed down her back in a wave. A long, dark blue robe covered her from neck to mid-calf, ermine fur at its cuffs and hem. White calfskin boots and breeches complemented the *Snegurochka* costume, and a white fur hat completed it.

She spun about and laughed gaily. Sequins had been sewn into the robe, glittering like ice crystals in the snow. A halo emitter was hidden in the hat, creating gentle falling snow around her. When Annika spun, the effect was a snow globe blizzard swirling around her. Andrei stood behind her, wearing a matching robe and hat. He had bleached his hair and beard a blazing white. "Now we are *Ded Moroz* and *Snegurochka!*" he laughed. "Come, Granddaughter, the children of the village await!"

A large, handsome sleigh awaited them. It was so tall, Andrei had to lift Annika into it. A pillow softened the bench for Annika to sit on, and a thick bearskin hide awaited. She pulled it over her shoulders and burrowed herself in its warmth. Andrei snapped a whip, roaring with joy. The large horses neighed and began trotting down the snowy lane. Strands of bells hung on the harness, the ribbons tied to their manes waved about as the horses trotted to the square.

The village square was gaily decorated for the holiday. A communal tree dominated it, heavily laden with lights and ornaments. Strands of evergreen and lights were hung over the streets. Smoke was at every chimney, smells of holiday cooking filled the air. Children came running from their homes upon hearing the bells on the sleigh of *Ded Moroz and Snegurochka.*

They cheered wildly as Andrei steered the sleigh into the square. He stood and roared "Happy Christmas, children. My granddaughter and I have heard there are some very good children in a village somewhere nearby. Would you happen to know where I can find it?"

"He-e-e-e-eere!" the children cried. "We all have been good, *Ded Moroz!*" Andrei reached into the bag next to him and flung handfuls of candy to the children. They cheered and scampered about, picking up the sweet treats.

Annika climbed down from the sledge and handed out small gifts and bags of even more treats, cooked lovingly in the Russolov's kitchen for many weeks. Small children approached her shyly; she embraced them and gave each one a candy. Parents had the smaller ones stand with her and take pictures. Annika laughed, thinking she would like this holiday, Christmas.

Yuri approached the sledge. Andrei spied him and called out, "Children, look! It is the handsome young boy come to kiss *Snegurochka* and melt her heart away!"

Yuri. He had been sad lately. Even now, he hung to the back of the crowd, looking so despondent. At *Ded Moroz'* prompting, the children swarmed, throwing snowballs at the young doctor. Yuri gave a shout, gathering snow and throwing at the children. *There's my Yuri! Happy at last. I wonder why he has been so sad lately.*

Andrei waved at her. Annika ran from the sleigh to "rescue" Yuri. "Children, stop!" she cried.

A snowball knocked her pretty hat from her head. Yuri was grinning, now, and stooped to scoop more snow.

Annika cried out and the bombardment began again. Outgunned, Yuri turned and ran. Annika and the children gave chase to the edge of the square.

The children waved "Bye-bye! Happy Christmas, *Snegurochka!*" as Annika chased Yuri down a side street. It was the end of the ritual.

Yuri was waiting for her, leaning on a post holding the overhang for a building. He opened his arms, she ran to him. The embraced, cheek to cheek.

"Annika." Yuri said. His eyes pointed upwards.

There was a sprig wrapped with a ribbon above them.

143

"What is that?" she asked.

"You don't know what mistletoe is?" his eyes were wide.

She shook her head.

"This." He pressed her lips to hers.

When they parted, Annika was breathing heavily. "Oh, my," she gasped, "I am liking this Christmas more and more every minute. So, this mistletoe means we must kiss, yes?"

"Only your true love."

"Well, then." They kissed again.

"Yuri," she said sadly, "I have to go off world. I need to go to school."

"I know," he responded, "and I want you to go. You have a destiny, my love. I want you to go fulfill it."

"Do you believe me when I tell you part of me doesn't want to go?" she asked.

"Of course," he responded, "But you have to go."

"Will you wait for me?" she asked anxiously.

He smiled, "For ten thousand years. When will you leave?"

"Spring. May, I think. After we go to the Temple of Angkor Khan."

"Are you sure you still want me to go?"

"Of course! And Master Tahn said you need to be there."

Snow began to fall. Mittened hands came together.

Snegurochka and her beloved walked away.

The Christmas party of Andrei and Clara Russolov was in full swing. Andrei had chosen the largest tree he could find and stood it in the parlor. When they were first married, the Russolovs made all their decorations. Tonight, those decorations were joined by two more generations of handmade ornaments. Painted clay figurines, sticks with yarn, tiny beaded balls - all were hung with care.

Annika studied the tree. The heirs had never had such a thing. There were few holidays and even fewer distractions. There was always a Christmas tree in the palace, of course. An immense thing, it was covered with complicated and ornate representations of all the Imperial worlds. It was a holo, and it meant nothing to the Eight.

This tree was different. It smelled, for one thing. Annika placed her nose next to a green sprig and inhaled. The sweet tang filled her nose. She could feel the pine slide into her lungs, tickling her. She eagerly inhaled again. She carefully picked up a decoration here and there, each with a tiny mark for who it represented.

There were glass birds all over the tree. Painted on the feet were initials. A.R., C.R. L.R. She wondered what they meant.

Clara joined her. "The birds, Clara, what do they represent?" Annika asked.

"Each bird represents a member of our family," Clara explained. "The initials are who each bird is. A.R. Andrei Russolov, C.R. is me, L.R. is Leonid Russolov, Yuri's great-great grandfather."

'How beautiful. We never had anything like this in the palace."

"Ah, how sad. Well, here you do, Child. This is from Andrei and me."

Clara handed Annika a wrapping of tissue paper. Gift exchanges were unheard of for the heirs. She held it carefully, examining every inch. The tissue was pretty, a pattern of pastel colors. a bit of tape held the package closed. Carefully, Annika pulled on the tape, trying to delicately open the gift.

"Oh, goodness, open it already!" laughed Clara. "You act as if you have never seen a Christmas gift before!"

"I haven't, Mama Clara," Annika admitted. "We didn't have Christmas at the palace. This is the first Christmas gift I have ever received."

Clara made an O with her mouth. "Dear, it is quite all right to tear the paper," she said warmly. "Yuri, when he was a boy, oh!

How he would tear into his gifts! He's not much better now. Please, don't worry. Tear away. Papa and I want you to see your gift!"

She tore the paper a bit, then a little more. "Well, hurry!" exclaimed Andrei, wandering over. "Mama isn't getting any younger you know." With his booming voice, the whole room went silent. Everyone watched the young princess.

The outer wrapping was finally loose. Carefully, Annika unrolled the inner tissue until the small brown wren was unveiled. On its feet were the initials A.R.

"Oh, Mama Clara, thank you!" Annika cried as she hugged Yuri's mother. She searched the tree, found the wise owl marked Y.R. and began to place her bird there.

"No, no, that's not who you're looking for," laughed Clara. "That is Yanko Roishenko, a cousin, quite an unpleasant fellow. But we love him anyway. No, here is Yuri."

He was a raven. Beautiful to be sure, but a crow? Annika scrunched her eyebrow.

Clara laughed again. "Yuri chose that himself. The raven is one of the smartest, most loyal of all the birds."

"It looks odd, surrounded by all the rest of the tree. But it fits him."

Annika's wren went on the branch next to Yuri's raven.

Supper was a free-for-all. Rather than sit formally, the Russolov Christmas table was laid out in the kitchen, buffet style. The traditional 12 dishes of the Apostles were the center of the table. All around were salads, steaming soups, and rolls... all the traditional holiday fare. Desserts were on their own table at one side.

"Yuri, Yuri, try this!" Annika fed him a rum ball from the dessert table. With far too much rum. "Moychya showed me how to make these! She liked them so much she said she'd serve it tonight!"

Moychya was known to enjoy a drink or two.

146

They couple loaded their plates and found a place to sit. It was not an easy task. All five of Yuri's brothers and sisters had come for the holiday, along with their children. Many of the house staff were there, adding their children to the mix. Unmarried field hands, with no family nearby joined in the festivities. Annika had been to many social gatherings growing up. But they were always staid, formal affairs.

Here, children were running through the rooms, flying various toy spacecraft. Games were being played in every room. Annika watched wistfully as a small knot of girls played with new dolls in a corner. Andrei had even set up a room to one side for the young people to entertain themselves…under his watchful eye.

There was much singing which Annika happily joined in. She didn't know any of the words, but sang along anyway, generally trying to anticipate the words and filling in with "La-la-la…" There was one song that offered up, "Fa-la-la-la-la-la-la-la-la-la." She leapt and danced about; the raucous singalong was fun!

Andrei tapped her shoulder and beckoned. "I have a surprise for you." Another surprise! Annika decided she did like this holiday, Christmas.

She followed them to the library. Seeing this room, she could understand where Yuri had found his love of books. Mahogany paneled, lush carpets to muffle any sound. Wide winged chairs, low tables for a drink. Old fashioned stand lamps at each chair.

And books by the thousands. The shelves lined all four walls from the floor to the ceiling. More stacks were piled on the floor.

Two women were in the room. The younger woman was wearing an Imperial Medical Corps uniform. In front of her was an ancient woman, wearing a support frame for her frail body and seated in a hover chair. On entering, she waved a finger and began rasping in a language Annika recognized as Old Russian.

Andrei shot back in the same tongue. They argued back and forth. Finally, the old woman waved her hand, dismissing him.

147

"Annika, this is my great-grandmother, Annika Sonya Russolov," said Andrei. "She wishes to speak to you alone." He led the nurse out.

Annika was nonplussed. She felt an annoying buzz in her head.

"I said, can you hear me?"

Annika startled. The old woman was using mindspeak?

Are you deaf or can you hear me? You don't look stupid, Child."

"I can hear you. You can mindspeak?"

"Gods above! I hadn't used this talent in so long, I thought I might have forgotten how!"

"This is wonderful, Grandmother! But I thought only heirs had mindspeak."

"Bah, child. It's not a common talent, but there are many non-royals who accomplish it. For me, it's because my great-great-great Grandfather was ne-Khan."

"I am honored. Grandmother!"

"You should be. So, you will be my Yuri's wife."

"I don't know, Grandmother."

"I do. I have the Third Eye, child. I see what others don't see. You will need him soon. And he will be there for you and the Empire.

I see great love between you. Great happiness, much joy. But much sadness, too. You can be so cruel, Daughter. So very cruel. Always remember, no matter how angry you get at Yuri, he loves you more than life itself. He would give his life for you."

"No, Grandmother. I could never be cruel Yuri. I couldn't ever hurt him."

"Not as you are now, no. But you are Becoming, Child. Soon, you will move from what you are to what you must be."

"What is it that I am to be?"

"Foolish girl! You know what that is. You are Khan.
You will rule this Empire beyond any glory you have imagined.
With my son, Yuri by your side."

"So, I must marry Yuri?"

"Soon, but not now."

"Grandmother, what must I do?"

"Have you gone to Temple yet?"

"In May."

"Yuri will be with you."

"Yes."

"Here, I have something for you."

She reached into the pouch attached to the arm of her chair
and handed Annika a brightly wrapped box. Annika thanked her and
opened the gift. It was a box of gaily decorated paper, envelopes and
a fine pen.

"Thank you, Grandmother. But what is it for?"

"It is stationery, child. You write letters to Yuri on it.
He, in turn, will write letters to you."

"Wouldn't a com message work better?"

The old woman pulled at her collar, disclosing a pendant.
When activated, a holo appeared, a powerful man in an old-style
Imperial Scout uniform.

"My Leonid. Dear, dear Leonid. After all these years,
oh, how I love him still." <

She tapped the pendant again; Leonid's head and shoulders
appeared. He had a strong jaw and piercing eyes. Annika smothered
a snicker. His nose. She could see where Yuri got his nose.

The elder Annika kissed the image of her missing husband.

"My Leonid was a deep scout. He went outward to the
rim and then inward, into the Spinward. No matter how far he
went, no matter the cost, he would mail me a letter. It could take
months for the next one to arrive, he would be so far out. But I
would get every letter he sent. I would hold each letter, knowing
Leonid had held it, written it. His tongue had sealed the flap.

149

He had kissed each one. The farther he went out, the longer it took for his letters arrive. I would hold each letter until the next arrived, then open the previous one."

She pulled an old, yellowed envelope from under her gown.

"I keep it here, close to my heart. Either I will open it when his next letter arrives or I will be buried with my husband's last words to me, unopened."

She replaced the letter and pendant.

"I am tired and wish to go back to my room on Luna. Promise me you will collect letters from your Yuri, for me?"

"I will, Grandmother."

"Now, send for my nurse, Child. And Happy Christmas."

"Happy Christmas, Grandmother."

Annika reached the door.

"Child?"

"Yes, Grandmother?"

The old woman stood and raised her arms. She wavered back and forth.

"VICTORY!" she shouted in Terran. "THE EMPRESS ANNIKA RAUDONA KHAN! FOR TEN THOUSAND YEARS, VICTORY!"

Chapter 19

Winter tightened its grip. Roaring like a freight train, a blast of
fierce weather rolled over the steppe. Snow piled high against every
building. Yuri and Annika's tiny home was nearly buried and
groaned at each icy gust.

It was dangerous to go outside. Andrei had braved the storm
a few days before, bringing supplies. "You should come up to the
main house," he told them. "It's warm and safe. We are having
much fun as a family." Annika gave him a quick scan. Andrei was
largely telling the truth. Mostly though, he and Clara were lonely for
the children.

She knew how he felt.

A wall had formed between her and Yuri. Outwardly, they
seemed fine. But her impending departure off-world for school
depressed them both. While trying to be as loving as she could,
Annika knew her decision was correct.

She sent application after application to off-world
Universities. Her applications were late, she knew, most worlds had
already set their summer quarter classes, but the Crown Princess was
banking on the cachet of her title. Her academic record was
flawless. There was no student anywhere who could compare with
her community services.

No one could deny her potential. Indeed, any University
would be proud to be the university of the future Empress.

Overtures poured back. Annika studied each offer. It was
more about the qualities of the education than the prestige of the
institutions.

"Have you made a decision?" Yuri slid next to her at the com
desk.

Annika sighed in frustration. "Three," Annika announced.
"Each has courses and instructors I want. Why can't they all be at a
single place where I want, so I can study what I want?"

Yuri chortled. "I suppose the free choice your Grandfather wrote into the law may be having something to do with it." She sat back against him; he wrapped his arms around her. "It's hard," she complained.

"You haven't told me one thing. What are the Universities themselves like?"

"How do you mean?"

"Are they on temperate worlds? Is there a community where you'll feel comfortable? Does the University participate in sport?"

"I am going to school to study, not watch movies or go to sport matches."

"You're going to university to grow and become a good citizen," he admonished. "Your education should be more than facts and figures. You will, for instance, meet lifelong friends. I had adventures and experiences that would…Well, let's just say it's better you can't read my thoughts." Yuri chuckled.

Annika rolled her eyes.

"You were a teenager when you were in college," she reminded him. "A young teenager at that. What kind of adventures could a fourteen-year-old have?"

Yuri kissed the top of her head. "That's right, fourteen. Means I'm still smarter than you."

He dodged the elbow she threw by escaping to answer the knock at the door.

A shivering young priest in the saffron robe of the Temple of Angkor stood there. "Gods below! Come in before you freeze!" cried Yuri. He half-dragged the priest in and closed the door against the bitter wind. Annika ran into their bedroom and brought out a quilt.

"What were you doing out in this weather?" she asked.

Still trembling wrapped in the blanket, the priest pulled out a packet and handed it to her. "Might I have some tea, please, Crown Princess?" he asked.

"Of course," she replied and nodded to Yuri.

Inside the innocuous paper packet were two data solids and a note: *May the 19th would be the most auspicious day. These data solids will tell you both what is expected. Until then, Tahn*

She got on the comm. "Major Campion? We have a guest. No, not a threat. I want you to return him to his home. Mongolia. Yes, that Mongolia. No, I don't know and would appreciate you don't ask him, either. Yes, thank you, Major."

"Please tell Master Tahn I agree and am eager for the time to arrive. My bodyguard shall escort you home," she told the messenger-priest.

"Thank you, Crown Princess. I am honored." He bowed his head.

After the priest left, Yuri held up his data solid. "What is this?"

"Instructions for my ascension to Crown Princess," she answered, loading the solid into a data reader. "I was to do this last year when I was named to the title. But circumstances precluded doing it then." She looked up from her data translation and beamed. "I am to become a Goddess/Queen!"

"A what?"

"A Goddess/Queen. In ancient times, the Khans were more than just the king or queen. They also ascended to the status of God when they were crowned. Angkor brought that back, declaring the new Crown Prince or Princess as God/Ruler of the Clan. It is my clan title until I become Empress," she explained.

"Ah. Good. So long as the new Goddess remembers it's her turn to do dishes tonight."

"I've decided." She projected the statement into thin air.

"Oh?" *Decided not to do dishes? What?*

"Yes. Saint Francis University on Vespa."

Oh, the school. "That's a Jesuit institution," he told her.

"It is."

"Papa will accuse you of being a Roman."

"Remind him I'm Mongolian," she retorted.

153

"He thinks Mongolians are Cossacks," Yuri said.

"He thinks everyone not Russian is a Cossack," she chuckled.

"He's right. Why Saint Francis?"

"It has an outstanding academic record." Annika ticked off on her fingers. "It is very organized and structured, something I am used to. There are some ethics and philosophy instructors I have researched and they intrigue me. And what should make you happy, I must spend my first year in a dormitory."

"What, no convent?"

She kissed his nose. "It will be good to be back in school. As much as I love the farm, I am missing the challenge of school. Vespa is also a world I visited when I was a child. It is a beautiful planet, temperate. I will have plenty to explore. Major Campion will be happy; there is a garrison near the school.

"And," she continued, "best of all for us is, it's only a two-day journey."

"That's wonderful!" Yuri smiled.

Annika was quite for long minutes before she spoke again. "I'm glad I decided finally. But I'm going to miss you."

"So close, our letters will be delivered in a day," he said.

"Not exactly Grandma Anni and Grandpa Leonid."

"No."

They were quiet for several minutes.

Then Yuri brightened. "I think the wind has let up. Grab your parka, let's go up to Mama and Papa's and see what is for supper tonight. I think they would be very pleased to see us on such a night as this."

Chapter 20

The scarred armored shuttle flew low over the Gobi Desert. Overhead, three full squadrons of Buccaneer fighters flew in swirling orbits, climbing, diving and looping around the Imperial ship. In orbit, a full battlegroup maintained a geosynchronous orbit over the path of the lone shuttle.

Even with this much protection, Campion fretted. The Crown Princess was not the head of state yet. She wouldn't become Empress for six more years.

But today, she was the most important being in the Empire. Tahn had been quite specific on this point. She and her consort must arrive safely today.

Nothing less than the future of the Empire depended on it.

In the center compartment of the ship Annika wore the white silken suit that Tahn had sent. A casual observer might comment on how calm and placid she appeared.

Unless they noticed how tight she gripped Yuri's hand.

They had read the briefing packets Tahn sent. Yuri wore a suit that matched Annika's, save it was desert brown. His briefing had been short. He was Annika's consort.

Her packet had been larger and more detailed. There were rituals to follow, prayers to be said. Annika must follow each precisely.

There are three rooms. The Room of Preparation, the Ossuary of the Emperors and the Room of the Khan. Servants will prepare each room for your ascension to Godhood. Only a Khan may enter all three.

Annika breathed slowly, calming her nerves. It wasn't the ceremony that concerned her. It was the last part of the message, a personal note from Tahn: *"Highness, following your ascendance, the File Council of Advisors would meet with you."*

155

File Council of Advisors. The convention of members from her government and other leaders who advised the File Committee. They had no real authority. What news would they have for her, their new Goddess/Queen?

Major Campion braced to attention in front of the couple. "Majesty, Sir," he reported. "We are entering the final approach to the temple complex."

"Thank you, Major." The compartment banked and dipped downward before righting itself. A roar came from outside the ship as it settled into a hover, then lowered. They heard the whine of hydraulics and the landing gear extending before the ship bounced slightly and its engines stopped.

The sun was rising in the east, its golden rays illuminating the red sandstone walls of the Temple of Angkor Khan cut in the side of the mountain. The walls and columns were roughhewn and irregular. Only the portals and walkways were smooth.

Thousands of saffron robed monks and nuns formed a passage from the shuttle to the temple. At the entryway were the eight members of the File Committee, similarly dressed, save for their ornate headpieces and colored sashes.

Yuri offered his arm and Annika took it with serene grace. He led her through the passage to the awaiting Bonzes. All bowed as the couple passed.

"What is this effect you have on people?" Yuri whispered.

"Shut up!" Annika hissed, trying hard not to giggle.

The procession arrived at the center of the Main Temple. A pair of gilded doors greeted them, a kneeling priest at each. Annika patted Yuri's arm and stood before the gilded portal.

She struck a defiant pose, her hand on her hips, head held high to her full four feet ten. She cried out in a loud voice," I am Annika Raudona Khan, preferred legatee to the crown of my ancestor, Angkor Khan. I require these doors open so I may join my progenitors in this holy place!"

The entire assembly knelt and bowed until their heads touched the floor. The doors slid open smoothly and a voice called out from beyond the doors. "Enter Annika Raudona Khan and be welcome. Your ancestors await."

Two attendants awaited her in the Room of Preparation. Swiftly, they stripped Annika of her white top and trousers, handed her soft leather breeches and calfskin riding boots.

The jacket they presented was called the Imperial Rainbow Robe. Its stiff brocade was a brilliant yellow to her waist. There it fanned into narrow stripes the colors of the eight heirs. Wide red cuffs adorned the sleeves, the left embroidered with a wild horse, the right with a golden dragon. A brimmed hat of black mink fur was placed on her head.

A cord was slung over her shoulder, a golden intricate braid. It held a gilded knife at her waist. One attendant handed her a small, glowing brand.

She bowed to them in thanks and assumed her defiant pose before the next door.

On it was depicted an ancient warrior, dressed as she was dressed, astride a white charger.

"Honored ancestors," she intoned, "it is I, Annika Raudona Khan. I ask your permission to enter this house and join your number with the Holy Blood."

The panel opened noiselessly and a woman's voice responded. "Welcome Annika Raudona Khan, Daughter."

The light of the room rose to the level of dusk. Before her were sixteen niches carved in the wall. The first fourteen contained a pair of funerary urns. The fifteenth had a single urn. The sixteenth was empty. Her breath caught. She was in the presence of her predecessors, the previous fifteen reincarnations of the Great Khan himself, and their partners. Two millennia of the royal line.

She covered her face and willed herself to breath.

Over each niche was a sealed box, bearing an image of the Khan who was interred at that spot. She went to the first box, lit the

157

incense stick left there by the nuns of the temple who prepared this place, bowed and prayed: "I humbly greet my ancestor Janus Arcadia Khan. I ask for him to look favorably upon my ascension, that he bid me to join the honored of the Khans of Terra. I ask he demands from beyond the Gods to look with favor on my Empire."

She moved down the line, bowing, lighting and praying at each of the boxes; Hinabrian, Gerta, Ho-Lua, James the First…Hesitating at the eighth, the emperor who would have no name. The incense was there, though the urns had been smashed and the image on the cabinet had been burned. She bowed and executed the ceremony.

Annika arrived at the last occupied niche. The image of Robert De L'Orange. He was young and beautiful, the very persona of the Terran Emperor. She delicately traced his face with a finger. How she longed to stay there with her father, stare into the image of his kind eyes. But she had the ceremony to complete. She bowed to her father's remains and repeated the ceremony.

She came to the last niche. Her niche. Where her remains would be for all eternity after her death. She opened the cabinet above her niche and removed a small vessel, took the ceremonial knife from its golden cord. "Honored ancestors, I now claim my place with you. With my blood drawn by my own hand here in this place, I declare by the Law of The Great Angkor Khan, that I am perfection of our bloodline. I now declare myself the sixteenth reincarnation of Angkor Khan."

She drew the knife across her left palm. Bright red blood gushed. She held it over the bowl, filling it halfway. According to her instructions, she placed bowl in the cabinet and closed the door.

There was the tinkling sound of a dozen small bells.

The cabinet's door now bore an image of Annika. From the day on Celtius 4, astride the horse, her hair streaming back, her eyes wide open and wild, her mouth screaming with joy: *VICTORIOUS! FOR TEN THOUSAND YEARS!"*

From a pocket in her Rainbow Robe, she drew a white cloth and wrapped her bleeding hand. On her left, the last door opened.

A voice, two thousand years in the grave spoke.

"Enter, Daughter."

The room was so bright, at first Annika had to cover her eyes.

The entire room, ceiling, floor, walls were gold. At the center of the room was a raised plinth, holding a crystal casket. She bowed her head as she approached.

Inside rested the two-thousand-year-old preserved remains of the first Khan, the Great Angkor Khan. He was dressed in the Rainbow Robe and furred hat. In his hands, he held an urn.

His wife, Sophia.

In a line across the top of the casket was a row of shallow dishes. Each contained a lock of hair tied with a ribbon and bore the name of a reincarnate of Angkor Khan. The last dish bore her name, *Annika Raudona Khan.*

Her Rainbow Robe was equipped for this ceremony, too. A red ribbon came from her pocket, which she tied to the end of her braid. She used the ceremonial knife to cut the tuft of hair, then placed it with reverence in the vessel bearing her name.

The walls were covered with writing. It was the Law of Angkor Khan, the codification which ran the Empire. In simple terms, it spelled out the responsibilities of the rulers and the citizens. Illuminations of various points in the Great Khan's life scattered throughout. Meeting Sophia. The Vinithri War. The peace he made with the First Daughter of the Vinithri. The first heirs.

His death.

These were the laws Annika had grown up learning. To her, they were the very foundation of her life.

She relit the flaming brand and circled the cist, igniting the sixteen incense sticks that had been placed there. She knelt on the floor before her ancestor and meditated for an hour.

Annika returned to the Room of Preparation. The attendants helped her remove the heavy robe. She stripped and they wiped her with damp towels, anointed her with oils and sweet perfumes. Her hand was bound, hair brushed and braided, cosmetics lightly applied. Dressed in a gown of shimmering gold, a golden cap was placed on her head and silken slippers on her feet.

At the door, she cried out, "I am Crown Princess Annika Raudona Khan, returned from the Gods as a God." The doors opened, all fell to the floor and prostrated themselves, save Yuri.

They smiled at one another and Yuri extended his arm. Gracefully, she placed her hand on his arm and they walked to the Throne Room of the Temple.

Annika was reminded of her Throne Room in Giza. The walls, ceiling and floor were white and filigreed in gold. Art work and tapestries were on every wall. At the far end of the room filled with a hundred prostrate subjects, a three-step dais held a plain cathedra. Yuri led Annika up to her throne. When she sat, everyone slid back on their heels.

"Rise," she commanded.

Tahn stepped forward and cried out, "The File Committee and the File Council of Advisors greet our new Goddess Queen, head of our Order and sixteenth reincarnation of our Founder. I give you Crown Princess Annika Raudona Khan."

The room raised its arms; "HooooOOOO! HooooOOOO! HooooOOOO!"

"I thank you, my loyal subjects. I vow to do my upmost to uphold the Law and prepare myself for my final ascension to Empress."

"My friends, I know we are here to celebrate the promise of a new dawn over our Empire," Tahn said. "But, we have more pressing matters to attend to immediately. Crown Princess, we were put in an untenable position when your father was murdered. You were not ready to assume your position and we had no recourse in the law. The solution we agreed to has exacerbated the issue of succession. There is also a danger we have failed to speak with you about. I invite Doctor Lucius Reynolds to speak."

A tall, grey haired man stepped forward. He had a patrician look, down to his long nose and firm chin. "I am Doctor Lucius Reynolds of Columbia University. My expertise is forensic genealogy. When the eighth Khan sought to destroy the Empire with his so-called democracy revolution, he tried to destroy his family line by murdering the heirs. He very nearly succeeded, killing all but two. With the death of He Who Shall Have No Name, his daughter became Empress Petra Khan. Fearing for his life, her brother, Thomas Blanc, hid from his sister, escaping to the rim to live out his days in obscurity.

"The File Council noticed a decline in the Empire after Petra Khan's reign. Perhaps she was inferior? We don't know for sure. The signs were unmistakable. While we were fulfilling the laws of Angkor Khan, the heirs were in decline, weakening the Empire."

Tahn interjected. "During the reign of Zander Khan, an errant gene sequence was identified as the root cause for the aberration in the pursuit of perfection. Our predecessors analyzed the sequence and believed they had made the necessary adjustments to eliminate erratic sequence. But the disastrous result was Kim Choi Khan."

"We isolated the errant gene," said Doctor Reynolds. "It was evident to us the mutation would require gradual modification. With Robert Khan, we achieved our goal. Unfortunately, he also carried the recessive gene sequence. We designed Annika Khan with the recessive sequence removed, replaced with a receptor sequence to restore the line. Since we couldn't create the needed sequence, the only solution was to find a descendant of Petra Khan's brother, Thomas. Evidence indicates he was the last heir not to carry the recessive gene. The search has been long and exhausting. But tonight, we have in the room a descendent of Petra Khan's brother, one who carries the gene sequence we need."

"Tell me, Doctor." The room went silent when Annika spoke. "This descendant, what is required of him?"

Tahn spoke in a quiet, but urgent tone. "By the law, Crown Princess, you would need to be bonded with the one, to create the next heir class."

"Bonded. You mean marry. Master Tahn, what if I had decided I don't wish to marry?"

"Majesty, it would be unseemly for you to produce heirs without a bonded mate," replied Tahn.

"So, you're more concerned with appearances than with my will," argued Annika

"It is not a matter of appearances," Than said. "It is a matter of survival."

"So, to save our species, I must give up my Rights of Privacy," Annika hissed.

Tahn looked sad. "Majesty, for our survival, sacrifices must be made."

"But this is my life we are talking about," Annika protested. "My body. My free will."

"It is not your body we are discussing," snapped Doctor Reynolds. "Only twenty-four of your eggs are needed for sequencing with the seed supplied by the descendant."

"Ah, so I am a hen to produce golden eggs for the Empire?" Annika waggled a finger. "Careful, Doctor, you are bordering on ugly ethics questions now."

"She needs to be told," said Tahn.

"Told what?" Annika demanded.

"Is that information you would want to know?" an anonymous voice asked.

"Know what?" interjected Yuri. "I am a doctor. Annika and I are very close. If this is medical information you are withholding, then I demand to know what that information is."

"You have no voice here, *Doctor*," came Reynolds icy reply. "This is File Council business, not the business of a starry-eyed boy." Jeers and shouted words filled the room.

"Enough," Tahn ordered. His voice sliced through the crowd and they fell silent. "Doctor Russolov is correct. And I would add, his relationship with Her Majesty is a critical factor.

"Majesty, this information, while common knowledge to this Council, is sensitive. I would prefer we discuss it in private?"

Annika rose, accepted Yuri's arm and strode regally from the room. Tahn led them to a cozy, open air balcony overlooking the western Gobi. An elderly nun in saffron robes offered them tea.

"Children, this is my wife, Ui," Tahn declared. "I asked her here today as she is my other half and may be able to find the words I cannot."

"What words would those be, Master?" inquired Annika.

Tahn took his wife's hand. "Ui and I have been married for seventy-five years now. We were younger than you two when we married. We will see perhaps as many as another fifty years together. That is the nature of man and woman. You find your other half, live your lives and pass. It is a great sorrow, but an even greater joy. I would drink the bitter tea all my days for each perfect dawn of my wife."

He sipped his tea, patted his wife's leg and continued. "Not all are as fortunate as Ui and I. Some never find their other half. They are the saddest of all. Some find their other half, but seek to sweeten their tea overmuch and in doing so, lose them. Still others find their other half, but only receive a half measure of life."

"One half dies before the other," Annika whispered.

"Yes."

A long silence ensued.

"How many years do I have, Master Tahn?" Annika asked.

"It is more complicated than that, Crown Princess. With luck, you will live to one hundred and twenty-five, one hundred fifty."

163

"That is an average lifespan," interjected Yuri.

"Yes. But there are...complications."

"I want the truth," Annika said flatly. "All of it, Tahn."

Tahn's sigh came as a half sob. "We have spoken many times of compromise, Daughter. When I designed you, I was creating the ultimate brain. In this, I have succeeded brilliantly. You have the most brilliant mind in the history of mankind. Unfortunately, you are transitional. A prototype. We made your brain as compact as we could, trading your physical size for brain capacity. Already, the base sequence that will create your children's brains is laid down. They will have brains at least the equal of yours; two will be superior. But for you, the physical strain on your brain structure was sacrificed. At some point, as early as age seventy to seventy-five, your brain will begin to deteriorate. Certainly, by eighty, the degradation will be noticeable. By ninety, you will be essentially incompetent to run the Empire. By ninety-five, you will be in a vegetative state."

"So, you see doctor, the Crown Princess living to one hundred twenty-five would be, for her, more a curse than a blessing."

"Gods below!" Annika breathed the curse. "Is there no hope? Is that to be my future?"

"Do not look at the bitter tea, Child," Ui spoke up. "Look to the countless dawns."

"They do not look so countless to me," Annika said bitterly. "Your husband has announced my doom."

"A single day is a lifetime for a June fly," Ui said calmly. "Yet it doesn't sit and bemoan its fate. It lives the day it was given, drinking the tea as it is served. What will you do with your day?"

They were quiet for a while. Then Annika said, "So, this is to be my fate. Why the rush, then, to mate me and establish my line?"

"The Empire is at a crossroads, Crown Princess," Ui answered. "I serve the Council as a political advisor. We have

164

enemies both without and within. Both have watched the Empire weaken the last seven hundred fifty years because of declining leadership from our Khans. Your father was to serve as a bridge between the ineffective Khans and you. Our enemies turned that plan on its head when they assassinated him. Because of this, we have been forced to accelerate your training.

"The schedule we designed for you would have had you becoming Empress at age forty-five, not twenty-five. Those twenty years would have given us sufficient time to ensure the proper development of your successor's superior brain."

"Then I am to be nothing more than a hen for the Empire," Annika asked the bitter question again.

"No!" insisted Tahn. "I created you for greatness, not a simple caretaker. Already you must have noticed how the military flocks to you. You will need them, Ming si will not give up the Empire now that he has a taste for power. Beyond that? Our enemies from without fear you for good reason."

"Master Tahn?" Yuri asked. "In all of this, what is my role to be?"

"Why, Doctor, your role is the most important of all to the future of the Empire," Tahn smiled.

"You are the descendent of Thomas Blanc."

It was decided quickly. Annika and Yuri would be married the next day before the File Council. Afterwards, the harvesting would be performed. The File Committee stayed up late into the night working on the final patterns, preparing to receive the eggs and seed needed to create the next perfect Khan.

The couple was placed in the opulent chambers of the Khan. While Yuri slept, Annika sat on the edge of the balcony. The night was moonless and the stars so bright she could make out details on the desert floor. But her attention was on the stars.

Terra's orbit this time of the year aimed the night side inward towards the galactic core. Spinward. Where Grandfather Leonid

165

had disappeared. In the direction of the Galactic Council, an entity that had started three declared wars against Terra.

She would only have sixty years to rule.

Annika counted one hundred fifty stars, more than her Empire. She could easily cover that many with her hand.

The Khan who replaces me must have a foundation to work with, one bigger than one hundred fifty worlds. If Terra is to survive, I must leave my child a larger Empire. An Empire that is safe for all Terrans.

She gathered herself and turned to leave, sending a silent vow into the void.

I will come. You can join me or you can stand against me. And if you stand against me, you will die.

She allowed herself a tiny smile. Annika raised her chin and stared at the Universe imperiously. She closed her eyes and thought of Yuri. Now he wasn't just her savior, he would be the savior of her Empire.

Chapter 21

The wedding was a simple ceremony. Annika wore the Imperial Rainbow Robe, Yuri his brown suit. The couple shared their vows in the Temple. Tahn bound their hands together and by the laws of the Khalkha, they were married.

Annika changed back into her customary white outfit and joined her new husband in the medical laboratory. Ui arrived, led her into a side room and closed the door. She emerged a few minutes later, nodding.

"She is ready."

Tahn and Doctor Reynolds entered the dim theater where Annika was waiting. She was lying on a firm but comfortable bed, raised to Tahn's waist level. Coverings lay across her chest and low at her waist. A light was focused on her exposed abdomen. A soft towel covered her eyes.

Tahn patted her bare shoulder. "This won't take long, Daughter."

The two men lay a thick beige mat over her exposed belly. It was slightly warm and remarkably light. Doctor Reynolds connected the pad to a handset. He tapped out instructions and the pad on her abdomen began to vibrate softly. "The extraction pad is a more comfortable, less invasive method for extracting live, human eggs," he explained. "The eggs in your ovaries are being accelerated to maturity, then drawn through your skin into the pad."

Tahn and the doctor worked in hushed tones. It was odd to Annika to think they were probing about inside of her. Once or twice she thought she might have felt...something. The feeling was fleeting

After an hour, Doctor Reynolds announced the twenty-fourth egg had been extracted. He and Tahn lifted the pad and delicately laid it on a cart. An attendant entered and took the cart from the room.

Tahn removed the cover from Annika's eyes and brushed her forehead. "It is over. You are free to go, Daughter. Ui has asked that you and Yuri join us tonight to celebrate your bonding."

"We would be honored, Master."

Tahn nodded. "As will we."

Annika dressed and returned to the lobby. Yuri joined her minutes later, red faced.

"Are you all right, my husband?"

"I don't want to talk about it." He stomped out of the room. "Traditional, my ass!"

Holding back a laugh, Annika followed.

The newlyweds spent the day exploring the temple complex. It was elegantly simple and functional. Openings in the cliff walls allowed sunlight in, which in turn reflected off carefully placed, shining surfaces, cleverly disguised in art work and statues. Other openings brought desert-fresh air into the facility constantly. Well-hidden heating coils, powered by concealed solar panels, warmed the air in the evenings.

The couple was surprised and pleased at the number of gardens in the complex. The inhabitants grew their own food and provided for the local tribes with their bounty.

They joined Tahn, Ui and two other couples for supper. It was a wonderful evening; all present enjoying a good meal and light conversation. Ui and Tahn had the party laughing at their antics over seventy years of marriage.

It grew late. The couples returned to their chambers. Annika changed into her nightgown and was staring out the window at the stars. Yuri joined her, wrapping her in his arms.

"What do you see out there?" he asked her.

"There is Vespa," she said, pointing, "The next step to my Becoming. And there," pointing at another star, "is Cadeau, where the Galactic Council meets. One is a pathway, the next is a gateway. That is where I see my future taking me," she spoke with resolve.

He nuzzled her neck. They kissed under the open window.

"Time for bed, my love," he whispered.

Nervous, she stood beside the bed, a golden-haired statue.

"Yuri, a few months ago, when I got upgraded, you saw me naked. You said I was beautiful."

She untied her gown and let it pool at her feet.

"Am I really beautiful?"

She was pressed back into her seat as the orbital lifted off from New Moscow spaceport. Annika was glad she didn't have a window seat. It had been hard enough to say good bye to Yuri as she boarded the ship.

Grandmother Annika's stationery was tucked in her bag. Annika removed a sheet and placed it on the table in front of her.

My dearest Yuri,

Today I have boarded a ship, leaving our home on Terra. Home is a word I've never thought about while growing up. There were the palaces my brothers, sisters and I lived during our childhood. But never a place that I thought of as home. When you and your family took me in, I found such a place. Such a precious thing you and your family has! I am honored you have brought me into our family.

Family.

I miss all my brothers and sisters. Anja most of all. We grew apart the closer we got to the Naming Day. After all of what has happened this past year, I find there are a million things I want to tell her...

The alarm screeched. As she had all her life, Annika was out of bed, racing to the bathroom to get ready for her day.

169

Marianne Wallace, her roommate, pulled the pillow over her head. Annika saw one foot uncovered. She grabbed the ankle and shook it as she hurried by.

"C'mon Mari, you'll be late again," admonished Annika.

"Not going!" came the muffled reply. "I'm quitting school."

"You can't. You quit yesterday. And the day before."

Marianne rolled over and glared at Annika. Her roommate had already donned her unitard and was pulling up her running shorts. "I hate you," Marianne hissed. "When are you going to learn to sleep in and be late once and a while?"

"When you learn to wake up and be on time occasionally," Annika retorted as she pulled on her shoes. "You could get up on time just once and go work out with me and the boys."

The boys. Annika's euphemism for her bodyguards.

"Gods, save me from me from motivated roommates with bodacious blokes chasing her around the campus," moaned Marianne.

"Slacker!" Annika was out the door.

It had taken the other dorm residents a few weeks to get used to the guard at Annika's door. It became a joke of sorts, a soldier protecting the Vault of Virtue.

Annika had tried to explain. Her family were wealthy industrialists; her father had insisted that she have around the clock bodyguards. The lie was believable enough. Many of the students at the University were from wealthy families.

No one bought her story. She was too well known.

The four soldiers were waiting. It wasn't just an honor to work out with the young princess, it was a matter of pride to be able to keep up with her. Following her experience last year with letting up on her training, Annika had become determined to outperform anyone who joined her workout.

During her first semester, some of the male students trying to catch her eye had attempted to work out with the fit, attractive young woman. They all fared poorly.

The quintet ran a 10-mile course around the classic brick buildings that made up the campus of Saint Francis College of Vespa. The buildings were a gothic mix with slate roofs and narrow windows. The priests and nuns lived at opposite ends of the campus, in a rectory to the east, the gated convent at the west.

The campus chapel charmed her the most. The spire soared seemingly forever and used real bronze and copper bells, rung by hand on the quarter hour. The interior was classic, naves running to either side of the main altar under the spire. The ceiling depicted the life of the Pope for whom the campus was named. Pope Francis the Fourth had been a Jesuit who opposed the Democratic Revolution of the Eighth Khan. For that, he had been martyred.

Tall stained-glass windows created a dancing kaleidoscope of color on the marble floor as the sun made its way across the sky. The pews were ancient pootawood, harvested from local forests, and had absorbed centuries of the odors of polishing oils, candle wax and incense.

She would lead her entourage to the gym on the post and would then either swim another five miles or weight train. She was thrilled with the way she looked and felt.

After a shower and change of clothes, she would have her morning electrolyte and light breakfast with Major Campion. He had let his hair grow out a little and Annika enjoyed teasing him about it. "Careful, Major, someone might confuse you with a civilian!" she would say.

"I have to look this way, Ma'am, to blend in with the large number of civilians on campus,." he always responded, albeit knowing full well there was no way anyone would ever believe the heavyset, scarred veteran was a college student.

Following breakfast, Anika had just had enough time to be driven to her morning classes. In the first two semesters, she had managed to complete all her required classes, leaving this semester for only electives. Philosophy and comparative religions were her favorite. She had also joined a class for choral singing. The structure of the chorus, the careful teamwork appealed to her.

Annika settled in the lecture hall for this day's Philosophy class. The classroom was intimate, holding twenty-five students in wooden benches and tables. The tables were ancient, naturally rubbed smooth by centuries of scholars. Looking under the tables, though, revealed the graffiti from hundreds of years of undergraduates who had studied in this room.

Annika was seated with two of her friends. Beck Riddle was from a LaGrange colony in the Vespa system. She was attending on scholarship. She was a pretty Terran girl who worked hard at both her studies and friendships. She had gravitated toward Annika out of curiosity, hearing rumor her classmate was a royal. She was happily surprised to find Annika was warm and friendly. They became immediate friends.

Louisa "Toady" Hanson was boisterous, athletic. She was from a high gravity world, rich with minerals. Her father owned several mine interests and paid her tuition himself. Toady enjoyed being the center of attention, surrounding herself with as many people as she could. Annika was sure Toady hung around her with the thought of becoming the confidante of a princess.

The three were waiting on Marianne. They had started a betting pool on Annika's roommate, who inevitably showed up late, eating an apple.

The bet was if Father James would notice. Eating in his lecture hall was forbidden.

The first time he caught her, he simply took the apple away. The second time, she protested. "But Father, it's a very good apple and it's a sin to throw away good food."

Father James took a bite from the apple and agreed it was a good apple. "But did you bring enough for everyone?" he asked. He discarded that apple, also.

The next day, Marianne brought in a bag of apples. Everyone agreed, including Father James, they were very good apples.

Today, Marianne arrived with a minute to spare. She was chewing the last bit of the core.

The campus bells tolled. On the echo of the ninth bell, the door to Father James office opened and he hurried in, his cassock furled around his legs. He pushed back the grey hood attached to his stole, the garment worn by the inhabitants of Mithrandir. It exposed his steel colored hair and pale blue skin. Students were fond of the eccentric Jesuit, although they wondered about a member of the Mithranderar race on Vespa, much less as a Jesuit priest.

Father James began the lesson, writing on the overhead display. He underlined each word as he read it aloud. "That which lives, grows. That which does not grow, dies." He clapped his hands together. "Origins? Meaning? Mr. Hilden."

"Origins, Terran Bible. Corinthians," answered the young man.

"Incorrect. First Corinthians: 'You fool, for does not the seed you plant die before it grows?' Miss Kohler?"

A studious girl in glasses stated, "Terran novel, late twentieth century. John M. Ford. A minor work from that period."

"Correct." Father James raised an eyebrow. "What about the statement? Valid or invalid? Miss Raudona?"

"Valid," declared Annika. "When something stops growing, it begins to die."

"Really?" Father James clasped his hands behind his back, "Please stand, Miss Raudona."

Annika rose. "How tall are you, exactly?" inquired the priest.

"I am four foot ten inches."

Father James nodded, "Four foot ten. Now, state your age."

"I will turn twenty this month," she answered.

"Indeed! Well, happy birthday, young lady. Back to the topic at hand. So, you are four foot ten inches tall and for all intents and purposes, twenty years old. Might I ask when you reached your present height?"

"I recall I stopped growing at sixteen."

"Ah," explained the priest, "So, if the statement is valid, then you died four years ago. You appear to be mighty lively for a woman dead the last four years." The class laughed.

"So, you are telling me that the statement is invalid?" queried Annika.

"I did not say that either, Miss Raudona," Father James responded. "I am merely pointing out where your reasoning may be invalid."

"I believe my reasoning is valid," Annika argued.

"Why?"

Annika's mouth opened and closed a few times. "I don't know," she admitted.

The class laughed again.

"The three hardest words to admit in any situation," responded Father James, "Miss Raudona, are there any ways, other than physically, that you have grown since you achieved your stature?"

"Certainly," she responded confidently. "I have learned more about the Universe around me. I am academically smarter than I was at sixteen. My body, while no taller, has matured."

"There! Right there!" the priest said, announcing it to the room. "That is the validation of your argument. While you assumed I was talking about physical growth, you neglected to consider the other kinds of growth. Age and wisdom are forms of growth. Particularly wisdom and the pursuit of knowledge. Mr. Ford could have put it simpler, yes? When we stop learning, we start to die."

"I think I understand," Annika said.

"Most students fail this class trying to find perception," Father James spoke again to the entire classroom. "I am not asking any of you for understanding. What I want you to do is to think."

Annika tapped on the door to Father James' office. "Enter," he called.

His office was neat, organized. She liked that. Other professors she had visited had messy, disorganized spaces. Father James' office would have pleased Miss Norris to no end.

"Miss Raudona. I'm pleased to see you. Have a seat; how may I help you?"

She fidgeted for a moment, then stated, "I'm still not sure I understand today's lesson. Was the statement valid or not?"

Father James steepled his fingers. "You were educated by Proctors using the direct download method, yes?"

"Why yes," she responded, surprised. "How do you know of this? I was told it is a secret."

"Amongst government and military departments, it is a big secret, yes," he told her. "But educators have been discussing it with your Proctors for years. Imagine, loading all the information anyone needs for a lifetime directly into a subject's brain, thus eliminating the need for a formal education. I believe you are experiencing the fault we found in educating this way."

"I can access the information and utilize it. But without direct experience, I have trouble understanding it," Annika said.

"Precisely. Consider Miss Wallace's apple," he suggested. "I could show you an image of the apple and I could show you the apple itself. I could describe how the apple tastes and the texture of the apple when I bite it. But how will you understand any of these things if you don't taste the apple yourself?"

"My education is inadequate, then?" asked Annika.

"Heavens, no!" exclaimed the priest. "I daresay most of the university's staff would love to have your knowledge! What we must achieve here for you is what can't be downloaded. The ability

175

to process and utilize the information, even if you don't have direct experience. Today's statement, for instance. You can't grasp when I say there is no right or wrong answer."

"But there must be a correct answer," Annika insisted. "Every question must have a correct answer."

"Not always," the priest said. "Once you have achieved your throne, you will find that there aren't always clear-cut answers to every problem. There will be many times when the best answer is the first idea that comes to you. Other times, you will simply have to do what seems most right at the time. But you will be wrong, more than once. In those times, you must learn from your wrong decisions and not repeat the same error."

"You don't understand, Father," Annika argued. "As Empress, whole worlds, even of whole species will depend on my every decision. If I am wrong, beings will die. I was raised to be perfect and I must make perfect decisions."

"No, Crown Princess. You have to be human," he said kindly.

Chapter 22

Dearest Yuri,

The spring quarter has finally finished! Everyone is celebrating, as you might imagine. I received your last letter about the offer to accompany Dr. Stevens on his fall tour of Imperial Military medical facilities at Valarius. I think that would be wonderful, as Valarius is adjacent to Vespa. We could spend more time together that way. Please do come to visit, Husband!

More exciting news! Marianne and I have decided to get an apartment for the fall quarter. Major Campion is objecting, of course. But I really want to do this, get out and live like an ordinary student.

I received a letter from my sister, Teresa. She has an invitation from the witches on Scarborough. I understand it involves her healing talent. Sadly, it is out near the rim, so she won't pass by here on her way out. Hopefully though, we will soon have a chance to see each other.

My friends and I are going camping this weekend in the mountains! Unlike when I was a child, we must carry all our own supplies.

After we return, my love, I will be eagerly waiting at the spaceport for you to arrive. Hurry, my love, I can hardly wait to be with you.

With all my love,

The view from the ridge was spectacular. Annika paused to admire the endless green forest spread across the rolling slopes below her. The air was perfumed with the sweet scent of the pootawood. The still air was broken only by the buzzing of insects and the occasional rustling as one of the hikers disturbed a bird or some other woodland creature. She sipped from her canteen. The water, fresh and cool, was taken from a stream further back on the trail. There was a crisp bite to it, so clear and clean. She almost regretted having to use some tomorrow to mix her electrolyte.

Marianne joined her.

"Beautiful, isn't it?" her friend said in a reverent tone. "The campsite is just down this ridge about a mile."

They reentered the tree line. Within the promised mile, a clearing appeared with a slow- moving stream emptying into an alpine lake. The afternoon sun illuminated pollen and seeds in an ethereal glow. Beck, Toady and four boys arrived and they set camp. Annika had her and Marianne's shelter up in record time. She grabbed a hatchet and soon had assembled an impressive pile of firewood.

Annika slept out in the open, under the starry night. The deep woods were darker than she would have imagined. She felt she were at the bottom of a vast pit, with the stars of the universe above her. Her hand went up and blocked the tiny number of stars she believed were the size of her Empire. She pondered the quote from Father James' class. "That which lives, grows. That which does not grow, dies."

The Empire was dying. Her uncle was failing to grow the Empire making it unsafe and unsustainable. Another indictment of his inferiority. One hundred fifty worlds were much too small. If her Empire were to survive, it must grow larger. Much larger. Allies would be needed. Enemies crushed.

She heard a noise. Soft padding of feet creeping toward the camp. The Crown Princess turned hunter, springing lightly into a crouch, drawing her knife.

A *vercha* cat stalked into the clearing. Long, and black, ears pressed back, it looked at the camp and opened its impressive maw, exposing long fangs and double rows of sharp yellow teeth. It panted and watched the slight Terran woman.

Annika never broke her stare. She reached out and touched the beast's mind. It wasn't hungry; it came here every night to drink from the lake. It was trying to decide if the strange shapes were a threat.

"I am only a threat to you if you threaten me. Drink your water and go.'

The beast blinked its eyes, confused. It slunk down to the edge of the water. Annika could hear it lapping. Finally sated, the beast looked to Annika and hissed. She opened her mouth wide, showed her teeth, and hissed back.

The other hunter retreated into the dark.

Annika smiled at the sounds of the day starting in the forest. Birds sang, tiny creatures scurried through the brush, searching for a meal. Yuri's arm was over her and she sighed happily as she nestled back against him.

Yuri? Yuri was not on Vespa. "God below!" she swore, grabbing the arm, flipping and twisting. She rolled the body onto its stomach, using her weight to drive the arm up further. Her knife was in her free hand, the tip pressed against the base of the skull of her attacker.

"Jesus, let up, will you? That really hurts!" It was Dolan, one of the boys on the trip. She released him and sprung to a crouch, her knife at the ready. "Christ, do you wake up every morning like that?"

"What do you think you were trying to do?"

"I got up to go use a bush. I saw you there, looking so calm and peaceful, I thought I'd join you," he explained. "That's all, no funny business intended."

Annika did a quick swipe of his mind. He was mostly truthful. He hadn't intended any "funny business." Not then and there. But he was hoping, maybe later...

His arm and shoulder really hurt. Good.

She helped him up. "Let's go get breakfast started," she said.

The others had aroused by now. Annika dug in her backpack, finding the mix for her electrolytes. She had started on a new regime, one that would last a few days, depending on her activity. *It's a vacation. A couple of days of rest and relaxation. I didn't stress myself too badly yesterday. I'll take it tomorrow,* she promised, stuffing the container into a pocket in her back pack.

The guys decided to go further up the trail and do some exploring. Beck and Toady opted to join them. Annika and Marianne decided to stay in camp, next to the lake. It promised to be a scorcher of a day.

The explorers trooped off while the roommates dragged a sleeping bag to the pond's edge and spread it out. For hours, they lay there, sunning themselves and talking.

Suddenly, Marianne popped up. "It's too hot and we have this lovely lake right here. Screw it, I'm going skinny dipping." She began to undress.

Annika asked nervously, "Mari, what if someone comes along?" The other girl laughed as she removed the last of her clothes.

"You'll deal with them, I'll be swimming!" She raced into the water, screaming.

It did look wonderful. And it was hot. Shyly, Annika disrobed and stepped into the water. *Gods below! It's COLD!* She waded out a few yards, then dove in. When she surfaced, her teeth chattered. It was wonderful! She chased Marianne around, splashing, ducking under and tripping her and, in turn, being flipped back into the water.

The explorers returned. They all quickly stripped down and soon all eight naked students were splashing and cavorting in the mountain lake.

Annika left the lake, the water sluicing down her slender body. *Like the Goddess stepping from the ocean.* She lay on the sleeping bag and took a nap, the sun drying her.

Evening came; the young people got dressed and had their supper. Dolan handed her tidbit he made. "Peace offering?" he asked. Annika nodded and moved over on the log she occupied. She nudged his mind again and decided he had learned his lesson.

She didn't object when he put his good arm around her, walked her to her tent and bid her goodnight.

"Why, Annika, Why?" Blaise stood on the stumps of his legs, his blood pooling beneath him. Gurgling, Victor's headless body, stumbled toward her. A red mist swirled; she could hear the mocking laughs of Jiro and Anja. She stumbled backwards into the soldier trying to hold his guts in. He grabbed her, yards of his intestine falling out. Thousands were around her now. Reaching, clutching, moaning and crying.

She screamed.

"GET THAT DUST-OFF IN HERE NOW!" The armored shuttle hovered over the camp, bright spotlights illuminating the clearing. Soldiers slashed open the tents, grabbing the students, moving them away as quickly as they could.

Annika sat in the remains of her tent, eyes opened wide, unseeing. Her hands tore at her hair, screaming a long, endless wail. She panted, took a deep breath and wailed again. Marianne was curled in a ball, her hands over her ears, herself screaming.

A medic raced in and grabbed Marianne, fit a neutralizer to her head and carried her off, getting her away from the Crown Princess. Even with his own neutralizer, he could feel the tickles of madness Annika's screams broadcast.

"The doctor isn't planetside yet. Recommend we tranq her," a medic reported over the com. That wasn't the report Campion wanted. He had seen for himself the effect Doctor Russolov had on the Crown Princess when she was like this. There were no other options right now.

"All right, do it," he ordered. The medic placed the neutralizer around Annika's head, took a syringe from his field pack and pressed it into her arm. And another. And another.

Annika toppled sideways, mouth still open, no longer screaming. She still pulled at her hair, but less energetically than before. Her breathing became a shallow pant.

A stretcher basket was lowered on a cable from the shuttle and her pliant body rolled onto it. Wide straps passed over her body and immobilized the Crown Princess. The medic clipped his belt to the cable and they were raised swiftly. The craft spun on itself and raced away.

"Where's that damned shuttle for the rest of these kids?" Campion screamed over his comm.

"Annika? Sweetheart, can you hear me? Squeeze my hand if you can hear me." It sounded like Yuri's voice. She focused on her hand and squeezed. "Ow! O.K. You can hear me, my love. Open your eyes now, Annika. Let me see your pretty green eyes."

She didn't want to open her eyes, terrified of what she would see. Still, it sounded like Yuri. Yuri was her hero. He would never let anything bad happen to her.

Annika slitted an eye. It was Yuri! "There you are, sleeping beauty! Can you open the other eye for me now?"

For Yuri, anything. She opened her other eye and smiled. "You're here," she said in a weak, tired voice.

Yuri stroked her head. "Of course, my love. Here for you for now and for always. I have a question for you, Annika. How much electrolyte did you take this morning?"

"It was too nice a day, Yuri. I felt so good, I didn't take any. I wasn't tired or anything from the hike."

He patted her hand. "That's good, Annika, that's very good," Yuri assured her. "Would you like some water?"

Annika nodded. Yuri helped her sit up. "Just a sip to start," he warned her. She tried to comply. But after three careful sips, she felt her bile rising.

"Oh, no!" she cried and then vomited.

"This confirms our suspicions." The voice sounded like her Proctor.

"I believe you're right. Let's convene the council as soon as possible," Yuri was saying.

"As you wish, Doctor Russolov," said the Proctor, "Shall we say eight hours?"

"Sooner, if we can manage."

"Indeed. Might I inquire as to the condition of the rest of the children?" the Proctor asked.

"A few scrapes and bruises. One or two will need extended counseling. Headaches all around, as you might expect." This from a stranger who had just then entered the room. "I am Doctor Aaron Thomas. The Crown Princess's tent mate seems to have taken the worst of it. However, she appears to be recovering quickly."

"Marianne? Did I hurt Marianne?" Annika exclaimed, "I must go see her." She tried to sit up.

"Get a hoverchair," ordered Yuri.

Escorted by her bodyguards, Annika was taken to the wards where her friends were admitted. Marianne was sleeping, a calm look on her face. "Her injuries, thankfully are limited to the forward cerebellum, mostly in short term memory." Doctor Thomas reported. "She will require counselling and aftercare, but no physical damage was inflicted. I anticipate a full recovery within a few days."

Annika held Marianne's hand and asked about the others.

"A much better prognosis," the doctor said. "Distance from the attack," (Annika winced at his choice of words) led to less damage. Most are fully recovered already and are waiting for their release."

She entered the next ward. Beck was sitting on the corner of a bed holding Toady. The four boys were arranged around the bedridden girl. "Hey, Gang." Annika called weakly.

"What are you doing in here?" shrieked Toady. "Get away from me! Haven't you done enough? You're a damn teep and you didn't bother telling anyone. Stay out of my head, FREAK!" Toady grabbed her pitcher of water and hurled it at Annika. The boys surrounded the bed, tensed and glaring. Two balled their up fists.

"Anni, you'd better leave," Beck said, standing between Annika and her friends. "We're all pretty scared right now. Give it a couple of days; I'll give you a call."

Annika hung her head. "Let's go, Yuri," she said sadly.

They were silent as she returned to her room. She gripped his neck when he lifted her from the chair and back into her bed. Yuri sat on the bed with her, gently stroking her hands. "My love, I need to know what you remember."

Annika related the events of the weekend. She spoke of the scenic hike, the glorious swim with Marianne and her friends. The warm campfire and closeness she had with those friends that night. Going to sleep and waking in the hospital.

Yuri had pulled out his tablet and pencil while she was talking and was jotting down notes. When she finished, he began to ask questions. How much had she eaten? When did she take her last electrolyte? Did everyone eat the food from the same container? Did anyone else drink the water? On and on, question after question.

Finally, he snapped the pad closed and put it in his pocket. He took her hands again and began to rub them. "I shouldn't be telling you this, my love. But you'll hear it in front of the members of the File Council who will be at the meeting in a few hours. We believe this was an assassination attempt. You were barely alive when you were delivered here. Doctor Thomas did an excellent job of purging your stomach, but we will most likely have to purge your electrolytic system to be sure all the poisons are out.

"I'm sure your friends weren't involved, but they'll have to be interviewed. We are checking samples from your electrolytes, to see if the poisons were administered that way."

He wrapped his arms around her, "My love, I came so close to losing you." Annika encircled Yuri in her arms, holding him in the way he held her so many times.

Chapter 23

The brownstone townhouse Major Campion found was better than Annika or Marianne could have imagined. Sitting on a broad, tree lined boulevard a block from the University, restaurants, markets, and theater were all within walking distance. Beck had rejoined their friendship. The house was plenty big enough; she agreed to move in with her friends.

What none of them knew was that all their friendly, attractive neighbors were members of Major Campion's guard for the Crown Princess.

Beck had a blossoming friendship with one of the boys from the camping trip, Devin. He was reserved around Annika, still a bit frightened from the incident. Marianne was as scattered as ever, having a boyfriend, then not having a boyfriend. For the other two girls, it was better drama than they could imagine.

With Yuri working so close on Valarius, he made the trip to Vespa every week-end. Saturdays were spent with the whole household on some adventure or another. They would troop down to the local park and engage in games the other students were playing - football, soccer, kick ball, or Yuri's favorite, baseball. There would be discussions, song circles and plays. Dinners were raucous affairs, at their home with friends or at someone else's home.

The couple reserved Sundays for themselves. Mostly, they would be seen sitting under a tree, Annika's head on Yuri's lap while he read to her. They would come back to the townhouse in the evening and retire to their room.

Gavin Howland requested a private meeting with the Crown Princess. "I have someone I believe you must meet," he told her. "Your Empire will depend upon it."

Annika accompanied the Defense Minister to the command post of the facility. Guards in Navy blue escorted them to a secure meeting room. The room was a prosaic conference room: a pootawood table with twenty swivel chairs dominated the center of the room. A large screen ran from floor to ceiling, wall to wall at the far end of the room.

A large, powerful man was facing the screen, his back to Annika and Garvin. His rich, baritone voice said, "Your decision to stay another minute at this college is tactically wrong." He turned and faced the girl.

Annika startled. Had she not known her father was interred at Angkor Khan's Temple, she would have sworn he was standing before her. "Crown Princess, it is my honor to present Fleet Admiral Thor Thiessen ne-Khan. Admiral, the Crown Princess," announced Howland.

Admiral Thiessen gave her a sharp salute. His hair was much shorter than her father's and graying. He was older, weathered.

But he had the Imperial emerald eyes with the Asiatic fold.

"Go ahead," he rumbled, "get it out of the way."

"What would that be, Admiral?"

"You wish to scan me," he said. "Do it now so we may get to business."

She performed a swipe of his thoughts.

He was beyond loyal. His passion for the Empire and the Laws of Angkor Khan was absolute.

"Uncle?"

" Yes, I am your uncle. Your father, Robert, was my brother."

"I thought all the elder heirs died at Giza."

" I stayed away. The Regent and I have... disagreements."

"Oh?"

" Yes. Had I known what he was capable of, I would have killed him years ago, the fat little pustule."

"I see we have something in common."

"There are many of us in the Empire who have this opinion of the Regent. But he is not our greatest threat," Thiessen growled. "You are."

"Me?" she startled. "Might I ask why?"

"When the time comes to follow the Law of Succession, I will be at your side," he stated. "The Empire needs a strong leader, especially now. We know of the enemies without; I have no fear of them. But the enemies within, they are a threat to you. You are not preparing yourself to deal with them."

"I think you had better explain yourself, Admiral," Annika said coldly.

"Every young person goes through the time of their life when they Become," Admiral Thiessen explained. "I did; you father did. Even Gavin did."

The Defense Minister chuckled.

"You are different from the rest of us. You were born into your role in the Empire."

"Crown Princess was hardly handed to me," Annika retorted.

"No," agreed the Admiral. "You were bred to it and have prepared superbly. I could see your father was born to be Khan. I used that as motivation to push him harder to be the superior. For myself, I studied and prepared myself for a life of service to the Empire and become a naval officer, the finest in several generations.

"Like Robert, you were bred and groomed to be the ultimate Khan, surpassing all the previous incarnates. Instead of preparing to secure your Empire, then lead us on a glorious conquest, you amuse yourself with petty indulgence and philosophy.

"Tell me, Child, when the time comes for you to order me to assault the Bougartd home world, will you do so in a fashion that my troops will rally to you and be willing to fling themselves from the airlocks of their ships and plunge naked through the atmosphere because you order them to do so? Or will you issue orders from the safety of your flowering gardens, pointing at a map section of sky at

189

a whim and directing Imperial solders to die because that pretty light appeals to you?"

"That's hardly fair, Admiral."

"My dear niece," he said, his very tone condescending, "in war, there is no room for fair. You either win or you die."

He stood. "I will be conducting exercises in the quadrant with my fleet for the next six months," he announced. "If you decide to heed my words, then Gavin will put you in contact with me on my flagship, the *Azahnti.* Do not dally with your decision, Crown Princess."

"Yuri, Yuri, Yuri!" Annika came dancing into their room.

It was December, the house was readying for Roman Christmas. The girls had found a pootawood tree that resembled a Terran Christmas tree and had been busying themselves decorating it and the rest of the house.

Annika danced a circle around Yuri, then grabbed him and planted a sloppy kiss on his lips. "Ask me why I am so happy!" she exclaimed.

"O.K. Why are you so happy?"

"Sister Marcia, the choir director has selected me, your amazing wife, to sing a solo at midnight mass on Christmas Eve! Me!" Annika kissed him again and danced out of their room to spread her happy news.

Everyone in the house was excited for the holiday. Bright packages appeared beneath the scrawny tree. Yuri brought home a gift from his lab. He had synthesized mistletoe for the holiday; it hung in the entryway. It would be pointed out to all their guests as they arrived. The three girls spent hours in the kitchen baking for the holiday feast.

Christmas Eve arrived. Annika left for Saint Francis chapel early, explaining, "I have to warm my voice up." Yuri teased her for being a diva. She sniffed, put her nose in the air and strode out the door.

Yuri had never been to a Roman Christmas mass. He found it was not much different than that to which he was accustomed. The chapel was adorned with expensive boughs of pine, imported for the occasion. Red ribbons and bows were evident everywhere. Banners hung on every wall and the sweet, rich smell of incense hung heavily in the air. The crèche was to the side of the main alter, the cradle empty.

The organ began to play and the mass began. Yuri was familiar enough with the ritual. The procession wound its way to the crèche. The organ stopped.

The light, airy music of a harp began. An angelic voice began to sing.

"Ave Maria. Gratia Plena..."

He had heard her voice a thousand times in the five years they had known each other. Never like this.

"Ave, ave dominus. Dominus tecum benedicta tu in mulierbus. Et benedictus..."

Yuri felt a surge of emotion well up in him. His eyes moistened.

"Et benedictus. Et benedictus. Et benedictus fructus ventris. Ventris tui, Jesus. Ave Maria..."

The man next to him patted his shoulder and whispered, "The voice of an angel, that one."

A tenor joined her then, but Yuri only heard the voice of his love.

They were a gay crowd romping down the street. Yuri had excused himself long enough to wash his face before greeting Annika. "Are you all right, my love?" she asked.

He could only smile and kiss her.

191

The couples had formed up as they left the church to have a late supper. Yuri and Annika led the way, followed by Marianne and her latest amour. Beck and Devin slowly strolled behind, arm in arm.

Annika heard a noise. She pushed Yuri away and spun around, pulling her knife.

There were four of them. Hulking men with devices replacing human flesh all over their bodies.

AUGMENTONS!

She didn't hesitate, leaping at the first one. Her small frame struck it in the solar plexus squarely, driving it back. She stabbed downward with the knife, feeling the satisfying crunch as it tore open the thing's knee. She dropped and rolled away from the falling, injured cyborg. Sweeping her leg, she tripped the next one, leapt and kicked it at the junction of its head and neck. Her knife punctured its skull; she wiggled it about, then rolled again.

Screams cut into the night and deep into Annika's heart. She heard an audible crunch, one scream whimpered away. The augmenton behind her was struggling to stand, so she mule kicked and it went down again. Her landing set her in position to fling herself at the third one. It caught her and raised her above its head. Gunfire from her escorts erupted and the augmenton collapsed beneath her.

Annika landed on her feet. Four augmentons lay on the ground, quivering and bleeding. Her heart caught in her throat.

Beck and Devin were clearly dead. Her head was twisted around in an unnatural angle. Marianne's date wasn't moving. Blood poured from his scalp. Marianne herself was writhing and grasping at her stomach, screaming.

Annika had never seen Yuri move so fast. He plunged his hands into her wounded stomach. "Annika, come here, now!" he shouted. "Put your hands here. Hold that, squeeze it hard. You've got to hold that so she doesn't bleed out." He yelled at Campion and two medics appeared, one at the boy she didn't know, the other helping Yuri.

The transport hovered overhead. Stretchers and more medics dropped all around. Marianne was loaded on a stretcher and lifted, her friend following swiftly. Yuri grabbed Annika's arm and gave her a quick kiss. "I have to go, my love," he told her. "She still has a fighting chance." Then he was gone.

A soldier had covered Beck and Devin. Annika stood over their bodies.

The augmenton. The one whose leg she had ruined. She stomped over to him, grabbed his neck. Lifted him.

"Who?" she demanded.

It moved its mouth in its approximation of a grin. "We killed some, yes? That was the job. Missed you, so sad, so sorry."

Her grip tightened. "Who sent you!" she screamed.

It gasped and creaked. It got out one word.

"Freak!"

Annika's knife sunk deep into its neck. She sawed at the windpipe, severing it completely. It gurgled and gasped, streams of fluids jetting out. Then it went limp.

She dropped it on the ground, then went to work with her knife. When she had finished, she lifted its decapitated head from its body and tossed it to the nearest soldier.

"Processing unit," Annika ordered. "Get it to Intelligence while it's still viable."

She joined Major Campion aboard the next shuttle.

Chapter 24

"I would see my Uncle. Immediately!"

Gavin Howland blinked. Bad news never arrived at a decent hour. The sight of the Crown Princess on his comm covered in blood, presumably not her own, qualified as official bad news.

"Yes, Highness," he told her. He checked his chrono. Gods below, it was two A.M. Christmas morning. He made the call. When Admiral Thiessen appeared on the screen he said, "She wants to see you. Immediately."

Admiral Thor Thiessen's face remained impassive. "It will be so. I can assume something has happened."

"Yes. She was covered with blood," Howland said.

Theisen turned from the screen for a moment. "The planetary Governor has declared an emergency and sealed the planet. I am placing my fleet in an over watch position. What has happened, Gavin?"

"I don't know. I'll find out and get back to you."

The Governor's call was seconds later. "Augmentons attacked the Crown Princess's party. She is uninjured. All the augmentons are dead. She killed two of them herself. Two of her party are dead, a third is in surgery now. I have sealed the planet and recalled Admiral Thiessen," the Governor reported. "I have also turned out the garrison and notified the local Intelligence office."

"Well done. I believe you will find Intelligence Master Blount is on-world and will co-ordinate with your local office. I will be in your office in one hour." Howland stabbed the comm unit with his finger. Gods below, the enemy had struck too close to home.

Annika sat, composed, in the same conference room where she had first met her uncle, the admiral, reviewing the events of the last three hours. Following the attack, she demanded Campion take her to her home. He argued, as she expected, but she was insistent. Arriving, they found a cohort of troops filled the neighborhood.

She stripped and showered first, pleased to note, unlike the attack two years ago, she did not slide into a state of shock. Methodically, she cleaned herself, braided her hair and dressed in sensible clothing.

She paused at the living room. The tree, all the gifts. None of that had been touched by the night's violence. It was as a dream to her, the perfect Christmas with her husband and their friends. Now, two of them were dead and one was fighting for her life. Annika offered a prayer for Marianne to the Gods above.

The Crown Princess and her escorts went to the command post. There she waited for the arrival of Admiral Thiessen and Howland.

Annika closed her eyes and replayed the attack. It had taken only seconds. She had reacted faster than any ordinary Terran could have. She had extracted the data processor from one of the augmentons before it could self-destruct.

Beck and Devin were dead, victims of augmentons. As fast as Annika reacted, there was no way even she could have saved them.

Marianne was still in surgery. Annika had tried calling Yuri, then called the hospital. Doctor Russolov was in emergency surgery with two other surgeons trying to save the life of a young girl viciously attacked, she was told by the operator. And on Christmas! The operator promised to have Yuri call her when he got out of surgery.

Admiral Thiessen and Gavin Howland entered. "Gentlemen, please." Annika indicated two chairs.

"I have been reviewing the incident this morning," Annika said. "I have examined what happened from my point of view, and offer you both a humble and sincere apology."

"For what, Majesty?" asked Gavin.

"You warned me about the gathering of my enemies, both from without and within. I am convinced we will find tonight's attack on me was from within, an enemy who has been stalking me for many years. It came at the cost of two, possibly three dear friends. My own husband is alive only because of my superior reactions and fighting skill. For that, I am grateful. Nevertheless, four people have suffered grievously because I have been selfishly seeking self-gratification instead of concerning myself with the needs of my Empire."

Both men nodded. "Very well, Crown Princess," stated the Defense Minister. "Have you decided on what service you will join?"

"I will be a pilot."

Thiessen snorted. "Wonderful!" he exclaimed. "Orbiting miles above the troops while they fight on the ground or die in a blaze of glory when your carrier is attacked by raiders. Not a choice I would make to prepare for your position, Niece."

"I will be a bomber pilot, flying close air support for those troops, Uncle," she answered.

"The Navy does not fly close air support."

"I did not say I would join the Navy," Annika said. "I will join the Army."

Gavin Howland slapped the table and let out a yell. "You see, Thor! I knew that's what she'd choose. I *knew* it!" He held out his hand, beckoning to Thiessen. "Come on, old buddy, pay up. Fifty credits."

The admiral reached into his jacket and handed Gavin his winnings. "I don't suppose she might be in shock? No? Damn."

The Admiral became serious. "Annika, you will, of course, have to attend Officer Training School on Sanderstrom VII. Then it will be off to flight school for another nine months. It will not be easy, especially at Officer Training. The instructors there hate telepaths, considering them lazy and untrustworthy. They will use banshees to keep you and any other telepath in line.

"And if they discover you are a royal..." his voice trailed off.

197

"It would be best you don't let slip your lineage until after you get to flight school," suggested Howland. "As your sponsor, I can only protect you so much."

"No," Annika said, "I have to do this on my own. If I'm going to lead, I must be able to do it myself, without help."

"Nonsense," Howland answered sharply. "I was in the army for forty years. I saw the wrong officers promoted and I remember the men who died for it. I saw more capable officers who tried to do it on their own and ended up dead, or worse, because they had no one watching over them. I'm not doing you any favors. I'm making sure you're getting a square deal and earn your way."

"It's too late for you to enroll this semester," Admiral Thiessen stated. "Go back to your home. You and Yuri must announce your marriage. This way, should anything happen…Well, we would have legal heirs, even if we had to wait another twenty-five years.

"I will arrange for you to report in March to Sanderstrom VII. I would suggest you cut your hair by then. Perhaps color it and change your name."

"One last question, Majesty," asked Howland. "You could have requested any job, any service. Why bombers?"

"I've survived four attempts on my life in the last fifteen years," Annika said in a low voice. She drew her knife and stabbed it in the table. "From this, to bombing, to poison, to the attack this evening." She stood, took her knife and stalked to the door. "Nearly every time, they struck at me and killed those precious around me. I want to put them and their loved ones in my bombsight. And blow the glarpshite out of them."

"Oh, Yuri!"

Marianne was covered with a sheet, elevated off her abdomen. Wires and tubes ran under the sheet and into her arms. A respirator hissed and clicked. One bare foot peeked out from under the sheet.

"Hey, Marianne, get moving," Annika whispered, shaking the foot and pulling the sheet over it.

"It's O.K., my love. We think she can hear you."

Annika brushed her best friend's hair from the pale forehead and gave her a kiss. "Hey, you need to wake up. We all miss you. I miss you. I need to know you're all right." Annika looked to Yuri. "She is going to be okay, isn't she?"

Yuri shook his head.

Marianne's parents, Fred and Leia, arrived. Annika had ordered a destroyer sent straight to their colony to fetch them and bring them straight to the hospital. Marianne's mother, an attractive woman whom Marianne greatly resembled, clung to Annika. Both women sobbed. "She was supposed to be safe here," Leia cried. "How could this have happened?"

Marianne's father, a tall, balding man, stood woodenly, unsure. Yuri escorted the couple into a quiet room and explained her injuries. What he had been able to repair. What she would likely lose.

"Thank you, Doctor," Fred managed to say. "I know you and your staff did the best you could. I'm a miner, so I understand there are limits. Believe me, I, we are grateful you're giving us back our little girl. Can we go see her?"

Yuri took them, returned and led Annika to a coffee shop. "Her injuries are very serious," he told her. "The weapon the augmentons used on her was designed to rip and shred, but not to kill. We had to rebuild her digestive tract and restore her blood supply as best we could to her lower extremities.

She'll never walk again," he sighed. "And she'll never have children."

"Oh, Yuri," Annika cried. "She dreamed of having children. She was going into social work and planned on having a large family. She was so jealous to hear I had so many brothers and sisters. Now what will she do?"

199

"She's alive." Yuri voice was firm. "When she decides to wake up, the doctors will remind her of that. She will have a major lifestyle change, but if she works hard with her therapists and counselors, I see no reason why she can't have a long and productive life."

"But no children."

"My Love, she'll find children to love. It seems to me the universe seems to make sure there are always enough orphans who need love."

The trip to Terra was quiet. The *Azahnti* was a warship, not a civilian transport. Their room was spartan. A small window revealed the universe beyond. A pair of comfortable lounges sat at either side of the window, facing a table between them. Annika spent the hours staring out the window at the stars. Yuri, sensing his wife needed time to process what had happened, read from a pad. It was a welcome respite.

They would arrive at Terra Station the next morning. A shuttle with escorts would take them to the farm.

That night, Annika rolled over in the tiny bed and faced her husband. "Yuri, I joined the Army," she told him.

"I know. I spoke with Gavin," he replied. "He was at the hospital visiting Marianne. He agreed to contact the Minister of Health on my behalf." He propped his head up with his elbow. "I'm joining the Medical Corps."

Annika's brow furrowed. "What about your clinic? I thought you were happy there?"

"I am. But I have been a little bored there, frankly," Yuri replied. "I had someone to come home to when you were there. But after you went away for school, I got lonely. I joined Doctor Steven's tour on Valarius for a change of pace. I found I really enjoyed going off-world and seeing how other cultures live and treat their sick. In Medical Corps, I will have that opportunity. And," his eyes glinted, "being in space, I can keep a close eye on my beautiful wife."

She giggled. His hand slipped under her gown. "Yuri, we need to announce our marriage. Our heir-children are ready to be born. All Tahn is waiting for is you and me to formally make the announcement. I leave for officer school in March and graduate in June."

"We should announce it on Christmas then, at Mama and Papa's," Yuri suggested. "Mama will be thrilled."

"How will they feel about being grandparents again so soon?" she asked. "And to eight new grandchildren?"

"They already have grandchildren. Eight more will make them eight times happier." He pulled her closer and nuzzled her neck. "I should think I will enjoy being Papa."

Annika moaned. "Yuri, are you paying attention?"

"Of course, I am, my dear," he answered. "I always pay attention to my loving wife. Marriage, war, children. Sounds like a wonderful plan."

Her hand slipped under his pajamas.

"Would you like to have children, Yuri?" she whispered. "Children of our own?"

"We have eight children already. See, I was listening," as he nibbled on her earlobe.

"I mean a natural child, one just between you and me."

"Can you?"

"I don't know," she admitted. "I've never discussed this matter with Master Tahn. I shall remember to ask him."

"In the meantime, my beautiful wife," as he slipped her gown off, "might I suggest we practice?"

Chapter 25

The day before Orthodox Christmas, they were transported to the farm. Clara, Andrei and the rest of the family were overjoyed to see the couple. Because the weather had been so severe, Annika and Yuri accepted a room in the main house. Clara and her staff laid out a grand feast for the evening.

Andrei, at the head of the table as was proper, had once again insisted Annika sit to his right. Yuri sat next to her, shuffling the whole side of the table down one seat. There was some good-natured grumbling until the feasting began.

After supper, the family retired to the parlor. Andrei had secured a large yule log and it burned cheerily, warming the room. Clara busied herself serving warmed winter punch and hot toddies. Annika curled up with Yuri on a loveseat, wrapped in his arms and sipping the spicy and sweet drink Clara had served her.

For the first time in her life, Annika felt completely at home.

Christmas morning! Annika and Yuri woke huddled deeply under their quilt. When she peeked out, only his great nose was sticking out from under the covers. She rolled on to him and kissed his schnozzle. "Wake up, sleepy head!" she announced. "It's Christmas!"

The blanket beneath his nose parted and he kissed his wife. "I am awake, silly girl," he said. "I'm just waiting here for *Ded Moroz* to bring me a warm sweater!"

There was a polite knock at the door. "Children?" called Clara, "Happy Christmas! Hurry now, breakfast will be on the table soon."

Annika smiled at Yuri mischievously. "Yes, Mama!" she called. She hopped out of bed, grabbing her robe and clothing, then raced out the door for the bathroom. Yuri sighed. Well, this got him another half hour in the bed, waiting for Annika to get ready.

Andrei and Annika reprised the traditional roles as *Ded Moroz and Snegurochka* for the village children. Andrei's robe was an elegant forest green, Annika's a bright red. Andrei had convinced Annika to have just the smallest nip of cognac before they departed. The sky was clear and blue as an iceberg. And just as cold. Just the nip was enough to redden her cheeks and the tip of her pug nose. She was a bit uneven and laughing as the two drove the gaily decorated sledge into the village. They huffed great clouds of fog as she led Andrei in the Christmas songs she had learned in choir. The jangle of bells, the clatter of the hooves of the horses on the icy road was a joyous accompaniment to the singers.

Andrei had had more than a nip of the cognac before they left and more along the way. He weaved and roared with laughter as *Ded Moroz* and the beautiful *Snegurochka* handed the eager children their small gifts and Christmas treats. Yuri appeared and Annika fell out of the sleigh, face first into the snow. The assembled children roared with delight, not knowing it wasn't part of the playacting. When Annika sprang to her feet and ran to Yuri, the children threw snowballs all the way. At the edge of the square, they stopped and waved as *Snegurochka* and her true love fled down the streets.

Yuri and Annika turned down the familiar side road, ducked under the porch. The mistletoe waited above, as it had the last Christmas. They kissed as lovers celebrating their first Christmas together. Breaking the kiss, Annika breathed, "Oh, Yuri, finally. We can finally tell everyone. Come, let's hurry."

"Wait!" he exclaimed. "I have a Christmas gift for you." He pulled his mittens off and reached into his pocket, drawing out a velvet bag. A slender gold ring fell into his palm. Annika gasped and pulled her right mitten off.

"With this small token," he said gently, "the whole of the universe will know that I, Yuri Russolov, love you, Annika Raudona Russolov." He slid the ring on her trembling finger.

Exuberantly, they raced hand in hand, skidding and falling on the icy streets, to their home.

Christmas at the Russolov household was as magical as Annika remembered. Dozens of children streamed through the house, screaming and playing with new toys. Clumps of adults sat or stood, talking and laughing. In the parlor, a cousin banged away on the piano and ten singers sang Christmas songs. Rich and spicy odors wafted from the dining room, where Clara had laid out the feast in buffet style. The tables fairly groaned under the bounty - meats, fowl, fish, and vegetables of Terra and off worlds. To the side, dazzling desserts of cakes, cookies, creams and trifle. Fruits galore. Candies of every shape and size.

Yuri found Annika at the desert table, where she had been hungrily eying a trifle of several chocolates, while dipping her finger into the frosting of a cake. He tapped his glass with a spoon and called "Everyone? Everyone! Shhh, shhh. Annika and I have an announcement."

With all the noise, no one paid any attention. Annika giggled and disappeared into the kitchen stopping only to grab a quick bite of fudge. She returned with two pot lids. She beat them together, calling out "Everyone? Yuri has something to say!"

With the clanging, the room got quieter. Yuri swallowed and stood on a table, lifting Annika up to him. "Family, friends, Mama, Papa. First, Annika and I wish all of you a Happy Christmas! May all your days be as bright and warming as today."

He took a quick drink. "Last year, Annika and I journeyed to the Temple of Angkor Khan." He raised her right hand for all to see. "She and I are married."

The room exploded with cheers and cries of *"Congratulations! "Well done!"* Andrei tossed relatives out of his way as he rushed the table. He lifted Annika high above his head in his beefy hands, lowered her kissed her. He set her on the ground, where Clara embraced her new daughter.

Yuri had clambered off the table, where his father engulfed him. Clara kissed her son, tears of joy streaming down her face.

"Why didn't you tell us before, children?" Andrei asked.

"It's complicated, Papa," Anika explained. "Politics is the biggest reason. But we have even more joyous news for you and Clara. In a few months, our eight heir children will be born!"

"Eight?" boomed Andrei. "You don't look like you could carry eight children."

"They're at the Temple, Papa," Yuri said. "I can explain it later."

Andrei eyed his son. "I am no fool," he said in a low voice. "I understand how your children are being gestated." He grabbed Yuri and hugged him fiercely. "I am so proud of you son. You and your beautiful wife."

"We have some sad news as well," Annika announced. "After our children are born, we will be leaving. I have joined the army to be a pilot. Yuri has joined the Medical Corps."

The room went silent. One of the children stepped up to Annika and pulled on her sleeve, asking in a bell-like voice, "Why do you have to go away? Don't you love us?"

The Crown Princess knelt and took the child in her arms. "I do love you," she said. "Just as I love our family and your new cousins waiting to be born. One day I will be Empress and I need to go away to learn how to do that. Because I also love our Empire. Do you understand little one?"

"No," the little girl pouted. "Promise you'll come home for Christmas with Uncle Yuri. Promise."

"I promise," Annika vowed. "Not every year, but every year we can."

Clara took Annika's arm. "I am not so sure about this army you are joining. Why aren't you and Yuri staying here? You could be very happy here. And your Mama. What will she think of all this army?" They found a quiet place and sat.

"Mama Clara, I have to do this," Annika explained. "I will be Empress soon. I need to know how to lead my army. My mother will understand." Reality struck her, and she blanched. "Mother. How am I to tell my mother of all this?"

"Go see her," Clara offered.

The Palace of Amaar on Argulea was different than she remembered. *It's been fifteen years. And I am just a little taller.* The sun had set and a light rain was falling. It couldn't wash away the sweet floral scent of millions of roses the Empress was said to adore. Annika found the odor soothing.

The guards were waiting for her. She was driven into the palace straightaway. Mother had sent a message welcoming her to Amaar, directing the time she would schedule for her daughter to visit. *I hope my being here isn't too much an inconvenience, Mother.*

Annika was made to sit on a plain wooden chair and wait outside the Empress's office for nearly an hour. Her secretary would occasionally sniff, but ignored Annika completely. The insult was clear. She was not wanted here; it was only by the greatest indulgence that the Empress would even agree to see her daughter.

A buzz came from the comm unit on the secretary's desk. She pushed a button and listened intently. Finally, the secretary was to allow her to enter the office. "Remember who she is and who you are," she warned. "She is the Empress of the Terran Empire. You...are not."

The office was smaller than she would have imagined. A floor to ceiling window to her left opened out on the cool Amaar evening. It was a pleasant enough evening, the room filled with vases and planters, giving the room a complex mix of earthy aromas. Annika drank in the rich, heady fragrance.

The Empress was seated on an elegant white silken divan, sipping from an opaque cup. Annika became aware of a low, annoying buzz. The banshee was sitting behind the Empress on a wooden chair. The brown-haired girl, *barely a teen*, Annika thought, was shivering, and barefoot. She was dirty and wearing a dress that could be better described as a sack. An obvious look of terror adorned her face.

"Really, Child, couldn't you have picked a decent hour to come visit your dear, loving mother?" the Empress asked. As though to prove the point, she wore a thick white brocade robe with golden patterns and golden slippers.

"I've been waiting an hour, Mother. Perhaps if you had been ready and on time." Thrust and counter thrust.

"Oh, pooh, silly girl," Her mother responded. "I had finished my day and was having supper with my dear friend Esmerelda here. You have met her, my friend I mean?" She beckoned to the banshee.

"What happened to Grenna, Mother?" Annika asked, "I thought you found her exquisite?" Annika taunted.

Annika felt a stab of pain. The poor banshee looked terrified.

Annika gritted her teeth. "Mother, stop. I came for altruistic reasons and you are hurting me. Can't we have a single conversation where you don't bring in your watch dogs?"

The pain decreased. Slightly.

"Whatever is it you decided to come all the way out here to visit your dear mother, Child? What could possibly be so important to you to take you away from your busy life?"

"I have come to tell you Yuri and I are married," Annika said in a rush. She had to get out of that room, away from that Eighth-be-damned servant. "And I will be going away in March to join the Army."

"Ah, your little Russian doctor boy," was her mother's catty reply. "A bit old for you, isn't he? I suppose I should have had Intelligence look into him years ago. Did he molest you when you were underage, hmmm?"

"Mother, enough." Annika stomped her foot. "I have come here to do the right thing and you have responded by injuring me with your banshee and wounding me with your words. Is there nothing decent you can say to your daughter?"

"Daughter?" the Empress shrieked. "Daughter? When did you decide to be my daughter? From the day I first met you on your Revelation Day, you have never treated me as your mother! Why should I even consider you as my daughter? What did I ever do to merit such resentment from you, Child?"

"You married an inferior!" Annika screamed. "My father was a powerful Khan and when he died, you replaced him with a small, vain, pitiful excuse in your bed. I could see that from the moment I laid eyes on him. How could you do that, Mother? How could you shame our family? How could you shame our line? How could you shame...ME?"

"There were forces at work you can't conceive, Girl."

"Forces? What forces? Had you married my Uncle Thiessen or turned the Empire over to the Imperial Council until I became of age, the Empire wouldn't be in the state it is today," Annika yelled.

"You can't imagine the pressure I was under. I had such grand plans for you children. They were being threatened." The Empress protested.

"Your plans?' Annika roared, "Your plans. You mean to tie yourself to my father, get credit for his successes? Now I see, Mother. You didn't love my father. You don't love your precious Regent. You love your title! Very well.

"When I reach twenty-five, as the File Committee has decreed, I will claim my rightful place as Khan. If the Regent opposes me, he will die. All who stand against me shall die. And since your title means so much to you, I will not accept the title of Empress. Until you die."

Annika spun on a heel and marched purposely away.

Chapter 26

Three years later.

The Third Fleet orbited Mykonos Three. Dreadnaughts climbed ponderously from the low orbits they'd used to pound the Mykonos cities.

Captain Annika "Mouse" Russolov tugged at the straps of her seat. She was flying the newest class of Imperial attack craft, the Icarus Bomber, with her Weapons Officer, Rita "Sweetie" Rivas.

Their ship was the latest in Imperial design. The Icarus was diamond shaped, struts on the aft end holding two powerful sub-light engines. On top of the hull and between the engines, sat a turret containing two meson rapid fire rifles. A third rifle was in the nose, for Annika's use. The large bomb bay in the belly contained six ground attack missiles.

Annika's and Rita's ship was painted mottled green and yellow. On the nose, the crew had painted "Red Queens" in bold letters.

Within the launch bay, a trolley moved the ship into position. The technicians looked the ship over and gave Annika a thumb up. "Ready, Sweetie?" she asked.

"Let's go!!"

Annika saluted sharply and the bomber was launched into space. They circled their carrier, the *ISS Vengeance,* one of four orbiting Mykonos Three, each launching forty attack craft to support the drop ships.

Today, Annika was Rook Three. Her flight formed up and prepared for insertion into the planet's atmosphere.

Annika checked instruments again. The flight leader, Major Tom "Flash" Morgan, called out, "Rook Flight, go for insertion. Call when in position and green."

"Rook Two."

"Rook Three," called Annika.

"Rook Four."

"Rook flight, here we go." The four ships pitched their noses up and fired the small motors on those noses. They slowed and penetrated the thickening atmosphere.

"WHEEEEEE!" cried Sweetie Rivas as the *Red Queens* plunged. Pink and orange plasma streamed past Annika's cockpit windows, but she scarcely noticed. Her eyes were glued to her instruments, adjusting the ship with light taps and wiggles on the controls. The glowing faded. Annika checked her instruments and called, "Rook three, green lights. Rook four, form up and let's get down in the weeds."

"Rook Four."

Lieutenant Rivas interfaced with command and located her first target. She entered the information into the attack computer, saying, "Bug on target, fly the bug." She went to work on the second target.

An indication appeared on the windscreen. Annika pointed her ship at the bug and dropped as low as she dared. This was a basic tech world, but it only took one dumb bullet to kill her. All the Rooks approached their first targets low and fast.

An indicator flashed, showing it was time to climb and release the first weapons. Annika eased back on the control stick, climbing to keep the ship centered on target.

"FLACK TOWER AT FOUR O'CLOCK!" screamed Rita. Annika rolled the ship to the right as she felt the "thump-thump-thump" of Rita firing her turret at the flack tower.

"One on our nose!" Annika cried. She wanted to dump the nose and streak away, but the target computer needed a few more seconds. Desperate, she mashed the trigger of her own weapon, hoping to throw the enemy gun off by spraying rounds around the tower. There was a tone, the bomb bay doors snapped open, released two weapons and snapped closed again. Annika kicked her rudder, centered the flak tower into her gun site; her forward firing meson cannon peppered the flak tower and made a satisfactory explosion.

Which was why she didn't see the third tower, which laced the *Red Queens* down its right side.

"Glarpshite!" Annika cursed. The right engine shuddered and lost power. She struggled to keep the ship aloft as alarms and warning lights demanded her attention.
She felt the "thump-thump-thump" again.

"Got it," grunted Rita. "Anni, we got orange fire on two. Get us upstairs!"

Orange fire was good. It meant fuel or fluids were burning. If it turned green or blue, it meant the engine case was on fire. That would mean ejecting. If they could get enough altitude, the escape pod could get picked up by shuttle. If not, there were a lot of angry bad guys down there, digging their butts out of just-bombed rubble.

She got the ship leveled and eased back on the stick. They began to climb. "Looking Glass, Rook Three. I've got an orange fire and climbing. Clear me for angels 350." The warning lights were flickering off one by one as Rita worked her way through the emergency checklist.

Twenty thousand feet. Sixty thousand feet. Looking Glass answered their desperate call, "Rook Three, negative on climbing to angel 350. You cut through the path of a drop. Suggest you alter course to two-seven-zero and resume climb to angels one five zero."

"Eight's ass. Move your drop path," Annika yelled. She clicked her comm switch and called, "Negative, Looking Glass. Rook Three is unable to comply. Angels one twenty and climbing for three fifty. Still on fire."

"Calm down, Mousey," chuckled Rita. "The fire is dying. Keep climbing." Calling her Mousey was a good sign. Rita was calm and trying to relax her pilot.

"Ditch the turret, Sweetie," Annika ordered. A resounding thump indicated Rita's immediate compliance. The ship, lightened by a ton and a half, accelerated.

"Mousey, ease us a little to the right, just a few degrees," Rita ordered. Annika lifted her foot just a bit off the left yaw peddle and eased the stick a tiny twitch right. She felt *Red Queens* slip, then steady. A large glowing object abruptly filled her windscreen. Before Annika could react, it thundered past, shoving the ship violently out of its way with its wake. Annika struggled to straighten out the *Red Queens*.

"Drop ship," Sweetie reported. "Missed us by, oh, fifty feet."

They continued their climb. By 200,000 feet, the fire died. Annika cautiously advanced her right throttle. The ship shuddered and vibrated. She retarded the throttle and pulled the fire handle.

"Gods below, we're getting clobbered down there," Rita reported. She was monitoring the comm. "Rook Two got hit and went in. Haven't heard from Bishop or Pawn flight." Annika grunted acknowledgment. She had to focus right now, get the ship in orbit.

Worry about missing friends later.

She eased the ship into a comfortable orbit at 350,000 feet. "Rook Three, angels 350," she reported. "One engine down, still packing four."

She wouldn't be allowed to land a damaged ship with ordinance aboard. "Rook Three, Looking Glass. Wait one, we'll find a target."

Moments later, Looking Glass called with a target. Rita programed the attack, the bomb bay doors swung open, released the weapons and snapped closed.

It was time to relax. The *Red Queens* was in a safe orbit, could wait for the other two ships from Rook flight to arrive, then make its way back to *Vengeance*. Annika monitored the comm. It wasn't good; there was a higher number distress signals than usual for an operation like this. The planet was too backward and the bombardment should have knocked out its defenses.

"Eight's crusty ass!" Rita exclaimed from her cockpit. "Mouse, look at this." On her display, Rita was running the turret's film of the attack. Anika was slightly disorientated watching the screen slide and roll while she was holding the ship level in real time. On the screen, blue/white balls danced across. The image rotated with the turret and she saw the flak tower. Rita stopped the film and zoomed in on the weapon site.

It was an Imperial anti-ship weapon.

An old one, at least ninety standard years old. But the Empire never discarded any weapon that was still usable and never sold them when they became obsolete, preferring always to recycle them.

So what was a ninety-year-old Imperial anti-ship gun doing on Mykonos Three?

The image changed. Now it was Annika's forward firing gun camera. The image slid as she rolled away from the bomb release and centered on the gun firing at the *Red Queens.*
It was a twin of the first. Annika yelped happily as the movie showed her destroying the gun.

The image shuddered and shifted back to the turret. They were bobbing and sliding all over the sky, but Rita could stop at a frame that showed the third gun was twin to the first two.

"What is going on here, Captain?" Rita's voice was furious. "How is a piddly ass, backward planet getting our own stuff to use against us?"

"Rook Three, Rook One." Flash Morgan sounded tired.

"Rook Three. Glad to see you, Flash," Annika replied.

"You too, Mouse. O.K. Let's head to the barn."

"Where are Two and Four?" Annika asked.

"They're down. Two is gone, four just about made orbit, but they're gone, too," came the flat reply.

"Eight's arse."

"Yeah. Form up, let's go home."

The flight back to *Vengeance* was short and quiet. As a damaged ship, *Red Queens* had to hold in the pattern while the undamaged ships landed. Of the forty that had launched, thirty-two returned.

All the undamaged raiders landed safely. Now Annika would be allowed to dock. With a dead engine, *Red Queens* wanted to slide to the right. Annika furiously worked the remaining throttle on her good engine and the attitude jets. *Red Queens* wallowed and swerved, then dropped laboriously onto the recovery sled. Mechanical clamps secured the ship to its transport carriage. Annika shut down the remaining engine as the transport bearing the damaged bomber trundled to its maintenance bay. Exiting the ship meant opening the hatch beneath her feet and crawling out through the bomb bay. She ducked out of *Red Queens,* ripped off her helmet and threw it, screaming. It skittered and bounced, coming to a spinning rest against a bulkhead.

"What in the Gods' names are you doing with your flight helmet?" came a roar.

Annika groaned. It was Colonel Rolando Byrd, Captain of the *Vengeance.* She stiffened to attention and saluted. "Is there something wrong with your helmet, Captain?" His voice dropped in volume only slightly.

"No, Sir," Annika said. "It, ah, slipped out of my hand while I was removing it."

"Slipped," the colonel repeated.

"Yes sir. Slipped," Annika confirmed.

"Halfway across my hangar deck."

"It was very slippery, Sir," Annika replied with a straight face.

"Well, Captain, since your hands seem to be so slippery this afternoon, I'm thinking some credits should slip out of your hand and buy a round in the wardroom tonight," Colonel Byrd stated. The corners of his mouth twitched upwards. Slightly.

Annika was beaten. Considering what the Colonel could have done, she was getting off easy. Although it would be expensive. "Yes sir, very fair," she answered.

She walked over to her helmet and bent to pick it up. And fainted.

Annika came to in the medical bay. Doctor Raymond Boyce's face hovered above her. "Welcome back to the land of the living, Captain." His smile was warm.

Of all the personnel aboard *Vengeance,* Doctor Boyce knew her best. Her unique physiology required his personal attention. He was calm, unassuming, treating Annika like a favorite daughter rather than an Imperial science experiment, as had other military doctors. She liked him immensely.

He handed her the electrolyte, which she drank eagerly. Doctor Boyce shook his head. "I have no idea how you tolerate that stuff," he commented. "I tried taking just a sip once, while you were downloading."

Annika giggled. "How sick did you get?"

Boyce chuckled. "I couldn't tell which was worse. Going down or coming up."

"My husband tried it once, too," Annika told him. "He was sick in bed for two days. Served him right. So, Doctor, why am I here?"

"You don't remember?" Boyce asked

"No. I was in the hangar bay, getting chewed out by Colonel Byrd," she stated. "Then I woke up here."

Doctor Boyce told her. "Well, in medical terms? You fainted."

"No, I didn't."

Doctor Boyd shook his head, "Yes, you did. Why else would you be here?"

"That doesn't make sense," she said, annoyed. "I have a superior body. My superior physique is too strong to faint."

"Under normal circumstance, I would agree with you," said the doctor.

"'Normal circumstance.'" Annika repeated. "What is that supposed to mean?"

He looked at her for a long moment, then asked, "Annika, when was the last time you saw your husband?"

"Four weeks ago, on Advance Station Thirteen," she answered. "He and I were able to get a twelve-hour liberty together."

"Four weeks, that's about right," Doctor Boyce said in a far-off voice. "Tell me, Annika, as your doctor, I'm assuming you were intimate."

Annika blushed. "Yes, we were."

The doctor looked relieved. "That's wonderful," he said. "Congratulations."

"For what?"

Doctor Boyce took the empty glass and handed her a glass of water.

"You're pregnant," he announced.

A macabre celebration in the ward room of the *Vengeance* happened that evening. Pawn flight was gone, all four ships were missing with their crews. The two ships missing from Rook flight. One ship each from Bishop and Knight Flights. Happily, three crewmen had been recovered. The rest were missing or confirmed dead. The ceremony had started off solemn enough for the missing thirteen shipmates. Now the party was in full swing, as the crews drank to forget they'd be flying into combat tomorrow.

Annika hadn't joined into the revelry. She stared out the window. Pregnant? How could that happen? She and Yuri were always so careful. She reviewed the shore leave. It had been so long, months, since they had been together. They didn't have long, only twelve hours. And she was so happy to be with Yuri.

It wouldn't affect her flight status for now. At four months, she would have to be removed from combat. She would remain on duty and eligible to fly shuttles until she delivered.

Politically, it made no difference. Their heir children had been "born." Having natural children had always been looked forward to by previous Khans and their partners. But, the timing was not good. Within the year, she would be twenty-five and ascend to the throne. She held no illusion that the Regent, Ming si, would meekly step down. Gavin Howland, Admiral Thiessen and Noire were preparing for the inevitable civil war to come.

And she was pregnant.

Annika dropped her head to the table and covered it with her arms. This was a disaster. Nothing less than a disaster. What would happen now? She couldn't see herself leading the charge up the steps of Argulea Palace, a rifle in one hand and a baby in the other.

Still, Yuri would be thrilled. She rolled her head into the crook of her arm. Truthfully, she was, too. Master Tahn had shrugged his shoulders when they asked him if it were possible for Annika to get pregnant. "I didn't modify your reproductive organs," he told her. "So, it will depend entirely on how your body reacts when the blessed day happens."

Rita plopped down across from her. "Hey, Mousey, why so glum?" Clearly, she had drunk more than the round Annika had purchased.

Annika lifted her glass of water. "Toast me, Sweetie."

Rita lifted her glass. "Okie-dokie. What am I toasting you for?"

"I'm going to be a mommy."

Rita snorted. "Some toast. You already have eight kids."

"No," Annika sighed, "I am going to be a mommy."

It took a second for the announcement to sink in. "How? What? Who…" Rita stammered. "Oh, Gods above, Mouse, this is WONDERFUL!"

Maybe from your point of view," Annika grumbled.

Rita stood on her chair. "Everyone!" she hollered. "I give you a toast to Captain Annika Russolov! And to her loving husband, Colonel-Doctor Yuri Russolov!"

"To the Russolovs!" cheered the entire room. They didn't care why. It was a toast.

Rita sat. "You really are crazy, Sweetie, you know," Annika grinned.

A shadow fell across the table. It was Colonel Byrd. "Captain, Lieutenant." He nodded to the women. "Russolov, come with me."

In the wardroom, three other colonels were waiting. "Captain," stated Colonel Byrd, "this is Colonel Scott of the *Victor,* Colonel Hannirabbian of the *Vulcan* and Colonel Lui of the *Valor.*" Scott was friendly-looking with a blonde lock of hair curled on his forehead. Hannirabbian was a dark Hindi. Lui was an Asian woman, older than the other colonels. She spoke first.

"Captain Russolov, you will brief us on your mission today," she demanded.

Annika did as she was ordered, from the launch through the attack and recovery. The colonels listened in silence.

"Why did you review the gun tape prior to landing?" asked Hannirabbian.

"My weapons officer noticed an anomaly with the enemy weapons during our attack," Annika reported. "She showed me for confirmation while we waited for our element."

"What was left of your element," challenged Lui.

"Rook element took heavy losses during the attack," interjected Colonel Byrd. "Pawn and Knight Elements also suffered heavy losses."

"We all suffered heavy losses," Hannirabbian countered. "Much higher than we were led to believe would be possible. Now, we may have our answer as to why. How did Mykonos obtain advanced technology?"

"Thank you, Captain Russolov," Colonel Scott sounded condescending. "I understand you fainted when you returned? Nothing serious?"

"No sir," Annika lied. "My electrolytes had gotten low. Doctor Boyce administered the necessary treatment."

"Admiral Theissen's fleet will arrive at fifteen hundred hours," Colonel Boyce announced. "Captain, you will take a shuttle over when he arrives. He will want to discuss this incident. Your weapons officer will accompany you. Dismissed, Captain."

Annika sat her desk, trying to pen a letter to Yuri. *My darling, I have wonderful news...* She wadded it up for the tenth time and threw it in the recycler. She had to tell him, of course; she wanted to tell him. She wanted to stand atop the Morning Tower at Giza and declare it to the universe. *I, Crown Princess Annika Raudona Russolov Khan, Goddess/Queen of Terra, am going to be a mother!*

But the words stuck in her throat.

In a few hours, she would face her uncle. How was she going to tell Admiral Thiessen? *Uncle, Yuri and I were just a bit irresponsible, so we'll have to put the revolution off until after my child is born.*

A tap at the door; Colonel Lui let herself in. "Listen carefully," she hissed. "There is a strike launching in fifteen minutes. An Icarus is waiting for you and your weapons officer. Your call sign will be Zulu Four. Form up and accompany the strike until the insertion. The *Azahnti* will be off your port side, twelve hundred fifty miles away. Waste no time, head straight to him and land immediately. Tell no one. Do you understand, Captain?"

What of the shuttle, Colonel?" Annika asked.

Colonel Lui responded with fury. "There is no time for discussion except to tell what Admiral Thiessen's message to me said, half an hour ago; 'The enemy within is set to strike,' Am I clear, Captain?" She spat the title.

"Yes, Colonel."

Colonel Lui glared, but raised her hands. "For ten thousand years, Highness," she said, and left.

Halfway to the hangar in her flight gear she heard a call. "Hey, Captain!" It was Colonel Scott, also wearing flight gear festooned with patches, denoting him as a Buccaneer fighter pilot. "I'm headed to the hangar, Captain. A little overdressed for a shuttle trip aren't you, Captain?"

"I was ordered after my meeting with Admiral Thiessen to transfer a replacement Icarus here to *Vengeance,*" Annika fibbed. "I was going to grab a bite to eat before reporting to the *Azahnti.*"

Colonel Scott asked, "Next year, when you turn twenty-five, do you expect to leave the army and ascend to Khan? Or will you continue your career and wait for the passing of the Regent, as per custom?"

"The law of my ancestor makes no provision for a Regent," Annika's voice was cool. "Therefore, I am bound by law to claim my title next summer."

Colonel Scott nodded his head, the lock of hair bouncing. "Ah, my launch bay. Good hunting, Captain."

She hurried to the launch bay assigned to her craft. Rita was already there, pre-flighting the ship. It was clear that this ship wasn't in pristine condition. But for a quick shuttle mission to the *Azahnti,* it would be adequate.

Rita was oddly quiet. She had finished and already wiggled her way into the aft cockpit. Annika donned her helmet and climbed up into her seat. The ship felt strange, like visiting a place that looked like home, but wasn't. The seat bottom had a strange feel. She wiggled her rump, but it still felt wrong.

She missed the *Red Queens.*

They went through their checklist while the technicians prepared the rest of the ship. They were trolleyed over to the launch tube. A yellow jersey handler signaled Annika.

Annika gave him a thumb up. He smiled and signaled the launch crew.

"Ready?" she called.

"Yeah, let's go," was Rita's quiet reply.

Something was bothering Sweetie. Annika saluted and the ship shot from its tube. She arced about and began the orbit around the *Vengeance,* searching for Zulu flight.

They formed up and headed toward the planet. Annika responded to all the callouts from the flight lead. She suppressed a touch of jealously. Zulu flight was getting back into the fight. She would have to wait for another day.

The call came and Zulu flight dropped into the atmosphere. Annika pulled up and looped around the planet. *"Azahnti* at point six," called Rita. "Light them up, let's get out of here."

No, Sweetie wasn't herself. Annika was now concerned. "Hey, Sweetie? Are you okay?" she asked.

"Yeah, yeah," was the terse reply. "Get us to the *Azahnti* as quick as you can." Soon they were on approach to the flag ship.

Azahnti was a heavy command attack carrier. His forward two thirds were star shaped when viewed from above, the forward arms drooping down, the two-aft curling upwards. Each arm flared into a launch bay larger than *Vengeance.* Aft of the launch bays, the ship rounded into a thick waist, carrying the largest missile battery Annika could recall ever seeing. The stern mounted a quartet of massive star drives. *Azahnti* wouldn't slug it out with other capital ships. Her eight hundred fighter and bombers would engage the enemy behind the thousands of missiles she would fire from her flanks.

"Land on the port side forward," Rita ordered.

That's curious. She's giving orders now?

She shot the perfect approach and recovery. As the ship was trolleyed, Rita spoke up. "Annika, stay put until I come get you." Again, with the orders! When did Sweetie start issuing orders?

Annika removed her helmet and set it on the cowl of the forward panel. She heard Rita's seat slide and her hatch cycle. She peered over the rail of the cockpit window, trying to see what Sweetie was up to.

Then Annika saw the squad of armed soldiers surrounding her ship.

What is going on? She drew her sidearm and patted the knife strapped to her left arm.

The hatch at her feet thumped. She slid her seat back, armed and cautious, and opened the hatch. Rita appeared and smiled. "We're all set, Mouse. Let's go."

Annika dropped through her hatch. The troops were there all right, their weapons drawn.

A familiar soldier walked up. "Major Campion!" Annika was pleased to see her old bodyguard. "Wonderful to see you again, Sir." She gave him a sharp salute.

"It's Lieutenant Colonel now, Captain," he replied, returning her salute. "The Admiral is waiting."

Annika had learned protocol. As her senior officer, she allowed Colonel Campion to lead her through the colossus.

"Well done getting her here, Lieutenant Rivas," Campion said.

"Thank you, Sir. It was a challenge," Rita answered.

"I can imagine. I had my turn trying to get her to comply." His tone was wry.

"Comply, who?" Annika asked. "What are you two talking about?"

Rita and Campion chuckled. "Sounds like you did better than I intended," Campion said. "Captain, Lieutenant Rivas is assigned to me. She has been your bodyguard since you two were assigned together."

"Surprise, Mousey!" Rita smiled a toothy grin.

The doors to the *Azanhti's* conference roof slid open. The brightly lit room boasted tall windows dominating the forward wall and half the ceiling. Various monitors and images were efficiently spread across the walls. A curved table of black stone was positioned in the middle of the room, surrounded by a dozen chairs. At the head of the table was a dark, upswept throne. From the entryway, the combination of the onyx table, the throne and the atrium of stars took Annika's breath away.

Defense Minister Howland and Admiral Thiessen were by the windows. "Did you know, from this angle, you can see into the whole of the Spinward?" asked Gavin Howland. "Imagine, all you see, standing right here, could be within your grasp."

"Annika," the admiral said in a low tone, "have you ever heard the testimony, 'Everything said under the stars is heard. And remembered.'?"

"Yes Uncle," she replied. "Long ago, a Proctor told me."

"Then listen carefully, my Khan. Very soon, this room will be filled with officers, beings whom I trust implicitly with both your life and my own. The disease that has infected our Empire has now reached the military and the highest levels of the government. We cannot wait any longer.

"Today, either you become the Khan or the entire Terran Empire will stumble and fall. So, I am asking you…"

"Wait," Annika said, "before you ask, I must tell you that I am pregnant."

Both men's faces lit up. "My Khan, this is *marvelous* news!" exclaimed Howland. "When did you find out?"

"J-just this afternoon." Annika told them. "I would have thought my being pregnant would be a detriment to this war."

Oh, quite the opposite!" exclaimed her Uncle. "In ancient times, our ancestors would mate with their partners before going to war to ensure the future prosperity of the tribe. Should they die in the war, the future of the tribe was assured, for the sons or daughters of the tribe would be the children of a warrior. This will rally many to your cause."

"You won't be leading any charges," Gavin told her. "We wouldn't have let you do that, anyway."

Annika turned once more to the stars. There were so many, right there, calling to her. She set her jaw. "Gentlemen. Let us make ready for my war."

Chapter 27

He sat in her stateroom, ruminating at the star field. The darkness matched his mood. He would prefer an additional year to complete his investigations. But the enemy within was making his first real play for power. They couldn't wait any longer.

She was ready. He knew she was ready. Another year would temper her edge just a bit sharper.

She had Become. It was time.

He sensed her coming and raised his defenses. She snapped, "Lights," as she crossed the threshold.

"Good Evening, my Khan."

"Noire!"

"Yes, my Khan."

"That's a neat trick. Have you just developed it?"

"It was suggested by my mentor, Kermit Blount. I have found it effective with those who can see and hear us this way."

"Interesting. Well, don't use it with me."

"Yes, my Khan. Do you wish to scan me now?"

"No. You are my oldest and most trusted servant. I am going to take a shower. Please order dinner for us."

"I have a surprise for you, Sister. You will find it in your stateroom when you finish."

She returned to the parlor brushing her hair, sniffing appreciatively at the odors rising from the covered dishes on the table's red linen cloth. She had donned the uniform he brought from Giza.

"Thank you Noire. It still fits!"

"I thought you'd like to have it. Especially now."

"Is that your report?"

He handed his pad to her as they sat. She read it as they ate.

"Interesting. The fourth and third names, I expected. The first...disappointing. As the second is for you, I am sure."

"Yes, my Khan. Unacceptable."

"I will personally handle one, three and four. Number two is Intelligence, so he is yours. My War Council will conduct court martials on the rest.

She stood, smoothed her jacket and strode from the room. **"We will start with number thirty-seven immediately."**

The War Council of Annika Raudona Russolov Khan met in the *Azahnti* council chamber. Admiral Thiessen and Gavin Howland were joined by Noire, fourteen Generals, Three Admirals, seven Naval Captains and Three Army Colonels. Annika knew the colonels, having met with them hours earlier.

The holo above the onyx table showed a shuttle bearing *Vengeance's* markings leaving him. It headed directly toward *Azahnti.* "The transfer is scheduled for a fifteen-minute flight," Noire said.

Five minutes into the flight, as the shuttle was arcing over Mykonos's polar cap, it exploded.

Admiral Thiessen stood. "I believe this confirms the evidence Agent Noire presented. The verdict?" He looked around the table. Each officer, in turn, slashed their right hand across their throat. Howland repeated the gesture. Admiral slashed his hand across his throat, then addressed Annika. "My Khan. The verdict is unanimous. Your orders?"

"Order him to land aboard *Azahnti* immediately. Once he is aboard, the *Victor* is to be boarded. Any officer or crewman who resists is to be detained. I do not want anyone killed or injured; they are still my soldiers and I will not allow them to be punished for the actions of traitors," Annika stated.

"As you order, my Khan." Admiral Thiessen pressed his comm button and gave the short, terse order.

Twenty short minutes later, the doors of the chamber opened. A furious Colonel Scott Hopkins was escorted in by two burly guards. He shook off their grips and demanded, "Admiral Thiessen!

What is the meaning of this? I am the senior on-scene commander of the accident involving the Khan's shuttle. I should be out there leading the search rather than here answering questions."

"An interesting choice of words, Colonel. Answering questions. I have a few questions of my own I would like answered." Annika rotated her throne from the star field outside the window. "What did it take for you to decide to betray me and my Empire?"

Colonel Hopkins was wide eyed. "M-m-my Khan," he stammered. "You're alive!" His hand snaked toward his sidearm.

And froze. She held him rigidly for three long minutes, then said, "You may breathe now. Admiral?"

Admiral Thiessen stood. "Colonel Scott Adam Hopkins, you have been tried and found guilty by the War Council of the Khan. The charges are treason, attempted murder of your Khan, conspiracy to commit mutiny and revolt against the Empire, murder of two Imperial officers piloting the shuttle and destruction of Imperial property. Have you anything to say for yourself before the Khan pronounces sentence?"

"You may speak," Annika granted.

"I do not recognize the authority of this council," Scott wheezed. "You cannot call for a War Council, Crown Princess. That is power reserved for the leader of the Empire."

"The Regent. Yes," Annika drawled. "I will be soon paying my Uncle a visit. As for my authority, I have the law of Angkor Khan giving me the all the authority I need as the fifteenth reincarnation of the Great Khan. These officers are honoring their oaths to the Law and the Empire, therefore honoring their oaths to me. That is all the authority my War Council needs.

Are you prepared to hear sentencing for your treachery?"

Colonel Scott's face writhed in fury. "Bitch!" was his reply.

Annika froze him again.

She settled back in her throne and crossed her legs. "I sentence you to spacing. It will occur on the *Victor* so any of your crew who is under your influence will be given the benefit of observing the consequence of standing against their Khan. Your body will be secured so that the ship may get some use out of recycling your otherwise worthless atoms. I claim your estate as mine. Your wife and children are now my property and will be sent to the mines." She leaned forward. "You are stripped of your rank. I take your name from you. You are nameless and honorless."

"Noire? I revoke this...thing's Right of Privacy. Empty it, then we will dispose of it."

"Now, normally I would have you settle onto a couch for a deep scan," Noire said in a pleasant voice. "It makes a deep scan a little easier if I have time and you are comfortable. But, time is of the essence. So, I'll just have to improvise.

"To start, you'll have no need for the uniform. As the Khan has stripped you of that honor, you should remove it." The former officer moved woodenly, removing his flight boots, then stripping the flight suit off.

"Waste not, want not," Noire raised a finger. "Dispose of that in the recycling slot."

"Watch, sister, I have been practicing this, just for you."

The nameless, rankless shell of a man bent and picked up his boots and flight suit. His feet slapped on the deck as he goose-stepped to the recycling slot and dumped his clothing into it.

"Hilarious, Brother! Thank you!"

"You're welcome, my Khan!"

His feet slapped again as he returned to Noire and stood, wooden, at attention.

"All righty, then, let's get started, shall we?" Noire removed a pad from his pocket. "You may feel just a little pressure." His eyes glazed over to black. The former officer's eyes went wide and his mouth gaped open, the cords in his neck stretched tight. He began to quiver. Noire's fingers tapped a staccato on his pad. The tortured man screeched for five long minutes.

Then Noire was finished. His eyes returned to the Imperial green. His pad went into his pocket. "Interesting," he stated to the room. "A few new names for your list, my Khan. I'll update it immediately."

"You will follow this guard to the shuttle bay," he instructed the former officer. "He will take you to *Victor* for your execution."

"Now, back to business." Admiral Thiessen said as he stood and signaled an aide. "We have the First of the Mykonos Three's government for you, my Khan."

A holo formed over the table of an elderly, canine being. A brown, peaked cap sat on its head between erect ears. Grey fur surrounded its muzzle. Its eyes were sharp as they darted back and forth. "I am Philemon, First of the Mykonos Elders," it stated. "And, very likely Philemon, the only of the Mykonos Elders. To whom am I speaking?" The voice was old, tired.

"I am Annika Raudona Russolov, Khan of the Terran Empire," she stated. "I am here to discuss your future, Philemon."

"My future?" His laugh was a dry rasping. "I think your invasion has pretty well secured my future, Miss Russolov."

"No. Your future is not yet determined," she told him. "I have two options for you, First of the Elders. One, you surrender immediately. My troops will occupy your cities and villages, such as they are. Order will be restored and maintained. Your local laws and customs remain in effect, save where they contradict the Laws of the Empire.

"The aliens on your world who supplied you with the advanced weapons are to be detained and turned over to my troops. Should they resist your detaining them, my troops will assist yours.

"I will order my Medical Corps to come to Mykonos Three immediately and care for your ill and wounded. My Corps of Engineers will meet with you and your selected leaders to rebuild your planet. I predict your society will soon recover from this unpleasantness. You have much you can add to my Empire. I would not be surprised to see Mykonos Three a client world within five years and a member of the Empire within the next fifty.

"You would go down in Mykonos Three's history as perhaps its finest leader."

"An attractive offer," Philemon stated. "And if I refuse?"

"Then my troops will withdraw from the planet's surface," Annika replied. "My main battle line will enter a low orbit and destroy anything larger than a privy. Your planet will burn, First Elder. Your people will scatter and become feral. My Empire will monitor and when all possibility of resistance, all possible sign of civilization is gone, we shall take your world and do with it as we see fit. You are an attractive species, First Elder. Perhaps my generals would come and hunt your kind in your forests. For sport.

What is your decision, First Elder of the Mykonos people?"

Its jaw snapped open and closed several times. Then it asked, "What title do your people bestow upon you, Miss Russolov?"

"I am Khan."

"Then we are your people, my Khan," Philemon declared.

That afternoon, the Terran fleet reformed. The decision was to strike quickly. Admiral Thiessen would lead the bulk of the fleet from *Azahnti*. He would strike for Argulea and the Regent. His orders were to capture the Regent and the Empress alive and return them to Terra for trial. Many of the traitors on Noire's list were located on Argulea; he was to capture them.

Annika would take five dreadnaughts with their escorts and strike for Terra. It was imperative she get there and claim her crown before the enemy could respond.

She selected the Dreadnaught *Lord Klerrks Revenge* as her flagship.

The ship was named for the greatest hero of the Democracy Revolution. Lord Stanly Klerrk had been the first noble to oppose the Eighth's bloody decision to violate the Laws of Angkor Khan.

He was arrested, his family murdered in front of him. He was condemned to toil in the mines until he died. It took Lord Klerrk fifteen grueling years to build a following and revolt, joining the resistance which defeated the obscenity on the throne.

Lord Klerrk, on the balcony of Giza Palace, personally strangled the despot. The rebels were prepared to declare him the new Khan on the spot. There was a howl of disbelief as Lord Klerrk drew his knife and cried out, "As a loyal follower of the Law of Angkor Khan, I now declare myself a traitor, for I have stood against the seventh reincarnation of Angkor Khan and murdered him. For this crime, the only punishment is death."

There, on the balcony, Lord Klerrk became a legend by opening his own throat.

The ship was three quarters of a mile long and slightly over a quarter mile wide and tall. Four of the largest star drives ever built were attached to its stern. The blocky hull supported two heavy turrets on the upper and lower spines of the ship, each turret holding two massive mason rifles.

The forward third of the ship flared out wide, then tapered to a point carrying two more meson rifles. Launch and recovery bays mounted to the lower, forward hull allowed the *Lord Klerrks Revenge* to operate two hundred fighters and bombers. Missile launchers, smaller weapons turrets dotted the rest of the black, silver and grey hull.

Lord Klerrks Revenge was the largest dreadnaughts in the Terran fleet.

It was now her flagship, and awaited her alongside *Azahnti.* Annika and Admiral Thiessen admired the menacing vessel. "An excellent choice, my Khan," commented Thiessen. "It sends exactly the right message."

"Thank you, Uncle." Annika was pleased with his approval. "He is a handsome ship. I expect we shall gather much glory and honor together."

233

A young officer signaled to them. "My Khan, Admiral, the signal from *Victor* you have been waiting for." A holographic image floated above the dark table. A middle-aged officer, his dark hair greying at the temples, spoke. "My Khan, Admiral. I am Major Francis Alberts, Engineering officer and temporary commanding officer of the carrier *Victor*. The operation to secure this vessel is complete. The X.O. and weapons officers were both involved with Colonel Hopkins' mutiny and have been detained by your boarding party. Only three of the rest of the crew are sympathetic with the Regent. They have been likewise detained. *Victor* stands with the Khan and is prepared to do her bidding."

"Are you prepared for the execution?"" Annika asked.

"Yes, my Khan," Major Alberts responded. "Understandably, he was quite angry when he came aboard. He offered bribes and issued threats. Even in the airlock, he is still trying to plead his case."

"What did he offer you, Major?" she asked.

"Half a million credits if I let him escape. Now it's a knife in my belly when he does escape. I fear he hasn't accepted his impending death."

"I'll do him one better," Annika declared. "You are now Colonel Alberts and I award you command of the *Victor*. Serve me well."

The new Colonel saluted. "It shall be as you order, my Khan. Shall we proceed with the execution?"

The hologram changed to the view inside the airlock. There room was bright, a red beacon rotated over the airlock's exterior door. The nameless traitor was secured by the waist to a steel chair that had been welded to the deck in the airlock for the occasion.

Colonel Albert's voice came over the airlock's intercom. "You have been sentenced to death for treason, fomenting rebellion and murder. Do you have any last words?"

"Yes! Tell that little bitch the Savior is coming!" he screamed. "He will smite her down and save all of Terra from the

234

mutants and freaks of the galaxy!" He puckered his lips and spat. "That's for you, FREAK!"

The warning alarm sounded. A countdown could be heard as he raged. He screamed one last insult as the external door opened. The rush of the air yanked him towards the void. Only the belt at his waist kept him from flying out of the ship. The last of the air was soon gone and a layer of frost began coating everything in the room.

A tiny puff of vapor escaped his nose and mouth. He gasped, then gasped again. His hands went to his neck as his chest tried to expand, seeking precious air. He writhed in the chair as scales of ice covered him. Blood seeped from the corners of his eyes and floated from his ears. The flashing red light at the bottom of the holo showed his heart accelerating. He convulsed and jerked, trying desperately to breathe. His motions stopped after five minutes. Four more minutes, the flashing red light stopped as well.

"Damnit," Annika swore. She handed Admiral Thiessen a fifty-credit chip. "I should have known better than to bet you, Uncle."

"Well, I've attended more spacings than you have, Annika," he replied as he pocketed the coin.

Lieutenant Rita Rivas bounded into the room. "Hey, Mousey," she called. "Shake a leg. *Lord Klerrks* called a half a dozen times wondering where we're at."

She noticed Admiral Thiessen. "Uh, um, Admiral." Rita stammered, "I just came by to get Mouse, I mean Captain Russo...Uh..."

"At ease, Lieutenant Rivas," the admiral smiled. "I know what you mean. The Khan will be ready momentarily.

Minister Howland will be with you on *Lord Klerrk,* " he said. "I would advise you listen to his directions and act accordingly. You have come so far, Annika. I will see you on Terra in five weeks."

"Five weeks, Uncle." She gathered Rita and left for her ship.

"You dumb pftooting, don't you ever look and see..." he heard Annika admonishing Rita as the doors closed.

She sat at the desk, her hands folded before her. Ten days before, the two main battle groups had departed Mykonos.

The Empire was uneasy. The news channels were full of conflicting reports about the happenings on Mykonos. The Regent's office was silent, declining to comment.

Defense Minister Howland was unavailable.

Prime Minister Moritz Stype had appeared on several news programs after a week of uncertainty. "There is nothing to be concerned with," he assured the reporters. "Mykonos was a minor operation. The lack of news is probably Fleet Admiral Thiessen performing a post attack inspection. This is a common practice after a military operation; it provides an excellent opportunity to identify mistakes made during the campaign and correct any deficiencies."

"We will have to replace him when we get to Terra." Howland said. "He knows something is going on and isn't doing a good job covering it up."

The broadcast was her idea. After watching the Prime Minister's performance, she fretted some of her military's consciences might be vacillating as to who had legal authority to lead the Empire. She didn't want to lose a single soldier to a mistake in judgement. The Law was on her side. She had to show that to the Empire.

Howland agreed. If a single soldier's life was saved, he was in favor of her broadcast.

She looked square into the camera lens and began.

"Greetings. I am Crown Princess Annika Raudona Russolov Khan, Goddess/Queen of Terra, Imperial Army Captain, on temporary assignment from my squadron, the 433rd Bombardment, based on the Imperial carrier, *Vengeance*.

"I am broadcasting to you, the loyal soldiers of my Army and my Fleet, so you understand precisely what is happening. Twenty-two years ago, a terrible crime was perpetrated against our Empire and against me personally. My father, Emperor Robert De

L'Orange Khan was murdered. The murder had never been satisfactorily investigated.

"My father was a great Khan, a fine man, loyal friend and dedicated servant to the Empire. When he was murdered, the Imperial Council panicked and appointed his brother, the inferior Ming si Haun, to be the new Khan. This was not in keeping with the Law my ancestor, the Great Khan, had laid down."

The corner of her mouth turned up slightly. "Nineteen years ago, you may recall, I pointed out that Ming si was unsuitable to be Khan. He was reduced to Regent by the council, even thought there was no provision in the Law for a Regent. Six years ago, a horrendous crime was again perpetrated against me and our Empire, with the mysterious raider attack during my Naming Ceremony. *One hundred forty thousand* of our citizens were murdered, including four of my brothers and my beloved sister. The Regent has never explained where these raiders came from, nor has anyone, save the officers who failed the Empire in the Command post, been identified or punished.

"The File Committee selected me to serve the Empire as Khan. I have served alongside you as a soldier and a pilot. I have dived through hostile atmospheres to drop bombs and fired my weapons at enemies who threatened my comrades. I have seen our lives thrown away needlessly by a gross inferior who is sitting on my throne, sending us to die for no reason. I have watched the decline of my Empire, the endless excuses his failures.

"I have watched my Empire dying."

"ENOUGH!" she thundered, slamming her fist on the desk. "I will not idly sit by one more day and watch a single soldier die because the Regent is more concerned with lining his pockets. I shall no longer sit back and watch my Empire grow weaker while our enemies grow stronger.

"The Law of Succession clearly states that when the Khan dies, the File Committee will name the new Khan. I am that Khan. I have formed my War Council. As per the Law, I order the Imperial

Council be dissolved and all the left-hand ministers arrested. This is to include Morris Stype.

"I appoint Admiral Thor Thiessen as my War Lord and order him to arrest the Regent Ming si Haun NeKhan and bring him before my War Council on Terra. I appoint Gavin Howland as my Minister of Civilian Affairs, to run my government.

"Each of you, sworn soldiers of my Army, of my Fleet. Officers and enlisted. Men, women and beings. Terran and non-Terran. Each of you swore an oath, the same oath I swore. We swore to follow the Law and defend the Empire against all enemies.

"The enemy is on the throne now. He has surrounded himself with traitors who will try to convince you I am not suitable to be Khan, that the Imperial Council's voice outweighs the Laws Angkor Khan gave us.

"They will try and convince you that I am the traitor.

"I ask each of you to look to the Law and ask yourself: Am I upholding the vow I took when I swore to defend the Empire? Or have I become a willing slave to those who waste my life because it would profit them, instead of my Empire?

"After this broadcast, you will receive a list. These are the officers confirmed to be traitors. If you are true to your oath, you will arrest and detain them. If those around you are forsaking their oaths, then you must resist them to your dying breath.

"To my enemies on Argulea and Terra, hear this. I am coming."

Chapter 28

Nothing good ever happens between midnight and dawn. Gavin Howland was taught that as a young officer. His experiences over the last fifty years had only confirmed it. The incessant pounding on the door of his stateroom onboard the *Lord Klerrks Revenge* at this hour could only mean bad news.

A black girl wearing ensign pips on her collar was waiting. "Sir," she said, "General Han is calling from Terra. Priority Epsilon, channel Villa One." Howland was awake. "Notify the Crown Princess. My respects, I'll meet her in the Command briefing room in ten minutes."

Bad news indeed; Priority Epsilon was just about as bad as it could get. And to risk using Villa One, the ultra-secret otherspace channel. Not even Intelligence knew of the Villa series of channels. He threw on his robe, splashed water on his face and smoothed back thinning grey hair.

His aging body hurried to the briefing room and had just arrived when the Crown Princess entered. Gavin wished he knew her secret. Her uniform was perfect, her golden hair impeccable. She settled into her place at the head of the table. "Minister Howland. I am assuming something has happened, to meet at this hour."

Howland nodded. "An Epsilon Priority message from Terra."

"Proceed."

He placed his hand flat on the onyx surface. "Howland, Gavin," he announced. "Execute priority Epsilon." A holo appeared on the table.

It had been six years since Annika had seen General Han. He hadn't aged a bit, still the stocky bald officer with a firm jaw and warm eyes. He bowed and announced, "Crown Princess. Minister

Howland. I have received a priority message from Celtius Four which requires your immediate attention."

A worn, tired vision appeared. "This is Rory Grant, of Celtius Station. We have had an outbreak of Tyrus Phage here on Celtius Four. I have initiated Omega protocol. We will have the information packet available for transmission as soon as the fleet arrives." The image winked out.

"Gods." breathed Gavin. "Tyrus Phage."

"Who is the closest Battlegroup, General Han?" asked the Crown Princess.

"Yours, Highness."

"Very well. Convey this message to Admiral Thiessen. Inform him we shall be delayed by…" she looked to Howland.

"To do the job properly," he pondered. "Seventy-two hours."

"Very well. Seventy-two hours. Orders to the fleet, maximum speed."

Annika put in a call for Yuri. A sunlit jungle loomed behind him. "Annika!" he grinned. "What a wonderful surprise! How is our child?"

She had told him a week ago. He was head over heels with joy over the wonderful news. He was being awfully silly about their child. Like today. The baby was barely a month formed. How could it possibly feel?

"We are well, my love. Yuri, I have terrible news. I just received a message from Terra Command. About Celtius Four." She swallowed. "It is Tyrus Phage."

His face paled. "Gods below," he breathed. "There's no mistake?"

Annika shook her head. "Rory Grant himself sent the message. He's instituted the Omega protocols."

Yuri lowered his head. "Yes, that's best. It's the only way. Who is the closest Battlegroup?"

"Mine."

Yuri's eyes locked with hers. "They'll be glad it's you, Annika," he said.

She sighed. "Do you want me to call you before...?"

Yuri shook his head. "No. Just do it. Show them mercy."

Tyrus Phage was a biological weapon from Terra's ancient wars. Designed for human physiology, it mutated, destroying any life form to which it was exposed. It attacked through skin, forming colonies under the epidermis, presenting as large red and green blotches. A week after exposure, the victims became catatonic as their internal organs were consumed. Days later, they died. Rather than dying with the host, the phage continued to multiply, feeding on the corpse. The entire body was consumed and a new colony formed. One hundred percent infectious, one hundred percent fatal. And the phage would live for years, feeding on its victim before going dormant.

The only effective way of treating the phage was immolation. Wars would be stopped and enemies would unify to burn every square inch of an infected planet.

Thirty hours after receiving the message from Terra, the *Lord Klerrks Revenge* Battle Group had arrived at Celtius Four.

A fatigued, red haired woman appeared on the holo. She was clearly infected, the red/green swelling of the Tyrus Phage in dark splotches on her face.

"Katy?" Annika asked.

Katy O'Brien gasped, then smiled. "Raudona. I'm so glad it's you."

"I'm glad to be here too, Katy. Do you have the records ready to transmit?" Annika asked.

"Transmitting now," Katy replied. "We've all followed you since your Naming Day. Imagine, our little Raudona, a princess and a war hero. You've made us all so proud."

241

"Did I ever thank you enough, Katy?" Annika asked. "You and Mrs. Adams and Mister Grant? All the rest? You all helped me so much to grow up."

"All teenagers go through it, Sweetie," the doomed woman responded. "But I'm glad we were there for you."

"Yuri and I will be having a baby." Annika said,

"Oh, Raudona, that's wonderful." Katy sighed. "The download is complete. Rory, before he died, wanted me to tell you that he included a vid of the ship that did this." Of course, there had to be a ship involved. The phage was a weapon.

"Raudona…" Katy's voice caught. "Raudona, it's time. Do the colony first."

Annika muted the comm. "Target the colony," she said, her voice husky, shaken. "Transfer fire control to my station." The weapons officer reported ready. She clicked the comm back on. "Good bye, Katy. I love you." She pressed the firing button. The eight meson rifles fired.

For three days, the fleet orbited Celtius Four, pounding the surface. The ships fired in a precisely plotted attack plan, ensuring that every inch of the planet's surface burned.

Midway through the second day, the planet's mantle split. Lava began to surge from its core.

Annika stood in the conference room window, arms crossed. A junior officer made the mistake of offering her a chair. Her backhand slap broke his jaw, sending him flying across the room.

Rita stood with her for hours on end. She would check Annika's electrolyte levels and offer her the necessary dose. Annika would drink her fluids, staring at the planet below as her Battlegroup's work went on unceasingly.

On the third afternoon, the atmosphere suddenly flared and burned off. The fleet continued to fire, making sure the phage was consumed. Precisely seventy-two hours after the Crown Princess pressed the firing stud, the weapons of the *Lord Klerrks Revenge* went silent.

Celtius Four was once again a lifeless world.

Gavin Howland joined Annika in the conference room. "The warning buoys have been set," he told her, "and the mines are all in place. The last ship will close off the planet when we leave." Four buoys would warn any ship away from the planet; thousands of mines now circled the Celtius system to ensure no being could ever land there and try to locate any sign of the phage.

"My regards to the Admiral," Annika said. "Set the fleet course for Terra. Maximum speed is ordered. Faster would be better. I have the future of my Empire to attend to." Her cogitating of the stars went on, unabated.

Admiral Thiessen's fleet had come to Argulea. The Crown Princess's message had clearly had an effect. Two full fleets, more than one hundred capital ships, had been sent by the Regent to intercept the Admiral's. With no exception, all joined the Khan.

Admiral Thiessen had acquired a pair of *Azanhti's* sister ships, the *Aziana* and the *Azakana*. Each brought a full Battle Group with them. In all, his fleet now had five thousand fighters and bombers.

The Admirals were all old friends. Hector Ruiz, whose granddaughter was the Khan's personal bodyguard, had been a classmate of Thiessen's at the academy. Laura Moss had served with both over the years.

Admiral Moss brought the information on Arguela. The Regent was having difficulty mustering anyone to his cause. Very few of the officers on the Khan's enemy list had actual combat experience. Most had been political appointees. None had fleet battle proficiency.

"Their ships are a mixed bag," Admiral Moss reported. "Plenty of cutters, six newer destroyers. The heavies are all museum pieces. They are converting civilian ships into fighters by attaching weapons to them. They have a handful of Buccaneers and several

243

squadrons of the old Scimitar fighters. They'll have to use cutters carrying missiles if they want to attack us with small ships.

"For Arguela's planetary defense, there are twin command stations in orbit and several manned outposts. They control at least fifty weapons platforms, ranging from missile batteries to old-fashioned lasers. They have several thousand mines, but the fools haven't deployed them yet.

"General Kelly refused to join the Regent after they heard the Khan's message. The Regent arrested him along with his senior staff. He has put junior officers and politicians in charge. A few of the regular army has joined them, most of the army mutinied a week ago and has dispersed into the civilian population. They have confined what's left of the army into their barracks. There is a fanatic militia band that call themselves the Imperial Guard. The Regent has been supporting them for years, they're well-armed and dug in around the Palace of Amaar. Most of the Imperial Guard have little or no combat experience. They seem to be mostly fanatics and week-end warrior types, but I wouldn't discount them. Some of their members are ex-army."

"So, we'll blow through their fleet, then dig them out of the palace," observed Ruiz. "I see a weakness we can exploit…"

Colonel Mickey Morando saluted the launch officer of the *Aziana*. The sled holding his heavy *Manta* bomber released and he guided it into open space. Half again as long and twice as wide as the Icarus, the Manta had a three-person crew and carried nearly five times as much weaponry as the Icarus.

Morando hadn't risen to command of a bomber wing by being imprudent. His mentors had pounded into his head repeatedly, *Perfect planning makes the perfect attack.* Admiral Ruiz had attended the briefing personally. "Their Fleet Commander is an old infantry officer," he had told them, "so he's used to thinking of a two-dimensional battlefield. We're taking advantage of this by introducing the old fool to the third dimension."

The Regent's fleet would be confronted by the *Azahnti* battle group. Admiral Thiessen was gambling the enemy would rush his ships to confront *Azahnti*. Meanwhile, the *Aziana* and *Azakana* battle groups would come out of otherspace on the far side of the system, obscured by the sun. Colonel Morando's strike would wait in the sun's photosphere until the attack order was given.

Admiral Thiessen settled into his command chair, ready for battle. As the fleet came out of otherspace, they began to launch fighters, part of the ruse to keep the enemy commander's attention. The holo above the command platform showed the enemy fleet positioning and launching its own fighters.

"Sir, signal coming from the Imperial Guard lead ship." The comm officer looked barely out of his teens. Thiessen shook his head. They were so young these days.

The holo reformed, showing an ancient officer, sporting a bushy white beard and matching eyebrows. His white uniform jacket was festooned with medals and a purple sash. "I am General Thomas Bramble," he said with bravado. "I am the commanding the defense of the Argulea system. What traitorous scum am I speaking with?"

"I am Admiral Thor Thiessen neKhan, Warlord for Her Royal Highness Crown Princess Annika Raudona Russolov Khan, Goddess/Queen of Terra and soon Empress of the Terran Empire. I will warn you once, Bramble. Stand down and I will spare your lives, though you will be punished for threatening the Khan. Resist and I promise those of you who die today will be shown greater mercy than those I kill tomorrow."

"That's GENERAL Bramble, young whelp!" he shouted, shaking a fist. "Resist? Damn right, we're going to resist! The Regent is the rightful heir to the Imperial Throne, not that tit sucking kitten of a Princess of yours!"

Thiessen steepled his fingers. "Tell me Bramble," he said evenly, "how much fleet experience do you have?"

"I was chosen for my leadership," the old man thundered. "I was leading troops into battle when you were still having your arse wiped, you insol…"

"None, then," the Admiral interrupted. "Then, Bumble, I suggest you prepare to die." Thiessen thumbed his comm unit and issued a single word order.

"KILL!"

The bombers left their hiding spots around the sun. The first wave destroyed the two command posts and all five manned stations in minutes. The second wave pressed their attack on the Imperial Guard fleet, firing their missiles from behind. The enemy disappeared in a massive fireball. When it subsided, all that was left was an ever-widening field of debris. Buccaneers swept through the system hunting down and destroying any Imperial Guard ships that had escaped the carnage.

Argulea lay defenseless from space. The Regent's "fleet" had been devastated: there were no survivors to be found. The only injury to Thiessen's forces was a cracked knuckle on Colonels Morando's right hand, where he had gleefully punched his canopy frame when it was clear how successful the trap had been.

Imperial Guard Sergeant Patroine Harvin tried to make himself smaller in his fighting hole. Headquarters had announced the Khan's fleet's arrival. They all eagerly awaited the news that their courage and bravery had driven the fleet away. But there had been no news.

The bombardment started, around the palace. Funny, they weren't shooting up the city, as he would have expected. Everything was directed against their positions around the palace. Patroine had been in combat a long time ago, during the disastrous reign of Emperor Kim Choi Khan. He had his share of free-falling from drop ships onto a hostile world. He had never been under an assault drop.

Until today. He could see the fiery trails as they twisted and arced across the sky. Each fireball carried fifty-five troopers.

Several hundred fell in the space of a few minutes. Then came the god-awful BOOM-BOOM as each shuttle passed through transonic speeds. He needed to piss. No privy or spider can, either. He was either going to hold it or… He felt instantly better.

"Here they come!" the call came over his helmet comm. He looked over the edge of his fighting hole. Someone was firing smoke. Patroine dropped the infrared lens. Better, he could see movement now. "Hold your fire," he whispered to his squad. Most were middle-aged men and boys rallied to the cause of the Regent. He wasn't feeling so sure about the Regent now. Sure, it had been fun to run about and pretend to shoot up Imperial troops. But now that the time was here…He began to wish he had thought this through a little more.

He heard a soft whirring noise. Cautiously he looked up. Crap! A hummerbee! Drones built to hover over a position, looking for signs of movement. It relayed a signal back to the squad controlling it. When movement was detected, it would fire a hundred flechettes into the position. "Nobody move," he hissed into his comm. The whining noise of the drone picked up slightly. "Stop! Stop moving!" he cried, "It picked you up." There was a pop, then screaming. Mercifully, it didn't last long.

More whining, a flock of the hummerbees appeared overhead. Where there was one fighting position, there would be more. He knew the guys would be squirming as the hunters searched for them. "Nobody move!" he pleaded. "They will find and kill you. Relax, when they leave the Imps will follow." There was a pop and a scream, then another. His squad was beginning to panic.

Patroine found himself praying to the gods. There were more important things in life than money and politics. If he had listened to his wife, he'd be at home and safe. Instead, he'd tried to relive old glories from when he was a younger man. He was going to die. Today in this piss filled hole.

He heard another noise. Cautiously, he looked up. The Imperial soldier was in front of him. Patroine hadn't seen or heard him coming. His armor was the modern chameleon suit, shifting colors and patterns to match his surrounds. Golden sensors were located on the helmet where his eyes would be. He looked more like an insect than a Terran and his weapon was pointed straight at Patroine's face. "Buh-bye, glarpshite!" he heard. The weapon flashed and Patroine Harvin, Sergeant of the Regent's Imperial Guard, was dead.

The palace was taken after a short, intense fight. General Kelly had fooled everyone. As the bombardment started, his loyal officers who had appeared to support the Regent released the General. Inside the defensive perimeter, Imperial Guards suddenly found army units they thought were loyal turning against the Guard. The loyal troops followed the orders of their Khan.

There were no prisoners.

General Kelly escorted Thiessen through the halls of the palace. It was every bit as decadent as he expected. He suspected he would need a bath after walking through this cesspool of opulent depravity.

Ming si Haun was discovered hiding in one of his own dank cells. The soldiers decided to leave the former ruler in the cell. He cowered on the cot, perspiration soaking the armpits of his brilliant white uniform, as Thiessen approached. "You!" he bawled. "You have brought this down on me! Why couldn't you just go off and play with your pretty ships and leave me alone! I didn't do anything to you! Why are you always picking on me?"

"I swore an oath, Brother." It galled Thiessen to have to call this wasted pile of flesh brother. "An oath to the Empire and to the Khan. I have dedicated my life to the Empire while you whined and sold yourself to your wealthy friends. No more. I am here to take you to the Khan."

"No!" Ming si whimpered, curling into a ball.

248

Lord Klerrks Revenge slid majestically on his flight path and settled next to the *Azahnti*. Annika stood on the bridge, hands on hips, admiring the magnificent vessel. She was home. And Yuri was down there waiting for her.

Duty first. A shuttle was waiting to carry her and Rita down to Giza. There she would assume her duties as Head of State. There were a myriad of details to attend to, securing the Empire, warning enemies off.

Revenge to be planned.

The vid Rory Grant had transmitted from Celtius left no doubt as to the perpetrators. The Bougartd were a humanoid race. Adults were over seven feet tall and heavily muscled. Their skin ranged from charcoal grey to black. Their lower mandibles housed yellow teeth several inches long. A brutal race, they preferred to bully and steal from the lesser races. Two thousand years ago, they were given permission by the Galactic Council to commit unrestricted warfare on Terra. The Bougartd didn't have a massive fleet, but they had hundreds of heavily armed raiders that wreaked havoc on the Empire, especially the frontier worlds. Emperor Kim Choi Khan begged the Galactic Council to stop the attacks. Emperor Robert De L'Orange threatened war if the raids didn't stop. As the Terran fleet grew, the raids lessened. Still, from time to time, the Bougartd would try a new tactic or weapon.

The vid showed a Bougartd raider dropping the phage weapon.

Annika vowed to put an end to the Bougartd.

The shuttle ride was quiet. Excited to be going to the fabled Giza Palace, Rita left Annika to her thoughts. Colonel Campion called her on the comm to check on the Khan's status and insinuated he might transfer her, keeping the job of personal guard of Annika himself. Rita was mortified. Not only did she take great pride in protecting the Khan, Mouse had become her best friend. She couldn't imagine not having Annika around. Rita caught the sly grin on her boss's face.

"Respectfully, Sir," Rita said in her most formal voice. "If you EVER try that kind of glarpshite on me again, you discover what taking a full clip from my rifle up your ass feels like!"

"You're late!" came the familiar greeting from Miss Norris as Annika rushed past. It was so good to be home, back amongst familiar people and surroundings.

"Tea, Miss Norris. I'll have several guests today," she called as she entered her office. Rita was stumped by the exchange; she would have thought Annika would have a more respectful staff in the palace.

Within minutes, Thor Thiessen and Gavin Howland arrived. Annika was seated behind her desk, not wasting any time getting to work. "Gentlemen," she greeted them, "what are the status of the trials?"

"They have begun, my Khan," reported Howland. "Minor officers and notable civilians to start. I expect to start the Regent's hearing within the week. I will have the recommended sentencing tomorrow morning."

"They are approved," she answered. "I will accede to the recommendations of my judges. Have number one and two been arrested yet?"

"Kermit Blount has been taken to the Intelligence Office at the order of your brother," Howland answered. "I can request he be transferred to our custody, if you wish."

Annika shook her head slightly. "No," she decided, "he is one of theirs. They will deal with him. What of number one?"

"Confined here in Giza," Thiessen stated. "Trying him could be problematic. He still wields considerable power and is nearly as popular as you."

Annika thought for a few minutes. "Leave him to me," she stated. "I will take care of it this afternoon."

Morris Stype sat on her couch as he had so many times before, looking kindly. Annika wished she could return to the time when she trusted this man. But the evidence proved otherwise. He was her enemy. He would die.

"I should suppose you would like an explanation," he said. "You deserve as much."

"I deserved your loyalty," she hissed. "What was it that turned your back against the Empire you've served for seventy years?"

"You have my loyalty, Majesty," he said smoothly, "but I have done what I have done for the good of the Empire. Your father would have taken us to war. Millions would have died. Now, you want to take us to war. Don't you see there is a better way? Given the chance, I could have ended all this hostility in our part of the galaxy. We would have peace, rather than this endless cycle of war."

"At the cost of our lives!" the Khan screamed. "Our freedoms, the order we enjoy that comes from the Laws my ancestor laid down. You wouldn't have given us peace! We would have fought each other to the death and allowed the lesser species steal from us what is ours!"

"So, you will go to war and steal what is theirs!" he shouted back.

"It is my birthright," was Annika's tight-lipped reply. "It is the duty Angkor Khan left for me. All that I do is for the good of my Empire and my people."

"Savior!" she snarled. "I see you for what you are. Weak. Inferior. You have made war against me, attempted to murder me. Lied to me. You deserve public humiliation and a painful death.

"But taking you to trial would be problematic. Instead, my bodyguard, Rita will escort you to a private room. She will leave you inside with a gun. One bullet.

"You will be taken down to the compost and buried there. It will be a fitting end for your transgressions. Be gone from my sight."

Morris Stype, number one, stood. "Might I use your personal weapon, Majesty?" He asked.

Annika removed her sidearm, ratcheted it several times until there was a single bullet in it. She handed it to Rita, who took Morris by the arm and dragged him out.

Annika sighed, for Miss Norris entered with another basket of paperwork.

Yuri waited in their apartment. Rita opened the door for her and there he was. "Yuri!" Annika cried, flinging herself into his arms. The palace could have exploded, the universe collapsed into a massive black hole and still Yuri and Annika would have stood there, her legs wrapped around his waist, his hands holding her ass.

"How is it every time I see you, you become even more beautiful?" marveled Yuri. "I tell myself it can't be possible, then there you are."

Annika grabbed the door and started to close it. She popped her head out and grinned at Rita. "If you hear screaming...Yeah, well, you know... Uh...yeah, see ya!" The door slammed shut and Rita heard the lock activate.

They were undressed before they got to the bedroom. The three months they had been apart wasn't the longest they had been separated. But the civil war and the Tyrus Phage drove them together as never before. Their lovemaking was frantic, as though it were to be the last time.

Afterwards, they lay tangled in the sheets. Yuri pressed his ear to Annika's stomach and whispered, "Do you hear me, Baby? I am your Papa. You are the child of the most beautiful woman in the universe, although you can only see her insides right now."

Annika tittered, "He can't hear you, silly! He's barely two months old."

Yuri shook his head and tilted his head with his nose in the air. "You forget who is older, wiser and smarter, my love. And who is the medical doctor here? Hmmmm?" Yuri kissed and spoke to her baby bump. "Baby, Papa knows you can hear him. You let your mama know, too."

Tears formed at the corners of Annika's eyes. She rolled on her side and Yuri cuddled with his wife. Their hands went to her belly. *So, this is love,* she thought as they drifted off to sleep: *This is my family.*

Annika wished she could be present for the trial of the Regent. Gavin Howland warned her away. "Your presence would be intimidating to the trial board," he explained. "We know he is guilty. The board will deliver us a conviction. We must maintain the correct image of the trials. The public won't stand for it if you appear to be influencing the process. Patience, my Khan. He will be delivered to you in good time."

She commandeered a small holo emitter for her office, and she and Rita watched the proceedings until Miss Norris brought more paperwork or announced some visitor. The efficient secretary would snap the holo off and Annika would go back to work, grousing under her breath.

She fretted about her appearance. She would study her growing belly in the mirror, turning side to side, rubbing her hands over the growing bump. "Yuri, am I fat?" she would ask. "I think I am looking fat." Yuri tried to avoid the question, but she would pester him.

"No, you are not fat," he would tell her. "I see our child growing inside you. Doctor Bond assures me our child is growing normally and is healthy."

Hmmmm…" she would answer. "Yes, that is what he told me. But I still think I am looking fat."

The trial ended. Annika hadn't been called as a witness, to her disappointment. She was dutifully working her way through the morning basket of reports when Gavin Howland burst unannounced into her office. He was wearing a large smile.

"Highness," he reported, "guilty, on all counts."

Annika whooped and leapt from her chair. She danced around her desk, grabbed Howland and whirled in circles, laughing.

"Howland, this is wonderful!" she exclaimed. "Assemble the War Council. No, better, assemble the court. This afternoon! In the Throne Room." She raced around her desk, calling "DOHLMAN!" He appeared at her elbow. "Uniform," she snapped, "summer weight. I'll change at lunch. Miss Norris, inform the court. I am calling an assembly in the Throne Room, one o'clock."

Annika changed into the black and green uniform, her Captain's bars muted on her collar, tiny gold wings on her left breast. She checked her appearance. Dohlman had done it cleverly again; her baby bump was hardly noticeable.

At precisely one o'clock, Rita opened the door for Annika. She strode quickly across her Throne Room, courtiers and officers bowing, curtseying or saluting as she passed. She settled into her throne with majestic grace. "Bring him," she ordered.

A door crashed open; two guards dragged the struggling Regent Ming si Haun across the hall, standing him before the Khan. He was still wearing his sparkling white uniform with the gold trim and braid. The collar was torn and missing; she assumed the guards had removed his undeserved rank. Gone, too, was his purple sash and elaborate display of equally undeserved medals. His eyes were wet with tears; even now his lower lips quivered and drooled at his niece's countenance.

"Uncle, what am I to do with you?" she asked. "My War Council has confirmed what I have known since I was five years old. You are worthless and weak, an inferior sitting on my throne.

"And you would try and make war with me! Oh, Uncle, how many of my loyal subjects fell victim to the belief of your wicked, wicked lies? Can you make restitution for them? No?

"And this," she slid her knife from its sheath. "Do you recognize this? It's the knife of the foul assassin you sent after me years ago.

"Uncle, you are family. I have learned much about family. Pity, you never met my husband's family. I am so blessed.

"I expect you anticipate this bond between us will warrant you some mercy from your Khan. I am prepared to be merciful. All you have to do, before this congregation, is admit to me you are inferior."

He looked as though she had slapped him. The unnerved look changed in milliseconds to one of fury. "Never!" he shouted. "You are a FREAK!" He cleared his throat and spat at the young Khan.

Her leap was too swift to follow. The knife in her right hand was pressed against his throat. She nodded to the guard on his right, who grabbed the hair on top of Ming si's head and pulled it back, exposing his throat. A trickle of blood blossomed under the tip of her knife.

"Uncle, I don't think I quite understand what you said," Annika purred. "Can you repeat that?"

Ming si's reply was a strangled growl.

Ah, I see your problem," Annika said brightly. "You're having trouble breathing! Here, let me see if I can help." With that, she pressed the knife slowly into his trachea. He struggled, making a gurgling noise.

"I simply cannot understand you!" Annika feigned exasperation. "Perhaps you're just not getting enough air?" She twisted the knife, opening the hole in his throat wider. Blood now

255

flowed freely, staining the front of his dandy uniform. He began to convulse.

"Ah-HA!" she announced. "A seizure! My husband is a doctor; he has taught me numerous things I can do to stop a seizure. Let me see…" Her tongue curled out like a school child focusing on a difficult task. The knife punctured the back of his throat and began to probe the spongy muscle behind it, tapping about on the vertebrae. "Ah, right there." The announcement was triumphant as the tip of the knife found its way between the bones.

"Hold still. I have to be very careful here," she said in mock seriousness. The knife entered Ming si's spinal column. Annika stared deep into his fluttering eyes. "Die, inferior!" she snarled as the knife wiggled side to side, severing the spine. Her uncle's eyes rolled back and he slumped. Annika pulled the knife to her right, slicing open the side of his neck, and jumped back. Blood sprayed as a squeak escaped from Ming si's mouth. The guard released him and he fell in a messy pile on the floor. Blood pooled under his body and around his head.

She stood over his body, breathing heavily. His blood had sprayed on her, a trickle ran down the side of her face. She licked and tasted it, then spat. The courtiers stepped back, for Annika's visage was wild, feral.

Dohlman appeared with a towel. She wiped her knife and returned it to its place on her arm.

She took her place at her throne. Two guards bent to drag the body away. "No," she ordered, "Leave it there for now. Summon my mother."

Lorraine entered Annika's Throne Room minutes later. Her hands were bound in front of her. Annika gave her a quick scan. Her mother's thoughts toward Annika were bitter, hateful. There was nothing left between them, save for resentment and animosity.

The Empress shrugged at the sight of the body of Ming si. She stepped back to avoid the pool of blood. "You little fool!" she

256

hissed, "He was a tool, but a useful tool. Now there is nothing I can do to save you."

"Save me?" Annika asked incredulously. "Save…me? From what? Your ambition? Your inferior plans? Just what were you going to save me from, Mother?" "

"All this!" The Empress Lorraine De L'Orange neKhan waved her hands. Bright sun reflected off the chains holding her, long fingernails glittering. "This joke they call a court. This illusion of power they've fed you since before you were born! You little freak, don't you realize you're nothing more than an obscene experiment? Do you really think you run anything here? You just murdered the last tool I had to protect you. You'll be on your own now, little Red. A pitiful toy in their sad little game."

She straightened herself regally. "Go ahead. Kill me. Kill me like you did your uncle. Kill me like all those poor souls you've murdered. What's one more dead body to a genetic freak show like you?"

"No, Mother, I won't kill you." Annika said. "I won't make you a martyr. Be grateful, such a small thing as an egg you donated bound us forever together. It is the only thing saving your life.

"My heirs won't have to suffer the way my brothers, sisters and I did. Your ambition outweighed any love you could have shown us. My husband and I will not repeat that mistake." Her hand unconsciously rubbed her belly.

"I have decided I will not kill my own mother, much as you deserve it," the Khan announced. "Nor will I take from you your title of Empress, since it seems to be the only thing you value in life.

"You are to go to the temple on Nikuman and there fulfill a life of silent service to the prisoner miners there. You will take a vow of silence and never speak again. I have instructed the bonzes if you cannot keep your mouth silent, then they are to remove your tongue. I will allow you to keep your title of Empress, but I strip you of your name. When you die, an empty urn will be placed beside the urn of my father, so he can say he had a wife. But your

257

body will be consigned to the compost heap, so my Empire may reap value from your worthless body. Be gone."

The nameless empress was led away, still regal as she went to her fate.

Annika stood. "I now claim my title and crown. There cannot be two Empresses in the Empire. Therefore, at my coronation, I will take the title of Queen."

Annika Raudona Russolov Khan, Goddess Queen of Terra, future Queen of the Terran Empire, straightened herself. She held her head imperiously high. She smoothed a hand over her uniform, Perfect. Her gold hair blazed in the sunlight as she marched out of her Throne Room.

Chapter 30

Thousands of workers, their gray uniforms adorned today with a red arm band, installed temporary seats to create a massive bowl on the Plaza of Giza Palace. The War Council knew it was critically important that every being in the known galaxy, particularly the governments surrounding the Terran Empire, see the coronation of the new Khan.

Four legions in combat gear marched into the Plaza. They formed long rows along the entire parade route. They were followed by crews from the fleet, then various service corps. Leaders of the Empire's worlds entered, each wearing cotton boots to comply with the Great Khan's order that no non-Terran foot ever again touch Terra's precious soil. First Daughter of the Vinithri, the Empires most valued ally, lead the procession, as was her right. Other non-human species, member worlds of the Empire, followed.

The affiliated worlds entered next. From smaller, less advanced planets in the Terran Empire, many had never been off their home worlds. Most, such as the Eldest of the Mykonos, craned their heads (or what passed for heads) about, marveling at the diversity of the Empire.

The delegation from the Galactic Council arrived. The president of that body was a Trilithon, a gaseous being wearing an encounter suit. S/he was accompanied by one hundred twenty-five beings from the council, including ten Bougartd. Security had wanted them fitted with tracking collars, but the Khan had forbidden it. "They are my guests," she informed Howland. "Let us be magnanimous and welcoming."

An ancient bugle sounded, cue for a column of a thousand horsemen to enter the Plaza. At the front was the Crown Princess. For the ceremony, she wore the traditional leather breeches and jerkin of her ancient ancestors, a skin cap and a cape of bear skin. A quiver of arrows and a bow adorned her saddle.

The thousand riders that accompanied her were dressed in variations of her uniform. Yuri rode at her right side. Admiral Thiessen and Gavin Howland were adjacent to Yuri. Behind them, a rider carried the horns and tail of the ox standard of the Khan. Once they passed the Necropolis entryway, there was a shout and Annika led her horde in a charge across the Plaza.

Annika, Yuri and her chiefs stormed up the stairway leading to the stage. Yuri leapt off his horse and helped his pregnant wife to dismount. Annika swaggered to the center of the stage, placed her hands on her hips and raised her chin imperiously. With her voice amplified by a concealed microphone, her loud declaration carried across the city and the Empire.

"I am Crown Princess Annika Raudona Russolov Khan. Goddess/Queen of Terra. I claim this Empire mine, for all my people. Is there anyone here who would challenge me for my crown?" It was theater, but of deadly earnestness. Years before, at her Great Grandfather Zanther Khan's coronation, a drunk had stumbled down to challenge the Khan. Zanther had slain him on the spot.

No being challenged the diminutive Khan. Her cape swirling, she spun, tramped to her throne and sat with a flourish.

Warlord Thor Thiessen ne-Khan stepped forward, bearing a plain, steel sword. "Highness, you are now the sword and shield of the Empire. Behind you stand ready the sons and daughters of all Terra. Let this sword serve to represent that you alone stand between your people and the evil which seeks to destroy us." Annika took the sword in her right hand, stabbing the tip into the floor.

Noire stepped before his sister, handing her a bullwhip. "My Khan, you are now the defender of our most sacred commandments, the Laws of Angkor Khan, greatest of all Khans. May this whip prompt you to uphold the law against all who would threaten or disobey." Annika accepted the whip. She stood, uncoiled it, then spun it around and cracked it.

All the Terrans, as well as the member world representatives, stood and bowed. In a single voice, they pledged, "I swear obedience, my Khan!" Annika coiled the whip and fastened it to her belt.

Teresa strode forward, bearing a falcon on her arm. "My Khan, you are our example of Terran pride, fierceness, honor and mercy. Be reminded by this falcon, to keep Terra forever mighty and free." Teresa placed the falcon on Annika's arm and removed the fierce raptor's hood. The crowd cheered, "HooooOOOO! HooooOOOO! HooooOOOO!"

Annika cried "VICTORIOUS! For ten thousand years!" The falcon flew from her arm with a powerful stroke.

The crown floated toward the Queen-to-be on a red pillow borne by an awestruck page boy. It gleamed in the sunlight, the steel circlet and hoops polished to a fine sheen. Its cap was now the blood red of Annika's file, replacing the burnt orange of her father.

Gavin Howland lifted the crown and held it high. "Crown Princess Annika Raudona Russolov Khan, fifteenth reincarnate of our beloved founder, Angkor Khan, the Gods who created you watched you carefully for imperfection, have declared you most perfect of all their children and selected you to succeed your father, Robert De L'Orange Khan. Do you now accept the mantle and crown as the Queen of the Terran Empire and Guardian of the Law?"

"I do," Annika declared, head held high. She knelt upon the red pillow the page had placed before the throne.

Gavin Howland cried out, "Gods above, Gods below, Gods of the wind and sky! Gods of the grasses and the endless steppes! Look with favor as I crown your daughter and declare her Queen Annika Raudona Russolov Khan of the Terran Empire!" He lowered the heavy crown on her head and seated it firmly.

He dropped to a knee and proffered his hand, helping the pregnant Queen rise. Once on her feet, she raised the sword to the crowd, as the whole of the Empire was seized with joyous rapture.

Her first order of business was to summon her War Council. The entire wing of the palace around the Council Chamber had been emptied and secured. The desks had been replaced with a large oval black topped table, holo emitters and imbedded keyboards. Vid screens were mounted to the walls, each imaging a planet or streaming statistics. The Khan had ordered all the council chambers to be so outfitted.

The War Council now stood at twenty-four, plus the Queen. She had changed into her Captain's uniform and taken her seat at the war table. Across her knees lay the sword of her office.

"My Empire must be secure," she declared. "We will never again let a single Terran die unavenged, nor allow any *Ouste-Woorldaire* to dictate to Terra. Never! What is our plan?"

Admiral Thiessen stood. "If it pleases your Majesty," he stated, "we have been working on such a strategy." The holo emitter displayed a star field, swathed in numerous colors. "This is the Sagittarius Arm," he indicated. "This blue streak is Terra. This red area here, the Bougartd. The yellow is the Galactic Council. As mighty as they are, the Bougartd has tied itself with the Galactic Council. And this works to our advantage. The Bougartd economy depends on the Council. Their industrial capability is limited because they would rather intimidate and steal. Intelligence is not highly valued by the Bougartd society. Brute strength and intimidation is. As such, the Galactic Council uses the Bougartd as their means of protection and to keep the other worlds in line.

"Presently, we are not prepared to defeat the Bougartd. We have the ships, yes. But the criminal actions by the Imperial Council have left us in a poor state of repair and training. Further, if you look closely at our Empire..." he touched a control on the table. The blue area representing Terra expanded, the rest of the map disappeared. There were dozens of dark spots riddling the representation. "There are too many unaffiliated systems within our borders. These provide prime jumping off points for Bougartd raiders.

"Our plan is to acquire these non-aligned worlds. They will be given the opportunity to join us willingly. But, should they refuse our offer, then they shall be put to the sword, thereby giving our Fleet and our Army needed training. I would estimate no more than twenty years will be sufficient to prepare for our all-out assault on Bougartd space. And once the Bougartd fall, the Galactic Council will crumble behind them." Thiessen sat.

Noire stood. "Imperial Intelligence has the necessary assets on most of the non-aligned worlds. I anticipate we will have successfully infiltrated the rest within the year. I have provided this War Council with the available information we have gathered on our neighbors. We also have sapper units on each world, prepared to start covert operations in support of our diplomats. Or our army." He returned to his seat.

"Ladies. Gentlemen." Annika leaned forward. "I approve this plan. Warn my enemies; I am coming."

Chapter 31

In the Giza nursery, the eight three-year-old children assembled. Their classes for the day had been cancelled. The children were taken back to the dormitory and made to dress in their finest clothing. *Stand straight! Chins up! Not a wrinkle on your uniforms, not a hair out of place!* The Proctors took note of which were handling the change in schedule and who was having difficulty.

The head Proctor spoke in gentle, but firm voice. "Children, you are being afforded a remarkable opportunity. Since the times of your Great Grandfather Angkor Khan, the children of the Khan have not met their parents until the Presentation Day at age five. However, your mother and father, Queen Annika and Prince Yuri, would very much like to meet you today. Isn't that exciting?"

The tiny girl with blonde hair and a blue dress wailed. "What did we do wrong, Proctor?" Her crying instigated mass weeping. The Proctors took notes, registering how the children reacted to this change.

"You have done nothing wrong," said the Proctor. "The Queen is quite interested in each of your development. And I believe she has a surprise for you. Now, hurry, and get in line. She is coming."

The door opened and a pretty lady with yellow hair entered with a tall man who had curly hair and moustache. The children all bowed, except the Blue, who stood, shaking, mouth open and eyes wide.

Annika knelt before the terrified little girl and took her in her arms. "Sweetie, Shhhhhh, it's all right," Annika cooed in the child's ear. "I'm your mommy. You don't have to be afraid." She kissed the Blue softly on the cheek. "This is your papa." Yuri knelt and wrapped his arms around the child.

"Hello," he said in a tender voice. "I have been so looking forward to meeting you."

Annika struggled to her feet. "We have looked forward to meeting all of you!" she exclaimed. A chair was provided and she sat. "Come, let me see you all." The children gathered around her, curious but cautious. She opened her arms and, in turn, hugged and kissed each one. Yuri still stood, holding Blue in his arms. Her head lay on his shoulder and she was smiling.

A boy wearing grey poked Annika in the stomach. "Mommy, you sure are fat."

"Silver!" a Proctor said sharply, "what have we said about touching people?"

"But she is fat!" the little boy protested.

Annika looked to the Proctor. *"Silver?"* she wondered. It was then she noticed there was no child wearing black.

"Silver, asking questions is good," his mother explained. "I am big right now. But that's one of the surprises your papa and I have for you. Who knows what pregnant means?"

The girl in yellow waved her hand. "It means when people are going to have a regular baby the regular way." Yellow couldn't hide her glee at being first to answer.

"Yes! Very good, Yellow!" Annika said. "Goodness, you remind me so much of your Aunt Teresa. She was Yellow File, too.

"So, children, the reason why Mommy is so big is - I'm going to have a baby. You will all have a younger brother in just a few months."

"Will he be an inferior?" asked the Green boy.

Annika shook her head. "He can't be Khan. But he will be every bit your younger brother. Your papa and I will love him as much as we love each of you."

Blue asked Yuri, "Is that true? Do you love me, Papa?"

"Of course, I do, little one," he replied. "I love each one of you. And your little brother inside your mommy. And I love your mommy very, very much."

"Now for our other surprise," announced Annika. "Christmas will be in two weeks. Your papa and I normally go back to Russia for the holiday. But this year, we have decided to have Christmas right here, in the palace! Grandpa Andrei and Grandmother Clara will be here. Oh, it will be such a grand time!"

Her daughter, in a dress of royal purple, pulled Annika's pant leg and asked, "Mommy, what is Christmas?"

It was a magical Christmas for the Russolov family. The heirs, never having been exposed to a holiday, gazed in wonder at the colossal tree their parents arranged. Recalling how she reacted to her first real Christmas tree, Annika was determined to have a live tree for the celebration. Grandmother Susan brought birds for each of the heirs to hang on the tree and spent several days after classes teaching them to make ornaments of their own.

Andrei was a doting grandfather, spending hours with his grandchildren on his knee, telling stories and teaching them old songs. Silver pulled on his grandfather's beard, disbelieving anyone really grew hair from his chin.

Christmas Eve came with the traditional feast. Clara had gone to the kitchens and made sure everything was prepared to her liking. Members of Annika's government arrived with their families, adding to the joy and happiness. Noire and Teresa attended. Noire was all smiles and laughing, singing with the carolers, chasing the children during their games.

"I have never seen you like this, Brother. It suits you."

"Ah, my Khan, life is too serious all the rest of the year. It is good when I can relax and be as other people."

"Are you that dissatisfied with being head of my Intelligence?"

"Gods, no! I am so excited to be doing the one job in the Empire I am so passionate about. Since the untimely death of Kermit Blount during his vivisection, I have come to appreciate the subtleties and details of my position. Indeed, this is truly what the File Committee designed me for. Thank you so much, my Khan!"

"Noire, for tonight, would you treat me as your sister?"

"Are you two going to talk shop all evening?"

Teresa strolled over, a champagne flute in her hand.

"Sister! I am so glad you could attend! Happy Christmas to you both!"

Annika's eight children went racing by, screaming. Behind them was Andrei, arms spread wide and roaring.

"If only we had holidays like this when we were young." <

"Yes. My children will."

"Promise me, Teresa, you'll come to the farm when the baby is born? Please? I can think of no on I trust more to deliver my son than you."

"Of course, Annika."

Spring came to the steppe. Andrei and Clara had given Yuri and Annika a one hundred acres parcel of land, cut from the Russolov family holding as a Christmas gift. As soon as the thaw came, he raced north to survey the property and get it ready for planting.

Annika remained in Giza through March, then moved to the farm in anticipation of the baby's birth. Yuri demanded she go to New Moscow for the delivery, while Annika insisted she wanted to have her child on the farm. They compromised. Annika would stay in the guest cottage they lived in when they first became a couple and she would not have Rita beat him up. Yuri would run the farm. They would both make plans for their new home.

Teresa arrived a few days before the due date, accompanied by two women in hooded robes. As they entered the house, Annika recoiled in horror!

"Banshees! You brought banshees into my home?"

"Relax, Sister. These are not banshees. The witches of Scarborough and I have developed these women. We call them sirens. They are empaths, not telepaths. Since they are a natural

talent, there is no need to fear them. We are working with them to use with our healing arts. To demonstrate."

Annika thought she could see the veil of one of the sirens move with exhaled breath. A feeling of wellbeing and comfort swept through her. "Oh my," she said, feeling sanguine, "that feels…wonderful."

"I thought you would like it. Childbirth is extremely stressful, both on mother and child. While it is the most natural thing for a Terran woman to experience, you are a special case, because of your superior breeding. I spoke with Tahn about this. He believes everything will be fine, but agrees we should take this precaution."

Days later, Annika awoke with terrible cramps. She struggled through the day uncomfortable and feeling sick. That evening, she wasn't hungry and went to bed early. Yuri convinced his wife to let him examine her. He called Teresa at the main house. "You should bring your friends over," he said. "I believe it will be time soon."

Annika was in labor for six hours. In the time, she alternated between angry rages and piteous weeping. Baby was uncomfortable too, not understanding why Mama was writhing and twisting him so. The sirens sang their soothing music, but mother and child were feeding off the anxiety of the other.

Teresa fitted Annika with a neutralizer. Her sister was a powerful broadcast telepath and she feared anyone within Annika's range would be in danger.

The time grew closer. Baby had turned and the natural process flowed smoothly. Annika regained her mental equilibrium and could follow the instructions from her sister. Yuri held her hand and wiped her brow.

"Push, Annika, push. He's crowning. Push, Sister!"

Annika screamed one last time. She could feel her son leave her, relief of the pressure. A moment later, she heard the gasp and tiny cry.

Teresa cleaned the child with practiced hands and lay him on his mother's chest.

She cradled him and said, "Look, Yuri. Our son. Our precious son, Robert...

"Anni, he is SO handsome!" Marianne exclaimed. Robert lay cradled in her arms, blinking his eyes and yawning.

"I think he's tired, Marianne; let me put him down." Her hover chair-bound friend reluctantly handed the baby over and sighed as Annika lay him in the bassinet Grandmother Clara had provided. "It has been in our family for generations," Annika said with pride. "Andrei is thrilled his grandson is sleeping where he once laid Yuri and where he himself once slept."

"So, tell me about him. Where did you meet? What does he do? Answers, Marianne, I need answers!" Annika demanded as she poured the tea and handed a cup to her oldest friend.

"I'm surprised you don't recognize him," Marianne replied. "He was with us the last night on Vespa..."

Annika's brow furrowed as she went over the faces from the horrible night. Then she gasped. "That boy! The medic who saved your life! One of my soldiers?"

Marianne giggled. "I did ask you to introduce me to one of your soldiers back at Saint Francis," she reminded her friend. "His name is Thomas Quinn. He is one of your soldiers for only six more months. Then, my dear friend, he and I are getting married!" She held up her left hand, showing off the starry ring. "He's already bought a sizable plot of land on Percii Seven. We'll have a farm. We're going to build a big house and orphanage."

"Percii is terribly close to the Galactic Council border," Annika fussed. "Particularly the Bougartd. Do you think moving there is a wise decision?"

Marianne shrugged, "It's where we'll be needed, Anni," she answered. "The Bougartd raids have left hundreds of orphans along the border. Thomas and I can't have children of our own. But we can care for the children who need love the most. You'll come to our wedding? Would you be my maid of honor?""

Annika clasped her friend's hand. "I wouldn't miss it for anything," she promised.

Chapter 32

Six summers came and six winters passed.

Annika and Yuri built a stately home on the land their parents had given them. Yuri left the running of the farm to Andrei and Clara. He returned to his beloved clinic, caring for the people in the region. He had purchased land and was building a fine, modern hospital.

For Annika, the farm was a godsend. She stayed in Giza to handle the affairs of her Empire. The expansion of her Empire to the outlying non-aligned worlds was going better than expected. Many of the worlds wouldn't fight, preferring to ally themselves with the young Queen rather than face her wrath. Yet, some worlds opposed her ambassador's advances. They soon found themselves visited by her Fleet and Army. The plan devised by the War Council was coming to fruition. The non-aligned worlds were joining the Empire. Or being invaded. Joining meant privilege. Defiance led to death and worse.

Giza afforded her time to spend time with her heir children. Annika marveled at how unique each child was. Green and little Blue were the superior brains. Annika knew one of them was destined to be the future Khan. Yellow was so like her Aunt Teresa, full of kindness, compassion and empathy. Red was an athlete, Orange a scholar. Purple and White spent hours together, mindspeaking quietly.

Silver worried her. His curiosity about everything around him was becoming dangerous at times. Already he had broken several bones from his "experiments," normally involving a risky derring-do.

She spent two weeks in three in Giza, the others at the farm. There, she had her office to get her work for the Empire done and still have time for Yuri and her family. She and Yuri had three new children: Anja Clara, Thor Gavin and Pia Rebecca, with another on the way.

Robert had started school and was taking after his father, brilliant and studious. Yuri was proud of his boy and spoke often of Robert following Yuri's path to Moscow University and becoming a prominent physician. Anja had started early school as well, she was so much like her namesake, the Queens own sister, Anja. Beautiful and strong willed.

Annika had the heirs at the farm as much as she was able. They had their schooling and required many off-world adventures. She remembered the trips fondly and would reluctantly allow the Proctors to marshal them about her Empire. On occasion, she or Yuri would accompany them. Yuri enjoyed the trips and would bring Robert, so the two of them could learn the marvels of other worlds.

It was such a fine summer day on the farm. Yuri had planted a beech grove and added plants from other worlds, including a savassava tree from distant Hydriaphon. The tree had a gnarled trunk and broad leaf covered branches. He and Annika spent hours under the tree together reading poetry. This morning was so promising, the family decided to have a picnic at the tiny forest. The household staff brought out baskets of food and arranged blankets in the grass.

The children's Proctor joined the family. This was not the same Proctor Annika had been raised with. He was astounded, and blinked when Yuri invited him. "Thank you," he said. "This will provide me with an excellent opportunity to study the children in an unstructured environment. "

He had brought along a folding stool and watched after lunch as the children laughed and ran about, playing games. Annika lay baby Thor and his new sister, Pia, on a blanket in the sun while she lay in the grass, her head resting on Yuri's lap. It was quite the placid scene; the Proctor took many notes.

The children huddled, whispering, then marched over. "Proctor, I have a question," announced Silver. "I heard Mommy use a naughty word at Papa the other day. He did this to her," he put a finger to his lips, "and nodded toward us. What I want to know is, what does 'by the bloody arse of the Eighth' mean?"

Annika buried her face in Yuri's lap, shuddering with suppressed laughter. "It's not funny!" he admonished her. "I told you kids their age will listen and pick things up."

"Yes, so what does it mean, Proctor?" the rest of the children echoed.

"Sit, sit," the Proctor instructed. "Let's see, what words do you know?"

"Bloody arse!" said Green. "It means…" he pointed to his bottom.

"Very good, Green," said the Proctor, "Now, what about the rest? What do you know of the Eighth?" The children all looked at each other, shrugging.

"There's eight of us, but I don't think Mommy was talking about us," said Violet.

"Majesty?" the Proctor asked.

Annika, finally recovered from her bout of laughter, agreed. "Better to learn from you."

Proctor began the tale to the eight assembled around him on the lawn. "Very well, children. You draw a direct lineage back two thousand years to the Great Khan himself. The Eighth Khan is your many times great-grandfather. His grandfather, Emperor James Green Khan II, lived many years longer than anyone thought possible. The Eighth Khan despaired ever becoming Khan, because his grandfather lived until he was two hundred and six. The Eighth Khan's own father had already died, leaving him as Crown Prince. When Emperor James Green Khan II died, the Eighth Khan was already one hundred and two and thought he would have a very short reign.

"While he was waiting to become Khan, the Eighth made an abundance of friends. Sadly, most of his friends were criminals and only interested in what wealth they could accumulate. Only a few of his friends were of royal blood or in the aristocracy. His criminal friends convinced the Eighth that when he became Emperor, he should reorganize the structure of our society. When his grandfather died, the Eighth immediately began to institute his new laws. Property was seized and was kept by the Emperor or given as gifts to his friends.

"To help run the government, they held "elections" which put his friends into power. Hence the term "Democracy Revolution." The Eighth began to make war on his own citizens, selling into slavery anyone who disagreed with him. Many stories are told, most verified, how he annihilated whole families and planets who stood against him."

Little mouths hung open, as Robert and the heirs sat in rapt attention to the Proctor's story. Blue arose and went to her parents. "I don't like this story," was her tiny-voiced complaint. She climbed on Yuri's lap and snuggled. Annika waited until her daughter was situated, then lay her head back down on Blue's lap. The girl sighed and played with her mother's long, golden hair. Anja grew bored and wandered off to pick wild flowers. The babies were oddly quiet.

"The aristocrats organized a rebellion; it was started in the mines by Lord Stanley Klerrk," the Proctor continued. "It took fifteen years, but Lord Klerrk himself strangled the Eighth on the steps of Giza Palace. It was a great day for the Empire. Its people decided they wanted to return to the times before the Eighth and crowned his heir daughter, Petra. She was the heir he had chosen to succeed him. He had hunted down and murdered most of the rest of the heirs. She was spared because he needed an heir and he felt his friends could control her after he died.

"Empress Petra entered the Temple of Angkor Khan and smashed the cenotaphs to her father. She also removed his name and

276

title, save for the term 'The Eighth.' As you know, this is a power restricted only to the Khan.

"So, when you hear anyone refer to anything involving the Eighth, the nameless one, they are invoking the most vile and evil thing in Terran society. Do you understand, children?"

Eight more years passed.

At the extraordinary age of one hundred seventy-nine, Great Grandmother Annika died. The whole of the Russolov family mourned the passing of their matriarch. At the reading of her will, her only wish was to be buried in space, in hope she could be reunited with her husband, Leonid. Annika ordered the records of Grandfather Leonid's last journey researched. She took the family on a three-month journey to the frontier and there fulfilled Grandmother's last request. The Russolov matriarch's remains went Spinward, fired in a probe toward the site of her husband's last mission.

The plan to secure the Empire was complete. The last of the non-aligned world joined, the final defiant worlds were enslaved. Annika ruled a peaceful, prosperous Empire. The worlds of the Galactic Council had taken notice. Several who shared a border or near the Empire sent emissaries, seeking to do business with the new power within the Sagittarius Arm.

The raids by the Bougartd continued. They would sneak into Terran space, attack a planet or convoy, then flee back across the border. The Queen was furious, demanding the War Council come up with a solution.

Admiral Thiessen and Minister Howland met with the Queen in her Giza office.

"Majesty," Howland stated, "as much as we need to strike the Bougartd, we cannot simply invade them without sufficient provocation."

Annika pounded her fist on her desk, "Two hundred dead on the colony ship *Elissa*. Twenty-five hundred dead on Rikers colony. How much provocation do we need?"

"The Bougartd are claiming the raids are being accomplished by privateers," explained Thiessen. "We are free to capture and try them, of course. We've closed off their hiding spots inside the Empire. They destroy themselves to elude capture, so we can't produce witnesses of their government's involvement. Without it, we bring the whole of the Galactic Council down upon us, along with several non-aligned worlds. Piecemeal, we can defeat them handily. If they find a way to co-operate and come after us..." his voice trailed off.

"I want that provocation, gentlemen," Annika said. "I don't care how. I want it."

Christmas passed without much fanfare. While the celebration seemed as spirited as ever, there was a tinge of sadness in the air. This spring, the heirs would select their names and in the eyes of the Law, become adults. One would be named her successor. Annika was positive it would be Green. He exuded natural leadership and charisma. As a superior brain, he was as intelligent as any of his brothers and sisters, maybe more so. Save one.

That one was who could not become heir, Robert. Not that it seemed to matter to him. He and Green had bonded, spending days together on the farm or during family outings. It seemed odd, in fact, to see one without the other.

Annika fretted about her sixteen-year old son. The closer the Naming Day came, the more unsettled he became.

The heirs gave their parents rocking chairs to sit in front of the hearth during the cold Russian winters. Annika and Yuri loved the gift, spending hours reading together or with the younger children. Anja was a teen now, preferring to spend time with her heir sisters or the village children. Annika worried about Anja. At fourteen, she was acting out and rebelling as Annika had done at the same age. Annika tried being strict, she tried being friendly. Nothing seemed to be working, although Anja got along with Yuri and Rita.

Robert stood before them as they rocked in silence. "Mother, Papa, May I have a word with you?" he asked.

"Certainly, Son," Yuri answered as he and his wife lay their books in their laps.

"As you are both aware, I have been working and studying hard. My instructors have been assigning me college work for several years now. I have met the basic requirements set down by the Education ministry several times over."

Before either parent could respond, nine-year-old Pia, all elbows and knees as Yuri often noted, danced into the room, carrying a comm. "Mommy, it's your gold channel." She handed her mother the comm, then pantomimed Annika as she spoke into the comm. "This is the Queen." Annika snapped her fingers at Pia and furrowed her brow as Pia spun out of the room.

"Majesty, this is Colonel D'Gembae of Terran Command," was the anxious voice on the comm. "We have received a message from Percii Central. They have been attacked by the Bougartd. Casualty reports are spotty but we believe them to be heavy." His voice caught, then he continued. "We have gotten a message from Percii Seven. They have instituted the Omega Protocols."

Annika's stomach clinched. *Marianne!* In a stern voice, she replied, "Who is the closest fleet, Colonel?"

"Admiral Harig, Third Combined," he reported. "We also have Vice Admiral Makati with Twenty-Seventh Heavy Bombardment within twelve hours."

"Very well. Send the orders on my authority. Contact Minister Howland, Admiral Thiessen and the rest of the War Council. Tell them I am ordering War Plan Red Queen. I will arrive in Giza within ten hours. Notify *Lord Klerrks Revenge.* My respects

279

to Vice Admiral Byrd; I expect the battlegroup to be ready to depart in twelve hours."

"It shall be as you ordered, my Queen." The comm went dead.

Annika moved to Yuri's lap. "Hold me tight, my love. It's begun. I am taking the Empire to war."

Chapter 33

"I am become Death. The destroyer of Worlds."
J. Robert Oppenheimer, theoretical physicist, early 20ᵗʰ century

The Queen's fleet appeared at the edge of the Cadeau System. The arrival of a Terran warship to any system was a concern. The arrival of her fifty-warship Battle Group was cause for panic.

From her flagship, Queen Annika Raudona Russolov Khan sent the message. She would address the council. Today. The fleet approached Cadeau 4 and entered orbit, ignoring all instructions from the system's traffic control. The Terran Battle Group created considerable confusion for the ships already in neat, orderly orbits around the Cadeau. There were several near collisions as the fifty warships advanced.

The fleet settled into a high orbit, its weapons trained on the planet and any ship that approached. Buccaneer fighters were launched and formed a protective barrier. From the *Lord Klerrks Revenge,* one hundred more fighters launched and escorted ten armed transports to the surface of the Seat of the Galactic Federation.

Queen Annika Raudona Russolov Khan had arrived.

Fifty Imperial troops in full battle gear surrounded her as she left her dropship, escorting her to the Galactic Council's chamber. Anxious clusters of council police tried to surround the group, but couldn't match the rapid march. Panicky politicians and council members assembled in their boxes, eager and dreading what the arrival of the Terran leader meant to each of their worlds. Not to mention to their personal safety. There had been rumors about this Queen. Only rumors, to be honest. But she was Terran, reason enough to be cautious. If half the rumors about her were true…

The avian ambassador of the Kyocera system protested that this Queen's appearance was improper. As a non-member world, Terra was not allowed to call a council meeting, much less be allowed to address the council, unless invited. There was protocol to follow before even a member world could address them. "By what right," the Kyocera ambassador asked, "does the barbarian queen address this august body?"

The Official Terran Observer to the Galactic Council pointed skyward. "Because none of you can stop her." The implied threat was clear enough.

As she entered the chamber with her escort of fifty armed soldiers (with more complaints called out over weapons in the council chamber), nearly everyone was taken aback with how *small* she was! Surely, this Queen could be no threat! In the eyes of most of the races represented, she was hardly bigger than a child. But her stride was confident and precise. Her pointed chin was firmly set and her green, almond shaped eyes looked neither left nor right as she strode purposefully down the aisle to the center rostrum of the main chamber.

The chamber of the Galactic Council was a menagerie of beings of the Sagittarius Arm. Scales and skin, feathers and quills were scattered throughout the two hundred races represented. Along the wall to her left was a series of tanks, containing aquatic and beings that required specialized environments. Behind her were a series of horizontal bars for the avians to perch and serpent races to wrap around. There were shouts, hisses and angry cries as the Khan and her escorts marched sharply down the aisle.

She reached the rostrum and said in a loud voice, "I am here to address this council. I will be heard!"

The chairperson, a nervous rodent from the Zionus system was anxious; there were no rules in place for a non-aligned world to demand this privilege. But he saw she would not yield and his courage left him. He nodded his assent and announced loudly, "The Chair recognizes the Leader of the Terran Empire. Your Majesty."

Annika ascended the stairs and moved behind the rostrum. She stood beside it, arms crossed, tapping her foot irritably. A trembling, rabbity aide brought a step; she could now see over the tall podium. In her Imperial Officer's uniform with the muted Captains bars on her collar and the golden pilot's wings on her left breast, she was a sight to behold on any world. She took measure of the assembly of races represented, then began to speak:

"I stand before you today, as the leader of an aggrieved people. I am Queen of the Terran Empire and of our member worlds, our allies, and our subjected worlds…"

"You mean slave worlds!" came a shout from the chamber.

"A curious accusation to come from the Hecht Homogony. As I recall, you have legalized slavery on your worlds, yes? Worlds you have invaded and enslaved yourself. Yet, you condemn us for doing what you yourself do." She raised her chin. "We're just much, much better at it.

"Which leads me to my address to you this afternoon." Annika continued. "Before I was so rudely interrupted, I was pointing out that not only am I the Leader of the Terran Empire, but that I am also Khan and Goddess Queen of Terra. The relationship between this Council and Terra has been, for the last two thousand years, more than a bit contentious. This council has, in fact, directed four wars against Terra. Not just my Empire, but Terra herself. Each of these wars were not wars of conquest, oh, no. They were wars waged against my people, my planet, for its very existence. Four times, this council has authorized and funded invasions of my world with the intent to exterminate the Terran people. The first was easily turned back. Even to this day, the Solarians have not recovered from their disastrous war with Terra. The second war this council declared was the Vinithri War. It turned out quite badly for you, didn't it? Not only did we stop the Vinithri assault, we became friends and allies! Today, the Terran/Venithrian Alliance is the strongest and tightest bond to be found in the known universe."

283

She paused for effect, then continued. "I suppose I should thank you for bringing Terra and the Vinithri together. It was the combination of Terran and Vinithri science that made me possible. So, for that, I thank you.

"The Hecht attack on my world was devastating, destroying five of our grandest cities and killing billions of innocents. We turned back your attack yet again. The harvest of technology advanced our war making ability a hundredfold. We rebuilt our cities. From where I stand, I see the Hecht still have failed to regain their standing within this council.

"But now to the crux of the matter," she went on. "Two thousand Terran years ago, this council gave permission to the Bougartd to begin an unlimited war of aggression against the Terran Empire. Many of your worlds have done more than give their blessings. You have, in fact, given the Bougartd financial and material support. You've given the raider ships free passage and shelter, shielded them when they exited Terran space after their raids. Purchased stolen Terran goods. And enslaved thousands of Terrans.

"My great grandfather stood on this very stage, on this very spot, and asked you, the Great Galactic Council, to stop the attacks in the interest of peace. My great grandfather was a builder and a man of peace. You forced him into a war he didn't want to fight.

"My father stood on this very stage, on this very spot and demanded you stop the war. You ignored him and he was forced to continue a war Terra didn't want to fight."

"Woman, get to the point!" came a voice from the Bougartd box. He stood, seven feet tall, charcoal grey skin, yellow eyes. Up from his jutting jaw were two, long yellow teeth. Around his neck hung a jeweled translator. "I have better things to do today than listen to your whining and crying on how unfair the universe is. Hey, I have an idea! Why don't you march your pretty little Terran ass over to my quarters? I know I have something that would make you feel all better." With that, all the Bougartd began to laugh.

284

"The animal will be silent!" roared the Queen. She composed herself. "I am not here to ask the council for anything. Nor am I here to make any demands. No..." her voice lowered.

"When vermin occupy your home, you have two choices. You can try and make peace with the vermin, which in turns leads to your house being vermin infested. Or, you hunt down and eradicate the vermin. Today, Terra is exterminating the vermin known as the Bougartd. As I speak, my fleets have taken up position around their home world and colonies. We have commenced our attack, then will move on to the rest of their colonies, stations, and ships. Wherever the vermin hide, we will locate and exterminate them. If any species attempts to aid the Bougartd, they will incur the wrath of my Empire. If any world gives aid or comfort to them, my fleet will raze the planet to ensure the vermin are dead. If any being attempts to hide even one Bougartd under their bed, we will burn that house down."

"What is the meaning of this!" roared the Bougartd Ambassador. Unlike his bare-chested companions, he wore a richly embroidered robe, of reds and purples, denoting his position in his government. His mandibles were jewel encrusted. "Bougartd has been an esteemed member of this assembly since its inception! Now this upstart comes in here and starts issuing threats? Against me and my people? For a few pirate raids that cannot possibly be seriously considered as endorsed by my government? What gives you the audacity, much less the right, to address me in this fashion?"

Annika's eyes blazed. "What gives me the right? As Queen of nine hundred worlds? As Khan of forty trillion Terrans? What gives me the right? The blood of the millions that is on your hands. Especially the blood of ones most dear to me. Marianne Quinn. Katy O'Brien. Rory Grant. Julia Adams. A few of the millions you murdered with Tyrus Phage, an unspeakable act to any civilized people."

She pulled a communicator from her pocket and commanded, "Execute." The external doors around the chamber flew open. Through them poured two hundred more Terran soldiers

285

in full battle dress. They blocked the doors while a group of them ran to the Bougartd box, leveled their weapons and fired. For thirty long seconds, weapons chattered and barked, tearing the Bougartd delegation to pieces. As the firing started, several delegations panicked and broke for the exits. The grim Terran soldiers stood firm, preventing escape. When the firing stopped, there were cries of terror and furniture toppled as nearly every race tried to escape the assault. Outside the hall, more firing could be heard from the direction of the Bougartd Consulate. The air vibrated, a ripping sound was heard as meson bolt after meson bolt tore through the atmosphere. Each ended with a heavy thud and explosion which shook the whole city.

"That will be the Bougartd Embassy," said the Queen. "I ordered my own ship to see to its destruction." She left the rostrum and, surrounded by her soldiers, moved toward the exit. The panicked beings were easily pushed aside as she made her way back up the aisle way. She stopped at the Bougartd carnage, whirled to face the council members, and said, "See this and trembly obey."

She left the stunned hall in silence.

The end of Terra/Vinithri War in 3053 A.D. was made possible by asteroid miners, who had covertly entered Vinithri Kuiper belt, attached powerful engines and guidance computers to heavy asteroids and sent them crashing into the Vinithri home world. Since that glorious day, asteroid miners had been held in the highest regard throughout the Empire as heroes and saviors.

Lieutenant General Mickey Morando, head of Imperial Army Special Operations, had devised a new method of the ancient miner's attack.

It had taken weeks to get *Genii* into position. Years before the Queen decided to go to war, Intelligence had determined that war with the Bougartd was inevitable. *Genii* was dispatched to penetrate and prepare for War Plan Red Queen from inside the Kuiper Belt. He had drifted in, unpowered, even though equipped with the most advanced stealth equipment in the Empire. General Morando had learned caution as a bomber pilot.

Once safely in and amongst the Kuiper asteroids, *Genii* spent months locating hundreds of asteroids, rocks of specific size and composition, namely, between five and ten metric tons and ninety per cent or greater of nickel-iron. The scouts found what was needed and cataloged each location. And waited.

The Bougartd had encapsulated their entire system with a network of listening stations outside its ten inhabited worlds. The outer two worlds were command posts for the outer ring of defensive satellites. The inner three worlds were the seat of Bougartd civilization. They had started on the smallest of the three planets and rapidly spread to the other two. Heavy weapon platforms ringed the valued worlds. Their fleet, such as it was, was moored there in two extensive shipyards. They had one hundred and forty capital ships and three thousand raider craft in the system. Powerful anti-ship weapons were mounted on all the planets.

The Terran Empire had more than two thousand ships, nearly half of which were heavy or medium warships, and well over seventy-five thousand fighter and bomber craft. The whole of the military had been fighting continually for the last fifteen years, consolidating the Empire.

The Planning Commission for the War Council had several members, including General Morando, who were astute students of history. They knew the Bougartd weren't industrialist, but preferred to trade or steal what they needed. Their Kuiper belt was relatively unexploited and unpopulated.

The plan was simple. The fleet would come out of otherspace in eight locations around the system and immediately launch a spread of five hundred missiles each. Mass drivers General Morando held in otherspace surrounding the Bougartd system would return to normal space, gather the asteroids the *Genii* had mapped out and fire them at the occupied worlds.

Using mass drivers against civilian worlds was strictly forbidden by the laws of the Galactic Council and most civilized worlds.

Terra had never signed the treaty.

Behind the first wave of missiles came a second, with fighters following them through, searching for enemy fighters and ships. The third wave consisted of medium and heavy bombers armed with merculite missiles, heavy ship killing weapons. They were to attack every ship, every satellite they saw.

Then would come the eight hundred warships committed to the invasion, making straight for the inhabited planets. This part of the plan needed no subtlety or great planning. They were to blast to rubble the Bougartd home worlds and every colony throughout the system. Occupation would come when there was no possibility of resistance.

As the great, twenty-ninth century Terran General LeGrie had said: "Courage and honor will always lose to overwhelming force." The Bougartd weren't brave and were about to be overwhelmed.

General Morando had *Genii* positioned behind an enormous rock in the Kuiper Belt. He awaited the "Go" order. As a student of history, General Morando had studied surprise attacks as far back as the nineteenth century. He found one in the mid- twentieth century that appealed to him, to his sense of history. He borrowed code words from that attack for this day.

"Prepare for attack," the Villa One channel squawked. General sent the coded message *"To-To-To"*. Minutes later, the fabric of space behind his ship began to unfold. A red light illuminated on the panel in front of him. General Morando picked up his comm and used the attack code not heard in three thousand years:

"TORA! TORA! TORA!"

Gragnar was bored. Stuck here on Listening Station Thirty, watching the gadneyk universe go by. Bofirn and Fewink were in the sleep furs, snoring away a good drunk. That was the only gadneyk thing to do on this damned station! Sit on watch, monitoring who and what went in and out of the system. Maybe watch some vid. And drink. Gragnar was pretty sure when his two-year tour on this yar-pho station was over, he would probably need a new liver. Maybe he could hook onto a raider ship and lay claim to a healthy Terran one. He heard they had a great capacity for drink.

Damn his sister! She had been caught in an affair with that gadneyk councilman and brought shame on the whole groppig family. Gragnar had lost his raider ship and been dumped here, a common punishment for someone who had been shamed by a family member. If he was lucky, maybe he would be able to kiss someone's snorgk and get back into space.

The board flashed once. A signal was incoming. Too short to trace, just three words, "*To-To-To*". It didn't make sense to him. He scanned the area where the signal originated. Some gadneyk big rocks, but no ships. He decided it was either a system glitch or random space noise. It had been known to happen.

Station Fourteen called. That fool, Muirygek, was signaling, "Hey, Gragnar, turn on your vid!"

Why?" grumbled the bored Gragnar.

"The Terran Queen is addressing the big council. She's a tiny thing, looks more like one of their gadneyk children than an adult. I wouldn't object to sharing this yar-pho station with her. Alone. Just to see how much roll and tickle she could take before I gadrog her."

Well, he was bored. Gragnar turned on his vid. The image showed a Terran. Muirygek was right, she was intriguingly small for a Terran. She had that long yellow fur he'd like to pull on while he gadrog her, then break her neck when he gadrogasse. He remembered one raid when…Terrans! Terran troops were shooting up the Bougartd delegation! The Terran woman yelled something in her language before she stomped out.

His scanner howled for attention. Another signal, as undecipherable as the first. *"Tora! Tora! Tora!"* What language was that; what was it supposed to mean? Then his proximity alarm screamed. He switched the vid to external view and froze.

Space unfolded before his eyes. More than two hundred Terran warships were exiting otherspace. Hundreds of missiles hurtled toward his station. He hit the alarm, waking his roommates just in time to experience the split-second immolation of Listening Station Thirty.

The outer worlds were slaughtered in the first minutes. Two listening posts managed to get off partial warnings before they became floating clouds of dust. The emergency grid designed to protect the outer planets was never activated. Command centers, weapons platforms, all were destroyed in the first minutes of the attack. Terra's four thousand remaining missiles of the first wave, followed by eight thousand in the second wave, headed to the inner system. The Bougartd had only a few minutes' warning before the first satellite was destroyed, but the inner system defensive grid was partially activated. They fired their own missiles and beam weapons at the shadow of destruction headed to the most densely populated worlds.

Most of the asteroids were deflected or destroyed. Five fell on the Bougartd Prime, creating immediate earthquake and tsunamis. The other two worlds were also hit, the smallest of the three absorbing ten impacts of five metric ton asteroids hurtling at half-light speed. Three punched completely through the original home world of the Bougartd. The planet was shattered into pieces in minutes.

The second wave of missiles came into play, escorted by fighters. Already battered, the Bougartd defensive system of stations and satellites collapsed. The system had taken more damage in minutes than it was created to expect over the course of days or weeks. Terran fighters darted about, looking for targets, harassing Bougartd defenses and adding to the confusion. A few Bougartd ships got underway, but were swarmed by the fighters now arriving on the scene.

The outer worlds fell under bombardment by the old and seasoned dreadnaughts. A Bougartd raider jumped into the system and rammed itself into one, the *Battleaxe*. The dreadnaught left orbit and burned fiercely for three days before the brave crew could put out the fires and regain control of their vessel. The proud *Battleaxe* returned to Jupiter station for repairs under his own power.

Newer ships with the latest technology positioned themselves over the two remaining inner worlds, Garssia and Womand. They trained meson weapons on the planets and began bombardment. Ground based weapons were destroyed first, then the industry. Finally, the cities felt Queen Annika's wrath. The dreadnaughts had been built to be weapons of terror. This day, they lived up to their reputation as every city, town and village on the two worlds was reduced to piles of rubble and ash. Smoke obscured the cities as they burned. Still, the dreadnaughts continued to fire.

After two days, surrender calls began to issue from the planets. Appeals for mercy begging, pleading for their lives were stoically ignored. The Terran fleet continued its bombardment.

On the morning of the fifth day, the guns went silent. Drop ships of troops, escorted by Buccaneer fighters, were deployed. There were small bands of survivors scattered about, they reported, but no resistance. The cities were nothing but vast fields of wreckage.

Sarcina and her small band of survivors clawed out of the shelter. Surveying what remained of Mornatd, she thought, *maybe we should crawl back underground and die there.* The city of her birth where she grew up, met and conjoined her mate and gave birth to their children, was a grey mound of rubble. Over it all lay a pallor and stench of smoke, penetrated in places by the sharp odor of ozone.

They all looked to her, the forty survivors from the shelter. She picked a direction she thought would take them from the city and struck out. Most followed her, but a dozen stayed behind, deciding then and there to die.

Small Terran ships flew overhead, but there were no more bombs, *thank the Maker.* They circled the motley group and flew off. Around noon, a shuttle hovered over them and in barely recognizable Bougartdesse ordered, "Continue to move south. There is camp two miles in that direction."

Sarcina had no better ideas, so they continued to march. More survivors dropped, exhausted, refusing to go on. She couldn't stop. Surely there would be food, water and shelter at this Terran camp.

They arrived. The guards didn't look like any Terrans she had seen on news broadcasts. They were all smaller than she, and wore green and brown mottled armor. Helmets enclosed their heads, making them look like upright insects. Two eerie, glowing, buttery eyes were on opposite sides of those helmets. They led Sarcina's little group to a tent, gave them water from a community cup, then examined each survivor. The sick and injured were separated, the remainder fitted with metal collars. One woman, her skin nearly white with exhaustion, held a hungry infant that wouldn't stop crying. A soldier took the child and cradled it, bounced it up and down for a few moments. When the baby Bougartd didn't stop squalling, the soldier snapped its neck and tossed it to one side.

They huddled outside as darkness fell. No food, no more water was given them. Third Season approached, and with it the evening rains. No shelter or blankets were offered.

Guards awakened them at dawn. Their small party had grown during the night; two or three hundred now huddled there. Helmeted soldiers herded them to an open area Sarcina recognized as a former parking lot. There sat a Terran armored vehicle with a Terran in his battle armor, minus his helmet.

"I am Major Bertrand Baker," announced the Terran speaking in a comm. There were speakers mounted to his vehicle. "I am military governor for what remains of this pitiful region. You are all now the property of the Queen Annika Raudona Russolov Khan. As her representative, I have a simple set of rules. Work and get fed. Don't work and die. The Queen has demanded her planet to be cleaned up and made orderly. That you will do. To begin, we shall separate the various resources here - steel, plastics and concrete - into piles which will be loaded for transport to recycling centers."

Work hard and you will be permitted to live. Don't work hard and..." He unholstered his sidearm and fired indiscriminately. A Bougartd girl, so young her skin was still mottled, collapsed, a bullet between her eyes.

"Today's quota is only twenty tons. I will double it for tomorrow if you make the quota by sundown. I will triple it if you do not. Now, get to work, animals," he ordered.

Chapter 34

The intercom chimed. "Majesty," called Miss Norris' voice, "Your son to see you."

"Thank you, Miss Norris." Annika answered. "Please see him in." The door opened and the sixteen-year-old ambled in.

"Robert! How wonderful to see you!" She hugged her child. "You need a haircut."

"Oh, Mom!" he sighed

He was growing up. Robert took after his grandfather, Andrei, towering over his mother. His hair was unruly, his jaw square and he had inherited his father's nose. But his eyes were his mother's, almond shaped and emerald green.

"Come, sit with me. Would you like some tea?" she asked.

"No, thanks, Mom."

He fidgeted his hands, looked down at them, not meeting his mother's eyes.

"Are you O.K., Dear? Is something bothering you? A girl, maybe?" Annika pressed.

"You're not scanning me, are you?" he shot back.

"That's a silly question. I'm your mother and I'm asking what's wrong. I won't scan you if you tell me," she promised.

"Well, I came down to Giza for the Naming and the memorial…"

The fleet had returned to Terra, victorious. The Bougartd were collapsing, their ships on the run. The battle groups were hunting them down as the Queen had ordered. Any survivors were being rounded up and shipped back to their home world, to the labor camps. The Queen had ordered the planet cleansed. Her army ensured that this was happening.

It was not a bloodless victory. Fifteen thousand members of the Army and the Fleet had died in the invasion of the Bougartd system, mostly from the suicide assault on the *Battleaxe*. Admiral Ross issued the order: she wanted all the bodies recovered. Or whatever was left to recover.

Samples were gathered and placed in a sarcophagus and the names of the fallen inscribed on the outside. The casket was then transported from the spaceport in Cairo to the Giza Necropolis, the route lined by the military to the beat of a solitary drum. The Queen, Minister Howland and Admiral Thiessen were waiting at the selected sepulcher. The casket was placed on a plinth. A holo emitter displayed an image of each one of the interred and each name was read, followed by the tolling of a bell. It went on for two and a half days. In the early morning hours, each heir and Robert had taken a turn, reading the names.

The Queen herself read the last names. As the last bell tolled, a musician played a mournful salute.

"I am so proud you participated. You didn't have to," she told him.

"I know, Mother. Respectfully, I did have to," his voice solemn.

"Oh?"

A deep breath. "I have been speaking with Admiral Thiessen. My grades are good and I have been taking college level classes for six years now. He has assured me, with your permission, that I can enter the Academy this semester."

"Your father has arranged for you to go to Moscow University," she reminded him.

"Father wishes me to be a doctor, like him," Robert chose his words with care. "I love Father, but I do not wish to be a doctor."

"I see. What do you want to be?"

"Green will be the next Khan. You will teach him to continue what you have started. If I follow Father's path, I will be a bystander to the future," he stated. "I do not want that. Uncle

Thiessen will teach me. When you die and my brother becomes Khan, I will be his War Lord."

"An ambitious plan. Are you serving yourself or serving the Empire?" she asked.

"Both. I have an advantage that no one else has," Robert countered. "Green was bred with a superior brain. I have the genes of your superior brain and my father's superior intellect. I cannot be Khan. But I will be the right hand of the Khan."

"What does your father think?"

"I have not told him. I was hoping..." the boy started.

"No!" Annika interrupted. "If you are going to stand up to your father, you cannot come running to me. You must confront your father, tell him the truth, and then execute this plan of yours. When do you plan on leaving for Sanderstrom?"

"After the Naming Ceremony. I will be enrolled as a first year."

"Then you tell your father," she ordered. "Tonight."

"Yes, Mother."

The sphinx stared into eternity. The three pyramids stood as silent monument of the greatness to the god/kings of this ancient land. Annika believed she was joined to the antediluvian stones. Her line was two thousand years, while the pharaohs had lasted more than five.

She had been looking forward to the lunch today with Archbishop James, the emissary from the Vatican. Affairs of state had kept Annika from meeting with her college advisor and friend as often as she would like. Today, she hoped, would give them a chance to catch up.

He arrived in his red trimmed cassock and grey stole. "It has been too long, Archbishop," she said as she hugged him. "What, fifteen years I believe?"

"Thereabouts," he agreed. "After the birth of your daughter? I returned to the University; with the war, it's been important to the

Holy Father we maintain normalcy both on the campus and throughout the church."

Father James brought her the latest from the Vatican. Annika shared about the coming and goings of her family. She sat silent for a moment, and spoke of Robert's decision. "How does this make you feel?" he asked.

"I am proud of him for making such an adult decision," she said carefully, "but I worry what will happen between him and his father. As a wife and a mother, I cannot get between them lest I lose both of them. Either way, Robert is quite determined and Yuri will be angry."

"Yuri," Father James muttered. "Annika, there is a reason I came to lunch today. His Holiness had instructed me to tell you he intends to send a mission to Bougartd."

Annika's head snapped around. "No," she decreed.

"You cannot stop us," Father James explained. "The Laws of Angkor Khan state you cannot monitor or block the actions of the church in missions of mercy. Bougartd desperately needs the aid of the church. There is great suffering there."

"I know there is great suffering there. I am the one creating that suffering." Her anger was rising. "They are paying for their sins. There will be no mercy!"

Father James whispered, "Vengeance is mine, saieth the Lord."

"And I am the article of vengeance your lord sent!" she shot back. "You're right, I can't interfere with you establishing your mission. But it must not interfere with any actions of my government. Further, you will receive no aid or protection. I will not allow you any support from Medical Corps. Your mission there will be alone amongst the animals. Will that suffice your holy pope?"

Father James responded. "Here is a list of physicians who have already signed aboard to support us."

Annika looked at the pad. At the first name, her face blanched. *GODS, NO!*

The Proctor's words from so many years ago on Celtius Four, "How do you feel?" repeated over and over in Annika's mind. The children had come down to Giza for a visit, so Yuri was asking each about their day exploring the palace. Robert fidgeted before addressing Yuri. "Father, I have an announcement."

"Good news, I hope?" Yuri said. "Your mother looks a bit unsettled this evening. I'm sure she needs some cheering up."

"Father, I have decided to enter university early. I have spoken with Uncle Thor and will be leaving in three days for Sanderson Seven." His voice was firm, resolved.

Yuri chewed for a few moments and replied, "Nonsense. You can start Moscow University in the fall. That was our plan."

"That was your plan, Father," Robert answered. "I love you, but I do not wish to be a doctor like you."

"So, you wish to go off and be a soldier like your mother?" Annika could hear anger in his voice.

"No, Father," said the boy. "I will be a naval officer, like Uncle Thor."

Yuri's fist hit the table, scattering silver and slopping the soup. "No!" he said. "You will forget this foolishness. You will leave after the Naming Ceremony and work the farm this summer. You will start university this fall in Moscow. That is that."

"In fall, Father, I will be in my second semester at the Academy," Robert answered.

"You do so without your mother's and my blessing," Yuri responded, now aloof. "Nor our help. You can ask your Uncle Thor for passage home when you fail at that institution."

Robert jumped to his feet. "I will not fail, Father." Annika could feel his anger barely in control. Her son excused himself and marched to his room.

The rest of the evening was tense. The children cleared the table and quietly went to their rooms. Annika tried to work on the reports she hadn't finished during her office hours. Yuri fumed on the veranda overlooking the plaza.

Annika grew weary and went to her bedroom. She piled pillows behind her in the bed and tried to finish the undone reports, but she couldn't focus. *How do you feel?*

Frustrated, she threw the folder on the floor. There was her pad; she selected twenty fifth century poetry. Usually that would calm and relax her. But not tonight. Over and over, the Proctor's words bored into her skull. *How do you feel?*

She dropped her pad, flattened the pillows and pulled up the covers while Yuri was in the bathroom preparing for bed. A soft sigh of the blankets shifting announced his presence in the bed. He called the lights down and they lay in the dark, Yuri on his back, Annika facing away from her husband.

"When were you going to tell me about Bougartd?" she asked. "Before or after you left?"

"I just signed on this morning," he replied calmly. "Robert's announcement upset me, so I am going to tell you now. Clearly, you already know."

"You cannot go, "Annika said. "I forbid it."

Yuri propped himself up on his elbow. "Is that my wife, Annika, speaking or my Khan?"

Annika rolled onto her back. "I will not let you go," she said, pointing her finger. "You did this knowing what I am doing on Bougartd is the right thing. They murdered my friends, Yuri. Your friends as well. Their voices are screaming for vengeance. I will not allow you to give those murdering animals a bandage or cup of water."

"You didn't answer my question," stated Yuri.

"I did answer," she rolled back on her side, away from him. "You may not go. You will not go." She shut her eyes and lay still as a stone.

Minutes passed before Yuri asked, "What is happening to us? I can understand your war. I can understand Robert and his foolish decision. But what I can't figure out is what is happening between us." He rolled on his side, away from his wife. "I have never seen you act this way before. Always in our bed, it has just been Yuri and Annika. Tonight, its Yuri and someone I don't know."

Annika woke with a headache. A dull throb in the front of her head, between her temples, in the place where she could hear her thoughts when she spoke to herself.

Yuri was already gone. She considered checking to make sure he hadn't left the planet. No, he wouldn't do that. He was angry, but he always restrained himself. It was a trait in her husband she admired. "Dohlman!" she cried. He appeared as always, unflappable and attentive. Annika explained her problem and Dohlman popped out and returned with a glass of clear liquid.

"Asperinium," he explained. "Doctor Bond's standing protocol for headaches."

It helped, slightly. Annika went through her day with the dull ache between her temples. Fortunately for her, the bulk of the day was preparing for tomorrow's Naming Day. At lunch, she went to the Grotto of the Blue Waters, always a place of calm water, darkness and cool temperatures. Normally, Yuri lunched with her, but he wasn't returning her calls today. His office reported he was in, but every time she called he was in conference or with a patient.

Supper was a strained, silent affair. Robert wasn't there and Yuri didn't ask anyone about their day. Annika's headache hadn't eased, so she excused herself and went to bed, pulling the covers over her head. Yuri joined her after a few hours. "Are you all right?" he asked. "I know you are angry with me, but you are acting strangely today."

"I have a headache," was the muffled reply from under the covers. "And yes, I am angry. You're not helping. Don't be such an arse and come to bed."

"Let me see your eyes." It was a firm command, Doctor Yuri speaking. Annika had heard that tone enough over the last twenty-five years. She made an exasperated noise as she extricated herself from her coverlet to sit up. His ever present and truly annoying flashlight shone in each eye, one at a time. "Hmmm," he remarked. "Normal. I shall ask Tahn and his Proctors to look, after the Naming Ceremony."

Annika burrowed beneath her covers once again. "It's just a headache, but if it will make you feel better," came her stifled voice. "Now, be quiet. I am trying to sleep."

Naming Day! The celebrated day across the Empire as the heirs were formally recognized as adults and the new Crown Prince or Princess was announced.

The plaza was impressive. The vast white stone had been cleaned and polished until it developed a pearlescent sheen. Banners of the previous Khans hung on the walls of the palace, demonstrating the history of the line and foretelling a promise of the future.

The Queen sat quietly, recalling her own Naming Day twenty-two years ago. So much had changed! She was forty now, no longer an impulsive, rebellious child. She was married and a mother. She had the Empire she had labored for the first half of her life. Everything she wanted was at her fingertips

Nearly everything. She sat in the antechamber, waiting for the ceremony to begin, Yuri sitting as far from her as possible. He was wearing a resplendent morning suit, as opposed to the Medical Corps uniform he was entitled to. Annika herself was wearing her uniform, as she felt she should in a time of war.

She suddenly felt foolish. When was there a time the Empire wasn't at war? Even on her own Naming Day, war wasn't far off. Indeed, her whole life centered on that horrid day. Ming si, perpetrator of the murders of her siblings, hadn't worn a uniform.

"Where are you going?" Yuri asked, still reading his pad.

302

"I think I should change," she said, "Maybe this uniform is wrong. I should be wearing something happy, joyful. I have a closet of nice dresses; Dohlman will know which would be best." She filled her lungs to call him.

There isn't time, my love," Yuri assured her. "The ceremony begins in a few minutes. You look just fine. Sit down and wait. How are you feeling? Do you still have your headache this morning?"

How am I feeling? That old question popped up again. "My headache is fine," she told him, pondering the question. She was forty. Her eldest children were about to embark on the rest of their lives. She had everything she could possibly want.

And she was miserable. Yes, that was the word. Miserable.

Dohlman appeared. "Ma'am, Sir, it is time." Yuri crossed the room and held out his hand. They stood at the graceful French doors, waiting. Annika looked up at her husband. "Yuri, am I still pretty?"

He kissed her bump of a nose as did the Yuri of old. "Of course, my love," he answered. "The most beautiful woman I have ever known."

The doors opened to a fanfare and they stepped out into the sun before the adoring multitude.

The ceremony was far longer than Annika remembered. She listened to the story she had loved as a child, the tale of the great Angkor Khan. That she was part of the long recitation as the fifteenth reincarnation took her breath away for a second. The children stepped forward and announced themselves to the universe: Randle Raudona-Russolov, Mary Raudona-Russolov, Belinda Raudona-Russolov, and Dorian Raudona-Russolov. Yuri's hand found hers: Violet Raudona-Russolov, Mercy Raudona-Russolov, Leonid Raudona-Russolov and finally Gart Raudona-Russolov. Never before had all the heirs done this honor to their parents. The couple were in tears of happiness.

Tahn led the File bonzes to the dais. "It has been my pleasure to have served the descendants of Angkor Khan for ninety-five years. Today, I will step down from the File Committee, with your permission, Highness, following our pronouncement." Annika nodded and Tahn stepped back in line. The ritual she had witnessed twenty-two years before was now performed in front of the trillions of the Empire. The chant, the golden envelopes, the tearing.

Eight green slips of paper.

Annika felt a twinge of jealously. His brothers and sisters bowed to him first while the Empire erupted with joy over the promise of the handsome, young Khan. This was his day, a day denied to her when the enemy within and without tried to assassinate her. The new Crown Prince was before his parents and bowing low. Could barely hear his mother direct, "Rise, Crown Prince Gart Raudona-Russolov." They embraced and she had to yell to be heard. "Go with Tahn and the others. Send my greetings to our ancestors."

Her remaining seven elder children were waiting for their parents in the family quarters. Annika sat in her chair amongst them. "Children, your mother and I are so proud of you," Yuri said. "Today, you are adults in the eyes of our people."

"But you will always be our children," Annika added. "Wherever your travels take you, whoever you become, your papa and I want you to know you'll always have a place in our home and in our hearts. We'd like to hear your plans."

Dorian and Violet were the first to stand. "Mother, Papa, we must take our leave, immediately. We are accompanying Master Tahn and the elders back to Angkor Khan's Temple," said Dorian. "I have been accepted as an adept. In two years, I will travel to Vinith to learn their bio-engineering technology. It is my hope to one day be on the File Committee. Violet has chosen to take the oath and become a servant of silence." Tearfully, Annika and Yuri held the two children. Violet mouthed "I love you, Mommy" as they exited.

Randle stood. "I have accepted a scholarship at Lee Military College in the Tarchment system. It is my hope to become an Army Officer. I will leave at the end of the summer."

"Aunt Teresa has spoken with the Witches at Scarborough," Mary's voice was bell-like to the ear. "I will journey there with her when she leaves and train to be a healer." With a smile on her face, she told her mother, "You said long ago I reminded you of her. I am honored to follow in her footsteps."

"I will be attending Moscow University," Belinda said, "close to Grandfather Andrei and Grandmother Clara. One day, I will manage the family farm."

"I will go to Vespa, Saint Francis University," Mercy spoke now. "I loved your stories of being there, Mother, and I have always loved visiting Vespa."

Leonid jumped to his feet. "All this talk of schooling and farming and such sounds wonderful," he exclaimed. "Me? I'm shipping out on a scout as an ordinary spaceman next week, headed for the Rim. I want to get out and see the universe before I settle down and find a j-o-b." His laugh was a perfect imitation of his grandfather Andrei's.

"We are both so very proud of you, "said Yuri. "Your mother and I love you. Please, come visit when you can and do be home for Christmas? Otherwise your mother will be so disappointed."

"Our children are leaving us, Yuri." She lay in bed, turned away again.

Yuri set down his pad. "It is what we have been doing for the last eighteen years," he told her, "Working, watching, teaching. So, when today came, they would be ready to move on to their future." He contemplated for a moment, and added "and the future is today. Is it what you expected?"

"No." she replied in a near whisper. "But I'm glad they selected Gart."

I expect he's leaving the Hall of the Khans now, yes?" he asked.

"It depends where his meditations lead him."

"Where did your meditations lead you?" he queried.

"Here," she answered, "This place. With you. With my family. Building my Empire. Right where I am supposed to be. Getting the Empire ready for when I hand it over to my son."

In her dreams, the solemn words from their wedding night came back to her: *Still others find their other half, but only receive a half measure of life.* Tahn's words.

"One half dies before the other," Annika said somberly.

"Yes."

There was a long silence.

"How many years do I have, Master Tahn?" Annika asked.

Their room felt so empty this morning. Yuri had been getting up and leaving early the last few days. Annika hoped he would be with her this morning. "Dohlman?" she called. When he appeared, she asked, "Where is my husband?"

"He left an hour ago," the holographic servant answered. "He was on his way to the spaceport."

He wouldn't! Annika's psyche was in an uproar. Yuri wouldn't sneak out and leave her, would he? Her headache returned, pounding and fierce. Her eyes rolled at its onset and she gasped.

"Ma'am?" Dohlman queried.

"Clothing, car," she breathed.

"What of your morning grooming and supplements?" asked Dohlman.

"Damn you, I said clothing and a car, NOW!" She was in physical agony. There was a ringing in her ears. When her clothing appeared, she dressed hurriedly and ran to her hovercar. Rita was waiting,

"What's going on, Mouse?" she asked.

Annika only said, "Spaceport," and climbed in the back of the car. Rita worried, as Annika was groaning and holding her head as they raced through the streets of Cairo.

"Mousey, what's going on? How can I help?" she asked. Annika pushed her away and continued to writhe and groan.

At the spaceport, Annika jumped out of the car before it stopped moving. The crowds gasped when they saw who was coming and moved out of her way.

The white and gold Vatican ship was near the far end of the terminal. Yuri was there, shaking hands and holding his small black bag. Annika strode up to her husband, grabbed his arm, spun him about and leveled him with a punch to his face. "Wha-what are you doing?" she screeched at his prone form. "I told you no, you can't go with them!"

Then the world began rocking back and forth, illuminated by bright flashes. "You. You…AH!" She screamed as her head felt as it were being ripped in two. In agony, she clapped her hands to her ears, trying to shut out the ringing. Dropped to a knee. She barely heard the voices calling to her.

Annika, Goddess/Queen of the Terran Empire, sank to the floor. The voices were in her head now, a disjointed reverberation screaming between her hands. Her eyes began to flicker, black to green and back again. She opened her mouth to scream as she flopped onto the floor and began to convulse. Yuri grabbed his wife, shouting her name. She could hear him, but couldn't understand what he was saying. She tried to call out to him, begging for help.

She heard a pop. Then coolness and grey. A blissful grey cloud enveloped her and gave her peace.

Chapter 35

This grey, foggy place was comfortable, serene. It smelled nice, also
- fresh, like the steppe after the first rain following a long dry spell.
She didn't feel anything save this warm, comfortable place of fluffy
grey.

"Annika!" That annoying sound again. It came and went.
She wished it would go away. She was happy here. Peaceful.

"Annika! My love, it's time to wake up. Please wake up? I
need to see your pretty green eyes. Please wake up."

The noise was familiar. It made her feel…loved? Safe? It
was a nice voice. Now she didn't mind it was disturbing her, not so
much. Maybe she would open her eyes.

Oh! It was bright! She snapped the eye closed, then opened
it again, cautiously. Someone hovered. He looked familiar. She
searched her mind, trying to remember. Yuri. Her secret place told
her that was Yuri.

She opened both eyes now. He wept, holding her hands.
"That's it, my love, open your eyes. Oh, Annika, I've missed you so
much." She smacked her lips; her mouth was so dry. While she
attempted to respond, a raspy croak was all she could manage.

A young girl appeared on her other side. "Here, Mother, let
me help." Something moist touched her lips. Annika closed her
mouth around it, sucked greedily. The sponge was withdrawn and
then returned, offering more of the minty, sweet moisture.

Now a cup appeared at her lips. Annika tried to gulp, and it
was removed. "That's better," he told her, "but not too much. Just a
bit, my love." She was remembering. This was Yuri. Her husband.
Her best friend. Her knight in shining armor. The girl
was…Belinda. Her daughter. She wanted to sit up. "Shhh, let me
get that, Mom," her daughter said. The bed whined and her upper
body was raised.

"Yuri." She reached out to him. He pressed her hand to his lips, salted it with his tears. "Where am I?" she asked.

"The Temple at Angkor Khan," he told her. "You collapsed at the spaceport. Fortunately, we had several neurosurgeons available. The Vatican ship was transporting a blue wave scanner; we determined your neural pathways had suffered an overload, and began a physical breakdown in your cerebrum. Your programing shut you down before too much damage was done. We flew you here so Tahn could examine you. He and the Proctors have repaired the damage. You're going to be better soon, my love."

Tahn and several Proctors entered the room. "Ah, wonderful, Daughter! You have regained consciousness. The repairs and reprograming has worked." Annika was awake now. On hearing the word "reprograming" something compelled her to look under the covers. She was wearing pajamas. A memory flashed and she smiled.

"What happened to me?" she asked her creator. Tahn sat on a chair offered by the Proctor.

"You had a stroke," he explained. "A series of events that we had not adequately prepared your programing for created a loop, trying to reconcile an unfamiliar set of data back on itself. The strain on your physical brain tore loose several capillaries. To protect itself, your programing shut you down. Your husband recognized what was happening and had you flown straight to us. We sealed off the damaged area and rerouted your neural pathways. From there, it's been all you, waiting for you to decide to regain consciousness."

Yuri squeezed her hand as he told her, "Two years. I've been waiting for you for two years.

She smiled and squeezed his hand. "But who's been running my Empire?" she asked.

"Gart," he told her. "You prepared him well. From the moment you collapsed, he seized control and ruled in your place. The transition was seamless; your government followed his orders as though they were coming from you. He has performed magnificently. You should be very proud. I know I am."

Physically, Annika recovered quickly. By the evening, she was taking her first, unsteady steps. The next morning, she had regained enough of her strength to accompany Yuri and Belinda to breakfast. Within a week, she was running five miles in the morning.

She felt she was foundering. Yuri was always at her side. She was comforted and grateful for his presence, but couldn't shake the feeling there was something not right between them. Her children were in and out on visits. Robert visited from the Academy. Gart Khan spent every moment he could from his duties in Giza. She counseled him on governing the Empire. Anja, discarding her rebellion, dropped in daily. Violet, the silent servant of the Temple and Dorian, the adept, spent the time between their duties with her.

Annika knew she loved her family, but there was no excitement, no joy in her when they arrived. She was anxious to return to Giza, to get back to work. Her Empire needed her. She expressed her frustration to Tahn.

"I was afraid of this," he told her. "The areas of your brain that suffered the most from your stroke was your emotional seat. I don't doubt you love Yuri and your children. But the part of your brain that feels that love is being bypassed right now."

"Will I ever recover that part of my brain?" wailed Annika. "I don't want to live knowing I loved Yuri, but not being able to feel that love." Her lip quivered and her eyes swelled with tears.

"I don't know," Tahn replied. "This will be your bitterest tea of all. I have no answer for you, Daughter. All I can offer is you know are loved. The love for your family is inside you. Finding this love will be the greatest challenge in the balance of your life. In the meantime, I think it's time for you to return to Giza, back to your duties as Queen."

311

Her office was familiar. Sadly, Miss Norris had died during the Queen's illness. Her replacement, Mrs. Wilson, was able enough. But Annika missed the dour secretary that she had worked with so long. In despair one afternoon, she called "Dohlman!" He appeared as always at her elbow. "Dohlman, you're a holographic servant attached to this place. Is it possible to have a holographic representation of Miss Norris to be my secretary?"

Dohlman shook his head. "Not legally, Ma'am," he told her. "I was a servant in this place nearly twelve hundred years ago. When I was dying, Emperor Jacober Khan asked my permission to become what you see today. I was only too glad to give my permission, serving the Khans and their families. You didn't have Miss Norris's permission, so the Right of Privacy prevents doing as you ask. I am sorry, Ma'am."

Noire made a surprise visit one afternoon shortly after she had returned, bounding unannounced into her office in Giza. It was a sweltering, summer day and she had the doors to her private patio open for fresh air. Noire was shining, joyful. He grabbed her out of her chair and fairly crushed her with a hug.

"Sister, so wonderful to see you! I have someone I want you to meet." She had so missed the warm embrace of her brother.

A small girl stepped from behind Noire. Barely three feet tall, she was rail thin with long, straight dark hair. Her face was thin and pointed, her skin translucent. But her eyes, large for her face, were almond shaped and Imperial green.

"Queen Annika Raudona Russolov Khan, I should like to introduce you to your niece, Eve. Eve, this is your Auntie Annika."

"Pleased to meet you Auntie." Even in mindspeak, the child's voice was like a small bird.

"I am so pleased to meet you, Eve. Come, give me a hug."

The Queen rose from her desk and came around to the child. She knelt and wrapped her arms around the tiny girl. She felt a light tickle in her mind and snapped down her defenses.

"Eve! What have I told you about probing other people without asking first?" Noire admonished.

"I'm sorry, Father, I didn't think..." The child's eyes welled with tears.

Annika patted Eve's cheek

"Shhhhhh, child. I know you meant no harm. But it is very rude to do without permission."

"Yes, Auntie"

"How about you go out on my patio and play while your father and I talk. I'll have Mrs. Wilson bring us a treat; I'll come out and enjoy it with you. O.K.?" Annika ran her hand through the waif's hair.

"May I, Father?" the child asked, excited.

"Of course. Run along, we'll be out in a few minutes."

The girl skipped through the patio door. Annika called Mrs. Wilson and ordered ice cream for the three of them, then sat with her brother.

"Your daughter?" Annika asked.

"The File Committee has determined that I am the penultimate Intelligence Master. As such, my file has been moved into a new category. Eve's design is based on my own pattern. She is three now and will replace me one day. Her child will replace her. It will be my legacy to your Empire." Noire's pride shone through the mindspeak.

"What of her mother?"

"Sister, some questions must never be asked." Noire's mind shields were firm. Annika let the slight pass.

The treat arrived. A servant pushed a pristine trolley, was motioned to the patio, deposited the ice cream and departed, all in silence.

"Come, Noire, I want to know your daughter better."

Chapter 36

Twenty-five years passed.

Robert's plan was coming to fruition. He had graduated at the first of his class. He joined the fleet and flourished. Within five years, he commanded his own frigate. His ship was badly damaged in combat during the invasion of the Hecht Homogeny. He continued the fight, gallantly attacking a Hecht destroyer, sacrificing his own ship to destroy the enemy. His mother personally pinned the medal to his chest when he returned to Terra. He was promoted to a cruiser, then to a dreadnaught, the *Behemoth*.

Gart made Annika proud, as well. He forged his own path, studying at Harvard University on Luna, and then joined the Army. He proved to be a skilled warrior, garnering the loyalty of his troops in many fierce combat drops. His brain didn't require the reprograming in adulthood that hers had. Instead, the weekly downloads to his brain sufficed. He met an attractive woman, Lyudmila, while on Christmas leave at the farm. In three years, they married and made the trip to the Temple of Angkor Khan. Her heir grandchildren delighted her to no end.

Belinda, Mary and Mercy had all married. So, had her natural born daughters, Anja and Pia, along with Thor and Yuri II. Annika and Yuri now had over thirty grandchildren and a handful of great-grandchildren.

Leonid had last passed through the Empire seven years before, bound for the Galactic Core. She received infrequent letters from him.

A candle sat in the window of their home during the holidays, along with an unused place at the table. Randle had led the first assault drop on the Hecht home world. His wave of drop ships entered a trap the Hecht had cleverly set. His own ship was hit on final approach and plummeted into the ground. The well-built ship protected most of the soldiers, but not all the ten ships were so lucky.

The Colonel and Major of his unit were killed. Randle rallied the survivors and held off Hecht attacks for three days. On the fourth, a rescue mission was launched. A sniper felled Randle as he boarded the last drop ship.

His remains held a place of honor reserved for the Queen's soldiers in the Necropolis.

Andrei and Clara had retired. At one hundred twenty, Andrei was still loud and boisterous, albeit much slower. His hair and beard were a broad sheet of iron grey around his head and chin. Susan was in a hoverchair, sharp as ever. Belinda and her family ran the farm now.

The war was going well. The invasion of the Hecht Homogeny had been touch and go. Admiral Thiessen had conceived a brilliant plan, but the Hecht were dug in and prepared. The battle to secure the home world lasted six months. Subduing the Hecht took three more years.

The losses on both sides were dreadful. The personal cost to Annika was tragic. Not only had Randle been killed, but her beloved Uncle and War Lord, Admiral Thor Thiessen had died in the final days. Annika named Admiral Laura Moss her new Warlord.

Tahn visited frequently. They were enjoying tea in the Tower of the Morning as the sun rose one spring day. The sunrise was perfect, as was the tea. Nevertheless, Annika was troubled. "Master," she asked after the sun had ascended, "after my stroke, you said my neural pathways would eventually find their way around the damage in my brain. Every morning I awake and tell myself I love Yuri. I know I do, but I still don't feel love. Not like I think I remember. When will I know indisputably that I love him?"

Tahn finished his tea and exhaled happily. He held up the tea cup and said casually, "Perfect. You see, Daughter? The perfect tea, in the perfect cup." He threw the cup and smashed it against the wall. "One more, please," he asked, holding out his hand. Annika reached for a fresh cup. "No," he said, "Please, gather the pieces of that perfect cup."

316

She stared at the splintered pieces. "Master, the cup is ruined," she pointed out. "There is no way to reassemble that cup. Please, let me serve you in a fresh cup." Tahn nodded and she prepared the drink. He accepted the tea, sipped and nodded. "Perfect. Thank you, Daughter. Do you understand now?"

"I think so. You are saying the relationship needs to be on different footing now?" she answered. "Because what was is gone now?"

Tahn shook his head. "Still, you are thinking too much," he said, regret in his voice. "And time is growing short.

"Daughter, there is an ancient tale of a milkman and his wife. They lived in a time where the two halves were brought together on their wedding day. They had five daughters. Instead of following tradition, each daughter married for love instead of who the papa had chosen for them. He was thinking about this, love versus tradition, when he realized he had never asked his wife if she loved him. The fell into an argument until they realized after twenty-five years, they did love each other.

"I would say to you, Daughter," he said as he rose to his feet for the journey down the long staircase, "you need to ask yourself the same question."

Today was a special day, Yuri's seventieth birthday. Annika rolled on her side and stared at her husband of nearly forty-five years. His hair had receded to a garland around his head, now grey, as was his damned moustache. Fifty years and she still couldn't stand his moustache. And his great nose. She giggled as his nose whistled and snorted in his sleep. She had once recorded it and played it for him at lunch.

She ran her hand over his bald pate and cradled his head to her chest. He mumbled and nuzzled her breast. She giggled again and held him tighter, kissing the top of his head. "You know, I could get used to waking up in a palace like this if I got to wake up

317

with a beautiful princess every morning." He was awake, his brown eyes shining at her.

"Well, I'd like to wake up one morning with a comfier pillow instead of your boney chest," she retorted. "Happy birthday, Husband."

"Harrumph!" he responded. "Tell me how happy you are when you turn seventy."

She playfully slapped the top of his head. "Be good, you," she admonished. "Our children and grandchildren will be here today just for you. Be pleasant and happy for them, old man."

He kissed her and said, "Yes, Mother. I promise to be good. Mostly," he grimaced as he stretched, "I have a doctor's appointment first thing this morning, dear wife."

Annika watched him shuffle to the bathroom, searched her feelings. She knew she loved Yuri. *How do you feel?* She couldn't find the answer.

She went to her bathroom and started her day. They kissed again after breakfast, then went their separate ways, he to the appointment, Annika to her office. Colonel Rita Ruiz accompanied her Queen as she had for thirty years. "One of these days, you're going to have to retire, Sweetie," said Annika.

"When they declare that so called superior brain of yours obsolete, then you won't need me anymore and I can happily retire to Luna Station or one of the pleasure worlds," Rita responded.

"Yes, but my job is for life," Annika reminded her.

"Mine, too," was her best friend's reply.

Mrs. Wilson stood and greeted the Queen when she arrived. How Annika missed Miss Norris' daily admonishment of "you're late!" Still, Mrs. Wilson was efficient. The samovar was already steaming. Annika brewed her tea and set to work. There were a few appointments this morning and with the family birthday party this afternoon, the day was a short one.

Gavin Howland was her last appointment. He still marched, his back ramrod straight, into her office. But he was approaching one hundred and had decided it was time for retirement. She left her formal desk and motioned him to the red couch.

"Highness, I have prepared this list for you, candidates for my potential replacement," he started. "All these persons would do a fine job. My recommendation would be Admiral Hinabrian. He has served the Empire for fifty years and was a finalist for your Warlord. He and Admiral Moss have known each other for nearly all that time and they have an excellent working relationship."

Annika pursed her lips. Admiral Hinabrian would be a fine minister, she was sure. "Set him up with an interview with me this week, Gavin," she told him. "I don't anticipate any issues, but I want to make sure. If I like what I see, then we'll schedule your retirement party for the next day. After you leave." They both chuckled, the meeting finished.

Her work day ended, Annika wandered up to the Grotto of the Blue Waters. It was still Yuri's favorite eatery in the palace complex. He was already there when she arrived, sipping from a tall glass and gazing into the flat waters.

"How was your morning, Yuri?" she asked. Her husband handed her a piece of paper from his inside jacket pocket.

"Gods, no…" she whispered. "There must be a mistake!"

Yuri shook his head slowly. I've known for some time, my love," he said sadly, "Doctor Hallal and I have run the test three times. It is Gilbert syndrome. There is no mistake." He took her hand and kissed it.

"It's not fair!" her voice cracked, "I am the one who is supposed to die first. "You're supposed to get another sixty years."

"Six months, my love," he said in a soft voice. "Maybe less. But no more than six months." he stared into the azure pool again. "If it's any consolation, there will be no pain."

A snap and crackle filled her head. "But what will I do?" she wailed, the tears flowing. All the feeling that had eluded her for years clamored for release. "You promised you'd be there for me! How will I go on without you?"

He pulled her close, her tears soaking his jacket, smoothing her long hair. "Annika, listen. I will be with you always. Whatever happens, wherever I go, I will be with you." Suppressing his own tears, he declared, "I love you, Annika Raudona Russolov, now and forever. Come now, wipe your eyes. Our children are all here, and their children, here for a happy birthday party. Let's go be happy together with our children."

The party was in the gaily decorated throne room. Nearly all the children had arrived, with the grandchildren. Noire and Teresa arrived together. **"I'll be with my cousins, Father,"** mindspoke Eve.

"Of course, Child. But remember, talking aloud here today," Noire advised. "Not everyone here can mindspeak. And no scanning without permission!" The young woman stuck her tongue out at her father and sauntered to a group of her cousins.

Dohlman's party was brilliant, as usual. Happy, gay music played. Jugglers, dancers and clowns entertained all the guests. The table groaned under the weight of the food he had arranged. The cake was tall and real chocolate. Annika sat with Yuri, holding his hand, watching their grandchildren as they ran around playing, shrieking and laughing.

It was time for the toast. Noire stood on a table and raised his glass and announced, "Today, we are here to salute my brother-in-law, Prince Doctor Yuri Andrei Russolov neKhan. And to think, there was a time, I was ready to kill you for marrying my sister." The room roared with laughter. ("Is that true?" whispered Eve to her Aunt Teresa.) "But today, I look around and see the results of that blessed union. And how happy you have made my sister. So, nieces and nephews, my sisters and my daughter, I give you the patriarch of our family and salute you on this, your seventieth birthday. May you live to see a hundred more!" The room cheered as Annika released Yuri's hand.

"Excuse me, my love," she said in a low voice. "I need a moment."

She exited the room, heading to the bathroom. She fumbled a moment with the door. "Are you all right, Mousey?" Rita asked. Annika's eyes welled, she slammed the door closed and latched it. With the water running at full force, Annika dropped to her knees, bawling. The feeling she had been seeking for twenty-five years came flooding back with her tears. *I love him. I love him...*

The report had said six months. The reality was only three. Yuri and Annika moved to the farm after his birthday party. He had gathered their children in the Garden of Eternity and explained what was to happen. "Your mother and I were happiest at the guest house at the farm," he explained. "She'll be able to handle the affairs of the Empire from the main house. But we'll stay at the guest house until…well, until I die. I want you to know I love you all, but your mother and I want to have these last few months for ourselves as much as possible. Belinda will keep you apprised of what happens. Aunt Teresa and Mary will be at the house. But I want you all to live your lives, make your old papa proud, O.K.?"

The summer was the finest they could recall at their old home. They took long walks in the grass. Yuri sat under the trees he had planted and read poetry to Annika as she lay her head on his lap. As the day ended, they would sit outside, hand in hand, watching the sun set.

One morning, Yuri couldn't get out of bed. Teresa and Mary answered Annika's panicky call. From that day on, they helped him from bed, cleaned and dressed him. Annika assisted where she could, usually fed her deteriorating husband. At night, she affixed the breather over his mighty nose and listened to make sure he breathed all night.

Yuri grew weaker and weaker. He lost his power of speech, communicating only with glances and blinks. Annika sat with him, rubbing his hands and hoping he knew she was still there.

His breathing was shallow the final night. Annika had succumbed to asleep, her head on his chest. It was time; the two healers could feel his spirit rousing and preparing to leave. Mary fitted the neutralizer to her mother's head with loving care, while Teresa summoned the sirens. They had only just arrived and started singing when Yuri drew his last breath and exhaled slowly.

"Yuri?" Annika was instantly awake, "Yuri?" She shook him. "Yuri, wake up! Yuri! No! Don't leave me Yuri!" Her anguished cry threatened to split the night sky. Teresa and Mary donned neutralizers and waited while Annika screamed and wailed, calling Yuri's name.

Suddenly, she straightened, tearless. Her emerald eyes flashed black.

"For Ten Thousand Years, Yuri! I will love you for ten thousand years." Then she collapsed.

Chapter 37

"I am all powerful time which destroys all things and I have come here to slay these men. Even if thou does not fight, all warriors facing me shall die."

-The Bhagavad Gita

Twenty years later

They gathered here under the naked stars. Each was aware of the gravity of this meeting, none save the stars would bear witness. The ancient monolith stood silent in the sands as it had for eleven thousand years. The three colossal tombs towered behind them.

They gathered in the silent darkness, for conspirators were always more secure when discussing such things in the dark. The whole of the family had been debating it amongst themselves. A decade ago, this would have been unspeakable. Tonight, the unspeakable had to be decided.

The eight were gathered in a circle. A ninth, unseen but felt, circled them watching for intruders. She was good at this kind of work, perhaps as good as her father. Time would tell.

They spoke in hushed voices. Mindspeaking could be overheard.

"It is decided then," said Noire.

"Nothing is decided, Uncle," countered Mercy. "We are here to discuss this thing, I thought."

"What is there left to discuss?" challenged the stranger. "We all know what has to be done.'

"We're talking about the Khan," Robert stated.

"Damn you, we're talking about my mother. Your mother, too." The Crown Prince glared at his brother and best friend.

"She is our sister, "Teresa's voice was soft. "Don't you think this pains us as well?"

323

"Noire, Teresa and I have known her the longest," spat the stranger. "She has much to answer for."

"Hasn't what she has done for the Empire atoned for any sin?" asked Noire.

"She has acquitted herself well, admirably." Teresa argued.

"I have forgiven her for what she has done," the stranger answered. "The Empire today is far safer than when she started. But her time has passed. She clings to power even as her mind is failing her. I cannot sit back and watch her destroy all she has created. I am dying already. Let my legacy save hers."

"Uncle, we are not asking you to do this," Pico spoke up.

"No, Niece, I am volunteering. It is a terrible thing we are contemplating. It violates the Laws of Angkor Khan. My death will be a relief."

"You cannot be a part of this," Noire told the Crown Prince

"I know. Nor can my brother. We stand too much to gain when she dies and far more to lose should our names be associated with her death."

"This is a family matter; we shall have the family deal with it," Noire stated.

"It is a matter of the Empire," argued Dorian.

"Exactly. And we must speak for the Empire. She is the legend that will be remembered. Who she has become must never be allowed to tarnish that reputation." The stranger was adamant.

"That which lives, grows. That which does not grow, dies." Pico quoted her grandmother.

"Yes, exactly, Niece. We have all heard her say that for decades. She is dying before us and the Empire. We must give her dignity." Noire sighed.

"Can this be a dignified thing?" Anja spoke for the first time.

"Is not doing this dignified? I fear we agree," Teresa announced

Nods all around signified agreement.

"When do we do this? "asked Pico.

"The sooner the better. I for one cannot bear to watch her like this another day. And my own time draws short." The stranger was curt.

"Today, then," announced Noire.

The conspirators went to make their preparations.

Silent, unjudging, the naked stars saw it all.

The War Council that morning was a disaster.

She was early, as always, waiting on them to file in as she studied the holo projected above the table of the Empire. Fifteen hundred stars, over ten thousand inhabited worlds and stations, projected in a grand blue streak across the Sagittarius Arm.

They stood by their chairs, waiting for her to start the meeting. Her emerald eyes bore into each of the twenty-four of them, seeking. Finally, she broke the terrible silence. "What is the status of the Bougartd?"

"The reclamation of their world stands at seventy per cent," reported General Ciejo. "I estimate we shall have the entire project completed on time in fifteen years. At that point, we project the system will produce a minimum of thirty five percent above initial estimates."

"Reclamation. Productivity estimations," her fist pounded the table. "That is not what I asked. What of the Bougartd problem? When do we expect their extinction?" There were worried looks around the table.

"Highness, the Bougartd are an enslaved race," explained General Ciejo. "As such, they have certain rights. They are at a manageable population now and have become a productive world."

"No!" she yelled again. "They are a vile, animal breed, beneath my contempt. They ought to have been exterminated by now. General Gart, what is the closest bombardment group to Bougartd?"

Gart pressed a key and responded, "The 496th, General Cornell," he reported. "But, my Khan, shouldn't we send a warning to Bougartd first? To allow our citizens and troops to get off world?"

"Those traitors?" she asked incredulously. "Those collaborators? They have been on Bougartd for how many years and failed to exterminate those foul beasts. No, let them die under my fury like the animals." She came around the table and patted her son on the cheek. "You see, my son, this is how a Khan acts," she said, condescension dripping from her voice.

"Authoritative, decisive, unrelenting. I was nearly murdered by these beasts on my Naming Day. My father was murdered by these beasts. There is evidence that they poisoned your father with Gilbert syndrome. I will eradicate the vermin that are the Bougartd. When you are Khan, you will understand."

Annika hobbled back to her throne. "What are you doing today to serve my Empire?" she demanded, lecturing, berating and screaming furiously at her War Council. None dared interrupt her when she was like this. A month ago, a General had interrupted her while she raged. She buried her knife in his throat and gloated while he died.

"And you, Admiral Thiessen, what do you have to say to these?" She stared into a vacant space next to her, nodded her head several times. "You see?" she pointed. "This is the mark of the Warlord for my Empire. This is the standard you should all aspire to. Why, if I had a dozen men like my Uncle no enemy could stand up to Terra! Instead, I am left with a bunch of stumblebums, geshaldocs and cowards." She limped toward the door. "PAH! I am done with all of you."

Pico entered the Throne Room through a side door. It seemed pretentious to her to enter through the grand entrance, the giant doors at the far end of the room. They were old and heavy, protesting with an annoying squeak any time they were opened. They hadn't been opened in years, so doubtlessly the hinges would gripe loudly if they had to do their job.

The Throne Room was so much smaller than she remembered. When she was a child, Grandmother and Grandfather had held elaborate parties for the family, particularly at Christmas.

After Grandfather Yuri died, Grandmother still held Christmas every January seventh, but rather than sing and dance with her grandchildren, she would sit on her throne, dressed all in black and watch the merrymaking. Pico brought her own children while they were young, to Grandmother's Christmas, but it got sadder and sadder every year. Finally, when Pico's oldest child left home, she and her husband stayed home for the holiday.

Her footsteps echoed through the grand hall. It was dank now, dark. Gauzy curtains hung over all the windows, filtering the sunlight. None of the chandeliers were lit. Shadows leading to alcoves and egresses littered what was once bright and grandiose.

The only noise, save for Pico's footsteps, was the steady sawing of the Queen's snoring. Her head was braced by her left arm, a steady buzz emitting from the old woman. Pico stood at the foot of the dais. Great Uncle Noire had warned her that Grandmother still retained her assassin's knife. Just last week, a maid had made the near fatal mistake of touching the Queen while she napped. The poor girl was expected to survive, but would bear the scar across her neck for the rest of her life.

"Grandmother? Are you awake, Grandmother?" asked Pico.

"Who wants to know?" grumbled the old woman.

"Pico, Grandmother. Your granddaughter."

I know you are my granddaughter. I'm ninety years old, not stupid. Why are you here?" Annika snapped.

"It's Tuesday, Grandmother. I come by every Tuesday to have lunch with you."

Annika straightened up, smiling. "That's right, Tuesday!" she sounded so happy. "I have lunch with my granddaughter Pico on Tuesday! But where is your mother, dear? I so much would like to see your mother today."

327

"Mama's dead, remember, Grandmother? She died on the rescue mission to Spencer station, ten years ago," Pico stifled a sob. Mother's death was painful still.

"Oh, yes, I remember now. Silly girl, your mother, I told her not to go. She never listened to me, you know. Still, I wish she were here. I would like to have lunch with her today. It's Tuesday."

Pico offered a supporting hand. The Queen took it and pulled herself to her feet, then balanced with it as she stepped down the dais. She held her granddaughter's arm on the trek through the palace.

"Foolish me. I didn't get up and do my stretching and exercise first thing when I got out of bed this morning," rambled Annika. "The Proctors warned me I must exercise every day. That's all I need, you know, just some exercise, and then you just watch me run circles around you!"

They arrived at the Garden of the Blue Waters.

"This was your grandfather's favorite place to eat. And today is Tuesday, so they're serving fish! I love fish. Yuri told me once, I think, that fish is good brain food."

The grandmother tapped her temple. "Master Tahn gave me the superior brain, but I have to take good care of it. That's why I like to eat a lot of fish."

Lunch was a poached salmon. The Queen was ecstatic, she loved salmon most of all. Pico was careful in selecting the meal for grandmother, today of all days. The salmon was genetically engineered and expensive, of course, since the last of that species had died off following the War of the Five Cities. The vegetables had been steamed to perfection. Dessert was a decadent chocolate cake. The Queen allowed herself to be convinced by Pico to have a second slice.

Pico felt the feathery touch in her mind.

"It is done, Cousin. Her guards are all immobilized. Father and his guest are waiting."

The Queen gave an immense yawn.

328

"I need to go to my room, Granddaughter. I want to take a nap."

"Let's go back to the Throne Room for just a minute, Grandmother. I have a surprise there for you." Pico's heart lurched.

"A surprise? For me?" gasped Annika. "It's not my birthday and it's not Christmas. What is it?"

"You'll have to come see."

"Can it wait until after my nap?"

"No, Grandmother. You'll want to see it before. Then I'll walk with you back to your room for your nap. Okay?"

"All right. I'll bet it's a good surprise." The Queen pushed back her chair and rose on shaky legs. "I like surprises and you always have had the best surprises, Pico. That's why Grandmother loves you so."

Pico's heart ached to hear Grandmother's declaration of love. Her part of the conspiracy was to tire grandmother out, weaken her defenses. While elderly and infirmed with her failing superior brain, the Queen was still a formidable telepath. Pico concentrated on keeping her mental shields in place.

They entered the dark hall. Pico saw them at the far doorway, sirens. Concealed around the room in the shadows, they began their slow, tranquil melody.

"Sirens! Oh, Pico, I love sirens. They make me feel so good, so happy. But why here in my throne room? Why not in my chambers where I could fall to sleep?" asked the puzzled old woman.

"They're not the surprise, Grandmother. There is your surprise, by the door."

Annika squinted. Her eyesight wasn't what it had once been. She could make out a pair of figures coming toward her.

"Noire! Teresa! So wonderful to see you! Is Eve with you?"

"She's nearby, Sister, watching the door."

329

"Oh, do have her come give her grandmother a kiss. But, I don't understand. I saw you all Sunday, for supper. What is my surprise?"

Wordlessly, Noire and Teresa stepped aside.

She hadn't seen him for seventy-two years. He was older now, his hair had thinned and gone grey. Clearly, he wasn't diligent with his exercises either, as he had a paunch.

But there was no mistaking him. He still wore white.

"T-T-Tomas? Gods above, is that you, Tomas?" gasped Annika.

"Hello Annika. Yes, it's me." The old man's eyes filled with tears.

"Tomas!"

She raced to him as fast as her timeworn legs would carry her. He held his arms open wide and she wrapped hers around his neck, crying and kissing, repeating his name. He wept as well, hugging her tightly. His left hand patted her back.

His right slid the concealed knife into her belly.

She gasped at the sudden pain. "Tomas?" she croaked. His tear-laden eyes bored into hers and she was drawn into him.

They were back at Giza. Naming Day. She was seeing the ceremony through his eyes, feeling his excitement. After today, he would be free! Everyone understood Red was to be the new Khan. To the heirs, it was plain the only choice would be their tiny sister. One or two grumbled about the choice, but not White.

After today, he could come and go as he pleased. Perhaps he would travel the Empire or maybe the Rim. There would always be opportunity for a telepath. While he wasn't as powerful as Red, Blue or even Black (whom he suspected of being far more powerful than anyone knew), he still had considerable abilities he could use.

He had studied the history of his family for centuries before he found the name he was seeking. Few would ever understand its meaning.

His turn came. "Know then, I am today Tomas Blanco." he cried. It was his declaration of freedom. A plain name, its meaning hidden away deep in the family history.

He was eager to go. Red chose a pretty name, Annika. Named for her boyfriend's grandmother, he had heard. Well, good for him! Tomas hoped he was prepared for all the attention that was going to come his way.

He heard the whistling noise at the same time as everyone.
"RUN!"

The bombs were falling. Teresa and Noire bolted. Annika leaped to one side. Tomas had turned and started to run when the bomb exploded behind him. He was addled for a few moments. He heard screaming and gunfire. Annika had found a weapon and was firing at the raiders as they flew overhead. Around her, Tomas could see tattered and bloody human remnants that only moments before had been his family.

Blaise was lying on the ground, his life draining from his missing legs. Screaming, she dropped to her dying brother.
"Why Annika, why?" His gaze shifted to Tomas.
Avenge us!"

Tomas felt his brother's spirit slip away. Annika was screaming and crying. Tomas saw his chance to escape. He struggled to his feet and limped away, joining a crowd of terrified spectators fleeing the plaza.

Annika slumped. Tomas's strong left arm kept her from falling completely. She tasted the coppery tang of her blood bubbling up her throat. "No, Tomas," she said, her voice scratching. "Not this. I don't want to see this."

Her secret place released the block. She saw Noire taking her to safety. She pulled away, seeking Yuri. She had to find Yuri! Tears rolled down her cheeks as she watched herself stumble and fall over the fallen remains of her butchered siblings.

"What of you, Tomas? Please show me what happened to you."

His face softened. He pulled her into his mind again.

Tomas shed his white jacket as he joined the flow of people escaping the charnel house. A young man stumbled in front of him. Before Tomas could help, the crowd surged. He stepped on the boy and stumbled along. Tomas could hear the boy screaming as he was trampled.

A raider flashed over, chased by an Imperial fighter. The bombing and strafing stopped. Soon the roars and explosions were replaced by the groan and cries of the dead and dying. Children, separated from their parents, were crushed when they stopped to cry for their mothers. Men fought men for a foot of space in the crowd, everyone desperately trying to survive.

When he finally reached the street, Tomas sought an aide station. They fixed his leg. He told them he was from Occident. They evacuated him to Seattle. In the confusing weeks that followed, he hid in the communities north of the old city. He survived by using his talents to cheat at gambling. He was caught once and received a beating. Certain Annika would be looking for him, as well as the gamblers he had cheated, he booked passage off Terra and headed for the Rim.

He moved from job to job for several years, finally settling at an outpost on Mead Nine, an unaffiliated world far out on the Rim. There, he established himself as a commercial telepath. He was an honest man and his business grew even as he was careful to stay unobtrusive and invisible to Imperial interests.

It was important to avoid Imperial entanglements. He didn't have the correct documentation to legally work as a telepath. He obtained counterfeit papers, preferring to service a cliental that asked few questions.

Tomas grew prosperous, married, had a family. He watched his sister, first out of fear, then out of admiration. She was certainly what the Empire needed to grow. His heart burst with pride when she executed their inferior Uncle and claimed her Throne.

As the years passed, his fear of Annika faded. He was less careful about hiding from the Empire. Noire found him. He was terrified when he was picked up by Imperial Intelligence and carried off to their offices. When the black door opened and Noire walked in to hug his brother…Tomas forgot he could cry so much.

Tomas was happy in his life, without the neKhan sur name, without the attention of the court.

"I don't understand, Tomas. Why did you spend so much time away, hiding from me…Oh, wait, your name? Oh, Tomas! Now I remember! Tomas Blanc!"

Tomas Blanc had been the brother of Petra Khan, heir of the Eighth Khan. He had spent years hiding from his murderous father. When the Eighth died, Tomas Blanc remained hidden, fearing his sister would seek retribution as his father tried. In the end, they both died within days of each other, never having reconciled.

"I had hoped to hide from you for the rest of my life. I am ashamed of my reactions of that terrible day. I saw what you were doing for the Empire. I am so proud, Sister. And so ashamed. And as this was happening to you…"

"What was happening, Brother? Show me."

Then Yuri died.

Tomas caught his sister as her legs failed her completely. "Yuri, Yuri…" she wept.

"I'm sorry I had to show you that. But you need to understand. I must show it all to you. It's important you understand why."

He pulled her back into his memory.

Noire reported to Tomas on his infrequent visits that Annika did well for the first two years after her husband passed. But he also revealed that Annika's brain was expected to start to fail when she reached eighty. As Tahn predicted, Annika began to be irrational and delusional. Tomas hired a pair of sirens and traveled to Terra to watch her in a public appearance. He was driven to tears at the sight of her physical decline.

Not that he was in good shape himself. Years of traveling in substandard ships had saddled him with severe radiation exposure. Due to the unique composition of his physiology, he declined at a slower rate than a common man. He knew he was to die in less than a year.

He contacted Noire and found the family was already deep in discussions about what should be done about the declining Khan. Gart was ready to ascend. With Robert as Warlord, there was no question that a new epoch for the Empire was ready to begin.

Tomas volunteered to do the deed. He would break the Law of Angkor, he knew. By the Law, he would deserve death. And by every moral standard, murdering his own sister also demanded his execution. But, as he pointed out, he was already a dead man. Tomas would also finally redeem himself. If just a little.

The story was told and Tomas was gone. Annika was in her own head, alone, again. Her legs no longer supported her slight body, and Tomas tenderly lowered her to the floor and withdrew the knife. She held herself up.

"Thank you, Tomas."

She looked around at her family.

"I'm sorry, all of you. I'm so sorry."

"We love you, Sister," Teresa lay a heeling hand of her sister's forehead, drawing away the worst of the pain. "That is why we have done this. We can't watch you deteriorate anymore."

"I know. For that, for not being strong enough, I am so sorry."

"You don't have to be sorry for growing old, Annika. We are all growing old," Tomas said

"I spoke with Dorian," Noire whispered. "You and Yuri knew this is what would come to pass."

"I had still hoped it would not. Oh, it's growing dark!"

Annika collapsed in a heap. Her eyes began to flash from emerald green, to black, to flat green and back to emerald.

"It will be soon. I need you all to know, I love you. Eve? I know you can hear me. I love you. Pico, tell your children Grandma loves them. Tomas? Teresa..."

Her body shuddered. A puddle of bright blood and thick, grey electrolyte formed beneath her. Garbled noise issued from her mouth.

"Noire? You most of all. I..."

She shuddered again. Her sightless eyes sought her brother. In a pained, halting, mechanical voice, she gasped, "Noire, I love you."

Her breathing was shallow, panting. It began to slow. Her mouth moved, then she bolted back up on one arm.

"Yuri?" she cried. "Yuri, is it you?"

She collapsed.

The Red Queen was dead.

The permeating odor was grass, just grass. She took another breath, inhaling rich, earthy smells and sweet grass. She felt a breeze, heard the rustling and sat up. It was a bright morning and she lay in a field of wildflowers. Red primroses, orange poppies, yellow daisies, paperwhites. Violet irises nodded their heads and bluebells danced in the breeze, partnered by graceful ferns. A black rose bush stood alone to one side, silent and watching.

She stood and stretched. Her hair was long and golden, unfettered and wafting in the breeze. She hadn't worn it this long since...she couldn't remember. She was wearing a peasant blouse and mid-calf skirt, like she wore that first summer on the farm. The

farm! Low hills surrounded her. Perhaps if she climbed one, she could see where she was. She was certain the farm was nearby.

Across the field she walked with ease, savoring the sunlight and sweet breeze. She left the flowers behind and walked barefoot in the grass. When had she felt this good, this happy, this satisfied? If only...

She saw him. Up on the hill. "Yuri?" she said, then called out loudly, "Yuri?"

It was Yuri, tall, strong and proud. His hair was thick and bushy, the damned moustache full under his wonderful nose. He was smiling a toothy grin and waving. She ran...She ran! Oh, how long since she could run? Up the hill and into his embrace, leaping and wrapping her legs around his long body, her arms around his neck. He fell and they rolled, laughing as they tumbled down the hill. When they landed, Yuri was on top of his bride, kissing her over and over.

"Gods, Yuri, is it you? Is it really you?"

It is my love, it is really me," he answered. "I have been waiting so long for you. And now you are here."

"But where are we, Yuri?" she asked.

"I don't know," he admitted, "but Annika, you're here now."

"Whatever shall we do, my love?"

"I don't know that either," Yuri replied. "But let's do it together."

Epilog

"Grief never ends...But it changes. It is a passage, not a place to stay. Grief is not a sign of weakness, not a lack of faith. It is the price of love."
Author unknown

The sun descended over the Gobi. Eve orbited the Temple complex and landed the shuttle a distance from the other multitude of ships parked here today. There were always those who feared seeing an Imperial Intelligence ship.

Some of them had a good reason to fear Imperial Intelligence.

Today was not a day for intimidation. Eve's father had culled her impatience, teaching her the value of placidly waiting for enemies to expose themselves.

She landed delicately, the ship settling without a bump. Noire sat in the cabin, eyes closed, meditating.

"We're here, Father," she whispered. A hovercar waited to carry them to the place of the ceremony. They passed four Legions of soldiers in formal dress. It was to be expected, the Queen was one of them.

The assembly formed one-hundred-yard circle around the funeral bier. The platform had been assembled with great precision. It stood six feet high and broad enough for the ritual. Prayer banners rippled in the wind; bright garlands of flowers arched around the platform.

"Brother, are you here?"

"Eve and I are, Teresa. We will be there in a minute."

"Well, hurry, it's almost time to start."

The family had assembled near the pathway leading from the Temple to the bier. Tomas had fallen ill after the killing. Fearing his life was coming to an end, Gart provided a fast scout so his uncle could return Nutrize 11, his home in the Rim, in time to die surrounded by his family.

Noire and Teresa stood in the front row, alone. Annika's heirs and children, save for the Khan, Dorian and Violet, stood behind them. The grandchildren and great grandchildren filled the rear rows. The public funeral had seen two million on the ground and trillions across the Empire by holo on the previous afternoon from the Giza Palace. Today was for family and close friends.

A gong's mournful clang tolled. Every twenty seconds, it resounded as long columns of priests and nuns of the temple came forth, surrounding the inner circle. After they were arranged, a soldier strode down the aisle way bearing the banner of the New Khan. Crown Prince Gart Russolov Khan followed twenty paces behind, wearing his dress army uniform. As his mother had, the badges and ropes of his General rank were muted and black.

Twenty paces behind the Khan came a second banner, borne by a veteran woman officer. The Colonel was crying as she held the banner high, leading her best friend on the final journey.

Cardinal James followed a twin row of saffron-wearing bonzes, each wearing a different colored sash and headpiece. The Cardinal and the eight bonzes waited at the base of the ramp leading up to the platform.

Eight soldiers bore the platform holding the Queen's remains. The bearskin she had worn so fiercely at her coronation covered her body. The procession ascended the bier, holding her body level, setting her remains on the altar with tenderness. The detail officer drew his sword and called out, "Salute!" Four Legions of soldiers raised their arms and cried in unison, "HooooOOOO! HooooOOOO! HooooOOOO!"

The holy men arranged themselves around the body and the hide was pulled back, exposing Annika to the open sky. Normally, the chieftain would wear ceremonial dress. The Queen wore her army uniform, her Captain's tabs muted on her collar, a pair of pilot's wings on her left breast. Cardinal James circled her body, chanting a prayer, waving an incense burner. He blessed her, bowed and left the platform.

The bonzes began a chant, raising their arms to the body, then to the four directions. They bowed a final time, then proceeded to their place with the priests of the Temple. The bonze wearing the orange headset stopped. His hand straightened a lock of hair that had strayed (*Not a hair out of place...*) then bent and kissed her forehead before he departed

The Khan ascended the ramp and stood next to his mother. He held a burning torch raised high as he cried, "Gods of the Grass! Gods of the Wind! Gods of the Sky! Gods of our endless Steppe! She has served you well and now she is finished. We return her to you now and demand you welcome her into your realm." He shoved the torch into the space under her body as he had been instructed, then leapt from the platform, joining his family. The woods of the bier were carefully dried pines and beeches. They would burn swift, hot and smell sweet. Oils and perfumes had been spread across the wood, sprinkled with spices and incense. The Queen's funeral odor would be pleasing to the Gods.

It erupted with such speed as to almost seem an explosion. The entire assembly knelt, out of respect and because the heat from the fire would wash over then. Not one mourner moved. After an hour, the pyre collapsed into a crackling heap, eliciting a low cry of surprise.

The fire burned until three hours before dawn, smoldering into a glowing pile of embers. Priests, wearing thick, padded shoes, entered the coals and journeyed to the center. There, using scoops, tongs and brushes, her ashes were collected and placed into an urn decorated with red flowers. Finished, they carried the urn to the Khan.

In turn, he carried her to Noire. "Here is all that is left of her, Elder," Gart told his uncle. "Please, honor me and our family. Take her to rest with our father."

Noire, now the patriarch, led his family into the Temple and entered the Ossuary with Teresa. Tradition said only siblings should be here for the interment. He and Teresa had agreed and let their defenses down so the whole of the family could bear witness through the mind link.

The urn was warm in his hands. Yuri was there, of course, resting in the niche, waiting for Annika. Noire placed her next to him, then had an inspiration. He pushed the urns until they were touching, removed the long cord from his hair and wrapped it around the bases, tying them together with a loose knot and bow.

"It's time to go, Brother," Teresa's words lay lightly, but painfully on his heart.

"In a moment," he told her. "I'm not ready yet."

Teresa patted his shoulder. **"I'll come see you in New York next week."**

He sat on the floor. The silence was a roaring in his ears and he began a recalling. That night, so many years ago, after they had been told of the death of their father. The Proctors had wakened the children, told them and sent them back to bed. He was terrified and found himself in Red's room, crying and lonely. She let him into her bed and held him.

"We're going to be fine, you know. I'll make sure we're all fine. I'll make it all okay, Black, you can trust me."

He had sworn himself to her that night and she kept her promise. Today, every Terran was safe, thanks to her. Queen Annika, the fifteenth reincarnation of the Great Khan, had secured all the Terran Empire's future.

Noire stood, clapped his hands and bowed. He saw the door to the next chamber. On it, Angkor Khan stood, fierce and proud. Beyond that door, the Great Khan himself slept. Noire ached to enter the door, to see with his own eyes the founder of his line.

But it was not to be. He was not Khan.

As he left the chamber, he thought felt a light touch on his mind, like a whisper in a fierce wind. *"Good bye, Brother."* He stopped and listened, but it must have been his imagination.

The family had departed, returning to their lives. He left the Temple and walked in the direction of his waiting ship. Eve was there and ready to leave.

It was an hour before dawn, now the darkest time of the moonless night. He paused and looked to the sky. It was spring and the whole of the Sagittarius Arm, down to the Galactic core, was visible. Noire held up his hand, blocking hundreds of stars from his view. *Covering more stars than the Empire had when she started. Now, we control nearly a quarter of the sky.*

A flash in the corner of his eye. He saw red, green and blue lights flare and disappear. The new Khan wasn't waiting, but sending his fleet against a new enemy to the Empire.

Annika would be so pleased.

Noire gazed again at the stars, He closed his eyes and saw Annika astride her horse on Celtius, her hair streaming behind her, her arms open, eyes wild. Screaming her challenge to the universe: *"VICTORY! FOR TEN THOUSAND YEARS, I AM VICTORIOUS!"*

"Goodbye, Annika," he whispered.

He hurried to the ship. **"Eve, prepare for departure immediately back to New York."**

With the new war, there would be much to do…

Books by David Winnie

Tales of the Spinward March Book 1 "The Great Khan"
Tales of the Spinward March Book 2 "The Red Queen"

Coming soon:
Tales of the Spinward March Book 3 "The Ballad of Katy
O'Hare"

Come visit and "like" the Tales of the Spinward March
Facebook page. Artwork, commentary and news of upcoming
books.

Made in the USA
Lexington, KY
17 September 2017